PRAIRIE FIRE

LUKE JENSEN
BOUNTY HUNTER
PRAIRIE FIRE

WILLIAM W.
JOHNSTONE
and J.A. JOHNSTONE

PINNACLE BOOKS
Kensington Publishing Corp.
www.kensingtonbooks.com

PINNACLE BOOKS are published by

Kensington Publishing Corp.
119 West 40th Street
New York, NY 10018

PUBLISHER'S NOTE
Following the death of William W. Johnstone, the Johnstone family is working with a carefully selected writer to organize and complete Mr. Johnstone's outlines and many unfinished manuscripts to create additional novels in all of his series like The Last Gunfighter, Mountain Man, and Eagles, among others. This novel was inspired by Mr. Johnstone's superb storytelling.

All Kensington titles, imprints, and distributed lines are available at special quantity discounts for bulk purchases for sales promotion, premiums, fund-raising, educational, or institutional use.

Special book excerpts or customized printings can also be created to fit specific needs. For details, write or phone the office of the Kensington Sales Manager: Attn.: Sales Department. Kensington Publishing Corp., 119 West 40th Street, New York, NY 10018. Phone: 1-800-221-2647.

PINNACLE BOOKS, the Pinnacle logo, and the WWJ steer head logo are Reg. U.S. Pat. & TM Off.

First Printing: February 2022
ISBN-13: 978-0-7860-4733-8
ISBN-13: 978-0-7860-4734-5 (eBook)

10 9 8 7 6 5 4 3 2 1

Printed in the United States of America

THE JENSEN FAMILY

FIRST FAMILY
OF THE AMERICAN FRONTIER

Smoke Jensen, *The Mountain Man.*

The youngest of three children and orphaned as a young boy, Smoke Jensen is considered one of the fastest draws in the West. His quest to tame the lawless West has become the stuff of legend. Smoke owns the Sugarloaf Ranch in Colorado. Married to Sally Jensen, father to Denise "Denny" and Louis.

Preacher, *The First Mountain Man.*

Though not a blood relative, grizzled frontiersman Preacher became a father figure to the young Smoke Jensen, teaching him how to survive in the brutal, often deadly Rocky Mountains. Preacher fought the battles that forged his destiny. Armed with a long gun, Preacher is as fierce as the land itself.

Matt Jensen, *The Last Mountain Man.*

Orphaned but taken in by Smoke Jensen, Matt Jensen has become like a younger brother to Smoke, and even took the Jensen name. And like Smoke, Matt has carved out his destiny on the American frontier. He lives by the gun and surrenders to no man.

Luke Jensen, *Bounty Hunter*.

Mountain Man Smoke Jensen's long-lost brother, Luke Jensen is scarred by war and a dead shot—the right skills to be a bounty hunter. And he's cunning and fierce enough to bring down the deadliest outlaws of his day.

Ace Jensen and Chance Jensen, *Those Jensen Boys*.

The untold story of Smoke Jensen's long-lost nephews, Ace and Chance, a pair of young-gun twins as reckless and wild as the frontier itself . . . Their father is Luke Jensen, thought killed in the Civil War. Their uncle Smoke Jensen is one of the fiercest gunfighters the West has ever known. It's no surprise that the inseparable Ace and Chance Jensen have a knack for taking risks—even if they have to blast their way out of them.

Denise "Denny" Jensen, and Louis Jensen,
***The Jensen Brand*.**

Denny and Louis are the adult children of Smoke and Sally Jensen. Denny is the wildcard tomboy, kept in line by the more level-headed Louis. The twins grew up mostly abroad, but never lost their love of the Sugarloaf Ranch, or lost sight of what it means to be a Jensen.

CHAPTER 1

Georgia, 1864

The Union burned Atlanta.

In the beginning, General William Tecumseh Sherman's army was intent on destroying only those buildings capable of supporting Confederate military operations. However, it wasn't long before roving bands of undisciplined soldiers, half-crazed from the death and destruction they had wrought already during their march across Georgia, spread the arson to civilian homes, and soon the city was an inferno.

Even as the funeral pyre that was Atlanta continued smoldering and thick columns of black smoke climbed into the sky, the Military Division of Mississippi, spearheaded by the Army of Georgia on General Sherman's right-wing, marched on toward the sea. The orders to show restraint in foraging for supplies and destroying only vital structures and military materials fragmented as quickly as they had in Atlanta.

Sherman's troops had burned Atlanta. Now they set the whole state of Georgia on fire. What became known as

"Sherman's March to the Sea" was the most brutal military strategy since the Romans burned and salted Carthage.

Which suited some of the Union officers just fine.

Colonel Neville Goldsmith loved fire. A company commander in the XIV Corps of the Army of Georgia, he hadn't yet seen nearly enough burning. Atlanta had been just about right, but there weren't enough Atlantas. Never *could* be enough, as far as Colonel Goldsmith was concerned.

Fire cleansed. It was a magical, living animal that breathed and ate to live. Fire purified as it destroyed, and to Colonel Goldsmith nothing needed purifying more than the hated Confederacy. Let the whole South burn away. Let it disappear in rising smoke, the ashes scattered by the wind.

This was exactly what Goldsmith intended to do.

He shifted on his mount, a strong, bay-colored Morgan horse, and watched his infantry marching past him along the road down the low hill from where he surveyed them. General Sherman's Special Field Order No. 120 had been clear. The advance army was to forage liberally for supplies. To that end, each command was to create scout units dedicated to the task of perpetual resupply.

Currently, Goldsmith waited for word from his own foragers. Beside him was a young lieutenant in charge of the reconnaissance platoon riding vanguard to the main troop column. Barely in his twenties, the lieutenant couldn't have grown a beard to save his life.

He finished his scouting report and sat patiently waiting for some comment from Goldsmith. The colonel felt the junior officer's eyes on him. Tall and whipcord lean, Goldsmith presented a startling figure to those unaccustomed to the sight of him.

As a child, he'd tried burning down his home while his family slept inside. He had set fires before, many of them, but never anything as big as a house. And never anything with something *living* inside it to serve as sacrifices to the hungry flames. Just the thought of that made his heart slug madly in his chest in anticipation.

But the lure of the blaze and the exquisite screaming from inside the house proved too mesmerizing, and he'd been caught off-guard by the rapid spread of the flames and been badly burned when he was too close to a collapsing wall. As a result, the left side of his body was a gnarled and twisted, pink mass of knotted scar tissue. It ran from his waist, up his arm from the back of his hand, across his neck to his face.

The facial scars twisted the corner of his mouth into a permanent sneer. He hadn't lost his eye, but the fire had damaged it so that the perpetually reddened orb constantly wept. His scalp was seared so that wispy hairs grew only sporadically on that side of his head.

When turned so that only his right profile was visible, he was still a handsome, if rather severe-looking, man.

But when he was angry, facing someone straight on, his face became truly terrifying.

Slowly, Goldsmith pulled a lucifer from his breast pocket and placed it carefully in the corner of his mouth. He turned his head. Realizing he'd been caught staring like a boy seeing his first naked girl, the lieutenant flushed in embarrassment and looked away. His mount, sensing his nervousness, snorted and stepped sideways, ready to bolt. The young officer was barely able to calm the horse.

"That will be all, Lieutenant," Goldsmith said.

The colonel's voice was hoarse and gravelly. The fire had damaged his vocal cords, too. When he spoke, it reminded men of the grinders in rock quarries, smashing stones to pebbles in a great grinding of gears. Goldsmith's words came out sounding rough-edged and uneven.

"Yes, sir!"

The lieutenant half-shouted the response in his haste to make his exit. He gave his horse its head and rode away at a gallop. His fear made Goldsmith grin. Goldsmith enjoyed the effect he had on others. He loved the terror he saw in the eyes of Southern civilians when his men rode onto their property.

I'm going to miss this war when it's over, he thought.

Just as the line of infantry gave way to the mule teams of the artillery platoons, Sergeant Major Jeremiah Trask rode up. Trask commanded the foragers, who'd earned the unofficial title of "bummers." In Goldsmith's opinion, no one was more suited to the task. He and the non-commissioned officer shared a love of spreading misery. Because of this, Goldsmith had given command of the unit to his sergeant major rather than an officer.

Trask reined in his horse and lifted a hand in a lazy salute, strictly for appearance's sake. A squat bear of a man, he was said to be strong enough to pick up and press the largest of blacksmith anvils over his head. The blunt features of his simian face were framed by a thick black beard that reached the middle of his chest.

"You have something for me, Sergeant Major?" Goldsmith asked.

"I got something I think you'll like," Trask replied.

He leaned to the side and spat tobacco on the ground. Jeremiah Trask kept a good-sized chaw of tobacco between his cheek and gum at all times, morning to night. He even slept with the plug, Goldsmith knew.

"Well, do tell . . ." Goldsmith said, feeling anticipation quicken inside him.

"Three miles over, on the river bend. We spotted some cotton fields and followed the road to a fair-sized plantation. It has a workin' cotton gin. The house's big enough to billet a company of the butternut grayback scoundrels."

Goldsmith licked his lips, a quick flickering of his tongue that betrayed his excitement. His hands massaged the pommel of his saddle horn as he squeezed his thighs tight against his horse.

"The house is big?"

"I imagine we'll find plenty of silver and there's bound to be some gold buried," Trask said. Then, because he knew Goldsmith really only cared about one thing, he added, "The house is two stories. So are the horse and storage barns." He grinned under the thick beard. "That place'll go up like Atlanta, sure enough."

"I think I better inspect this myself before I give a report to the brigade commander." Goldsmith rolled the lucifer from one corner of his mouth to the other.

"Yes, sir."

The men turned their horses away from the road and the marching army. They rode out of the hills and into the river bottoms that gave way to pasture land and then cotton fields now lying fallow. After a short time, they came to the plantation.

The plantation house was palatial, made of red brick with white trim, a thing of Georgian columns and Palladian-style wings as additions to the main house. Trask's men held the occupants at gunpoint. Off to one side, a cluster of shotgun shacks stood around a circle of sugar kettles. The slaves stood there, solemnly and silently watching the unfolding events.

Goldsmith rode his horse slowly up to the lavish front porch. On it, a tall woman with flame red hair stood stiffly waiting for him. She rested her hands on the shoulders of a ten-year-old boy who wore an expression of hatred so fierce it almost inspired a grudging admiration from Goldsmith.

Beside the woman and boy stood a teenage girl with the same red hair as her mother. She wore a simple but elegant gown that also matched her mother's. Off to one side stood several slaves dressed in formal livery, the household servants.

Goldsmith stopped his mount in front of the woman and touched his hand to the brim of his hat. As he did so, he turned his face so she got a nice long look at his scars. His smile widened when he saw the involuntary look of revulsion flash across her own face.

"Ma'am," he said. "I am Colonel Neville Goldsmith, XIV Corps, Army of Georgia."

"You ain't no army of Georgia!" the boy suddenly shouted. "Georgia fights for the Confederacy!"

"Hush," ordered his mother as she tightened her grip on his shoulders.

"It's all right," Goldsmith chuckled. "I can respect spirit in a boy."

The woman pressed her mouth into a firm line. Finally, she spoke to him, her voice as stiff as her spine.

"My name is Mrs. Scott. Patricia Scott. This is my home. What is the meaning of this incursion?"

"Pleased to meet you, Mrs. Scott. I realize it's about dinnertime, so I'm sorry if we've interrupted your meal."

"Beg pardon, ma'am," Trask chimed in. He smirked behind his beard.

"Is it necessary to have your men point their guns at us?" the daughter spoke up.

"You'll have to excuse them, young lady," Trask said. "They've been a little on edge since we've marched south. What with the yellow-livered Johnny Rebs shootin' at us and all. I reckon that goes double for your traitor scum pa, you little slut."

Grinning, he leaned over and spat a stream of brown tobacco juice onto the porch, almost hitting the girl's slipper-shod feet. She drew back quickly in disgust and Mrs. Scott turned to Goldsmith, her cheeks burning with anger.

"I would like you to please leave my property. At the very least, control your men, Colonel!"

Reluctantly, Goldsmith pulled his eyes away from the architecture of the plantation house. He imagined it burning, flames spilling from windows as columns of thick black smoke lifted toward the autumn sky.

He regarded the indignant Mrs. Scott with a cruel gaze. Pulling the lucifer match from his mouth, he pointed it at her.

"Pursuant to Special Field Order Number 120, and in accordance with laws of the United States of America, I hereby requisition all goods, materials, livestock, foodstuffs, or equipment capable of assisting in the military campaign to defeat the Confederacy, home of cowards and whores."

Smirking, he replaced the match in his mouth.

"You heard the Colonel," Sergeant Major Trask shouted at the troops. "Get to it!"

The sergeant major's eyes burned with avarice as he swung down out of the saddle. He bounded onto the porch and lunged at Mrs. Scott's daughter. His hand shot out and snatched a gold locket from around her slim neck. She cried out in pain and protest as the thin gold chain snapped.

"That includes all forms of currency." Trask smiled through tobacco-stained teeth. "Like this here gold necklace."

Her brother launched himself at Trask, a wolverine of windmilling punches. Laughing, Trask backhanded the ten-year-old across the face, knocking him to the porch at his mother's feet.

"You damned Yankee pig!" Mrs. Scott swore. She produced a Sharps Pepperbox derringer from the pocket of her dress and leveled it at the startled Trask. "Stay away from my children or I swear to God—"

Atop his horse, Goldsmith drew his Colt Army Model 1860 in a lazy motion. As he leveled the long barrel, he thumbed back the hammer on the single-action revolver. The .44 caliber cap-and-ball pistol roared as he pulled the trigger. A cloud of coarse black powder smoke geysered from the barrel and cylinder and hung in the air in a dark haze.

A scarlet rose of blood blossomed high on Mrs. Scott's chest as the woman gasped in surprise. She stumbled backward and collapsed loosely to the porch floor. Her eyes remained open, fixed and staring blankly. A soft, almost gentle sigh escaped her mouth. She was dead.

"She raised a weapon against soldiers of the Union and made herself a combatant," Goldsmith announced. "May God almighty have mercy on her soul."

Still off to one side, the house slaves stared in shock.

The shriek that wrenched from the lips of the Scott daughter was anguished, a cry of pure animal pain. Her face went white with grief and her mouth worked soundlessly, trying to form words that wouldn't come. Her brother threw himself at his mother's body, desperately pleading with her to be all right.

"Mama! Mama!" he cried.

"Let this be a lesson to all present," Goldsmith continued pompously. "Do not bear arms against the Union, under penalty of death."

Ignoring the sobs of the children, he looked around. His men, veterans of numerous such raids, had immediately sprung into action. Milk cows and horses were brought out and tied to the back of supply wagons. They found a brace of healthy-looking mules, and Goldsmith made a mental note to assign them to the artillery corps.

Soldiers emerged from sheds with clucking chickens held upside down in each hand, or bags of cornmeal and flour over their shoulders. The blue-clad troops took stolen sledgehammers to the machinery of a cotton gin set up inside an outbuilding off from the main house. Men emerged from the main house, arms filled with silver utensils and teapots, which held no military applications whatsoever.

"These buildings are hereby deemed essential to the Confederate War effort!" Goldsmith shouted. "Burn them!"

He had to stop talking. His throat had choked up thick with his desire to see the flames let loose. He made a fist with his free hand as he holstered his pistol, trying to bleed off some of the overpowering arousal at the idea.

"Give us a chance to find more valuables!" Trask protested.

He seemed half-panicked at the thought he might miss out on the looting. A female slave in a gingham dress and white pinafore apron fell to her knees and began loudly praying.

"Billy, no!" the Scott daughter suddenly screamed.

Goldsmith turned and saw the boy racing toward him, his mother's fallen Pepperbox in his hands, his tear-streaked face twisted with rage intense beyond his years. The girl lunged after him, trying desperately to stop the child.

Goldsmith clawed for his pistol which he'd holstered. He realized with disbelief that he wasn't going to make it in time. The boy stopped, took the Pepperbox in both hands, and thumbed back the hammer on the little 4-barrel pistol.

Someone taught the boy to shoot, he had time to think. The observation was not without approval.

The boy was picked up and thrown to the dirt at the feet of Goldsmith's mount. The boom of Trask's Army Colt sounded like a cannon. The .44 caliber ball ripped into the boy's back with unforgiving force and smashed through his spine. The child's blood rapidly spread across the ground in a pool as he lay facedown, never to move again.

"Billy!" Sobbing, the girl threw herself at her brother, calling his name again and again.

"She's going for the Pepperbox!" Trask hooted.

His Colt roared again. The Scott girl was flung to the side, long red hair spilling from the loose bun she wore it in. She landed hard in the dirt, eyes staring wide. Her mouth worked again, but only a bubble of blood emerged. It popped and a trickle of crimson leaked from the corner of her soft lips. By the wheezing, Goldsmith knew her lung had been shredded.

He watched the light fade from her eyes. He knew she hadn't actually been going for the derringer. Not that it mattered.

"Well," he told his sergeant major, "I do appreciate the assist, but the men are going to be mighty disappointed that we did away with both mother and daughter."

Trask spat. The tobacco juice splashed the bloody backs of the murdered children. "That's a soldier's life for you." He spat on the corpses again. "Besides, there's still the darkies. Their women'll do just fine."

"True." Goldsmith dismounted. Pointing at a private who'd just emerged from the front doors loaded down with several silver picture frames, a gold snuff box, and a pair of silver candlestick holders, he ordered, "Fetch me kerosene, Private."

"Right away, sir!"

Goldsmith went up the porch steps and into the antebellum mansion. Behind him, the slaves cried in fear and outrage as the Union foragers began picking out women and girls for their use. His men saw little need to be gentle.

He walked slowly through the entryway, taking note of the numerous oil paintings, expensive furniture, and the handcrafted banister of the dramatic split-staircase leading to the second floor. He noted the heavy curtains with something like physical hunger.

"That's what you call 'ladder fuels' right there," he murmured.

Everything was so combustible, so deliciously *burnable*. He trembled with the anticipation of it. Trask had gotten a silk pillowcase from somewhere and was in a small, formal tea room off the main hall. He merrily stuffed anything of value he could find into the makeshift sack.

"Best hurry," Goldsmith warned him. "I got a powerful need to burn."

Saying nothing, Trask moved faster. He was well acquainted with his superior's predilection for fire.

The private returned with the kerosene; Goldsmith snatched the metal can from his hands like a starving man grasping for food. The private let go and stepped back in undisguised horror. Goldsmith's face was twisted up with lunatic joy.

"Private," Goldsmith said.

"Yes, sir?"

"When I come out of this house, I best see every building burning."

"What about the slave quarters?" he asked. "They'll need—"

"*Every* damn building," Goldsmith snapped.

"Sir, yes, sir!"

The man practically ran to the door as Goldsmith started splashing kerosene onto a French Renaissance–inspired settee. To his ears, the metal jug gurgled like a happy baby as he poured it across the polished walnut of a finely crafted side table. Dribbling a little trail as he went, Goldsmith wandered over to the heavy brocade curtains and liberally soaked them.

Trask had gone upstairs in search of loot. He came back down now, boots tromping loudly on the steps, a disgruntled look on his ugly face. He spat tobacco juice on the gilded wallpaper.

"Didn't find much," he groused. "I bet that red-haired bitch buried her husband's hard currency somewhere. I imagine one of the house slaves knows where."

Splashing the last of the astringent smelling kerosene on several of the oil painting portraits, Goldsmith waved him away.

"Go to it, Sergeant," he said. "Beat the old man on the porch and he'll talk. Failing that, get yourself a woman from the slaves." He grinned, throwing the empty kerosene can to the floor with a clatter. "Rank has its privileges, after all."

Sour, Trask nodded. "Girl," he corrected absently. "I'll

pick me out a nice girl. If I'm going to eat dark meat, I want it tender." A grudging smile tugged at the corners of his mouth as he thought about the idea.

The air was thick with kerosene fumes. The entryway would light up like a bonfire. The condensed pocket of heat would rapidly carry the flames throughout the mansion. Goldsmith pulled the lucifer from his mouth. Trask hurried from the house.

Alone with his desires, a giggling Goldsmith popped the sulfur head of the match with one hoary thumbnail. It snapped to life. Goldsmith felt a line of drool spill over his rubbery, fire-scarred lips and run down his chin.

He dropped the match and it caught with a *whoosh*. Fire exploded in the antechamber. It raced along rivers of kerosene, igniting furniture and floorboards. Yellow flames licked at the walls hungrily. The conflagration found the curtains, and fire raced upward. In moments the fire roared into a holocaust of heat and flame.

As the inferno raged, Colonel Neville Goldsmith stood, arms outstretched, and laughed.

CHAPTER 2

Kansas, sixteen years later

Luke Jensen slow-walked his horse into the town.

A tall, well-built man dressed in black from head to foot, he rode easy and loose, just another saddle tramp wandering through on his way to no place in particular. And Craig's Fork, judging by the looks of it, was just a step above no place.

The settlement had started life before the war as an Indian trading post, swapping whiskey, steel knives, and Sharps rifles for furs and hides. First, the trade was for beaver pelts, then buffalo skins. Then the furs and hides ran out, the end of the war pushed the frontier farther west, until the Lakota Sioux and the other tribes rose up fiercer than ever.

Craig's Fork had always been home to rougher elements. The fur trapper brigades, mountain men, buffalo hunters, and riverboat men using the Kansas River to move goods all mixing with natives looking to trade. Not to mention the whores who serviced all comers during any boom. These weren't the breed of men with much use for civilization or any laws that came with it.

As the trade in northern Kansas petered out, the rough but generally honest element gave way to outlaws and desperate men. Craig's Fork became known as a place where owlhoots and gunhawks could congregate without fear of interference from the law. Justice was determined by being the quickest to kill or by making violent allies to watch your back and impose fear.

Luke had followed a trail of rumors to Craig's Fork, searching for a wily half-breed killer named Daniel Yellow Dog who led a mix of ex-Comancheros, young braves off the Indian Territory reservations, and hardened killers on the run from the law. They raided west, into the mining and ranching towns of Colorado, then ran for the contested lands of western Kansas where they hoped fear of Sioux war parties would stop any pursuit.

Luke turned his head slowly from side to side as he rode. He saw a boarded-up assayer's office left over from more prosperous times next to a rundown hotel that probably doubled as the local cathouse.

Those were the only two buildings made of wood. Lumber was expensive in treeless Kansas. The rest of the buildings were constructed out of sod.

Several hogs rooted through a rubbish heap. Their squeals and grunts were the only sounds except for the high-pitched whistle of the wind coming off the sea of grass. Down the passage between two sod houses, one with its roof caved in, Luke looked out onto the prairie. Dully white against the gray sky and brown grass stood two pyramids of buffalo skulls. Thousands of them. The top of the mounds had to be four stories high.

Luke had seen such sights before, but the grisly awesomeness of them never failed to impress him. These plains had seen a powerful lot of buffalo killing—and no doubt would continue to do so until the last of the vast herds had migrated south.

He stopped at a corral placed on the edge of the river. Holding several horses, it was part of the original way station and Indian trading post that had been the start of the town. It seemed ludicrous now to imagine any stagecoach ending up here on purpose. Still seeing no people, he looked around again as he swung down out of his saddle.

Two or three of the sod houses, built in a row like army bunkers, had thin trickles of brown smoke leaking from their chimneys. The trading post held the town saloon, such as it was. It seemed likely Daniel Yellow Dog would be either there or with the whores.

Luke casually flipped the ends of his reins over the post at the water trough to let his horse drink. The animal was well trained and would not wander.

Pulling his Winchester from its saddle boot, he turned to the building. A battered plank door, likely salvaged from the wood of a freight wagon, stood open. It was marked by several bullet holes. A bead curtain hung inside the door, intended to cut the ever-prevalent wind.

Luke approached the curtain slowly, Winchester kept casually by his side. He didn't expect to be recognized, but he had a reputation as a man tracker and bounty killer that would not serve him well in this haven of cutthroats and sidewinding gunslicks. He stopped just outside the curtain, listening.

Hearing nothing, he parted the hanging beads and pushed his way inside. He stepped to one side to avoid silhouetting himself in the doorway.

It was gloomy as a cave inside the sod building. There were two windows, one to each side of the large open room, but they were grimy to the point of opaqueness.

"Hello, stranger," a deep voice said from across the room. "I hope you didn't come in here looking to use that thing."

Luke took a step forward, his eyes adjusting to the dim light. The bartender and likely owner of the no-name saloon stood behind a bar constructed out of an old door laid across two whiskey barrels. The room stank like smoke, rotgut whiskey, and a decade's worth of unwashed men.

"Not directly," Luke answered, hedging a little. "I just didn't want to leave it outside."

That wasn't exactly a lie. Years of riding the same dangerous trails as the owlhoots he pursued had taught Luke the value of being well-armed. In addition to the Winchester, he carried two long-barreled Remington revolvers in cross-draw holsters, and farther back on his left hip was a sheath with a heavy-bladed knife in it. He had a derringer in the top of his right boot, a small dirk in a sheath inside the left one.

All those weapons might make some people say he was armed for bear. Luke thought of it more as being well-prepared for any trouble that might arise.

The bartender was a rough, round barrel of a man with a bushy, drooping mustache and prominent buck teeth. He looked at Luke with his head cocked to one side to compensate for his wandering right eye. He wore an Arkansas toothpick damn near big as a cavalry sword on his belt. Balding, his head was ringed by a matted crown of filthy hair. A Navy Colt sat tucked into the front of his pants. The handle was all but enveloped by his prodigious belly. He grudgingly nodded at Luke's answer.

"Fair enough, I guess."

Luke looked around. He didn't find any friendly faces.

An Indian, maybe Kiowa by the beadwork and fringe on his stained buckskin shirt, lay as if poleaxed against one dirt wall. There was a rough kitchen table Luke suspected had started its journey west on the back of a covered wagon along the Oregon Trail before being abandoned because of its weight. Around this table, three men sat playing a game of cards.

Luke recognized one of them as Martin Hascomb, called Ole Dirty on the trail by his wanted poster. He was thin as sugarcane and had a nose like a vulture's beak. Known backshooter worth $250.

If that was Ole Dirty, then the obese Mexican with the pockmarked face sitting next to him had to be Juan Cortez. Known as Fat Juan, he was wanted for rustling and rape in Texas. He must have figured he'd be safe from the Rangers this far north. But there were a whole hell of a lot fewer Mexicans in northern Kansas than along the Pecos or the Rio Grande, so he stood out. He glared at Luke and smoked a quirley.

Both men were known to ride with Daniel Yellow Dog.

The third man sported a worn and patched dress coat dusted with dandruff on the too shiny shoulders. It wasn't Yellow Dog, Luke saw. The hair tucked into a rawhide bound ponytail was dirty blond. Or maybe just blond *and* dirty, he reflected.

He pretended to ignore the men, even though he had taken in all those details at a glance.

"Whiskey?" he asked.

The bartender grunted in response and put a labelless bottle on the makeshift bar. The liquid inside was the right color, but when the man yanked the cork out it smelled a lot closer to turpentine than Who-Hit-John. When the bartender put a dented tin mug on the bar, Luke was glad the liquor was so strong; at least it would sterilize the filthy cup. The bartender splashed a generous enough shot into it.

"Fifty cents," he declared.

"That's a steep price for something that smells about like moonshine," Luke told him.

The man grinned, revealing yellow, rabbit-like teeth. The easy grin didn't reach his muddy brown eyes.

"I guess you could go somewhere else . . ."

"If there were somewhere else to go," Luke finished for him.

The man scowled at having his punchline stolen.

Luke placed a silver dollar on the bar. He swirled the cup after he picked it up, making sure any lingering small-pox, or rat feces for that matter, left in the tin mug was killed off by the astringent liquor. He threw it back in a single swallow.

Setting it down, he nodded. The bartender poured another. This one, Luke noted, was less generous.

"Where you headed, mister?" a nasal voice asked. It was Ole Dirty.

Luke frowned. He'd hoped to take his drinks to allay suspicion, then claim to want a woman so he had an excuse to leave and check for Daniel Yellow Dog in the cathouse. Didn't seem like that was going to work.

Owlhoots look for trouble, it's what they do, he reminded himself. He set down the cup.

"I guess I'm going someplace where people mind their own business," he answered.

These men were snakes. They murdered at the slightest provocation. But showing weakness to them—and common manners were a sign of weakness in an outlaw town—invited attack.

Besides, if he were being honest, he didn't have much

patience with trying to appease men like these, even if it was only to fool them.

"You mouthy sonofa—" Old Dirty snarled.

Out of the corner of his eye, Luke saw the outlaw rising. He whirled, swinging the Winchester up and around. The metallic *clack* as he jacked the lever was loud in the enclosed space. Ole Dirty froze, halfway out of his seat, eyes wide.

"Anyone so much as shifts their leg to break wind," Luke warned, "and they get a slug in the chest." A cold, humorless smile appeared on his weathered, craggy face. "Go on, try me."

He took a step backward, bringing the bucktoothed bartender into sight. The man had his hand halfway to the pistol butt in his belt. He froze when he realized Luke was watching him.

"You've had your drink, mister," he rasped. "Maybe you should go."

"Can't say as I care much for the company anyway," Luke said. "I'm going to back out that door now. I've been riding for a long time, and I want a woman. I see any of you again, I'll assume you're there to kill me. I will just start shooting, I promise you that."

"You should ride far away from here, *pendejo*," Fat Juan said.

His long, thick mustache was so bushy it barely moved when he spoke. His eyes, beady as the feral hogs outside, were almost swallowed up by his fat, pock-scarred cheeks.

"Someone take a cheese grater to your face, *Gordo*?" Luke asked.

Fat Juan snarled in response. Not a curse, but an actual growl, like some rabid cur. Luke felt the beaded curtain at his back. He stepped back with one leg then stopped and lifted the rifle to his shoulder.

"You, long hair," he said to the blond man still sitting with his back to him. "You think you can turn around quick enough to beat the bullet I'll put in the back of your head, you just keep reaching for that hogleg."

Grudgingly, the blond man lifted his hands so Luke could see them. The bounty hunter stepped through the curtain and then to the side. The rotgut burned in his stomach. It had in no way been any sort of fifty-cent-a-shot liquor.

"I'll be watching this door," Luke warned. "The first person who shows themselves before I'm knee-deep in whatever passes for women around here gets shot."

He stepped farther to the side, putting the sod wall between himself and any clear aim. He slammed shut the door he figured was only closed when the bartender slept, or in the winter.

A wise man would get on his horse and ride hell-bent for leather. Men like those three nursed grudges like expensive liquor and were stone-cold bushwhackers.

But a salty gunhand, like say a John Wesley Hardin, wouldn't think twice about staying in the town. A practiced don't-give-a-damn killer would dare lesser trail scum like Yellow Dog's gang to come after him. Luke Jensen wasn't leaving Craig's Fork without Daniel Yellow Dog. So it was a lot safer if everyone here thought he was a mean pistoleer instead of an outgunned hunter of wanted men.

He had a hunch his troubles were just starting.

CHAPTER 3

Going to the far side of his horse, Luke walked up the street, keeping his mount between him and the trading post door. Holding the Winchester at the ready, he walked the animal toward the derelict looking hotel. When he got there, he took his horse down an alley between it and another of the town's ubiquitous sod buildings.

Going around to the rear, he found the hotel's back door. Several yards away stood an outhouse. Off a little way from it hung a clothesline, heavy with bed sheets rustling softly in the wind.

Holding the Winchester down at his side, Luke entered the hotel through the rear door. He walked with a light step down a narrow hall, past a row of hanging rain slickers. He came out into what had been the hotel lobby some time ago, when the armies of buffalo hunters and hide skinners had been active.

A tall, older black man with iron gray hair, wearing homespun clothes, used a straw broom to idly sweep the floor. He stopped what he was doing when Luke appeared and stared openly at the bounty hunter.

Two soiled doves lounged on an ancient striped divan

on the other side of the lobby. The women wore threadbare dresses a far cry from the spangled saloon-girl outfits he'd seen on whores in the cow and mining boomtown meccas of Deadwood, Kansas City, or Denver.

As worn as their clothes were, they perfectly matched the women wearing them. Young, pretty whores didn't end up in dying towns like Craig's Fork, for the most part. To his surprise, Luke knew one of them. Upon reflection, he realized he shouldn't be as surprised as he was by that fact.

The frontier was a vast, wild space, millions of square miles in size. But people congregated in the towns and the denizens of boomtowns tended to be nomadic, migrating as one lively town died down and another popped up somewhere else. Whores were no different from gunmen, gamblers, or dry-goods merchants; they all followed the money.

The woman's name was Sally Masters, but when he'd known her in Abilene, Texas, and Silver City, New Mexico, she'd been famous under the moniker of Buffalo Hump. She claimed it was because for $10—or a double eagle if the town was truly booming—she'd "hump you like a dern buffalo cow." While he couldn't speak personally to her enthusiasm or skill, Luke thought the nickname might have as much to do with her prodigious size as anything else.

When he'd last seen her in Silver City, Buffalo Hump had been well over three hundred pounds at barely five feet tall. Now, she was positively svelte by comparison, a relatively slim two-hundred-twenty pounds or so. Buffalo Hump was going hungry, he realized.

Not only that, but her left eye was purple and black,

puffy with swelling. She'd tried hiding it with rouge, pan-cake makeup, and eyeshadow the same garish red shade as her henna-dyed hair.

Someone had smacked her around a good bit. Luke thought he knew who. As he watched, she poured a slug of something brown and thick from a patent medicine bottle into a spoon and slurped it down.

The face of the woman sitting next to Buffalo Hump was just as battered. Besides sharing a shiner, the woman was almost comically opposite the much larger woman in every way. Tall, she was thin and bony to the point of gaunt-ness. She smoked a fat cigar with disinterested apathy. A bottle of trading-post whiskey sat on the dusty floor be-tween her feet.

Luke stood still for a moment, unsure of how to best play the situation. Daniel Yellow Dog wasn't anywhere in sight. He assumed the murderer was upstairs with another woman. But Buffalo Hump knew Luke Jensen well. She knew he was a bounty hunter and as unlikely a man to ride the outlaw trail as ever was. Once she recognized him, the charade of him as a desperate gunhawk come to Craig's Fork, same as any other saddle tramp, was over.

"Howdy, sir," the black man said, speaking with a pure Alabama river-bottom accent.

At the sound of his voice, both of the women looked over. Immediately Buffalo Hump's eyes widened in recog-nition.

"Why, I declare," she exclaimed. Her words slurred together. "As I live and breathe, Luke Jensen!"

The scrawny prairie hen of a whore next to Buffalo Hump regarded the tall newcomer with interest. As far as potential customers went, this drifter was a rather large step up from the usual Craig's Fork clientele.

"Hey there, stranger," she said around her stogie. "Are you looking to enjoy some female company for a while?"

Luke sighed. "Not this time, ladies."

"The Luke Jensen I know didn't mind seeing the elephant with a sporting girl," Buffalo Hump giggled, "or two."

"I'm here for business." No sense beating around the bush, he figured. "Not pleasure, I'm afraid."

Buffalo Hump lost her smile. Her eyes, pupils contracted to pinpoints by whatever narcotic was in the snake oil she drank, flickered toward the stairs leading up to the second floor. *Buffalo Hump was a lot of things*, Luke thought, *but stupid wasn't one of them*. She had wasted no time putting together why he was here.

"What kind of business, mister?" the skinny whore asked.

"Luke Jensen only knows one kind of business," Buffalo Hump said. "And that's gun business. He's a bounty hunter, Misty May."

Now Misty May's eyes grew large. In an almost comical mirror of Buffalo Hump, her eyes also flickered upstairs. Unconsciously, she began puffing on her cigar faster, putting out smoke like a locomotive engine.

"Oh," she replied in a small voice.

Forgoing the spoon this time, Buffalo Hump took a slurp straight from her medicine bottle. When she lowered the bottle, her face was set in a hard scowl, and Luke caught a glimpse of the strong woman he'd known during better times.

"I hope you *kill* that half-breed skunk," she spat. "Kill him dead then hang his body from a tree."

"He's upstairs, then," Luke confirmed. "Daniel Yellow Dog."

"Upstairs beating on Lil' Kate," Misty May said, sullen.

"First room," Buffalo Hump added. "You be careful when you start throwing lead, Luke," she said. "Katey ain't even eighteen years old yet."

"I'm always careful," Luke told her. "*Especially* when I'm throwing lead." Suddenly he realized something was wrong. The black man's broom was leaning against the wall and he was nowhere to be seen. "Where did the fella who was sweeping up go to?"

"Snuck out the damn window," Buffalo Hump said. "Luke, that owlhoot Yellow Dog has a gang with him."

"Yeah, they're down to the old trading post, drinking. Old Moses is looking to get free drinks from the owner. Those bandits is friends of his," Misty May added.

"I know about Yellow Dog's gang," Luke said. "You ladies best make yourselves scarce."

"You heard the man," Buffalo Hump told Misty May.

Heaving her considerable bulk off the sagging couch, Buffalo Hump took hold of her friend's hand and pulled her up.

"I don't need to be told twice," Misty May protested. "I'm coming!"

The skinny whore grabbed the bottle of whiskey off the floor as she rose and the two painted ladies made for a door set in the wall behind the front desk. Luke turned and looked up the staircase as they disappeared.

What he'd come for was right up those steps.

* * *

At the top of the steps ran a short balcony with a railing on one side and several doors opposite. Luke climbed the stairs slowly, rifle ready. Soon Yellow Dog's men would be coming, and he wanted to face them from a position of strength.

Halfway up the stairs, sound began bleeding out from behind the first door: the telltale sound of mattress springs singing as someone put them through their paces. A few more steps and Luke heard the woman crying despite the racket the bed made. Clearly, she wasn't enjoying herself.

Luke frowned. He didn't like seeing women mistreated. That went for sporting girls as well as proper ladies. Whores led rough enough lives as it was. Yellow Dog and his men had obviously been very hard on the women. Reaching the top of the stairs, he paused outside the door, listening.

The squeak of the bed springs was louder here. So was the woman's crying. Mixed in, Luke made out a series of low grunts coming from a deep, male voice. Rage welled up inside him. His hand went to the doorknob, found it locked.

He switched the Winchester to his left hand.

Snarling, he stepped back and brought the heel of one boot up and kicked hard. He put his foot just inches from the handle and ripped the lock from the doorframe with a loud, flat *bang* like a gunshot. The door exploded inward and Luke stepped into the room.

He automatically scanned the room for threats, devising tactics on the move.

The room was tiny. A battered dresser stood to his right as he entered. The top of it held a collection of perfume bottles and glass phials. In front of him a nightstand was shoved against the wall. On it was a mirror and metal washbasin next to a clay pitcher. He recognized two or three empty patent medicine bottles like the one Buffalo Hump drank from. Directly opposite the room door was an open window, ratty curtains flapping lazily in the breeze.

Taking up the middle of the cramped room sat a worn, iron frame bed with dirty sheets on a sagging mattress. The whore named Katey lay facedown on it, sobbing. Daniel Yellow Dog covered her naked body like a blanket.

Startled and angered by the door being kicked in, he whipped his head around and shouted, "Who the hell—"

On the far side of the bed sat a wooden chair. On it lay Yellow Dog's filthy dungarees and leather gunbelt. In the holster was a bone handled Colt Peacemaker.

"Get your hands up!" Luke barked.

Instead, Yellow Dog lunged for the .45 with his left hand. Luke stepped around the bed and whipped down the barrel of the Winchester. It struck the outlaw's forearm with a meaty *thwack,* and Yellow Dog cried out in pain.

"Next time you get a bullet," Luke warned. "Now get off that girl and stand in the corner by the dresser. Go on."

Yellow Dog was a big man. Tall enough to look Luke in the eye. His large frame was heavily muscled. Several nasty scars showed on his coppery skin. He moved slowly to get off the bed, and when he shifted, Luke saw Katey for the first time.

She was young. Younger by far than Buffalo Hump or Misty May. Her body was covered with bruises and bite marks, her makeup ran in streaks from her tears. She continued sobbing. Her nose was broken, leaving dark bruises under both her blue eyes. Her lip was swollen and split.

Seeing the abuse, Luke decided Yellow Dog wasn't moving fast enough. He clubbed him across the face with the Winchester barrel. Yellow Dog's head snapped around as blood and teeth fragments flew from his mouth. The outlaw staggered, still naked, into the corner.

Luke leveled the Winchester.

"Give me an excuse," he all but pleaded. "You breathe the wrong way and I'll put holes in you."

"Go to hell, lawman," Yellow Dog answered.

He may have been cruel and a bully, but he was clearly no coward, for all his mistreatment of women. His black eyes burned with hate, and Luke knew if he hadn't caught him with his pants down, the killer would have gone down fighting.

"Katey," Luke asked, voice gentle, "can you get up?"

The girl looked at him blankly. Luke feared the shock of his entrance after Yellow Dog's mistreatment had been too much for her. Her eyes were unfocused as if her mind were far away. She seemed to be staring out through the window curtains and into the vast space of the prairie beyond.

"Katey?" Luke repeated softly. "Katey, can you hear me? Honey, I need you to get up now."

"Can't wait to take your turn, lawman?" Yellow Dog taunted. Turning his square, brutish head, he spat out a stream of blood.

"I'm not a lawdog," Luke told him. "I hunt bounties. Since yours gets paid off dead just as well as alive, I'd consider shutting your damn mouth."

"You're never making it out of this dung heap alive."

"You're not making it out of this room alive if I have to tell you to shut the hell up one more time."

The outlaw glared at him but kept silent. For the moment.

"Katey?" Luke urged. He feared he didn't have long until Yellow Dog's men showed up.

The young girl blinked and the focus slowly returned to her eyes. She still lay prone on the bed, trembling. Without moving, she looked away from the window and found where Luke stood.

"Is he gone?"

Her voice sounded small and soft. But when Yellow Dog began laughing at her question, a look of terror seized her face and she fell silent again.

Downstairs the front door slammed open and Luke heard several boots pounding the floorboards. Cursing, he looked at the outlaw. Yellow Dog smiled. He knew as well as Luke did that his men had arrived. There was no time to waste.

Moving quickly, Luke leaned his Winchester against the wall behind him and took hold of Katey's arm. He hauled her upright and stood her next to him while keeping his eye on Yellow Dog. Katey started crying again as her knees buckled and she stumbled against him.

He caught her easily enough, but in the half-second he looked away from Yellow Dog, the outlaw sprang. If he'd tried diving for the door, Luke would have killed him easily enough. Instead, he leaped forward, screaming a warning to his men.

"Up here!"

Luke fired, but Yellow Dog was already lunging under the muzzle of the Remington. The naked killer slammed into Katey and drove her slight body into Luke's. Luke staggered backward, and his shoulders rammed against the wall.

Katey screamed in terror and confusion as Luke, desperate now, tried pushing her clear. Outside the door, footsteps clomped up the steps at a run. Yellow Dog snatched his Peacemaker clear of the holster resting on the chair.

Luke slung Katey to the side, throwing her sprawling across the bed. Yellow Dog was already turned and leveling the Colt .45 at the bounty hunter. In the doorway, Ole Dirty appeared with a hogleg Colt Dragoon .44 caliber pistol in his hands.

Luke threw himself to the side, covering Katey's body with his own as he fired. The Remington barked and jumped in his hand. The Peacemaker belched flame at the same time, and the double report echoed loudly in the tiny room.

A bullet punched into the mattress next to Luke's head, kicking up a confetti-like snow of ticking and fiber. Katey screamed. Yellow Dog's throat exploded, spraying blood and gristle across the wall. He slumped, eyes crossed as if trying to see the wound that killed him, and fell.

Luke rolled toward the foot of the bed, still shielding the girl's body with his own. He brought his pistol around with him.

Ole Dirty was in the room. The Dragoon looked like a cannon in his skeleton-thin hands. Luke aimed the Remington and fanned the hammer. The gun boomed in his hand, muzzle spitting flame. From point-blank range, three slugs drilled the skinny owlhoot.

Bright blossoms of scarlet opened on his chest, and his knees buckled. Two of the heavy-caliber bullets burst out his back and shattered the mirror on the night table with a crash. Martin Hascomb fell hard, and the last beats of his heart pumped blood from his wounds with enough force to splash the dresser.

Luke stayed in motion, rolling over until his stomach

was on the bed. He held the Remington one handed and fired the last two shots at Fat Juan as he drew his second pistol.

"Get on the floor, Katey!" he shouted.

His shots took the Mexican bandit in the belly, and the killer triggered his pistol into the ceiling as he spun. Right behind him was the bartender, the bucktoothed man holding a Greener double-barrel .12 gauge.

He jumped to avoid the big Mexican's falling body and tried swinging the shotgun to bear, but Luke had pulled the second Remington. Katey screamed again. The cry was a high, piercing sound that echoed as loudly as the guns. Gunsmoke hung in an acrid, miasmic cloud.

Squinting through the haze, Luke sighted down the barrel of his pistol.

Stumbling, the bartender came up against the top step and waved one arm in a looping windmill motion to try and keep his balance. Luke took deliberate aim. The man started toppling backward as the bounty hunter fired. An untidy third eye opened in his broad forehead.

The proprietor of the Craig's Fork trading post tumbled out of sight. He struck the steps hard, body boneless in death, and bounced to the bottom of the staircase like a sack of loose meat. Luke rose, pistol ready. On the bed, Katey cried softly. Gunsmoke and fading echoes of gun-thunder filled the room.

"It's over," he told the girl. "You're safe."

Suddenly she was in his arms, head buried in his chest as she wept. After a moment he hugged her back with his free arm, the other hand keeping the Remington ready. Her tears made his black shirt damp, and she shuddered with the force of her sobs. He held her, making gentle noises, until her crying faded. The fact that she was nude never entered his mind or, more than likely, hers.

"None of those owlhoots will bother you again," he told her.

The jangle of spurs saved his life. He turned toward the sound in time to see the blond outlaw with the ponytail creeping up the stairs. His hatchet sharp face was bisected by a lightning bolt of scar tissue. His .44 caliber hogleg was leveled.

Luke fired as flame erupted from the muzzle of the outlaw's gun. Fired again and emptied his second pistol. The window glass behind him shattered with a crash as the outlaw's bullet smashed through it. Luke's bullets caught the man in the heart with a shot pattern tight enough to hide beneath a tea cup.

The blond outlaw fell back against the wall and slowly slid down, leaving a crimson smear behind him. Gravity took hold as Luke watched, and the body rolled down to land on top of the bartender's.

"I'm sorry I spoke too soon," he said to the girl frozen in his arms. "That was the last of them."

Seemingly cried out, Katey nodded, gathering herself. He let her go, and she began slowly, still in shock, to dress. Keeping an eye on the stairs, just in case, Luke quickly reloaded before he holstered the Remingtons. He didn't intend to get caught sleeping by some unknown party with allegiance to the men he'd just killed.

"Whatever money these men are carrying," he said, "take it. I don't know how much they already spent, but they just got off a spree of stagecoach robberies. There should be enough to get you to a better town than this cesspit."

"Thank you," she whispered.

"That colored man, Buffalo Hump called him Moses," Luke said. "He went to tell Yellow Dog's boys I was here. They already knew, but he didn't know that. Is he tight with this bunch? Will he try and come gunning for me?"

Walking to her night table, Katey dipped a lace handkerchief into the basin of water. She wrung it out and began washing her face clear of smeared makeup.

"I don't think so," she answered. "Moses got no reason to love them. He was just looking for a payoff."

Luke looked at the blood splattered walls and dead corpses strung around like a child's neglected toys.

"Well, for his sake, I hope he got paid first."

CHAPTER 4

It took a while for the citizens of Craig's Fork to make an appearance. In that time, Luke helped Katey empty the pockets of the dead outlaws. He had no compunctions whatsoever about looting from dead men, especially varmints like these. The frontier was a wild, unforgiving place. If the money could do a little bit of good for one of its many victims, then so much the better. He asked Moses to help him round up the outlaws' horses and then heave the outlaws up across their saddles.

Under the circumstances, Moses didn't hesitate to co-operate. When the job was done, the black man said with an embarrassed expression on his face, "I sure am sorry about that, mister. Didn't have nothin' against you, but I figured those boys'd slip me a few coins if'n I was to tell 'em what was goin' on." Moses spat in the direction of the horses and their grisly burdens. "They already knowed. Not only did they not pay me a damn thing, they called me names, to boot, and derned near run me over leavin' the saloon."

"Sometimes the luck just doesn't go our way," Luke said dryly.

"Yeah, I—" Moses stopped short and glared at him. "You're funnin' me, mister. But I reckon *I'm* lucky you don't do worse'n that."

Luke fished a five-dollar gold piece from his pocket and flipped it to the black man, who caught it deftly.

"There you go," Luke said. "So your day's not a total loss."

Moses still looked ashamed, but that didn't stop him from biting the gold piece to make sure it was genuine and then slipping it into his pocket.

Daniel Yellow Dog had a finely crafted Bowie knife on his gunbelt. Luke thought it superior to the one he carried and transferred it to his possession. It didn't pay to let opportunity go to waste on the frontier.

The prostitutes stood in the door of the hotel and watched the grim work. Buffalo Hump had finished her bottle of medicine and started another. Misty May drank most of what was left of her whiskey and swayed on her feet as she chain-smoked cigars. There were a handful of other citizens of Craig's Fork who watched from the safety of their doors. After determining they were little or no threat, Luke ignored them.

Swinging into his saddle, he looked back at his grisly mule train of bodies. His business was hunting, and business had been good. He wasn't sure he'd ever made more money from bounties in one shot than this. When he factored in what he'd get for the outlaws' horses, he was looking at a very tidy sum.

Don't go counting your money yet, he chastised himself. *You still got to get these bodies south to claim the reward.*

Once he was set, he spoke to Buffalo Hump. The woman stood with one sympathetic arm around Katey, who wore a blanket draped around her thin shoulders. Next to the obese woman, the young whore looked positively child-like. All three of the soiled doves looked like they'd gone ten rounds in a prize fight and lost.

"What will you do?" he asked.

"I'm going to run that trading post," Buffalo Hump declared. "I now own the two most successful businesses in Craig's Fork. I'm going to retire a respectable woman. Hell, I might run for mayor!"

Luke laughed. "Sounds like you've got things well in hand." He looked at Katey and Misty May. "What about you girls?"

"I heard they done struck silver in Wyoming," Misty May said. "They got a boomtown called Golgotha Rock. Reckon Katey and I have enough money to make another start, thanks to you."

"Yes, thank you, Luke," Katey said.

He ticked a finger against his hat brim in a final salute. "Ladies."

"You want a free poke for killing them varmints, honey?" Misty May asked. Her words were steady but her eyes were heavy lidded and shiny from drink.

"Uh . . . no, thank you," Luke managed to reply. He cleared his throat, not wanting to appear rude. "I'm in a hurry to get these bodies south before they turn and the horses won't have anything to do with them."

Misty May shrugged. "Your loss."

"Yes, ma'am."

He touched his hat a last time and then gigged his mount. He rode out of Craig's Fork and didn't look back.

Following the North Fork of the Solomon River to where it ran into the South Fork and heading southeast, he made it to Salina in less than a week. Once, he spotted a line of Cheyenne warriors against the sky, riding slowly. He took his little remuda into a copse of willow trees down where the river had dug out a hollow. He made a cold camp there, giving the Indians plenty of time to ride on. In the morning he pushed into the town.

Salina didn't have a railroad spur of its own. Despite this, the railroad's Land Company had invested in the building of a hotel to go with the one room courthouse for the county seat. There was a post office in the general store, a blacksmith, and two livery stables. Not that long ago, during the summer months the dance halls and whorehouses did most of their business servicing cowboys on the drive up from Texas. Those cattle drives were mostly a thing of the past now. At the moment the town was quiet.

The sheriff was a quiet man with steel gray hair, the beginnings of a paunch, and a noticeable limp. He'd started his career as a deputy for Bat Masterson in Dodge City before going to Lincoln to work as a sheriff.

During a disputed card game between drunk cowboys from separate outfits, he caught a bullet in the knee. While convalescing, he met a widow from Red Willow County and decided his drifting days were over. Once able to walk on his own again, he took the sheriff job in Salina after the man before him was fired for perpetual drunkenness.

"He'd been at Bull Run, and then Vicksburg," the sheriff explained. "He couldn't stop dreaming about the war."

Luke nodded. It was a common enough problem for veterans, on both sides. He had his share of memories as well, and very few of them were good. He'd found hunting bad men did more to help him escape the unending loop of those memories than to drink.

"I doubt the County Clerk has enough cash on hand to

cover a payout this large," the sheriff said with a dubious frown.

"I doubt I can haul those bodies much further," Luke pointed out. "They're already starting to get pretty ripe."

"We'll get the clerk to write out a check, and I'll write you a letter of introduction to the officials of whichever town you're headed to next."

Luke nodded his agreement. "I guess that'll do. I imagine Lincoln would be where I'd go next."

"You going to keep hunting bounties?"

"I am. Why?"

"Because you might want to consider going to Carlton from everything I've been hearing."

Luke had been through Carlton. A cowtown of ill repute, it had been dubbed "Bloody Carlton" on account of its lawlessness. Such places usually offered a bounty hunter plenty of work.

"I know Carlton," he said. "I know the sheriff there well enough. You mean in general, or is there something specific?"

The sheriff leaned back and put his feet up on his desk. A drunk snored loudly behind him in the jail cell. Linking his fingers behind his head, the man went on.

"There was a grass fire up that way, not in Carlton, but close by, to the north. Bad one. The whole town turned out to fight the blaze, and while folks was concentrating on not losing everything they had, some owlhoots rode in and robbed the bank. They looted a good number of the other businesses as well."

"They set the fire as a deliberate distraction?" Luke guessed.

The sheriff shrugged. "Nobody knows. They get thunderstorms like the wrath of God on the prairie. A lightning strike can smolder around in wet grass for days, then cut loose when the weather dries it out enough. And you know how the wind gets out there. But either way, the fire torched several buildings and a few people died. They were lucky it wasn't a lot worse."

"The townsfolk posse up and go after the robbers?"

"Sure," the sheriff allowed. "Didn't do them no good. Those bandits was salty dogs. They lost 'em crossing the Little Arkansas River. Rode circles around the local vigilance committee, it seems."

Luke was silent for a moment. Something tugged at the back of his mind. He couldn't put his finger on the memory and filed it away for later consideration.

"Well, I appreciate the suggestion," he said. "I guess I just might check Carlton out."

"I reckon if you could pick up the trail of those bank robbers, it'd pay off enough to be worth your time."

Outfitted with his check and a letter from the sheriff, Luke sold the five horses he'd taken from Daniel Yellow Dog's gang. The man at the livery stable sensed that he was in a hurry and so he didn't get top dollar, but since the horses were found property, it was all profit.

Yellow Dog and his men wound up at the undertaker's, bound for unmarked and unmourned graves. At that, it was more than they deserved, Luke reflected. Men like that were only fit for buzzard bait.

With his business concluded, Luke took a bath, saw a barber, ate a prime meal, drank good whiskey, and then slept in clean sheets. He was up early in the morning and on his way after breakfast.

* * *

He made Carlton in two easy days, saving the horse for harder riding that might be coming in the future once he zeroed in on a bounty. As he rode into town from the east before lunch, he found a typical cattle boom town now growing into its maturity.

Carlton survived when the great Texas cattle drives ended in 1871, in part because of the railroad spur. But it had sprung up in the same fashion as those that had faded away.

Main Street was like any of a hundred he'd seen: general store, hotel, post office, bank, apothecary, a stable on either end, two barber shops, and five saloons. Right at the edge of town was a stagecoach station with a large barn and corral.

Luke spotted what was left of three buildings on the northern outskirts that had burned down. The charred debris hadn't been cleared off yet. Looking beyond, he saw a darker sweep of prairie extending to the north. Patches of bright green dotted the ground here and there.

Luke had seen the aftermath of prairie fires before. The grass had burned off, leaving the ground dark and sooty, but indomitable nature was repairing the damage already. New grass was sprouting in.

Those were the only visible signs of the blaze and the raid on the town. Luke felt quite a few suspicious stares directed toward him, though. Folks here hadn't forgotten their recent troubles.

He turned his attention back to the businesses, searching for something in particular. Each building had an elaborate façade that hid the generally cheap, quickly done construction inside. Elevated boardwalks on either side kept the dust and mud where it belonged, in the

street. Above the walks, wooden awnings provided shade.
A set of stairs led up to a doctor's office in a second-floor
room on one end of the street, and a lawyer on the other.

There was also exactly what he was looking for—a
newspaper office.

Newspapers were ubiquitous on the frontier. The government provided land for $1.25 an acre to speculators and
founders. First came brothels and saloons. But almost
immediately a newspaper office was added. The editor set
up his printing press in a tent or hastily knocked together
shack and began running copy singing the praises of the
area to out-of-town readers.

Land could easily go for between ten and a hundred times
its initial price if a town proved viable. Town newspapers
reached much farther than their local area as news-hungry
communities traded with each other.

Luke found a wizened gnome of an old-timer in a white,
button-up shirt, green eyeshade, and garter on his right
arm. The man's nose was a craggy rock outcropping, ruddy
from a lifetime of drinking, and he wore an ink-stained
apron. Standing at a printing press, he gave Luke a sour
look when he entered the one-room operation of the Carlton *Chronicle*.

"You the manager?"

"Manager, editor, head reporter . . . and I sweep out the
place."

"You the news for the whole area?"

"Well, I ain't giving the Kansas City *Times* a run for
their money," he snapped. "But I guess around here most
folks who get the news get it from me."

"Out-of-state news?"

The old codger squinted at him like he was stupid.
"Ain't enough happening around here to fill out a news-

paper." He paused to consider, then added, "Leastwise if 'n you don't count the constable blotter."

"I was hoping to take a look at some of your back issues."

"Are you thinking of taking out an ad-*vert*-IS-ment?" he asked. He suddenly seemed a lot more interested.

"No, just looking for a story."

Obviously disappointed, and halfway to disgusted, the old man waved a dismissive hand in Luke's general direction. Opening a desk drawer, he removed a bottle and poured himself a drink. He didn't offer his guest one.

"I guess I can't find a reason to say no," he finally allowed. "The morgue is in the closet," he groused. "Help yourself."

"Morgue?"

"That's what you call where you store old editions of newspapers, you idjit!"

Luke, knowing the old-timer would be mortally offended if he burst out laughing at his curmudgeonly antics, fought to keep a straight face.

"Yes, sir," he managed. It physically hurt not to laugh.

Having clearly dismissed the stranger, the codger returned to arranging the blocks of metal letters on his printing press. His foot pumped the pedal and the contraption rotated, stamping into blank sheets of thin paper. The headline read:

CHEYENNE ATTACKS CONTINUE!

Luke opened the closet and found a tall filing cabinet of pine wood knocked together by an indifferent carpenter. Opening the drawers, he found the newest edition and began methodically working backward. It didn't take him long to find what he was looking for.

"Don't you mess up the order!" the codger bellowed.

Fully engaged with solving this mystery, Luke waved a hand in distracted acknowledgment.

In the end, what surprised him the most was how far back the attacks went. Once you understood the pattern it was easy to spot. The paper went back a little over a decade. Every year there was at least one robbery that coincided with a big grass fire. He took note of the amounts listed as stolen in the robberies. A pattern within the pattern emerged. When the amounts of cash were larger, the incidents were farther apart, when the payouts were smaller, they occurred closer together. They always occurred during summer or very early fall months.

As far as he could tell, they began in Missouri a couple of years after the war. They could have started earlier, but the *Chronicle* only went back to '69. The James-Younger gang had been robbing banks for three years at that point. When that group of ex-Confederate guerrillas struck Liberty, Missouri, in '66, they spawned a whole host of imitators.

Few outlaws had the military experience or discipline to turn a stick-up into a clockwork raid the way the James boys did. Their robberies were really nothing more than extensions of the lightning strike assaults they executed during the war.

This Prairie Fire gang seemed to be operating on a similar level. Possibly border ruffians, like the Jameses and Youngers, former Cavalry troops, or at the very least Dragoons. He frowned, shuffling through the papers he'd pulled out of the morgue.

The raids started in Missouri, close to the Kansas border. They moved north to the corner of Iowa in the area where the state border converged with those of Nebraska and the Dakota Territory. Then they marched east to west across the southern part of the Territory.

From the Territory the pattern wound down into Nebraska proper. The latest raid had come across the Kansas border and penetrated as far as Carlton. Luke chewed his lip, thinking. He turned to ask the old man a question.

The codger had one ink-grubby finger up his beak of a nose to the second knuckle. As Luke watched, fascinated by the casually vulgar display, the man pulled his finger, gnarled as an old branch, revealing a glistening green lump. The globule was as big as a child's marble. Casually, the newspaperman wiped it on the underside of his desk.

Luke imagined there were so many of the deposits under there that they looked like green stalactites hanging from the roof of a cave. He felt a little queasy. The old man looked up, eyebrows as bushy and matted as a rabbit tail. If he was embarrassed, he didn't show it.

"You been struck dumb, son?"

Luke cleared his throat to give him a moment to recover. He shook his head. "You got a map?" he asked.

Using his gold-digging finger, the codger pointed at a wall. Luke looked. Tacked to the wall was an official U.S. Census map. Luke hurried over and studied it carefully. The arsonist outlaws preferred smaller towns, but large enough to have a bank or primary business like a mine or mill with a steady payroll delivery.

In chronological order, he traced his finger from the first incident through to the last attack, the one here in

Carlton. Then he noticed another town to the west, Hatchet Creek.

"Hey, old-timer," he said over one shoulder. "How big is Hatchet Creek?"

"Not big. Of course, that's depending on the time of year."

"How so?"

"The Kansas Pacific put in a spike into Ellsworth. It's a cowtown as wild as Dodge City ever was. Hell, so many herds converge on the area, little ol' Hatchet Creek has two dance halls and a bank to handle the overflow." He paused, then added, "It ain't like the old days, mind you. It's just the local ranches driving the beef in. But it still gets a mite rowdy."

The last piece of the puzzle fell into place. Luke would have bet the Jensen family farm back in the Missouri Ozarks that the next place the outlaws would strike was Hatchet Creek. He thought about the fat payout he'd just gotten for Yellow Dog's gang. This fire-happy bunch had looted even more banks and trains.

If he could bring this bunch down, he suspected the combined rewards would dwarf what he'd just gotten. He could take some time off, head down to New Orleans or maybe San Francisco. He'd play cards for a while maybe.

Glad to have a target firmly in his sights, Luke gave the old man his thanks and turned toward the door.

"Where you going?" the codger demanded.

"To make the news, old-timer," Luke grinned.

"Don't let the door hit you in the butt on the way out."

CHAPTER 5

Luke outfitted himself before he set off for Hatchet Creek. He made sure he had enough ammunition to fight a small war if needed. Cheyenne war parties were raiding across the plains, up from the Indian Territories.

Many of the Northern Cheyenne who'd signed peace treaties when Crazy Horse surrendered had been put onto a reservation there near Fort Reno. The quiet barely lasted a year. Now Broken Wing, a warrior under the famous chief, Dull Knife, had taken bands north of the Arkansas river and into Kansas. Travelers and homesteaders, along with remote ranches, had felt their fury. If the army didn't corner them soon, the depredations would likely go on until the snow fell.

It also didn't help that it was the height of twister season. Early summer storms were brutal, unforgiving affairs on the plains. If Luke was lucky, he'd face nothing more than thunderstorms. He wasn't about to let the weather interfere with his man-hunting, however.

Following the Smoky Hill River and riding west, he kept up a brisk pace. There were storm clouds building in the north, and he wanted to cover as much ground as he could before he was forced to hunker down.

Using the Winchester, he shot a small pronghorn antelope on his third day and dressed it out. That night he made camp in a stand of cottonwoods a little ways from a small creek feeding into the Smoky Hill River. He ate the steaks with some wild onions he found growing along the water. He smoked several long strips of meat for travel.

Washing his knife down by the creek, he heard a rustling in the bushes and went still, hand on the Winchester next to him. The babbling of the water made sound uncertain, but whatever was snapping through the branches was big. It could just be a mule deer looking to drink, but it could just as easily be a man.

More branches snapped. Whatever was coming wasn't trying to be particularly stealthy. Easing back from the water, Luke lifted the Winchester. With a final crash, the bushes on the other side of the creek parted in a rush.

Luke brought the rifle to his shoulder.

A horse plunged into view. A little sorrel mare, she was riderless and lathered up from a hard sprint, spittle forming clumps as it chomped at the bit. Jumping into the creek without hesitation, she barreled directly toward Luke. He saw her terrified, rolling eyes and realized the animal was running in a blind panic.

He dove out of the way and the horse thundered past.

A step slower and he'd have been trampled. As the animal scrambled up the grassy incline and out of the cottonwoods, he got a good look. The horse might have been riderless, but it had a good working saddle adorned with silver conchos the way prosperous Texas cowboys liked to dress them up.

It also had two arrows buried in the cantle.

He hurried back to his own camp to make sure the spooked animal hadn't upset his own horse. He thought it prudent to put out his fire. He waited for a long while, letting his eyes adjust to the darkness. Hobbling the horse, he sat quietly, Winchester ready.

After a little bit, the wind from the north picked up, combing the tops of the prairie grass into rustling waves. A party of a dozen Cheyenne braves, or more, was not something he wanted to run into if he could avoid it. No matter how ornery these fire-happy outlaws turned out to be, Luke doubted they were the fighters the Cheyenne were. In his opinion, Cheyenne Dog Soldiers were some of the best warriors of the horse tribes. He felt they were more than a match for the typical Sioux, though he doubted the Comanche would fear them.

The Comanche feared no one. What was left of them anyway.

After a while the wind pushed in storm clouds. He watched a wall of thunderheads building to the north. Lightning jumped in brilliant flashes, but the storm was too far away for him to hear the thunder. When the sky to the east began to lighten and turn orange, he ate a cold breakfast of antelope steak, then mounted up and rode.

He came across the ambushed freighters at noon.

Two buckboards sat in the middle of the prairie, traces empty and the bodies of the draft horses drawing flies a little ways away. Indians counted wealth in horses, and stealing as many as possible was top priority in any raid. But, as he learned during the war, horses were big animals and when lead was flying had a tendency to catch bullets. When that happened out here, horseflesh was a favorite native food.

His mount didn't like the smell of horse blood and wanted to shy. Keeping it from bolting, he let it dance sideways until it seemed unlikely to panic. His eyes scanned the undulating grass for danger. Once the animal was calmer, he dismounted and approached.

The buzzing of flies was a deafening drone. They rose off the horses in great black clouds. Disgusted, he gave the dead animals a wide berth as he went to inspect the wagons. One of the buckboards was overturned, maybe on purpose for use as a makeshift fort. Also maybe when a freighter had tried turning around in too-tight a radius while attempting to flee.

Whichever, nothing had done the men any good. They lay among the spilled dry goods like rag dolls. The attackers had ripped open sacks of flour and dumped them on the men so that it made a pinkish paste where it clung in clotted lumps to their wounds.

The men had been scalped, and flies were as thick on their heads as they were on the dead horses. Stepping over a consignment of spilled shovels likely too cumbersome for the Cheyenne to consider valuable, he forced himself to check the men. Sometimes folks survived. Rarely.

There were five bodies in all. The stink forced him to pull his bandana up over his nose like he was riding in a dust storm. Stripped naked, they had sizable wounds where the Cheyenne had yanked arrows free, though most victims had been shot with rifles, as well. The dead men's guns were gone.

"Hell of a price to pay for thirty-five dollars a month in wages," Luke muttered to himself.

The bodies lay stiff as wooden puppets. He'd seen enough death in his time to guess they'd been killed as recently as last night. Maybe right around twelve hours based on the rigor mortis. He stopped walking and muttered a curse that sounded more like a prayer.

The woman, like the men, had been stripped naked and covered in flour. She'd also been scalped. There were the remains of a small fire beside her body where the raiders broke up crates and casks for fuel. Judging by the burns on her body, the woman had lived longer than the men and had been tortured more. Luke turned away, feeling a murderous rage at the dead men.

"Why the hell you bring her along?" he demanded of the corpses.

They didn't answer.

He felt less anger toward the Indians. Not because he forgave the cruelty, but because he saw the tribes as forces of nature like storms or grizzly bears. When you were in bear country, you took precautions and planned accordingly. When it rained, you dressed for the weather unless you were a fool. When braves were riding the warpath, you kept your womenfolk close to civilization.

If the army didn't mobilize soon, he reflected, the Cheyenne would be lords of these plains once more and shut commerce down to nothing.

Using their own shovels, Luke buried the party. When he was finished, the grave mounds ran in a neat row of sorrow. In a year's time there'd be no sign they had existed at all. He didn't know any of their names but made crude markers out of boards from the wagons and carved epitaphs with his sheath knife.

DIED. INDIAN ATTACK

After pounding the last one, the woman's, into the ground, he tossed the shovel aside and stood in silence for a moment. When he lifted his head, he saw a cloud of smoke rising on the western horizon. It was shaping up to be a real bad day.

First the runaway horse, then the ambushed wagons, and now the homestead. From the order he'd found the depredations in, it seemed obvious the war party was pushing west. A little way from the wagons he cut sign of horses, unshod. They ran unfailingly in the direction of the smoke.

Dreading what he would find, Luke had no choice but to continue. Someone could need his help; it was as simple as that. Always had been. He was a Jensen. Jensens did good whenever and however they could.

As he followed the tracks toward the rising smoke, the front end of the storm moved in. The wind picked up, whipping the grass like ragged banners. It dispersed the smoke column to a large degree, but he wasn't likely to lose course now anyway. He was too close.

He came up over the gentle undulation of a small hill and saw the prairie spreading out in a shallow slope before him. One of the numerous creeks feeding the Smoky Hill wound through the wide-open landscape, and a stand of Eastern Redbud and Bur Oak, shrubs more than trees like he'd known back in the Missouri Ozarks, stood in a cluster.

Smoke smeared the sky above the copse, and he just made out the collapsed structure of a sod house. The wind picked up and it began spitting a light rain. Pulling his horse up, Luke studied the trees and ruins. Could have been a hundred Dog Soldiers in there and he doubted he'd have seen any of them before it was too late.

He pulled the Winchester from its boot. Feeling his tension, his horse danced sideways.

"What?" he asked the animal. "Don't you think you'd like to be an Indian pony? Why, they'd let a stud like you have his pick of Kiowa mares."

Rain began falling harder, and the wind threatened to take his hat. He tugged it down tighter on his head. The horse knickered.

"Yeah, I know," he said. "But who wants to live forever?"

He put his heels to the horse's flanks and started toward the sod house at a canter.

The old joke was as rare as trees in Kansas.

It was true for as far as it went, but the state wasn't totally without trees. What trees there were tended more toward shorter, brushy species, but you could find cottonwood and poplar among others, just not in large numbers.

It was at the edge of one of these uncommon stands that the people who owned the sod house had built their home. Luke made for it as he realized the weather had truly taken a turn for the worse. The wind picked up, and the rain turned to hail. That was never a good sign.

The horse neighed as ice chips the size of quarters pelted them. He gigged the animal into a trot and they made for the dubious shelter of the trees. The hail stung as they rode, slapping into him with increasing force. The sound of it falling was a deafening cacophony. In the time it took for six strides of the horse, the ground was littered with the ice pebbles.

The horse was galloping now. A flash of motion on the horizon caught Luke's attention. He turned to look and what he saw filled him with dread. The clouds swirled tightly like a whirlpool in the sky. The bottom of the formation dropped toward the earth in a tightening spiral.

Twister.

CHAPTER 6

He was almost to the trees when he looked to the plain on the left of him and saw two more tornadoes touch down, trapping him in a triangle of howling death. The hail stopped as if someone had thrown a switch, and the rising, screaming wind pushed so hard against his chest he thought it'd pluck him from his horse.

Branches whipped Luke's body as the horse made the thicket and plunged in. He put an arm up to protect his face and hauled back on the reins with his other. The horse stopped but whinnied in fear. The sound was picked up and thrown into the sky by the wind. Swinging out of his saddle, he tried to find the sod house.

If it hadn't been totally destroyed, it most likely offered the best shelter. His hat was ripped from his head and when he turned to snatch at it, a fruitless gesture if ever there was one, he saw the dark black funnel of the twister barreling toward him.

He turned and saw the sod house through the cluster of tree trunks. He hauled on the reins to get his horse to follow, and grudgingly it stepped after him. Someone had tried burning the structure and there were large swaths of blackened grass, but it obviously hadn't caught fire very well. The house was caved in on one side, the door collapsed, leaving only a window left to show into the darkness of the ruin.

He couldn't get his horse inside. For better or worse the animal would have to remain in the thicket for what protection it could offer. Wind bent the trees double and he heard them snap like gunshots as they broke in two or were yanked from the earth. The twister sounded like a locomotive engine bearing down on him, and the thicket had gone dark as twilight.

Yanking his Winchester from its saddle boot, he let the horse go and ran toward the partially collapsed sod house.

Gunshots crashed close by. Three in a row, .44 caliber, one after the other. It was answered by the unmistakable bangs of a Sharps rifle. These weren't breaking trees and popping branches, this was the sound of battle.

The Cheyenne.

He didn't see any muzzle flashes coming from the sod house. The wind pummeled his back, shoving him forward. As he scrambled into the dark hole of the window, it fairly picked him up and tossed him through.

He came down in a tumble, the barrel of his Winchester slamming into his mouth, and he tasted blood. There was a flurry of gunshots outside but they sounded muted, nearly drowned out by the tornado wind.

Scooting back to face the window, he felt around for his rifle. The interior of the house smelled like earth and reeked of smoke. Hard wind pushed in through the window carved out of the sod, throwing dirt like shotgun pellets into his face.

Suddenly a figure blocked out the light of the window. Giving up on his Winchester, Luke drew his Remington,

The man scrutinized him, sizing him up. There was a tense moment of silence, and then the man seemed to relax. He nodded.

"Well, we're obliged to you for helping the boy," he said. "Josh's pa rode with me in the war. Lost his legs south of Atlanta. I feel mighty responsible for him." He rolled the lucifer to the other side of his mouth. "I'm Neville Goldsmith, formerly colonel, Army of Georgia. This is my sergeant major, Jeremiah Trask." He nodded toward the bearded man.

"Sir, he rode with Marshall Cleveland's boys during the war," Josh spoke up.

Goldsmith rolled his lucifer back and forth again, seeming to turn that nugget of information over in his mind.

"That so?" he asked.

"Cleveland at the start," Luke said. "They claim those James boys invented bank robbery, but that's a damned lie. We were robbing Missouri banks back in '61."

"Didn't his own boys kill Cleveland?" the one called Trask asked. Demanded was more like it. His tone was as surly as his gaze.

Cleveland had been such a ruffian and robber that in fact he *had* been killed by Union forces, although the circumstances hadn't been exactly as Trask had indicated. That was part of why Luke had chosen to say he rode with Cleveland. That allowed him to establish his owlhoot bonafides without explicitly mentioning any particular crime.

He grinned. Having had many a hardcase smile at him right before the lead started flying, he knew exactly how to smirk.

"Sure," he nodded. "Sixth Kansas cavalry caught up with us down around the Marais des Cygnes River. Ol' Marshall wasn't so good at reading maps, it seems. Come

As such, soldiers tended to be meticulous in their care and more lackadaisical of their own.

Luke touched the brim of his hat. "Howdy."

"This here is Luke." Josh performed the introduction eagerly. "The one I told you about, Colonel. The one that kilt them Injuns with the slickest gun-handling you ever saw!"

Luke felt the scar-faced man studying him intently as Josh babbled on, describing his prowess in bringing down five Dog Soldiers. The scar-faced man chewed on the end of a lucifer match. It was the brute of a man beside him who spoke first, though.

"Quiet, boy."

Josh instantly shut up.

The kid's friendly smile melted off his face. Luke shifted slightly in his saddle. If things went sideways, he wasn't going to be able to bring down thirty-five men so easily. He decided he'd charge, shooting, and try and break through them if it came to that. It wasn't a great plan, but he'd rather go down fighting than fleeing.

"That true, mister?" the scar-faced man asked. "You kill five of those red devils so slick-like?"

He wore a black cavalry slouch hat with distinct gold brocade and wide, hand rolled kettle brim. His body was covered in a worn but well-made duster. He wore a Peacemaker on his hip and there was a gleaming Henry .44 lever action carbine in his saddle boot.

"There's five dead in that sod house back yonder," Luke said. "I killed them." He offered a small smile. "I don't know how slick it was, though. It got a little close there at times, if I'm being honest. They came in expecting just to find Josh and that helped some. They were as surprised as I was."

CHAPTER 6

He was almost to the trees when he looked to the plain on the left of him and saw two more tornadoes touch down, trapping him in a triangle of howling death. The hail stopped as if someone had thrown a switch, and the rising, screaming wind pushed so hard against his chest he thought it'd pluck him from his horse.

Branches whipped Luke's body as the horse made the thicket and plunged in. He put an arm up to protect his face and hauled back on the reins with his other. The horse stopped but whinnied in fear. The sound was picked up and thrown into the sky by the wind. Swinging out of his saddle, he tried to find the sod house.

If it hadn't been totally destroyed, it most likely offered the best shelter. His hat was ripped from his head and when he turned to snatch at it, a fruitless gesture if ever there was one, he saw the dark black funnel of the twister barreling toward him.

He turned and saw the sod house through the cluster of tree trunks. He hauled on the reins to get his horse to follow, and grudgingly it stepped after him. Someone had tried burning the structure and there were large swaths

of blackened grass, but it obviously hadn't caught fire
very well. The house was caved in on one side, the door
collapsed, leaving only a window left to show into the
darkness of the ruin.

He couldn't get his horse inside. For better or worse the
animal would have to remain in the thicket for what protection it could offer. Wind bent the trees double and he
heard them snap like gunshots as they broke in two or were
yanked from the earth. The twister sounded like a locomotive engine bearing down on him, and the thicket had gone
dark as twilight.

Yanking his Winchester from its saddle boot, he let the
horse go and ran toward the partially collapsed sod house.

Gunshots crashed close by. Three in a row, .44 caliber,
one after the other. It was answered by the unmistakable
bangs of a Sharps rifle. These weren't breaking trees and
popping branches, this was the sound of battle.

The Cheyenne.

He didn't see any muzzle flashes coming from the sod
house. The wind pummeled his back, shoving him forward. As he scrambled into the dark hole of the window, it
fairly picked him up and tossed him through.

He came down in a tumble, the barrel of his Winchester
slamming into his mouth, and he tasted blood. There was
a flurry of gunshots outside but they sounded muted,
nearly drowned out by the tornado wind.

Scooting back to face the window, he felt around for
his rifle. The interior of the house smelled like earth and
reeked of smoke. Hard wind pushed in through the window
carved out of the sod, throwing dirt like shotgun pellets
into his face.

Suddenly a figure blocked out the light of the window.
Giving up on his Winchester, Luke drew his Remington,

thumbing back the hammer. But the figure was screaming in a male voice, screaming in English, no less.

"White man!" he shouted. "Don't shoot! Please!"

Luke tried diving out of the way, but he'd hesitated when the man had screamed. The figure's momentum sent him crashing into the bounty hunter. Luke fell backward, holding on to his pistol. His head slammed into something hard and he saw stars for a moment.

Furious, he shoved hard against the man with his free hand. The man grunted at the impact and half rolled across Luke's legs. The weak, gray bar of illumination coming in from the eroding window flickered. Luke looked up in time to see a second and then a third figure dive through the opening.

One of the figures lifted off the ground and his silhouette revealed a feather sticking from his hair. Luke fired. The head disappeared, but he didn't think he'd hit his target.

"They're in here!" he shouted.

The man trying to untangle himself from Luke's legs threw himself to the side and Luke was free. The twister was directly over them now. Swirling clouds filled the window, plunging the interior of the sod house even further into darkness.

One of the Cheyenne snarled something in his language. Luke started to fire at the sound but realized he couldn't risk it. He swung out blindly with the heavy iron in his hand. He struck someone and heard a grunt. A body fell into him, and the stench of buffalo grease filled his nostrils.

Something hard, he thought it was a shoulder, rammed into his chin. The blow drove his head back and he saw another figure scramble in through the window. Yet another silhouette appeared in the opening, but then it cried out in a terrified wail made so faint by the roaring wind it was snatched away in an instant. In the next moment, the figure outside the window was gone, lifted into the maw of the deadly cyclone.

Luke twisted his arm, trying to bring the muzzle of his Remington .45 around. He couldn't hear anything but the howling gale. The edge of the sod house roof began peeling back like the lid of a can. Gloomy light spilled through the cracks. Clots of dirt and splinters of trees knifed through the air.

The Indian on top of him twisted and there was enough light for Luke to see the knife in his hand. Black and red streaks of war paint made a mask of the native's face. Luke got his free hand up in time to stop the downward thrust and close a grip on the wrist. They strained against each other, sinew to sinew.

More of the roof flew off, letting in more light. The warrior had all the leverage. The wicked tip of the cheap trading-post knife descended inch by inch toward Luke's face. He squeezed the wrist with everything he had and fought back the knife blade.

The Indian showed his teeth in a snarl. Luke brought the Remington up and laid the metal of the barrel alongside his face. The warrior sagged under the impact, spitting blood that sprayed Luke's face.

Luke swung again, connected again, the end of the barrel clocking squarely into the Cheyenne warrior's temple. The Indian crumpled and Luke abruptly had room to bring the pistol to bear. The gun went off like a cannon between them. The muzzle flash sparked so close to the warrior Luke smelled burnt flesh. The slug struck the Indian in the chest and smashed through his ribs to core out his heart.

The gunsmoke was sucked away along with the rest of the sod house roof. Twilight illumination spilled into the ruin. Dust and debris filled the air, stinging faces. Luke squinted, casting about for the other warriors in the house with them.

They had found their prey.

Two painted braves had a boy in his late teens in the corner. One was reaching for a Sharps 1863 carbine adorned with beadwork on the stock and several hawk feathers dangling from the barrel. The other had a tomahawk lifted over his head. The boy threw his arms up and ducked his face, squinching his eyes shut so he wouldn't see his own death coming.

Luke fired twice. The slugs caught the Indian with the tomahawk between his shoulder blades. Blood from the exit wounds sprayed the cowering boy's face. The brave tumbled forward on top of the boy.

The third Indian snatched up his rifle and yanked back the hammer on the breech. A distant part of Luke's mind realized he'd heard the greasy metallic *snap* of the hammer with no problem. The twister had moved past them.

The Indian lifted the Sharps to his shoulder and swung the muzzle toward where Luke sat against a half crushed wooden chest. The bounty hunter slapped his hammer three times with the flat of his other hand. The pistol jumped like a wild horse in his grip. The three slugs formed an uneven triangle in the Dog Soldier's abdomen and chest. The Cheyenne crumpled and sprawled loosely across the flinching kid.

As the weight struck him, he cried out. Luke, figuring he'd realize the brave was dead on his own, ignored him and pushed himself to his feet. Suddenly buckshot loads of hail whipped down into them through the torn-open roof.

Luke staggered in surprise. Stepping back, his foot caught the limp, dead weight of one of the Cheyenne warrior's legs and he went down. Luke felt something part his hair—the wind-rip of a bullet coming much too close for comfort. The gunshot took him completely by surprise and he looked around.

There was another Cheyenne at the window, his face painted yellow and black. He wore the claws of a black bear around his neck on either side of his medicine bag and several eagle feathers in his hair. They locked eyes for a moment. The warrior snapped the trigger guard lever down on his Lyman Sharps carbine, ejecting the spent shell.

Luke straight armed his Remington up, thumbing back the hammer as he lifted the pistol. The Indian was already ducking away as he fired. The bullet took the brave in the side of his neck and blood spurted out to be immediately dispersed by the wind into a fine mist.

The Cheyenne warrior cried out as he fell back. Hail continued pelting Luke and the boy. In a single breath, Luke was soaked to the bone by the melting ice pellets. Jumping forward, he holstered his empty pistol and drew the other. He looked out the window then jerked his head back in case someone had a bead drawn.

In his quick peek he'd seen the Indian he'd shot in the neck lying on the ground, wide, sightless eyes filling with hail as he stared into nothing. Beyond the dead Cheyenne he saw the thicket, trees ripped from the ground, branches and trunks snapped like matchsticks, denuded of leaves.

He hadn't seen any more Indians, but he was worried about his horse. He liked that horse. It was a good horse.

"Holy cow, mister," the kid shouted. "You done kilt 'em all! That was some slick shootin', I tell you what!"

Luke edged up to the window, still worried about another Dog Soldier popping up like some children's jack-in-the-box.

"How many of those Cheyenne were after you when the storm hit?"

"Six, maybe seven," the kid said.

"That it?"

"My outfit crossed the trace of a larger band. Four, maybe five times that number. The ones I ran into at the river might have been scouts."

Figure seven, Luke thought. *Safer to assume the worst. I got five dead right here. I need to account for the other two.*

He remembered the last figure that had appeared in the window and then disappeared. It was possible the twister had sucked him up. A tornado could fling a milk cow two counties over if it had a mind to. More than one man had been sent flying in just such a manner.

But then the one he'd shot in the neck had appeared once the funnel rode over them. That could have been the one he saw disappear. Which left two.

"Mister?"

"Yeah?" Worried about the Cheyenne, he was only half listening to the kid.

"My name is Josh, Josh Palmer, sir. I want to thank you for saving my life."

"Well, I'm not sure it *is* saved just yet," Luke said, "seeing as how you said seven Indians and I only count five dead. Call me Luke."

"Okay, Luke. I lost my rifle crossing the creek, but I still got the Army Colt my daddy gave me."

"Keep it close. See if you can find my Winchester in this mess."

"I got it. It's right here."

"Okay, good."

Luke holstered his pistol and stepped back from the window. He turned his head slowly, taking stock of the room. Icy water trailed down his back, but in the next moment, just as suddenly as it started, the hail stopped.

Outside, the pitch of the wind changed, slowing to something less than a tempest. The low, angry clouds still hung in blocky gray fortresses above them, but there was the feeling of peace that followed every bad storm he'd ever been caught in. It didn't matter if it was desert, plains, or mountains, the feeling of the entire natural world seeming to hold its breath, waiting to make sure the storm had truly passed, was universal.

Luke reloaded his pistols.

"Cover me from the window with my Winchester," Luke told the kid. "Keep back from it a bit but move back and forth so you get a wide view. I'm going over the top of the roof."

"Yes, sir."

Seeing the dresser the Indian had pinned him against, Luke opened the drawers in a staggered fashion and used them like steps to climb on top of it. Putting his hand against the wall, he carefully peeked over the edge of the missing roof.

He had a better view from here. One of the Cheyenne was twelve feet in the air at the top of a Sycamore tree. Three stout branches, sheared into stakes by the twister, impaled the Dog Soldier like cavalry sabers. Blood dribbled steadily out of the wounds to drip off the ends of the busted limbs.

Okay, he thought, *that's six.*

He climbed over the lip, hung by his fingers, then dropped the short distance to the ground outside. Landing, he went to one knee and drew his Remington. Broken branches stuck in the ground like picket fences. The sod roof was nowhere to be seen.

"You see anything, Josh?"

"Nothing."

Luke walked around the corner of the ruin, scanning the thicket for trouble. Deciding it was safe enough for the moment and growing increasingly concerned for his horse, he holstered the Remington. He walked to the window, which looked a lot worse for the wear.

"Hand me the Winchester," he told the kid.

Josh pushed the rifle through the window and Luke took it. He took one last look around, then decided they couldn't stay hunkered down in the ruin forever.

"I guess you'd better climb on out," he said.

As Josh clambered out, Luke walked toward the creek, rifle ready but pointed down. He whistled sharply for his horse but didn't hear an answering nicker. The whole area smelled like a freshly plowed field, the ground was so torn up. The earth beneath his feet was damp from melting hail, which still stood in snow-like patches here and there.

The place reminded him of a battlefield once the fighting was over and the survivors were left wandering in shock among the dead. Josh walked slowly toward him, his Colt still drawn, obviously impressed by the devastation. Seeing the impaled Cheyenne warrior, he let out a long, low whistle of amazement.

"Whoo-ee! Well, that's one less red Injun for us to have to shoot."

"Could still be one more somewhere," Luke reminded him. "You said seven."

"I said *maybe* seven." Josh laughed. "Truth? I might have been a little scared when I was doing my 'rithmetic."

Luke smiled. "I guess I could understand that." Something Josh had said earlier registered with him. "What'd you mean by 'your outfit'?" he asked. "You get separated from friends?"

The instincts from more than a decade of man-hunting made Luke scrutinize the kid's face when Josh hesitated to answer.

"Uh, yeah," he stammered slightly. "I guess maybe outfit is too strong a word. Just some pardners who ride together."

"How many partners?"

"Well, that can kind of depend."

"Depend on what?"

"Oh, different things I guess."

Luke's suspicious nature was fully aroused now. The young man was definitely giving him the runaround.

"Well," Luke smiled, "how many are riding with y'all at this particular time."

Josh was quiet for a moment. It stretched on so long that Luke actually thought the boy might refuse to answer. Then he mumbled his answer.

"What?" Luke asked. "I didn't catch that, Josh."

"I said thirty-five."

Luke absorbed the information. Thirty-five men not working for a particular outfit or on a drive was damn near unheard of. Since the last big Texas drive had been almost a decade ago, what seemed more likely was that he'd somehow found himself in the company of an outlaw separated from his gang.

Josh didn't strike him as a cold-blooded owlhoot. But then, it didn't take a lot for men to cross the line on the frontier. Sometimes it was nothing more than partnering up for safety while traveling with the wrong element. Sometimes all it took was for a misunderstanding to escalate to a sudden moment of violence. Every man was armed, and frequently drunk.

Either way, it was apparent that Luke was going to guess what Josh's pards were, based on the size of their group alone. Only outlaws or posses caused men to ride in groups that large. Things could turn awkward between him and the kid, and more so if the kid's friends turned up looking for him.

In a flash of inspiration Luke came up with a plan. The kid's accent was pure midwestern, likely Indiana. That state had played an important role during the war while fighting for the Union. But that didn't mean the older men riding with the gang would be Union veterans.

He had to be sure before he tried out his lie.

"I guess that's a pretty sizable collection of pals. I guess I ain't rode with that many pards since the war. I guess you must have a few veterans in your group."

"Hell," the kid laughed, "it's almost all veterans, mister. I got in because my pa served under the colonel during the March to the Sea."

Sherman's March, Luke thought. *Union veterans then.*

"I never got that far east," he said. "I spent my time during the war fighting in Kansas and Missouri. First with Marshall Cleveland and later with the Red Legs."

Jayhawkers like Cleveland, and the Red Leg militias, had been the pro-Union version of the Missouri-Kansas border ruffians like William Quantrill and Bloody Bill Anderson. If the James-Younger gang came out of that tradition, he figured Union veterans riding the owlhoot trail would think a man coming from the opposite side of the same coin might be worth riding with. Both sides had well-earned reputations for murder and thievery, as well as being deadly, hard-riding pistoleers.

Josh seemed properly impressed. "Whoo-ee," he said. "I heard you Red Legs was some rough old cobs."

"We held our own," Luke said. "Of course, all it left me good for was using these pistols and riding hell-bent for leather."

"Lucky for me, I guess." Josh grinned. Luke took that as proof that his story had been believed. The kid considered him for a minute. "Say," he said. "You should think about joining up with us. Colonel Goldsmith is always looking for steady gunhands. I reckon there ain't no steadier gunhand than an ex-guerrilla."

Time to reel the kid in.

"Well," Luke said, "I ain't exactly flush, and I ain't exactly looking to become no damn sodbuster."

Josh grinned. "You're going to fit right in, Luke."

CHAPTER 7

The two of them separated and walked up and down the creek bed, looking for their horses. By some miracle of dumb luck, Luke found both animals grazing about a mile and a half beyond the ruined sod house. Both were white-eyed and tense with the stress of the storm. He didn't even attempt to approach Josh's horse, focusing on calming his own mount instead.

"Easy, big fella," he said, keeping his voice low and soothing as he sidled up to his mount. "I was only kidding about how much you'd like being an Indian pony."

After a little while, the horse let him approach and run his hands along him to check for injuries. The animal needed a good brushing, but other than nerves it seemed fine, thankfully. When he swung up into the saddle and started back toward the ruins, Josh's horse, a bay gelding, didn't seem to want to be separated from the other animal and followed along easily enough.

He found Josh half a mile down the creek in the other direction from the sod house. The kid was no longer alone. His outfit had found him.

Thirty-five men ranged along the bank of the stream,

watering their horses. As Luke approached, the rag-tag bunch watched him with suspicious gazes. Most kept carbines handy over their saddles, ready to be brought up at a moment's notice.

Luke kept his hands visible and approached at a slow amble. Josh stood in front of two men on horseback. One was a burly character with a bear-like build and a wild black beard that nearly reached his belt.

The other was older and much leaner, and something about him reminded Luke of a wolf. Even from a distance Luke could see the scars on the man's face where he'd been burned. Both men regarded him with wary expressions that bordered on downright unfriendly as he approached.

Seeing his owner, Josh's horse whinnied in recognition. The kid broke into a grin and hurried toward his mount.

"You found my horse!"

Luke reined in. "He was with mine, down the creek a ways." He looked at the two men who seemed obvious choices for leaders of the band and nodded in greeting.

The group was a rough-looking bunch. Multiple knives and pistols hung from gunbelts. Every man carried a rifle of some sort. Dirty and ill-kept the men might be, but their weapons looked clean and well maintained, Luke noticed.

He saw scars, missing fingers, the occasional black eyepatch, and plenty of missing teeth. The smell of unwashed men was strong enough to get up and walk around on its own two feet. Their horses, like their weapons, looked healthy and well-cared-for, the saddles well-oiled and burnished.

He'd seen the same sharp contrast in army units on the frontier. Soldiers were often the flotsam and jetsam of society, but their lives depended on their horses and guns.

shoot and we'd killed more separatists than any regular unit at that point. Long story short"—*which is good,* he thought, *because I'm just about out of knowledge on this matter*—"I ended up riding with Jennison. I was a Red Leg for the rest of the war."

While Marshall Cleveland's antics had been criminal from the start, with raids and thievery that had adversely affected both sides, Jayhawkers in general had been more like privateers with Letters of Marque giving them legal standing as long as they stole from the *right* ships. But of the Jayhawkers who rode the Kansas-Missouri border, it was the Red Legs who were loathed the most. A Red Leg veteran was a perfect candidate for the life of western outlaw; the war had given them all the training they needed.

"Well," Goldsmith said, "I guess we need to say thank you for keeping our young Josh here alive. And any man who can do for five hostile redskins in one fight is someone I'd be happy to have at my bivouac. Mister, ah, I didn't catch your name . . ."

"Miller," Luke said. "Luke Miller."

For a long time after the war, before Luke was reunited with his family, including twin sons he hadn't known he had fathered, he had used the name Luke Smith, not wanting the shame of what some considered the sordid profession of bounty hunting to rub off on the Jensen clan. So whenever he needed to use a nondescript alias these days, he had to pick something other than Smith.

"All right, Mr. Miller," Goldsmith went on. "Why don't you come on back to our camp? I believe some of the boys have enough good whiskey to knock the taste of that twister out of our mouths."

"Yes, sir," Luke said. "I do appreciate the invite."

As they rode away, Luke felt Trask watching him.

to find out, the last two banks we robbed turned out to have been in Kansas. Those Union soldier boys didn't care for that."

That comment drew rough laughter from the nearby men. It even got a ghost of a smile from Trask. It didn't last long.

"How'd you escape?" he demanded.

"I didn't have no truck with killing Union soldiers," said Luke, who'd killed his fair share of men in battle while serving the South. "I assumed orders was orders when we took them banks. I'll kill a Johnny Reb if he was eating dinner, but I don't want to be shooting boys on my own side just because they were in uniform and I was an irregular."

Just as his joke had elicited laughter, this comment drew mutters and nods of approval from the men around him. Luke paused for a moment to let that comment settle with the group. After a moment he continued.

"When the Sixth Kansas caught up with us, we assumed there was going to be a talking to, or a dressing down. At worst they would escort Captain Cleveland back and maybe break up the group." He sighed in a what-are-you-going-to-do way. "But the captain was a stubborn man, prone to outbursts. He also liked to punctuate points by drawing his pistols and waving them around." He shrugged. "They shot him down. So there I was, pretty young. And the next thing I know, Cleveland's dead and they're riding us back to what I figured would be a hang rope."

"So how'd you escape the noose?" Trask asked.

"By the skin of my teeth, if I'm being honest. They needed men in the border region. The West wasn't a prime concern for the generals back East. We may have been wild as red savages back then, but we could ride and

Usually they kept a hideout somewhere or scattered once a job was done, not regrouping until it was time to pull another robbery.

This group seemed set up like a military force on an extended expedition. They even referred to themselves as a "unit" rather than a gang.

Considering that they were capable of killing him where he sat, Goldsmith's riders were friendly enough. Still, he was a stranger, and untested.

Quickly enough, Luke found himself alone with only Josh for company. It seemed even more obvious that the kid felt out of place here. He wore a lost, lonely expression as he stared into the flickering flames.

Luke could have told him that it wasn't wise to do that. Nothing ruined a man's night vision quicker than gazing into a campfire. Luke never allowed his gaze to rest on the flames for more than a second.

"You don't mind my asking," he said to Josh, "how exactly did you end up with these boys? Seems to me the greater part of them rode under Goldsmith in the war. Even those that didn't are veterans."

Josh stared into the fire. He sat quietly for so long that Luke thought he wasn't going to answer the question. Finally, he spoke. His voice was low, moving with undercurrents of emotion Luke doubted the kid himself knew were there.

"My pa, I guess," he said. He kept his voice quiet. "Like I told you, he rode with Colonel Goldsmith when they marched through Georgia under Sherman. My pa lost his legs at Bentonville. The damn war was pretty near done at that point and he got shot through one leg and into the other. He said them army docs was always quick on the saw."

"Your pa gone now?"

Josh smiled a little. "No, he's still alive. Back home in

CHAPTER 8

By pure chance, Luke had found the very outlaws he was looking for. But now he was surrounded by them, and his only chance at survival was to gain their trust and acceptance. Providence had delivered them to him, though, and he wasn't going to waste the opportunity.

Still, he figured, *it's not the worst plan in the world.* Also, he didn't really have another choice.

He accepted a jug of corn whiskey and took a slug. He had to keep his wits about him, but he also had to win the men's trust. Refusing a drink didn't establish rapport. So he drank. Josh sat beside him at the fire in the outlaws' camp, and he began to suspect that the kid felt out of place in this gang of hardcases.

They were holed up in an old buffalo wallow deep enough to provide some cover for the light of their campfire. On the plains at night, you could see light for almost unbelievable distances. Campfires could look as bright as stars scattered across the grassland.

The outfit seemed well-supplied, Luke noted. In addition to extra horses for each man, they had a small mule train. Such organization in an outlaw gang was surprising.

Indiana." The smile faded. "Though sometimes I think he does wish he was dead. Mama swears he ain't known a happy day since March of '65."

Luke grunted. There were innumerable veterans, on both sides, who felt the same way, he was sure.

"So he sent you to ride with Goldsmith?"

"*Colonel* Goldsmith," Josh firmly corrected.

"So he sent you to ride with Colonel Goldsmith?"

"No, it was my idea, I guess, more or less." Josh drank some corn liquor from a tin cup. "This country turned its back on veterans. They were loyal and then the country wasn't loyal to them. You imagine a man who fought from Bull Run to Appomattox reduced to begging for the rest of his life? It ain't right."

Luke kept silent. He felt strongly, though, that those weren't the words of the kid himself, but rather an echo of his eternally angry father. A lot of sour plants of hate and rage had grown from seeds of truth.

"One day a member of his old unit came back asking to spend the night and told him he was going west to join up with the colonel again. When he heard Colonel Goldsmith and Sergeant Major Trask were set to ride again like they done in Georgia and the Carolinas, he was pretty damn happy, for once. I thought he'd forgotten how to smile. 'You watch, son,' he said. 'The colonel's going to bring hell to all the ex-Confederates, draft dodgers, and those that abandoned us after the war who thought they could run away to the frontier."

There it was again. The voice of the kid's father masquerading as his own. Josh seemed completely unaware of it.

"I decided I couldn't pass up the chance. So when my dad's army friend started out in the morning, I made up my mind and went with him. I figured it was a son's duty to avenge his father."

"Your daddy's friend still here?"

"No, he was killed up to Dakota Territory. But I'd already ridden on three raids by then."

Luke nodded. He felt sad for the kid. His father's poison had sent his son down the owlhoot path. That trail ended in gunfire or the rope. Josh's father thought he'd just lost his legs to the war. In the end, it would likely cost him his son, as well.

Luke brooded. Maybe there was a way he could convince Josh to leave the gang. He'd like to see the kid spared the hellfire that was coming for these men. But the boy was a man, he'd made a man's decisions and he rode with hardcases. It might already be too late, Luke reflected.

He said good night and settled down in his bedroll. Exhausted by the day's events, sleep came easily enough to him. But his dreams were troubled.

Luke knew the men didn't trust him yet. Especially Trask. He figured they'd test him somehow in an attempt to get him to prove his loyalty and reliability.

The test came sooner than he'd expected, though.

Breakfast was bacon, biscuits, and strong coffee. Luke ate his share. After a bit, the men began drifting off to tend to the horses, swap out pickets set during the night, and pack up their gear. Trask came over and spoke with Luke and Josh.

"Colonel's got a little mission for us," he said. "Finish up and let's go see the man."

"Yes, Sergeant Major," Josh said without hesitation.

Luke nodded and tossed the last of his coffee onto the ground. "Sounds good," he said.

He was troubled that Josh seemed to have been lumped in with him. Maybe they figured that because the kid had brought him in that he was responsible for Luke's actions. That idea troubled him, because, when push came to shove, these outlaws weren't going to like his behavior. Not one little bit.

Equally troubling, though in a different way, was the idea that he and the boy had been grouped together because Goldsmith and his men still didn't trust Josh. That spelled danger for the kid.

He made his bed, Luke told himself, *he's got to lie in it.*

But the thought still troubled him.

Goldsmith waited for them. He'd traded his ever-present lucifer match for a cigar. Luke hadn't grown used to the sight of Goldsmith's disfigurement yet, so he made a studied practice of looking the man in the eyes when he spoke. It was his practice anyway, but he knew men with facial scars were often touchy about them. Goldsmith's scars were no minor matter. The left side of his face looked like a melted candle.

Trask stood off to one side, arms crossed over his barrel chest. He wore a regular holster on his right hip, a cross-draw cavalry model on the left, and had a .454 Colt Dragoon stuck through his belt. A sheathed Bowie knife with a nearly foot-long blade hung off his gunbelt, and the bone handle of a second knife stuck up from his boot top.

The burly varmint isn't likely to be confused for a traveling preacher any time soon, Luke thought.

He also realized that when it came time, Trask was unlikely to surrender. Sooner or later, if he wanted to stop the gang, Luke was going to have to kill the man.

"The sergeant major and I have been talking," Goldsmith said. His eyes scrutinized Luke as he spoke. "We need to perform some reconnaissance and consider our options before we act."

"Makes sense," Luke acknowledged. "What'd you have in mind?"

"You and young Josh here are going to accompany the sergeant major into a nearby settlement called Hatchet Creek. We need to get an idea of how many deputies the sheriff has, how many men are likely to take up arms in an emergency, and where the likeliest places to hit for cash money are."

"Yes, sir!" Josh said.

Luke nodded to show he understood. "We're going to hit Hatchet Creek next, then," he said.

"*We* ain't necessarily doing a damn thing, Red Leg," Trask said suddenly. His voice was basso profundo deep and gravelly as a desert gully. "*We* don't know how *you* handle yourself or even if you're who you say you are."

Luke looked him in the eye. "I can handle myself just fine," he said, voice even. "I'm ready to prove that anytime with anyone."

The tension between the two men sparked like electricity. Like a building storm it threatened to break loose at any second. Rarely had Luke met a man who pushed him so close to violence so quickly. Abrupt violence was a hallmark of his life as a bounty hunter, but Trask seemed belligerent beyond the norm of even casually violent men.

"At ease," Goldsmith said. He didn't shout, but his tone had enough steel in it to catch anyone's attention.

Trask paused for a moment then looked away. He spat. "Yes, sir, Colonel," he said.

Luke knew he had to cooperate if he was going to survive. "Yes, sir," he acknowledged.

"This is a learning experience for young Josh," Goldsmith explained. "A chance for him to show he can be trusted with jobs harder than watching the horses when the rest of the men go to work."

Josh looked proud fit to burst. He nodded energetically. "Yes, sir, Colonel. I won't let you down!"

"I know, son," Goldsmith smiled. He drew on his cigar, the breeze immediately snatching the smoke away. He looked at Luke. "You understand we can't just take Josh's word for everything. Most of these boys have been together since the war started. The ones who didn't ride with me for Sherman have been with us a good spell. We know they're solid. If we're going to trust you, we need to see how you handle yourself."

Luke nodded. "That makes sense," he acknowledged. "I appreciate the opportunity to prove myself."

"One of the fastest ways to earn our trust is showing you're able to follow the chain of command. That means listening to the sergeant major."

Luke let his mouth settle into a hard, flat line. He nodded sharply, playing the role of hardcase trying to earn his way into a new gang.

"I get that," he said. "I know how to ride with an outfit."

Goldsmith nodded. "And that's just what we are, Luke," he said. "We're an outfit, a unit, just like the Red Legs. We're taking our Jayhawking to ex-rebels who think their crimes have been forgiven. We're taking our Jayhawking to those who turned their backs on us after the war."

"That sounds all right by me, Colonel," Luke lied.

Goldsmith smoked his cigar. He looked satisfied. "Good," he said. "Then get to it."

CHAPTER 9

As Luke approached Hatchet Creek with Josh and Trask, he realized that he had been through the settlement a couple of years earlier, although as far as he remembered he had never heard the name of the place.

It had been a lot smaller then, too, barely more than a wide place in the trail. As that crotchety old newspaperman back in Carlton had told him, Hatchet City had grown a lot since the railroad reached Ellsworth, not far away. Now it was starting to look like a real town.

Luke hadn't interacted with a lot of the folks here, just picked up a few supplies at a trading post and moved on. Nobody in Hatchet Creek had any reason to remember him or know that he was a bounty hunter. But after so many years of roaming around the frontier, it was impossible to guarantee he wouldn't run into somebody who would recognize him.

He had made a few friends over the years . . . and a whole heap of enemies.

He turned this potential problem over in his mind as the three men rode into the prairie town, but eventually he settled on a cold truth.

If things fell apart, he'd kill Trask as quick as he could and then attempt to arrest Josh. Then he would go after the gang. That was what was going to happen sooner or later anyway.

It was probably just as well he made peace with this fact, because things went to hell pretty damn fast.

They made the town by early afternoon. And when things quickly went wrong and spun out of control, it wasn't because anyone recognized Luke.

It happened because of a girl.

The town was booming. A large company of freight haulers had arrived with supplies. The streets were crowded with people shopping, and the platoons of bullwhackers and muleskinners looking to blow off steam after an arduous and dangerous trip. Muleskinners were freighters who drove wagons pulled by mules. Bullwhackers were those freighters who used teams of oxen.

Neither group of laborers was considered the cream of society.

Luke, Trask, and Josh had come into town in the opposite direction Luke had used on his last visit. As such, they were able to corral their mounts without incident. They walked slowly up and down the main street, Luke sweating them running into the sheriff the whole time. The way lawmen moved around, the local star packer might well be the most likely person in town to remember his face.

That didn't happen, however, and after thoroughly walking the town, Trask seemed satisfied for the moment.

The bank was the primary target, but Trask also picked out the largest general store. It might have a safe so that the owner could lock away a day's receipts and not take them to the bank until the next morning. They went inside to have a look around.

"You got any money on you, kid?" Trask rumbled at Josh.

"Yeah, why?" Josh sounded surprised by the question.

"Go buy some candy."

Josh's jaw tightened. His expression stiffened. In a quiet but angry voice, he began, "I'm not some kid—"

"I don't want that clerk gettin' suspicious of us," Trask cut in. "We'll give him a reason for us bein' in here."

"Oh." Josh nodded. "I understand now. Sorry if I—"

Trask interrupted him again. "Just do what I told you."

Apparently idly, Josh wandered over to a glass-fronted case that held various types of candy. The apron-clad clerk finished with a sale and came to see what Josh wanted. While Josh was pointing out a couple of different kinds of candy, Luke and Trask ambled along the rear counter.

There was a safe back there, all right, a small, square job with one of those newfangled combination locks. You didn't see many of them on the frontier, especially outside of banks.

Josh had finished buying his candy. He headed for the door. Luke and Trask followed him.

Once they were outside, Josh asked, "You want some of this licorice, Sergeant?"

"No, damn it," Trask replied through clenched teeth. "And don't call me sergeant!"

Josh swallowed hard, nodded, muttered, "Sorry. I forgot."

"Let's finish taking our look around," Luke suggested.

The next obvious targets were the saloons and brothels. The establishments were booming and likely had considerable amounts of money stashed away. But being able to loot them depended heavily on how many customers and employees left to fight the fire Luke knew the gang would set as a distraction.

Being forced to shoot their way through an outfit of stupid cowboys looking to protect the honor of their favorite whores could greatly compromise the plan.

"Maybe we should pick out one, or maybe at most two places with setups that look particularly lucrative," Luke suggested. "One of us can check as we ride in and if there aren't too many people hanging around, we take 'em while the rest do for the bank."

Trask pursed his lips, turning the idea over. He stopped in front of a busy saloon and spat a long stream of tobacco juice into the dirt. He indicated the saloon with a thrust of his lushly bearded chin.

"I suppose that could work. We'll have to take closer looks at them before we make up our minds, though. Make sure we've got our eyes on the best places."

"If we're doing that, we'll need to blend in," Josh said eagerly. "We don't want to stand out. We'll need to drink, maybe buy a girl, stuff like that."

He grinned the way only young men thinking of fast women can grin.

His enthusiasm was so sincere it was contagious. Trask almost smiled. He turned the kid's words over for a moment, playing up his authority. Luke wasn't fooled. He'd seen the way Trask had eyed a stable of Chinese girls set up in a tent behind the laundry. If it was up to Trask, they would check out that place eventually, but the saloon in front of which they found themselves appeared considerably more prosperous.

"Beer only," Trask said as they paused on the boardwalk. "Keep your eyes peeled for where they keep the safe."

Outside the batwing doors hung a painted sign with a surprisingly good depiction of a rooster riding the back of a cat. No words were written on it, but they weren't necessary.

"That's real funny," Josh said as he looked at the sign. "You get it?"

"Yeah, kid," Luke noted dryly. "I'm pretty sure everybody gets it."

Josh laughed. Trask scowled. The three men went inside. Even though it was a weekday, the place was busy. In fact, it seemed rowdy to a point just short of a riot. Rough-looking men in dirty clothes filled the room. The bull-whackers who had brought the freight wagons into town lined the long bar where saloon girls goaded them into buying drinks. The freighters took up the tables as well, some of them playing cards.

A roulette wheel and two Faro tables sat on one side of the room. Those were filled with more shouting, laughing men than the bar. More saloon girls mixed with the gamblers, wearing low cut and corseted dresses, egging the men on to reckless bets and even more shots of whiskey.

A black man banged out songs on an old piano, stopping every now and then to take swigs from a beer and count his tips. Sawdust was scattered on the floor, tobacco smoke hung in a fog just over the heads of the customers, and as Luke watched, an endless parade of men entered and left the upstairs rooms where scantily clad women waited in their doorways.

"Beer only," Trask repeated.

He spat tobacco juice on the floor, not even attempting to get it in any of the spittoons placed around the room. From what Luke could tell, he was hardly alone in that habit. The floor was as sticky as a field of mud under his boots.

Easing their way through the crowd, they managed to reach the bar. The bartender was an abnormally tall and pale man with oiled-down hair and a handlebar mustache waxed to points sharp as arrowheads. He wore a red-and-white striped button-up shirt under a tan apron. When he spoke, Luke saw that half the teeth in his head were gold.

"What you gents drinking?"

"Beer," Trask announced.

"Coming up."

The service was fast despite the crowd. Luke took a few big swallows, clearing the trail dust out of his throat. The beer was flat and room temperature. It made him think of the refrigerated beer he'd had in Denver and St. Louis. It was becoming just enough of a common commodity that he noticed the difference when he couldn't get it.

Josh drank half his beer in an eager gulp. "This place is hopping!" He grinned.

Luke smiled. The kid's good nature was infectious. Not all of his basic wonder at the world had been knocked out of him yet. It'd happen soon enough, riding with such a crew of hardcases, though, Luke knew. The war had pretty much done for Luke's own naivety by the time all was said and done. Its loss made him appreciate it when he came across such optimism. In his experience it was an exceedingly rare commodity.

"You ain't here on no damn vacation," Trask snapped.

"Ahh, we got time to see a girl, don't we?" Josh asked. "I mean, we're already in town."

Luke saw his opening. Following his instincts, he leaned over closer to Trask. "Let the kid have some fun," he suggested. "I'll stick with him and sort of hurry him along.

Give you a chance to do some business without having to nursemaid him. It'll give you a chance to see I can follow orders."

Trask was a first-rate killer and a steady hand at cold-blooded outlaw work, but he wasn't complicated. He didn't guard his expression like some riverboat gambler with a winning hand. His thoughts cascaded across his face without guile. He was thinking about those Chinese girls. Unconsciously, his tongue flickered out and moistened his lips.

"I guess that makes sense," he allowed, voice grudging. "I wanted to double-check something anyhow."

Luke nodded, face solemn. "Probably wise. We need to do as thorough a job as we can."

Trask spat, stroked his beard, weighing the decision over in his mind. "I think I might just get my shirts laundered."

Luke, realizing the man was talking himself into the idea, kept quiet. After a moment Trask jabbed him in the chest with a blunt finger.

"You're responsible for the kid," he said. "Make sure he don't go shooting his damn fool mouth off."

"Not a problem," Luke said.

It turned out to be a problem.

CHAPTER 10

Trouble hit almost as soon as Trask made it out the door.

Saloon girls had a very specific job. They flirted with customers and encouraged the men to purchase drinks for them. Drinks for the girls were usually a little bit more expensive. Frequently the bartender gave them watered-down drinks or even tea in place of whiskey so the ladies could function all night. Sometimes they were prostitutes hustling for business, as well, but frequently they were not. In establishments where both kinds of women worked, being a saloon girl was often how a young woman eased herself into the business of whoring.

From what Luke had seen so far, the sporting ladies in this saloon worked both sides of the job.

One of them approached Josh. She was a pretty little thing, no more than nineteen at the most, with an elfin face and a curvy but compact figure. Her hair was the color of summer wheat and her eyes a startling shade of cornflower blue.

"Hey there, cowboy," she said. She draped her body against Josh's. "My name's Sarah. Buy a girl a drink?"

Josh turned beet red and tried stammering out an answer. Rolling his eyes, Luke turned and signaled the bartender for another beer. Still, the best way to learn was by doing, so he didn't try to save the kid. Of course, if Trask showed up and found the kid drunk as a skunk, there might be trouble.

He leaned over to Josh. "We're just drinking beer," he stressed so the girl heard him.

She showed a smile as bright as the noonday sun. It was dazzling. Luke wasn't sure it reached her eyes, however.

"Why shoot," she said. "That's fine by me! Why, I get plumb crazy when I drink too much." She ran a finger up and down Josh's arm. "There's no telling what I might do if I got drunk."

"Whiskey for the lady!" Josh said in a too loud voice. He colored and looked at Luke bashfully. "I'll stick to beer," he assured Luke.

Luke snorted. You couldn't save the young from themselves.

"Come here, gal," a gruff voice bellowed. "A pretty thing like you needs to be with a real man, not some damn pup."

Luke turned at the sound of the insulting challenge.

He saw a giant of a bullwhacker standing before them. The man stood six and a half feet tall, towering over Josh, who was average height. His frame was heavy and his hands large as dinner plates. A filthy, knotted beard spread in a fan over his deep chest and a shapeless black hat kept a rat's nest of long, greasy black hair in check.

There was a .44 Henry revolver pushed behind his broad leather belt, as well as an Arkansas toothpick with a fourteen-inch double-edged blade. Luke was certain those weren't the only weapons the bullwhacker carried. He was loud, clearly drunk, and just as clearly used to getting what he wanted by virtue of his massive size.

With one grubby paw, he snatched up the girl's arm, yanking her to him. The saloon girl was like a child compared to him. She bounced into his body and he pressed her close, leering at Josh over her head.

"You like that, little girl? Big Edgar knows what the pretty girls like!"

His grin revealed square yellow teeth so large and blunt they would look at home in the mouth of the oxen that pulled his freight-hauling Conestoga wagon across the plains. He laughed like a donkey braying.

"Let me go, you damn jackass!" Sarah shouted.

Josh spun. He might be young, but he'd been riding the outlaw trail among men who killed for much smaller offenses. His hand went for the Army Colt at his waist. Luke stopped him.

"Easy," he warned. He dropped his voice. "The trail boss," he said, referring to Trask, "isn't going to appreciate you getting pinched into the hoosegow right before it's time to go to work."

The kid relaxed. Luke noted the discipline Goldsmith had ironed into his outfit. It explained their continued success in an occupation more known for early deaths than long careers. That was one of the reasons it was so important to stop them.

But Big Edgar had seen Josh's initial move and responded. He threw the girl to one side and drew the Henry .44. Luke stepped around Josh, his hand like lightning as he moved. The Henry had just cleared the bullwhacker's belt when Luke shoved the barrel of his Remington up under the man's chin.

The bullwhacker froze. Luke used his free hand to lock up the wrist holding the pistol.

"Easy," he warned. "We don't want this getting out of hand."

Silence spread through the saloon like a brush fire. The piano player continued banging away for a moment until he, too, sensed something was wrong and turned his head to look. His hand slipped and the wrong note echoed discordantly. He stopped playing.

"That's right, gentlemen," the bartender said. "*We* don't want this getting out of hand."

Luke heard the distinct metallic *snap* of shotgun hammers locking back. He glanced over. The bartender had a Greener side-by-side 10-gauge with the barrels sawed down flush with the forestock. If he triggered the cannon from this range, the shot would take off both men's heads.

Luke noticed that where it had been shoulder-to-shoulder standing room at the bar only a moment before, now there was plenty of empty space around them.

"Willy," the saloon girl told the bartender, "it was that stinking bullwhacker who started it!"

Willy wasn't moved. "You drink with the customers, Sarah, whoever the customer is. You don't like that, I figure you can work someplace else."

"Yeah," Edgar said. "I was just offering to buy the little miss a drink is all."

The bartender ignored him. "Both of you holster them big irons. Now."

Luke released Edgar's hand. Carefully, glaring at each other, the men put their revolvers away.

"I'm drinking with the girl," Josh said. His voice was stubborn.

"She's drinking with me, boy."

Luke looked sideways as he stepped back. The girl stood quietly. There were high points of color on her cheeks and Luke had to admit she was an exceptional beauty. He scanned the saloon, taking stock of those watching. There were plenty of bullwhackers, but they didn't seem particularly interested in backing their compatriot. At least not vocally.

Big Edgar must not be too well liked by his coworkers, Luke thought. That was something at least. Maybe this thing could be contained.

"It's a free country," he said. "The lady can choose who she drinks with."

"That's right!" Josh agreed.

"The hell she can," the bullwhacker roared. "My money spends as well as this here boy's. Willy, you know I bring plenty of money in here every month when I bring my boys to town. I'm a good regular customer, not some no-account drifter."

Luke frowned. The man ran his own freight company. That might change things.

Men would stay loyal to the one who paid them, even if they couldn't stand him. To a point anyway. And a regular customer who was free with his money went a long way toward earning a proprietor's sympathy. What was fair just didn't figure into things when money got involved.

"She's drinking with me," Josh said. His voice was tight with fury.

He was hot enough to get them both killed over this saloon girl, Luke saw. He caught the bartender's eye.

"I don't see how you explaining a bunch of dead men in your place to the sheriff, no matter who or why they're dead, is going to help you do business. He's liable to shut the place down."

He was taking a gamble using that logic. In the early days of places like Kansas City, Deadwood, and Tombstone, nothing stopped the drinking or whoring or gambling. Dead men were carted outside or put in the icehouse. Business didn't stop for blood.

But usually, once a place settled down a bit, even one that remained rowdy overall, something as uncouth as gunplay and murder could close an establishment, at least for the night. He hoped Hatchet Creek had progressed to that point.

After a long, tense moment, a look of consternation appeared on Willy the bartender's face. He lowered the Greener and looked around. Luke could almost read his mind; men waiting for a gun duel weren't busily spending money on cards or liquor or women.

"If you boys want to fight over her, I won't let her go with either one of you. I'll send my colored boy to fetch the sheriff and have both of you thrown behind bars."

"This ain't settled," Edgar growled.

"Then you can settle it with cards," Willy told him. The bartender's face lit up with inspiration. "Play a hand of Faro for her, winner take all. The loser goes someplace else to drink."

"Fine by me!" Josh snapped. "Let's do it."

What the hell is happening here? Luke wondered.

The situation had shifted and changed and gone off the rails so rapidly in so many directions he felt like he was getting a stiff neck. He also wasn't sure that Josh could just walk away and leave the saloon girl to drink with a varmint like Edgar, or that someone like the bullwhacker would admit he was beaten even if he was.

The situation still had potential violence stamped all over it.

"I ain't scared of nothin'," Edgar declared.

The crowd standing around them cheered. It was a ragged, boozy rallying cry, but the situation had drawn the whole saloon's interest. Luke doubted he could have put a stop to it even if he could talk the kid into walking away.

Josh sauntered over toward the Faro table, grinning big. He seemed to be enjoying all the attention. Luke hoped his luck held.

Faro was a simple game. It was that very simplicity that contributed to its popularity. It was exceedingly hard to cheat, and it could be played almost blind drunk. Going from Ace through the numbered cards to the King, thirteen cards of one suit, almost always spades, were laid down in two rows of six with the seven of spades put off just to the immediate side.

This was the game board. Players picked the card with the face value (Ace through King) they thought would win and put their money or chips on that card. The dealer took a regular fifty-two card deck and turned over the first card, showed the players, then discarded that draw.

The game started. The dealer flipped over two cards. The first card was the losing draw. Anyone except the banker with bets on that card lost. The second card was the winning draw. Any player with bets on a card of the same face value doubled his money. The rest drew even.

Once the two drawn cards were put in a bone pile to one side, players were free to change their bets to different cards or double down on the choice they'd already made. Discarded cards were left face up and clearly visible. The dealer then drew two more cards. If both drawn cards were the same face value, the dealer took half of the money on that card.

The house held the advantage. But there was still a

reasonable chance of winning. Luke had heard it likened to playing roulette with cards.

"Why don't you get us some drinks, darling?" Josh told Sarah. He gave her some money, and she went to the bar.

Josh immediately turned to Luke.

"Uh, I hate to ask," he said, voice low, "but you couldn't see your way to maybe lending me a little money, could you?" He hurried on when he saw the doubt in Luke's eyes. "Please, it ain't right that such a nice girl should have to go with a no-account bit of trash like him."

Luke could see that the irony of an outlaw calling a man with an honest job "trash" was lost on Josh. He supposed that, gainful employment aside, the mark of a man was how he treated women and those in less fortunate positions than themselves. By that marker, the bullwhacker was indeed trash.

Young men on the frontier falling in love with whores was hardly uncommon. Once Sarah took him upstairs and bounced him off the mattress springs, it was only going to make it worse.

But Luke had to admit that in his lonely life of riding and killing, he'd sometimes taken the same comfort. There was a certain red-haired madam he'd left behind in Deadwood who'd been his good friend and companion for a while. Maybe Sarah was as good a gal as Maggie. He guessed he'd want someone good to stick up for Maggie if she ever found herself facing the same problem.

He sighed like a man contemplating a long, uphill walk.

"Fine," he said.

"Thanks, pard!"

Luke handed over a $20 bank note. "Buy chips from the dealer with this."

"You ready to lose your money, boy?" Edgar demanded.

His face was a sneering mask of condescension. The bullying nature of the bullwhacker set Luke's teeth on edge. "Once I'm done cleaning you out, I'll show that little piece of fluff how a man does it!"

"Beat this buffalo patty until he cries, Josh," Luke snapped, his patience wearing thin.

"You calling someone a buffalo patty?" Edgar demanded.

Luke met his eyes, face expressionless. "I guess if I'm talking to you, you'll know it."

The two men glared at each other for a moment. The bullwhacker saw something in Luke's eyes he didn't like and looked away. Insulting boys was one thing. Mouthing off to obvious hardcase gunhands was quite another.

"Are we going to play or not!" he shouted.

"Ready when you are, sir," the dealer said.

Sarah returned with drinks. Luke noted with approval that she'd been savvy enough to bring beer instead of whiskey. Let the bullwhacker get drunk and impulsive. If Josh was going to win, he needed to play with a clear head.

Luke had an uneasy feeling about how this was all going to turn out.

CHAPTER 11

Josh gave the dealer his cash and took chips in turn. In smaller or newer towns, players placed their bets with money. Once an establishment or township had been around for a while, as Hatchet Creek had, most businesses went over to chips. Edgar scowled when he saw how many chips Josh had staked in front of him.

Josh put the cheroot he'd purchased in his mouth and Sarah lit it for him. She hung on his arm and whispered encouragement in his ear. Luke was a man-hunter by trade. Some of that involved tracking in the traditional sense, but a lot of it came down to reading people. He was good at it. But he couldn't seem to get a gut-feeling about the girl.

He couldn't tell if she was good-hearted and had latched on to Josh because she sensed his kindness, or if she was a professional manipulating a mark. It bothered him he couldn't tell, but he found himself wanting to give the soiled dove the benefit of the doubt.

Edgar slapped a bulging leather sack onto the table. The drawstring on the top came loose and several silver *reales* spilled onto the table.

"We're playing until one of us is bust!"

"The hell we are," Josh protested. "One hand, winner take all."

Edgar grinned, showing those mule teeth. "All right. But you gotta match my bet."

"I can't cover that all at once," Josh sputtered.

Luke turned to Willy the bartender. "This isn't what we agreed on."

The bartender had locked his gaze on the bag of silver the bullwhacker had put on the Faro table. Greed shone in his eyes like light from a lantern in a deep cave. The law of averages that kept these games of "chance" profitable for the owners was clear; the more these two drunk fools bet, the more the house stood to gain.

"I reckon I think it's fair to let things play out," Willy said.

He stuck his thumbs underneath his suspenders and stretched them out in a pompous display. Luke turned away, disgusted. Josh was looking up at him pleadingly. Sarah had a near petrified look on her pretty young face. He sighed.

Reaching into his shirt pocket he pulled out a roll of $20 and $50 government notes. He wasn't a banker, or an assayer for that matter, but every newspaper worth its salt carried the latest exchange rates as they were understood. Luke kept up with such things well enough that he had a decent idea what the silver exchange rate was. He figured the amount of his bounty money roughly covered what the bullwhacker had shown in silver.

"Beat him, Josh," he said.

The crowd exploded in cheers. Rough hands slapped Luke's back and suddenly a slinky looking saloon girl in a red satin corset petticoat and knee high, lace up the front, high heeled boots sidled up to him. She smelled like lavender and had huge brown eyes. Hugging his arm, she gently pressed the swell of her generous and very much on display bosom against him.

"Buy a girl a drink?" she asked. "Gambling is thirsty work."

The lady was good. She somehow turned *thirsty* into the most obscene word he'd ever heard. A chill ran up and down the length of his spine. He was on the verge of sending her politely away when Josh, with Sarah laughing in delight, shoved the entire kitty Luke had just staked him across the table to the dealer who began counting out chips.

Watching almost his entire poke disappear, Luke sighed. "I must need my head examined," he muttered. Not for the first time.

"What's that, mister?" the lanky saloon girl asked.

"I said, get us a bottle," he said. He handed her his last $10 government note. "And hope for both of our sakes the kid wins."

She took the money from his grip with a sensual smirk and disappeared. *If the kid loses, I may* have *to turn owlhoot for real,* he thought sourly. He turned back to the table. Edgar and Josh were placing their bets.

"All bets final," the dealer said.

He was a portly little dandy-looking fellow with a blue garter on the arm of his dirty ruffled shirt and a pork pie hat with black silk band sporting a peacock feather. He had a nose with prominent red veins like a river delta.

Taking up the deck, he began a smooth Faro shuffle. He split the deck in half and made a show of neatly tapping the bottom of one half with the top of the other. Once that was done, he settled the halves one atop the other and wove them down into each other about a quarter of the way. Then he bent them and let them shuffle quickly into place.

The crowd had grown quiet enough that the spectators could hear the whisper of the cards as they settled back into a single deck. He repeated the process three more times and then carefully set the deck down.

"Satisfied?" he asked.

"It's fine," Edgar half-snarled. "Get on with it already!" He turned toward the bar and shouted, "Whiskey!"

The crowd roared in approval. Luke figured this kind of contest constituted first-class entertainment around these parts. So much for keeping a low profile. Trask was not going to be happy when he heard about this.

The girl appeared at Luke's arm. She handed him a shot glass. He tossed the drink back without looking at the bottle she held. It went down with surprising smoothness. He looked at the girl in surprise. Grinning mischievously, she held up a bottle of Kessler whiskey. Made in Denver, it went as high as $2 for three fingers. She grinned.

Nodding toward the bartender who was watching the Faro game intently, she leaned in close and whispered into his ear.

"I guess if old-limp-carrot-Willy ain't paying attention it won't hurt nothing for us to drink quality."

Her breath blew warm across his ear. Once again, he felt the press of her breasts. *She's about as subtle as a sledgehammer,* he thought, *but a sledgehammer doesn't need to be subtle to knock you on your butt.*

He felt a schoolboy grin pull the corners of his mouth back. He held out his shot glass and she filled it. She matched his grin with a wink.

"Call me Jenny," she said.

"Here's to you, Jenny." They toasted, her with the bottle and he with the shot glass.

When that was done, he swallowed his second drink and she took a healthy slug from the bottle. *So much for "beer only,"* he thought. *I'll probably end up having to shoot Trask sooner rather than later.* The whiskey spread a warm, relaxed feeling through his body. *Oh, well.*

"Place your bets," the dealer said.

Josh and Edgar began putting chips on cards. Edgar threw back two more whiskey shots, one after the other, smooth as a piston on a steam engine. By Luke's reckoning, he'd already been well-lubricated before this whole situation had unfolded. He looked bleary-eyed and unsteady on his feet.

His betting system seemed to be to spread as many bets as possible across multiple cards. Josh, seeing what he was doing, was forced to place an equal amount of bets in order not to fall behind. At this rate, they'd burn through their stakes quickly.

"No more bets," the dealer told the players.

The dealer turned over the top card. A three of hearts. He moved the card to the side and started his bone pile. He turned over the first card, the losing card. King of diamonds. Edgar had placed a stack of chips on the king. He cursed out loud as the dealer took his chips from the table.

The dealer turned over the winning card. King of spades. Edgar hooted with delight. He'd lost more than he'd won— but he'd won more than Josh.

"Don't worry," Sarah told the kid. "I'll bring you good luck." She rubbed his shoulders.

A moment of clarity struck Luke.

Perhaps this had all been a setup. The bartender had the girl pick an easy mark. The bullwhacker, in on the con, offered insult, the bartender stepped in smoothly and proposed an alternative to bloodshed. Then the dealer dealt into the bullwhacker's bets while another saloon girl distracted the mark's friends.

Luke blinked.

He frowned, turning over the play in his head. It wouldn't even need to hinge on the dealer's ability to draw the correct cards. The house held the advantage on every bet. With one of the players working with them and splitting the pot afterward, that advantage went up to something like more than two-thirds.

The dealer put the cards, face up, in the bone pile. The two men placed their bets while the crowd shouted encouragement. Jenny leaned her soft body against Luke, slipping an arm around his waist. She smelled good. She felt good. Waving away her offer of another drink, he watched the play. He needed to focus.

The dealer turned over the losing card. A five of clubs. This time Edgar cursed as the dealer took his chips. The dealer turned over the winning card. A king of clubs. Josh and Sarah hooted in victory as he doubled his bet. Jenny hugged him.

They're uncommonly good actors if I'm right, Luke thought. Of course, lying to men came easily enough to most prostitutes. It was often a question of survival.

The game went back and forth for several hands as the deck whittled down. Josh won a huge round when the dealer turned up the king of hearts as the winning card. Edgar swore loudly and glowered. He took two more shots. He was definitely drunk.

"Bah," he slurred out in an angry, belligerent voice, "this is all crap!"

Luke wasn't even sure what that statement meant, but

what he was sure of was that Edgar had just put several chips down on the king despite there being four kings in the bone pile. He went to grab Josh's shoulder and alert him to the fact, but to his surprise Sarah beat him to it.

The girl leaned in close and grabbed his thigh, whispering into the kid's ear. Josh reacted like a man electrocuted. He sat up like a pistol shot, excitement electric in his voice.

"Dead bet!" he hollered.

"What are you talking about?" Edgar demanded. "I didn't put down no dead bet!"

"Dead bet on king," the dealer called.

Grinning, Josh scooped the chips off the king card.

He handed them over to Sarah, who kissed them and then slid them away between her ample breasts. Luke frowned. That wasn't the action of someone on a hustle. Perhaps he'd just been paranoid. Sarah wouldn't be the first saloon girl to take a shine to a cowboy who treated her nice in an establishment filled with rough, ill-mannered yahoos.

He turned to Jenny. "I do believe I'll have another shot now," he said. She poured, he drank.

The game went up and down as the deck of cards whittled to the end. Edgar placed no more dead bets and the two men held more or less even with neither holding a clear advantage, though Josh overall won more rounds. Soon the number of dead cards in the bone pile grew, forcing the gamblers to more narrowly place their bets as they ran out of choices. Edgar drank more.

Finally, the dealer got to the last three cards in the deck.

"Last cards," he announced.

"I'm damn well done with this nonsense," Edgar slur-growled. "I got better things to do than teaching some damn puppy how to play cards all night."

"You cashing it in?" Josh asked.

Edgar scowled. "Not by a damn sight. The day Edgar cashes out of a contest with some wet-behind-the ears little puppy-boy is the day he screws an ox."

"Well, there has been talk . . ." Luke said.

He realized that under the gentle and charismatic influence of the beautiful Jenny, he'd really blown Trask's rule right to hell. He was a little drunk.

Red in the face with effort of suppressing his rage, Edgar shook one blunt finger at Luke.

"You and I are not finished, not by a sight!" Before Luke could reply, the bullwhacker had turned to Josh. "Let's finish this," he snarled. "Last three cards, winner take all."

The crowd fell silent at the escalation. The game had started to lag a bit with neither player gaining the upper hand. Those kinds of games could go on all night. But what the bullwhacker suggested now was a little more interesting, a little more *immediate*.

In Faro when a deck was run down to the last three cards before a reshuffle of the bone pile into a new deck, a side bet was possible. The players could bet on the order in which each of the last three cards would be turned over and put into play.

"Fine," Sarah spoke up. "But he gets to choose first." She leaned against Josh. "Sorry, honey, I got a little carried away."

Josh grinned. The smile was stupid but genuine. "That's all right, darling," he said. "I ain't backing down from this son of a gun."

Luke rested his hand on the butt of his pistol. It was an unconscious gesture. *Is this the play?* he wondered.

A smooth dealer could easily put any three cards he wanted on the bottom of the deck. Trying to stack the deck play-by-play in Faro was impossible. But this one all-or-nothing bet was far from impossible.

"Josh—" he started to say.

"I'm in!" Josh shouted. He didn't bother studying the bone pile. Instead, he turned to Sarah who was now sitting sideways in his lap. "You pick, darling," he said. "You're my good luck."

She kissed him hard on the mouth as the crowd cheered and Edgar fumed.

"Josh—" Luke repeated.

"Ten, eight, three!" Sarah laughed.

"Bet made!" the dealer shouted.

It was done.

CHAPTER 12

Luke felt a cold fire burn in his belly. Once the dealer announced, the play was in action. If Josh pulled out, he'd concede defeat and lose the girl. Luke would have still opted for that if it saved their money, but the kid was too far smitten to listen to reason. He'd never willingly give up the saloon girl now.

He looked into the beautiful, smiling face of Jenny. The saloon girl's hustle was easy to fall for. You *wanted* to believe. She squeezed his hand and then tilted the whiskey bottle back and drank down two shots.

Mama warned me about gambling and fast women, he thought. *I guess it's my own damn fault.*

"Ten, eight, three," the dealer repeated. "Dealing."

He turned over the first card.

"Ten."

The crowd cheered. Edgar cursed. Sarah giggled happily and kissed Josh hard on the mouth. *Sure,* Luke thought, *give him the first card to make it look good.*

The dealer reached for the card. This was the pivotal card, the one in play that would actually dictate who won.

Either way, once the second card was flipped, the third card was simply a formality. Either it was an eight, or Josh lost.

The dealer flipped the card.

"Eight!"

The crowd erupted in boozy cheers, and several rough hands pounded Josh on the back. Luke let out a breath he hadn't realized he was holding. This hadn't been a setup. He almost sagged with relief.

Jenny thrust her body against his and, growing more elated by the second, Luke hugged her back. He smiled. Josh and Sarah were in a happy embrace. He doubted Edgar was anywhere near this happy. Suddenly worried about the man's reaction, Luke's hand dropped to his gun again as he looked to the bullwhacker.

The burly man had gone deathly white and trembled with fury. His hands came up and made great claws that he squeezed into fists so tight his knuckles popped like gunshots. His mouth twisted up into a snarl. He glared at Josh and Sarah.

The kid seemed oblivious, Luke realized. That was a potentially lethal state of affairs. He went to nudge Josh hard to get him out of his dazed celebration, but then Edgar swore again and stomped off, shoving his way through the crowd.

Luke stepped up and began heaping the chips into a pile for the dealer to cash out. Once he had the money, he counted out his loan and handed Josh his winnings. They must have bankrupted the bullwhacker, because Josh's pot was considerable.

"Thanks for believing in me, Luke," the kid said. His earnestness over his good fortune was almost childlike. "Sarah's going to show me her room," he gushed.

Luke, who'd been "shown" the rooms of more than one

saloon girl, just nodded. "You came out on top this time, kid. Enjoy it. It doesn't always play out that way."

Josh waved acknowledgment as Sarah dragged him toward the stairs. *She didn't have to cheat him at cards,* Luke thought. *The kid'll most likely just give her all of his money and do it with a smile.*

That was the kid's business. A man had to learn about women on his own. Some lessons were more painful than others.

Jenny snuggled in close, pressing her body into his.

"How 'bout you?" she purred. "You willing to spend some of those winnings on an old St. George?"

He broke out into laughter. The legendary St. George was famous for having ridden a dragon. When a sporting lady said it, she meant she was going to ride you like St. George rode the dragon.

"I can think of worse ways to spend my money."

Jenny was nothing if not enthusiastic. He reflected that should she want to give up the sporting life, she could make a good living breaking horses. He lay on the bed in her room and caught his breath. He'd deal with Trask in the morning, he promised himself as he dozed off.

Angry shouts rang out and Luke came awake with a start. It was pitch black in Jenny's room, and he had no idea what time it was or how long he had been asleep. He was still more than a little drunk. As he sat up, he heard the door in the room next to his splinter as a heavy boot kicked it open.

The kid!

He was out of bed, the Remington in his hand and cocked before he consciously thought of moving. He made it across the room as Jenny came away, groggy and confused. He found the doorknob.

Gunshots in rapid succession. A shotgun went off. Sarah began screaming. Luke yanked the door open and stepped naked into the hall. The Remington was up and ready in his fist, hammer cocked back.

He saw Edgar stumbling backward, away from the door to Sarah's crib.

The bullwhacker held a 10-gauge William Moore & Co. side-by-side. With eighteen-inch barrels, the shotgun was a pure lethal mankiller.

Luke was already firing by the time he realized Edgar had already been shot. His Remington barked, and the muzzle flash lit up the gloomy hallway like a lightning strike. His bullet caught the stumbling man in the side, and Edgar staggered and grunted under the impact. Luke fired again just as a pistol boomed from inside Sarah's crib. Blood splashed from Edgar's belly as Luke's second round struck him in the side of the neck.

Edgar went up on his toes as the thick, meaty muscles along the side of his throat unraveled and splattered bright red arterial blood across the walls and wainscoting behind him. As he turned, falling, Luke triggered a final round. As he did so, he saw two wounds in the bullwhacker's gut he hadn't been able to see initially.

Edgar stuck up against the wall, the 10-gauge coach gun clattering to the floorboards. Edgar looked over at Luke, an expression of stupid shock on his face. He leaked from half a dozen holes like some fancy town fountain. Gravity pulled on him, and he slid down the wall, leaving a crimson smear behind him. He landed heavily on the floor.

He went to say something and blood spilled out of his mouth and soaked his beard. The great bear of a man gave a last shuddering sigh and then his muddy brown eyes glassed over as he died.

"Josh?" Luke called. He could hear Sarah crying. "It's me, kid, don't shoot."

He entered the room. Enough light from the outside filtered in for him to see. Josh sat on the edge of the bed, white as a ghost. His Army Colt was in his hand. Sarah, wrapped only in a sheet, leaned against him, crying hard enough to cause her makeup to run. There was a hole the size of a teapot in the ceiling where the buckshot had blasted it.

"Kid?" Luke said. "You okay?"

Josh looked up at him. The expression on the kid's face was almost a mirror of the one that Edgar had worn. Shock. Luke edged forward. When he spoke, he kept his voice low and calm. Behind him he heard voices from downstairs and from some of the other rooms along the hall shouting out questions.

"Kid!" he snapped.

Josh looked up at him, blinking his way out of the confusion. "I ain't never killed a man before," he said. He turned his eyes to the hallway behind Luke where Edgar's corpse bled out.

"You get used to it," Luke told him. That was true enough for how far it went. "But I need you to get yourself together. The law will be here in a minute."

That seemed to get through to him. He looked back at Luke, his face intensely earnest. "The skunk burst in here and tried to kill us! It was self-defense!" He grabbed Luke's arm. "You have to believe me!"

"Settle down, kid," Luke said. "That's obvious. You aren't going to be in any trouble," he assured him. He paused, then added, "Except with Trask, I expect."

"To hell with Trask and Goldsmith, too!" Josh swore.

Luke blinked in surprise at the vehemence behind Josh's words. The kid looked so angry, he thought Josh might have killed another man if Trask happened to show up just then.

People were coming toward the scene of the shoot-out. Luke looked down and remembered that he was naked.

"Get dressed," he snapped. "We'll figure out Trask after we deal with the law."

"Here," Jenny said from behind him, "I'll take care of Sarah. You do what Luke says now, kid."

The saloon girl wore her blanket around her shoulders and Luke stepped back to let her comfort Sarah as Josh hurriedly began dressing. Seeing things were in hand, Luke went next door and quickly pulled on his own clothes.

He heard the bartender from earlier loudly demanding answers. There were other men's voices, as well. That worried Luke. Edgar hadn't seemed that popular in the freight hauler community, but not siding with the man in a dispute over a prostitute was one thing, being indifferent about his death by gunplay was something else. It was possible there could be trouble from the other bullwhackers.

Buckling on the Remingtons, he entered the hall again, ready for trouble. Several girls he'd seen downstairs stood around in various stages of undress. Their customers—all armed, Luke noted—were mixed in. He'd never seen such a collection of grubby long handle underwear in one place.

"Dang," one scrawny prairie chicken of a man said as he stared down at Edgar's corpse. "He sure enough got enough bullet holes in him."

"Yeah," agreed a bucktoothed whore, "I think I can see the wall behind him through his guts."

Luke spoke up. "Everyone who was here tonight knows this bullwhacker was gunning for the kid. He tried to murder him in his sleep."

"It's true," Jenny spoke up. "Ask Sarah, she saw him."

Luke watched the crowd closely. The bystanders seemed to be open to the story. It was no more than the truth, and there was very little to question about why Edgar would have been upstairs with a shotgun. Men interested in visiting whores were usually a lot more concerned with other things.

Luke thought that if Josh stuck with the truth he'd be fine. But if the sheriff found Luke Jensen, bounty hunter, here with the kid, then explanations could get awkward. He needed to maintain his ruse for just a little while longer.

He pulled Josh to one side and spoke quietly in his ear. "Listen," he said. "I might have problems with the law in this town. I don't think it'll be such a good idea if I'm still here when the sheriff gets here."

Seeing the startled look on Josh's face at this bit of news, Luke pushed on, voice urgent as he kept one ear cocked for the sound of the sheriff arriving to investigate the trouble.

"You'll be fine, kid. Just tell the truth. You got half-a-hundred witnesses to how he was hoorawing you earlier and how mad he was about losing. Sarah is important to the bartender's business, so there's no way he's going to want her swept up in any legal trouble."

Josh's face clouded darkly at this bit of commonsense observation, and Luke had his first inkling of the trouble that was going to unfold later.

"I'll go get Trask," Luke went on. "I'll tell him what happened and send him around to stick up for you. You didn't do anything but defend yourself. Everyone knows that."

After a moment, Josh nodded in agreement. "Go on, Luke. I can handle this." He put an arm on Sarah's shoulder. "Sarah will help me."

She smiled from Jenny's arms, face tear streaked but looking resolute. "You're damn right I'll help," she declared.

They heard the bartender's voice at the top of the stairs. "There you are, sheriff, took long enough. It's up here!"

Luke got his belongings and went toward the window at the end of the hallway. As he passed by Willy the bartender, he slipped the man a $20 government note.

"I wasn't here."

Willy took the money, made it disappear. He nodded once.

Luke got the hell out of there.

CHAPTER 13

He needed to find Trask.

He was fairly certain killing a bullwhacker in a crowded saloon and brothel wasn't what the sergeant major had meant by keeping a low profile. Despite that, the big army veteran would need to adapt to the situation, and Luke figured it was better if the news came from him, rather than Trask hearing about it on the street.

Trask was going to be angry as a bee-stung bull, but the quicker the situation was behind them the better.

Luke started toward the tent beyond the sod building that housed the Chinese laundry. If he was lucky, the outlaw would be passed out drunk. Luke pulled his turnip watch from his pocket and flipped it open to check the time. Three o'clock in the morning. The town was still awake, though less busy. Saloons and gambling halls remained open and crowded. A few drunks and vagrants slept in doorways and alcoves.

He crossed the street to avoid two drunk bullwhackers loudly arguing over some nonsense he had no interest in. The laundry was closed, but he saw a red lantern light glowing down the alley between the laundry and a feed store.

Whorehouses frequently used red lights to indicate that they were open. The practice had begun as the railroad moved across the country. By using railroad lanterns, the prostitutes had signaled to the workers that they were open for business. The practice became so widespread the areas where brothels congregated in a town started being called "red light districts."

As he entered the alley, someone lay propped against the laundry wall, legs sticking out into the passage. Luke stepped over them and kept walking. The figure was so still he couldn't tell if the man was dead or just drunk. He guessed it didn't matter that much.

At the far end of the alley, a scrawny cur with a spotted hide and one mangled ear nosed through a refuse pile. The dog growled a warning low in its throat as Luke approached. He didn't want to share whatever he might find in the garbage.

"Go on, get!" Luke snapped. He waved his hand at the animal.

Deciding the prize wasn't worth the battle, the dog slunk away and Luke strode into a courtyard space between the back of the laundry and the front of a large tent on a wooden frame. Several red lanterns sat on the ground or hung from poles. He hadn't seen a tent this large since the ones used by the surgeons during the war.

Two Chinese men sat on overturned whiskey barrels. One man was skinny with a pockmarked face and the other portly as a railroad baron. They were dressed in traditional, indigo-dyed linen trousers and loose-fitting shirts that had always reminded Luke of pajamas. Instead of western-style hats, both wore the straw coolie hats of their own culture. He guessed the head covers were just as effective as sombreros for keeping the sun off, but they didn't exactly make them inconspicuous.

The men stared at him, faces expressionless. Both wore long-barreled .454 Colt Dragoons stuck in red sashes wrapped around their waists. Each had a hatchet tucked in there as well. The hatchets were common weapons among the Chinese, but it was rare to see any of them packing iron, despite the fact that gunpowder had been invented in their homeland. A battered tin pail filled with beer sat on the ground between them.

Luke had little doubt they would be quick to use the weapons if they thought they needed to. Depending on who they killed and how much they were kicking back to the sheriff, they might even get away with it.

"I'm looking for a friend," Luke told them.

"You want girl?" the fat one asked.

"No. I'm trying to find my friend. He's a little shorter than me and about twice as wide. He's got a long, black beard, wild as hell." Realizing he'd started pantomiming his words in frustration, Luke forced himself to stop.

"Plenty girls here."

"Eight dollar," the skinny one added.

"You want opium?"

Opium and morphine were incredibly easy for patent medicine companies to get hold of as ingredients for their "tonics." So many veterans returned from the war addicted to morphine, it had become known as the "soldier's disease." But Chinese merchants seemed to have a good supply, too, and were the only ones selling it in a form that could be smoked.

"No," he said. "No opium. No girls."

"Laundry closed," the fat one said.

Luke sighed. Pulling out two uncashed in chips from the saloon, he held them up.

"Can I look around?"

The skinny one looked at the fat one. After a moment he nodded and the skinny one held out his hand. Luke placed the chips into his palm and they disappeared into the man's sash. Stepping past the guards, Luke pushed the tent flap out of the way and entered. He smelled burning opium. It wasn't a scent he knew well, but it also wasn't something you forgot.

He stopped for a moment just inside the door to let his eyes adjust. The tent was poorly illuminated and smoke hung thickly in the air. He coughed a little. Though it was gloomy as a cave in here, his eyes adjusted soon enough and he began picking his way carefully forward.

The floor of the tent was made out of shipping pallets obviously stolen or purchased from the railroad. To either side of a center aisle, rugs had been thrown over the wooden slats. Sheets strung on lines divided the main area into a series of narrow cribs. Beaded curtains hung in front of some of the little areas.

Chinese girls sitting on cots looked at him, watching him as he walked past them. In one of the cribs, a young Chinese girl, no more than fifteen years old, held a heavy, ornate pipe to the lips of an almost comatose man. He inhaled deeply and his eyelids grew so heavy he looked like he was sleeping. Smoke leaked from his nostrils as if from the chimney of a locomotive engine. He wasn't the man Luke was looking for.

"Trask," Luke called.

He moved deeper into the tent. Lanterns hanging from the ceiling shed weak, flickering yellow light. Impassive girls sat in their cribs, waiting for customers. All of them were young. Some were pretty. They smoked pipes or hand-rolled cigarettes and stared at him with bored expressions.

"Hey, big spender," a girl spoke up.

Hoping she spoke more English than just that phrase, Luke turned toward her. Her right eye was swollen shut, the bruising a deep purple. A Siamese cat sat purring in her lap as she stroked its fur. Its tail lashed back and forth as it studied Luke with inscrutable yellow eyes.

"I'm looking for my friend," he said.

"I will be your friend," she answered. "Ten dollars."

"You speak English?" he asked. "More than that, I mean."

"I speak the best." She sounded insulted he'd asked.

"Good. I'm trying to find my friend. I'll pay you a double eagle if you help me."

He held up the big $20 gold coin. Showing money in a place like this was dangerous, but he didn't think he had much choice.

"I show you a good time." She patted the space beside her on the cot covered with rough-spun military blankets.

"No, I'm looking for a friend."

"Friend? Another girl costs more money."

"Never mind," he said.

He let out a disgusted sigh and started to put the coin away, but she stopped him. She stood up quickly, dumping the cat on the ground. It yowled in protest and scampered away. The girl reached out and caught hold of Luke's hand that had the double eagle in it.

Her hand looked doll-like as it grasped his. He looked at her, saw in her eyes that most of what had just occurred had been an act. She knew what he wanted. He opened his hand and held it palm up. She took the coin.

"What your friend look like?"

"Big son of a gun," Luke said. "Wide as a barn door. He's got a beard down to his belt."

The Chinese girl pointed at her black eye. "I know him," she said. Anger and dislike were plain to hear in her voice.

"Where did he go?" Luke asked.

She pointed toward the back of the tent. "He's still here. He went to chase the dragon."

"What does that mean?"

"He went to the tent to smoke opium. The tent in the back."

"There's a tent behind this one?"

She nodded, obviously already bored with the conversation. "No girls there," she said. "Just opium. Those who are *feixing* don't care about having girl."

"Fei—," he mangled the Cantonese word and sighed in exasperation. "What does that mean?"

She held out her arms and flapped them up and down. *"Feixing,"* she repeated. "Like a bird."

"Flying," he clarified.

She shrugged. "He's in the back tent," she repeated. "But only those who buy opium get in."

"All right, thank you."

By the time he turned around the girl had already forgotten him. She sat back down on the cot and called softly, "Here, kitty, kitty . . ."

Luke went to the rear of the tent brothel and pushed past the flap. Stepping outside into the night air, he suddenly felt considerably more alert. The density of smoke and human stink in the place had clouded his head. He inhaled deeply, feeding his lungs fresh air.

He looked around.

A second tent about half the size was set up behind the first. On one side, a series of clotheslines were set up, hung with sheets from beds in the brothel. On the other a rope was strung between the structures and three bull's-eye lanterns like those used by railroad brakemen hung.

A white man in a pinstripe vest, sack coat, and derby hat stumbled into Luke. Sporting an intricately crafted walrus mustache, he reeked of bay rum as if he'd bribed the town barber to splash the whole bottle on his weak, double chins.

"Watch where you're going!" the man slurred, eyes so red it seemed he'd cry blood instead of tears.

The man pulled himself up straight, face a doughy approximation of indignant. The bounty hunter resisted the urge to lay out the weaving fool. There was a gold watch on a chain tucked into the pocket of his vest. He made a show of pompously checking it. It reminded Luke of the White Rabbit in that book by the Carroll fellow that had come out at the end of the war and been in newspaper cartoons ever since.

The man steadied himself. Narrowing his eyes, he regarded Luke like a farmer discovering a new species of slug infesting his crops.

"Do you know how much money I'm worth, you saddle tramp?"

Luke looked at him, nonplussed. He could see the door to the tent behind the man. He was almost there. He needed to find Trask and as carefully as possible break the news of the situation with the kid. He didn't have the time or the inclination to deal with this opium-muddled blockhead.

The man jabbed a finger into Luke's chest.

"Did you hear me ask you a question, sir?" he demanded. "I run the largest bank in this town and I—"

With a sigh, Luke decided he didn't have time for this.

He pulled back his fist and drove it into the man's jaw. The banker went down like a poleaxed steer. He slumped on the ground in a loose pile, head lolling bonelessly on his chubby neck. For a moment, his body was so slack that Luke feared he'd killed the man. Then the banker cut loose with a deafening snore and Luke knew he was still alive.

Muttering in exasperation, he stepped over the man's body and entered the opium tent.

CHAPTER 14

A huge, heavily muscled black man sat on a stool just inside the door, lantern light gleaming on his hairless head. He'd obviously been chosen for his size. His arms and shoulders strained the fabric of the homespun shirt he wore. Even sitting on the high stool, he was a head taller than Luke. His torso was broad enough to rival Trask, and his arms would have been at home on a grizzly.

Standing in the dirt beside him, within easy reach, was a sledgehammer. Twine had been wrapped around the ash handle halfway down the haft to offer a more secure grip. A lantern burned on the ground beside it, and in the yellow illumination it was easy to see caked blood and random hairs stuck to the steel head.

The hilt of a big butcher knife stuck from the top of the man's massive stovepipe boots. The handle of a Navy Colt, looking almost ridiculously small next to the big man, stuck from a pocket of his dungarees. Beside his stool was a battered table with an iron strongbox on it.

"No girls in here," the man informed Luke in a rumbling basso profundo.

"I know what's in here," Luke told him. "How much?"

"No less than five dollars."

Luke handed him a Liberty gold coin. The man studied it then bit it to test the authenticity. Satisfied, he put the coin in a slot in the top of the strongbox. He handed Luke a brownish lump of opium then jerked a thumb the size of a dinner knife back over one shoulder.

"There are pipes next to the couches."

Luke nodded. He found the tacky feel of the drug in his hand distasteful and stuck it into his shirt pocket. Playing the role of an eager addict, he didn't reply to the bouncer's instructions but instead headed straight to the back.

The opium den was the purest example of equality Luke had ever seen, though he didn't necessarily recognize it as such. But both men and women, of every race and creed, sat or lay near each other in the throes of opium bliss. The air was so thick with the smoke of the drug that everything seemed sleepy and soft.

Forcing himself to concentrate, Luke searched among the rugs and couches and cots for Trask. Silk drapes had been hung at strange intervals, creating partitions that offered some sense of privacy. People were congregated singly and in small groups, all in various stages of inebriation.

He found the sergeant major sleeping blissfully on a bearskin thrown over an old army cot. A long, hand-carved pipe lay on his stomach, the bowl thick with burned resin. A line of tobacco-brown spittle glistened along his beard where he'd drooled in his sleep.

A young girl sat on the floor. Naked under a sheet wrapped around her shoulders, she looked terrified. Luke couldn't blame her.

"Go," he told her. "I'll handle him."

She didn't hesitate. Springing to her feet, she was up

and gone before Luke could blink. Amazed at her agility, he turned his head to watch her flee. She disappeared behind several hanging silk curtains and was gone on silent feet. He looked back at Trask.

"You got a real way with the ladies, Sergeant Major," he said. "I think you and Big Edgar would have got along real fine."

Trask cut loose with a ripping snore. Luke sighed, then kicked Trask in the boot. Nothing. He kicked again. This time Trask stirred a little, a look of consternation on his ugly face. Luke kicked him a third time.

"Trask, get the hell up."

Trask opened his eyes. They looked unfocused and bloodshot. He blinked several times as if willing himself to wake up. Narrowing his gaze, he appeared to study Luke's face, confusion making him look stupid.

"Trask, wake up. There's been trouble. I think it's going to be all right, but the kid is with the sheriff."

Trask ran his tongue across his teeth and tried sitting up. It was like watching a drunk try to get to his feet in a rowboat. Luke made no move to help him.

"Miller?" he asked.

"Yes, it's me. Did you hear what I said?"

Trask made it up on his second attempt. He paused for a moment, breathing heavily. His eyes still looked glazed. The opium pipe fell to the floor and bounced. Trask spat a stream of tobacco juice onto the rug.

"Where's the girl?" he asked. His face darkened. "I told that little slut to stay put." Like sun burning through storm clouds, the anger on his face changed to a smile of pure happiness. "I guess I'm going to have to discipline her some now, for disobeying."

"Trask—"

"The good book says spare the rod and spoil the whore."

"Trask, damn it, pay attention," Luke snapped.

Trask blinked and looked at him as if really understanding what his eyes were telling him for the first time.

"What the hell is it?" he demanded. "Why are you bothering me when I'm at my leisure?"

"The kid killed a bullwhacker in a fight over a whore."

"What?" That had his attention. "You mean Josh?"

"Yeah, he's with the sheriff now."

"What?"

"It wasn't his fault, the blockhead tried to kill him when he was in bed with a whore. The man kicked in his door and tried to blast him with a 10-gauge. It's a clear case of self-defense, but it's brought him to everyone's attention . . . including the sheriff's."

Trask was furious. "You were supposed to have looked out for this kind of crap!"

Rising, he shrugged back into his suspenders and looked around for his hat. Growing more clear-headed and animated by the second, Trask began checking his weapons. Satisfied that they were all right, he put his hat on.

"Let's go," he growled.

"That's a problem," Luke said.

That brought Trask up short. "What problem?"

"I'm not wanted in Hatchet Creek," Luke said. "But I don't want the sheriff to know I'm here. It could cause complications you wouldn't want."

"Why?"

"Now's not the time to get into it. He might recognize me, he might not, but it's better if he doesn't have the chance to."

That sounded like the sort of worry an actual outlaw might have, Luke thought. He hoped Trask wouldn't realize that being recognized by the local star packer could apply to a man on the right side of the law, as well.

"We have to make sure everything goes all right with Josh," Luke went on.

"This isn't over," Trask warned with a dark scowl. "But take me to the kid."

At first Luke thought his luck had held up extremely well.

It had taken long enough for him to find Trask that by the time they returned to the saloon the circus had ended. The place was empty, lanterns turned low.

Luke and Trask arrived just as the bartender was putting the last of the chairs on the tables and was about to retire. They pounded on the door, explained who they were, and demanded to be let in. Willy unlocked the door and opened it, but only after Trask threatened to burn the place down. With a sullen look on his face, the bartender explained why the saloon was closed.

Men had carried Edgar's body to the ice house, and the sheriff had chosen not to arrest Josh based on witness testimony that the shooting had been a clear case of self-defense. If the sheriff was worried about anything, it was retaliation by drunk bullwhackers. So he had closed the saloon down for the night to prevent any sort of continuation of the conflict from occurring.

Josh was in the back of the saloon shooting billiards by himself. Sarah was nowhere to be seen, and Luke suspected that was no accident. Josh stopped playing as they approached and leaned on his cue.

"Sergeant Major," he acknowledged.

"I don't blame you for killing that damn fool bull-whacker," Trask rumbled. "But I sure as hell didn't need you gettin' in a fight over some stupid whore to begin with and gettin' the sheriff wise to who you are."

"Don't call her a whore," Josh said. His voice was tight, but he was firm.

Trask was so busy planning things out in his head that he didn't immediately register the implications of what Josh had said. Luke did. He silently cursed, thinking that he would have to kill Trask now to keep the massive outlaw from killing Josh. His plan wasn't going to have a chance to succeed.

"What's done is done," Trask continued, surprising Luke with his uncharacteristic tolerance of Josh's defiance. "I killed my share of idjits in my day, too, so we'll let it go. We've gotta get out of town and back to camp."

"I'm not going," Josh said.

Trask looked confused. He wasn't used to having his orders disobeyed. It took a moment for Josh's refusal to sink in. He blinked. His face turned red and tobacco juice spilled from his lips as he shouted, "What did you say?"

"I'm not going. I'm done."

"You will damn well follow orders!" Trask bellowed.

"The hell I will," Josh shouted right back.

Luke was taken a bit aback by the kid's courage. Either he'd fallen into an altered mental state because of his feelings for Sarah, or killing that bullwhacker when it counted most had imbued him with new confidence. Perhaps it was both.

The burly man backhanded the kid hard across the

face, and the blow lifted him onto his heels then sent him tumbling over backward. Josh looked up at Trask in shock. Blood trickled from his lip, and he angrily wiped his mouth with the back of his hand.

A curse spewed from his lips, then he said, "I'm done with you and done with Goldsmith. You can all rot in hell for all I care!"

Luke came around the table to put himself between Trask and the kid, but Trask was quick for his size. He drove the toe of his boot into Josh's chin, ramming his head into the wall. Josh's skull bounced hard and the kid went out like someone snuffing a candle.

Luke shoved Trask away from the unconscious youngster. It was like pushing a brick wall, but he managed to knock him back against the edge of the billiard table. Trask clawed at his gun handle. Luke stopped his draw with an iron grip on his wrist.

For a moment, the two men struggled against each other. Trask began moving his hand toward the butt of his pistol. He couldn't loosen Luke's grip, but Luke couldn't stop the man from reaching his pistol.

"That was your last mistake, Miller," Trask said through gritted teeth.

Suddenly he struck Luke in the face with his other hand, driving his fist into the bounty hunter's jaw like a miner pounding rock. The punch drove Luke backward. He tasted blood in his mouth.

Falling back, Luke snatched up a billiard ball from the table and flung it at Trask with a sidearm throw as the man used the space to pull his revolver. The hard ceramic ball smashed into Trask's face, bursting his nose so that blood squirted like pulp from fruit. The sergeant major roared and staggered.

Luke used the moment to draw and fire his right-hand Remington, but Trask staggered again at just the right instant to avoid the bullet. Trask caught his balance and turned, again with surprising speed, and eared back the hammer on his Army Colt as he did so.

Luke threw himself to the side as Trask's gun thundered. He landed on the table and rolled across it. Billiard balls went spilling in a clatter.

Luke came down on the other side as a bullet hummed through the air just over his head, and the report of Trask's shot echoed sharply. Luke fired but was off balance and out of position. His bullet shattered a window in the wall to Trask's left.

Trask thrust out his arm and Luke ducked. The outlaw's gun roared twice more. Head still down, Luke fired twice over the top of the table in the general area of where he thought Trask was. The move was designed to harass Trask so Luke could get in a better position to make a more accurate shot.

Hard on the heels of the last shot, Luke popped up, hunting for a better angle. Gunsmoke hung thick in the air, irritating his eyes and burning the inside of his nostrils as he breathed it in. Trask was retreating toward the back door. He saw Luke and fired, but Luke was quicker on the trigger.

Luke's round struck Trask in the left shoulder, and blood splashed as the burly man jerked under the impact. His Army Colt hammered out another shot, driving Luke back behind the table. Luke holstered the Remington and drew its mate.

Luke shuffled to the side and popped up, gun ready. The back door stood open. Trask was gone. Cursing, Luke jumped up and made for the door. He almost barreled through in his haste to chase after the outlaw, but instinct stopped him just in time.

He stepped through the door then jerked back inside. Molding from the doorframe exploded into splinters as Trask's shot rang out. A lightning strike of muzzle flash lit up the night from out in the dark. Luke turned and fired back into the room. His bullet smashed the lantern hanging over the billiard table and plunged the room into darkness.

No longer silhouetted by the light, Luke went through the door in a rush and immediately cut left. He looked to where he'd seen the muzzle flash and saw nothing. No shot rang out. He fought to keep his breathing under control. Head turned to one side, he listened.

There.

He heard the pounding of footsteps on hard-packed ground running flat out between two sod buildings. He raced after the sound. He came around the corner of the building and saw Trask's unmistakable outline between the two structures. They each fired on the run, missing.

Trask darted left and was gone. Reckless, hungry for vengeance, Luke chased after him. He came to the end of the alley and quickly stuck his head around. No one shot at him and he ran toward the stable, thinking Trask was trying to get to his horse.

A mounted Trask burst from the space between the mercantile and the next building. Luke dropped to a knee behind a post, lifting the Remington. Trask fired, his face lit up by muzzle flash. Bullets hammered into the boardwalk and support post causing Luke to grimace as he crouched lower.

Trask turned the animal and leaned low, riding flat out

for the edge of town. Cursing, Luke rose and ran into the street, firing after the fleeing man. But Trask was gone.

Men were shouting and lantern light began appearing in windows. Doors flew open and people spilled into the street. Luke spat, furious. Holstering his pistol, he turned and began striding up the street. He needed to check on Josh.

The game was up, and it was time to tell the sheriff the town was in danger.

CHAPTER 15

Angry citizens gathered outside the sheriff's office—those that weren't drunk, anyway. Luke and Josh waited in the office while the lawman gave instructions to his deputies to disperse the crowd. He looked put out. Luke had barely had time to tell Josh to back him no matter what he said before the sheriff lit into them.

"Seems to me you boys have a lot of explaining to do," he said. "And you should start, *now*. What the hell are you messed up in, Luke?"

As Luke had worried might turn out to be the case, the sheriff was an acquaintance. Luke wouldn't have called him a friend, but they had crossed trails several times in the past, when Red Conwell had been packing a badge in other towns and Luke had brought in wanted outlaws to collect the rewards for them. The man was honest and tried to do his job. Sometimes that meant catering to the merchants more than Luke would have been able to stomach, but that was the price of being a town lawman.

Conwell had ridden with the cavalry in General Joseph Hooker's command at the Battle of Chancellorsville. He was a stocky man with dark red hair, what was left of it. His hairline had receded well past the middle of his head.

"Red, the kid's with me," Luke said. "I owed his daddy, and I'm helping him earn some money to establish himself. You've got a gang of bad owlhoots outside of town, and you need to get ready because I believe they're going to hit this town."

"How do you know all this?"

"Because I managed to infiltrate them."

Josh opened his mouth to say something and Luke shot him a look. Obviously confused, the kid closed his mouth, but Luke knew that sooner or later, Josh was going to want an explanation.

"What's their game then?" Conwell asked.

"The man I chased off earlier cased the bank and every safe worth taking in the whole town."

"The whole town?" the sheriff almost shouted. "What the hell? How many of these owlhoots are there?"

"A full platoon's worth," Luke replied grimly. "Most of them are steady gun hands, veterans. Their usual plan is to set a fire near a settlement to draw most of the menfolk away. I may have ruined that plan this time, but I believe they'll still hit you, try to clean out the bank, at least. We need to show them we're ready."

The door to the office swung open as a deputy rushed in. "Sheriff!" he shouted.

"Damn it, Oxford," the sheriff snapped as he turned around, "I'm doing something important."

"But this is important. There's a big grass fire just north of town. It's running with the wind and headed right toward us. If we don't stop it, it's gonna get into town quick."

Luke felt as if he'd been punched in the gut. It wasn't

just that Goldsmith was using a tactic he now knew his enemy expected, it was the speed at which he'd implemented the plan. The outlaws had to have been in position already, just waiting for the order to start the blaze.

Probably as insurance if I proved untrustworthy, Luke thought.

"They're coming," he told Red Conwell. "You got to get these people ready for a shooting war, *now.*"

"Yeah, but that fire is still a real threat," Red told him. "We know it's a distraction and it doesn't matter, because it'll burn this place to the ground just the same."

He pushed past the frightened deputy and hurried out of the office. Luke followed him outside.

As they looked to the north, it was immediately apparent that Goldsmith had compensated for his lack of surprise by sheer volume. The horizon was on fire as far as Luke could see. The wind came steadily from the north and already smoke was filling the town. Luke couldn't get over how big the blaze was, maybe half a mile across, maybe more.

It would hit Hatchet Creek like a furnace.

"Fire!" Red bellowed.

The call was taken up quickly by the citizens. The sheriff turned to the deputy named Oxford. "We got gunmen coming. They won't come ahead of the fire because most of us will be out there fighting it. They'll circle around and ride in from the south. Get yourself eight men and some rifles and take up positions to guard the south end of town. I'll join you once I get men out there to fight that fire."

"Eight men?" the deputy protested. "Is that enough?"

"No, but the fire is the more immediate danger, believe it or not. We just need to make those owlhoots realize this town ain't easy pickings. They'll ride off looking for a better target."

"I'll help the deputy," Luke said.

"So will I," Josh immediately echoed.

Luke glanced at him. The kid was still confused, but he had said to hell with Trask and Goldsmith, and evidently he'd meant it. Luke gave him a nod, glad that Josh had decided to stand with him.

Red Conwell nodded, too. He said, "I doubt many men here have as much experience with killing as you do, Jensen. Get to it."

A line of citizens had formed outside some of the mercantiles and general stores. The owners passed out shovels and picks and steel-headed rakes. If they could scratch a fire line out of the prairie before the flames reached the town, there was a chance to stop the fire in its tracks. *If* the wind didn't pick up.

"Go get our rifles, kid," Luke said. "I'm going to the edge of town and picking a good spot. Hurry."

"The sheriff knows you and called you Jensen," Josh said. "You're some sort of lawman, aren't you?"

"Long story," Luke said. "Just get the rifles."

Josh hesitated, but only for a second. Then he nodded and ran off to fetch the weapons.

Goldsmith brought his men in like a cavalry charge. They came running flat out, horses pounding the ground with their hooves like thunder. This was a military raid, Luke realized. They were coming in fast and shooting. They sought to wipe out the resistance in one violent assault and then loot the corpses.

There were plenty of places on the frontier where the people in a town saw themselves as a community, as citizens. A newly burgeoning boomtown like Hatchet Creek wasn't one of those places. A store owner might fight like hell to save his property, but it wasn't a certainty that every cowboy in a saloon would jump in as if they were fighting for their own outfit.

The West was filled with capable men hardened to violence, but even out here they weren't the majority. Steady gun hands were outnumbered by laborers fifty or a hundred to one. A man who'd served valiantly on either side of battles like Shiloh or Bull Run wasn't looking to die in a scummy little skirmish with owlhoots.

If Goldsmith cowed the town, he could do whatever he liked while people hunkered down behind cover and waited for the outlaws to leave. This thing could unravel fast, and Luke knew it.

"Stand steady, boys!" he shouted to his fellow defenders of Hatchet Creek.

He worked the lever on his Winchester. As a unit, the charging mass of outlaw riders shifted to the left, going off the wagon road and onto the prairie. Luke saw what they'd done in an instant. With one maneuver, they'd cut off almost half the guns defending the town.

"Get to the other side!" he shouted.

Men hastened to obey him and the deputies already in position on the other side began firing. Behind them the sky was red and the glow of the racing fire grew enough to start casting a ghastly illumination crawling with flickering shadows. The smoke grew thicker.

Luke made it to the stage depot. The depot itself was a small sod building. There was a corral between it and the stationmaster's house, which shared a wall with the stable that opened into the corral. There were five horses in the corral and a pair of oxen. All the animals began calling out in fear as gunshots echoed and the smell of the fire grew in intensity. He saw riders racing past, pistols in hands, faces hid by bandanas and flour sacks. Night riders, raiders, home burners, and killers. The worst the frontier had to offer.

Someone fired from the top window of the saloon. Luke knew at a glance it was Sarah's room. Josh had gone to protect her. He was in love and that was where his priority lay. Luke couldn't begrudge that. A rider's horse screamed and went down as the kid's rifle bullet found it, and the outlaw was thrown.

The group of riders around the fallen horse returned fire at the window. Bullets slammed into the wall and shattered the glass. Luke stepped up on the bottom rung of the corral fence at the far side while the men were distracted and killed two of them with a pair of swift shots from the Winchester aimed over the heads of the horses and oxen. The group was still riding hard and they swept past the corral, not even realizing that two of their number at the back were no longer with them.

The man who'd had his horse shot out from under him staggered to his feet. Luke tried drawing a bead through the milling animals in the corral. Couldn't find one before the man made it away and to the back door of the saloon.

Cursing, Luke jumped from the fence and ran toward the front of the stationmaster's house. Goldsmith's men were in the town now, horses racing up and down the street, men exchanging gunfire. He didn't recognize any of the masked men as Goldsmith, but he saw Trask's unmistakable form kicking in the door to the saloon. Muzzle flash lit up the cave-darkness through the windows though he couldn't hear the shot.

He saw the raiders breaking off into well organized and smoothly executed teams. Most to the bank, several smaller groups hitting each business. A small contingent continued battling the townspeople and deputies firing at them.

Using the steep front steps of the stationmaster's house as cover, Luke killed a man firing on the defenders. His round caught the raider squarely between the shoulder blades and put him facedown in the dirt of the street.

There was a momentary lull in the swirling chaos of the gunfight, and Luke took the opportunity to run toward the saloon. He bounded onto the boardwalk and put his back against the wall, then took a quick look through the big front window.

The man wearing a red bandana over the lower half of his face was definitely Trask. There was no mistaking the murderer's burly shape or the beard that jutted out from under the bandana. The raider whose horse had been shot out from beneath him was beside Trask. Both men were behind the bar and firing up the stairs toward where the prostitutes' rooms were.

Willy the bartender lay sprawled over a poker table, eyes open and staring, shotgun on the floor beside him. He was dead, and blood ran in bright red rivulets from the table and dripped onto the floor where fresh sawdust collected it. The flash of gunfire blinked on and off from the staircase, and Luke heard the kid's Henry rifle barking as he returned fire.

Trask popped up over the bar and fired twice up the stairs. He dropped back down, and the second outlaw did the same. Luke slapped the barrel of his own rifle against the window and shattered the glass. Shoving the barrel through the opening, he fired, worked the action, fired again.

Both shots missed, gouging out half-dollar sized chunks from the bar. Trask came up quick and fired in his direction, forcing Luke to jerk his head back. Crouching with his back to the wall of the saloon, Luke realized he was caught with enemies on both sides.

He threw himself back around the corner as two attackers caught a deputy fighting from the door of the feed store in a crossfire and gunned him down. Luke shot at both, hit the first in the hip and spun him to the ground but missed the second. The first tried to return fire from the dirt but was in too much pain to aim accurately. The other ran for the door where the deputy's body lay.

Luke's round caught the man down in the street in the head and blew a crater in his face. The second gunman reached the door. Luke tried getting a shot off but couldn't tell where it landed. A moment later, the outlaw fired from inside the building. There was more smoke in the street, from the fire or the gunbattle, Luke wasn't sure.

Rifle up and ready, he ran down the alley between the saloon and the stationmaster's house. Rounding the corner, he entered the saloon through the same door he had pursued Trask out of, what seemed a lifetime ago.

Gunshots crashed heavily in the building. He heard Sarah screaming and the Henry rifle going off. Somehow in the time it took him to flank the building, Trask and the second raider had managed to make it up the stairs. Probably the kid had run out of shells in the rifle, unable to return fire, as one of the two advanced while the other kept him pinned down.

Whatever had happened, both men were upstairs now. Luke came around the staircase and saw Jenny lying dead at the top of the steps. Her eyes were open wide, staring into nothing. A four-shot derringer dangled from her hand. Blood trickled out of her mouth and ran down the steps.

White hot rage burned through him, and in an instant Luke was on the stairs. He flung the rifle from him and drew the Remingtons in each hand. Pounding up the steps, he thumbed both hammers back. He was without fear, filled only with an all-consuming rage.

Halfway up the stairs he gained enough height to see the men standing in the hall. Both of them pumped shot after shot through the door to Sarah's crib. The wooden barrier rattled and jumped under the unrelenting fire. Holes blasted through it, and splinters ripped free.

Lifting both pistols, Luke fired one, shifted his aim, and fired the other. The rounds caught both Trask and the other outlaw in the back. They twisted as they fell, still firing. The outlaw in the flour-sack hood triggered his round into the wall and then coughed up a torrent of blood as his lung collapsed.

Trask's wild shot caught Luke high in the right shoulder. The force of the Colt Dragoon's heavy round slammed into him like a mule kicking. Grunting under the impact, Luke staggered. He didn't know how Trask was still moving. The man's strength was seemingly inhuman.

Trask roared incoherently, a bull-like bellow of pure hate. He swayed, somehow staying on his feet, and although his gun sagged for a second, he managed to lift it again for another shot.

At the same time, Luke was struggling to stay on his feet. After being hit in the shoulder, he had to force his right arm to function. But his indomitable will was enough to make his muscles work. Both Remingtons came up again.

Trask fired again just as Luke pulled both triggers. The

Remingtons roared and bucked in his hands. Trask's shot struck in almost the exact same place as the first wound, and Luke's arm went numb. The Remington tumbled out of that hand.

He staggered as his boot came down in a pool of Jenny's blood and went out from underneath him. Hit the stair awkwardly and lost his other pistol as he bounced down the stairs, each step-edge like a hammer blow to his head and back.

Trask stumbled to the top of the staircase. One of Luke's rounds had struck Trask in the left arm, causing a rose of blood to bloom on the big man's jacket sleeve. He'd ripped his handkerchief mask away, and despite his injuries, he was grinning as he cocked the Colt Dragoon.

Luke hit the bottom of the stairs in a jumble. He tried to flip over and roll out of the way, but he had landed on his wounded side, and his body wouldn't obey. Pain lanced through his body with such intensity that he gagged, almost vomiting.

Shots rang out. Luke twisted his neck, looking back up the stairs. Trask was leaning against the railing where the bullet impacts had flung him. Josh appeared in the hallway, already bleeding from several wounds. Gunsmoke hung thick as London fog in the hall. Josh pointed the gun in his hand at Trask and pulled the trigger again, but nothing happened except the hammer fell on an empty chamber.

Trask's gun went off and the bullet punched a hole through the left side of Josh's chest. The kid's mouth made a surprised "O" as he jerked under the impact. His eyes, filled with terror, found Luke's across the distance, and then he fell forward. His body struck Trask as the man tried pushing himself off the railing. Cursing, Trask swung his arm out, flinging the kid off him. Josh's body thumped down the steps like a rag doll. Trask turned, hunting Luke, his pistol ready.

The time it took for Trask to push the kid away was all the bounty hunter needed to find one of his pistols and scoop it up in his left hand. As Trask staggered, Luke took aim and fired three times.

Two of the three slugs blew snowball-sized holes in Trask's throat. The third smashed his heavy jaw under the wild beard and angled up into his brain.

Trask crumpled at the knees and pitched forward. It was like seeing a redwood topple. He hit the stairs and slid down, tangling up with Josh's corpse, arms akimbo, one leg caught between the wooden dowel balusters of the railing.

"Kid?"

Luke groaned as he managed to get himself into a sitting position. His good arm trembled supporting his weight and he realized he was bleeding badly. No one moved upstairs. There was the sound of gunfire from outside.

Reaching out, Luke jerked the flour sack off the dead raider's head and pressed it against his wound. He'd been shot more than his share over the years. Had made it right up until the end of the war without catching a round and then been left almost crippled. Since then, he'd been on death's door more than once. He knew the feeling well. He could survive these wounds, but only if he got help. His shirt was soaked with blood now.

The windows blew out and the door rattled in its frame as a fusillade of bullets struck it. Thundering hoofbeats pounded by, and Luke saw the outlaws fleeing town in mass. They'd gotten what they'd come for and now were leaving.

He gasped in pain, then started crawling into the bar. He found a chair and used it to help him stand. The pain radiated down from his shoulder where his arm hung useless as a butchered carcass. Gritting his teeth, he found his feet and stood, swaying.

The kid was dead. Jenny was dead. From the funeral silence upstairs, he was pretty sure Sarah was dead. At least Trask was dead.

People often pointed out that vengeance didn't bring back the people you'd lost or lessen the pain of that loss. That was true, as far as it went. But there was more than one kind of pain when someone you cared about was taken from you. There was the pain of the loss, but also the pain of realizing the person who'd killed them was still living. Killing that person didn't ease the first pain, but it sure as hell eased the second. It was, in fact, the only thing that *could* ease it.

Luke Jensen had more killing to do.

Staggering to the entrance, he leaned heavily against the doorframe. His breaths came as shallow pants. Several bodies lay sprawled in the streets. Smoke burned his lungs. He coughed harshly and then almost screamed from the pain of his wound. More blood, hot and slippery, ran down the inside of his shirt.

"Maybe I'll just sit down for a minute," he whispered to himself.

Darkness took him, and he fell to the boardwalk.

CHAPTER 16

Three weeks later

Luke found the bodies hanging from the tree. It was a family and they'd been burned before they were strung up. The woman and little girl still had parts of their bonnets intact, but their dresses had melted away. Their skin was streaked red and raw where it wasn't crusted black.

Goldsmith had wiped their eyes with grease so that they popped when they burned and all five of the bodies showed empty melted sockets.

How they must have screamed, Luke thought as he cut them down. A shiver of pure hate went through him. Anybody who could do this wasn't even human anymore. Maybe never had been . . .

He was by himself, so there was no dignified way to do it. He used his clasp knife to sever the ropes and the bodies struck the ground like sacks of loose meat, the wet *thumps* punctuated by the crunching of bones. The sickly sweet smell of burned flesh hung in the air like a perfume of flowers, making Luke gag until he was forced to put his bandana around his mouth and nose.

The family had used a lean-to to shelter the animals and it was a blackened ruin with the charred corpse of a mule and an ox underneath the collapsed roof. But luck, such as it was, was with him, and he found a shovel more or less intact. He buried the family.

Death was everywhere on the frontier. People died from murderous violence. Minor wounds became infected, and fevers took them away. Accidents occurred with relentless repetition. Women suffered and died in childbirth. Snake bit, thrown from ill-broke horses, disease, the list of lethal encounters could fill pages. Many ended their hardships by hanging themselves or using their firearms one last time. Medical care was crude and even that could be hard to find in an emergency.

Half a day's ride from a town and someone could find themselves in a primitive, savage, and lawless place that reduced people into two types, the quick and the dead. Such an environment suited him more than he cared to admit. He admired, for example, what his brother Smoke had built, and even envied him the love he shared with his wife.

But push come to shove, Luke had realized he wasn't built that way. Something was fundamentally different inside him. He longed for the loneliness of the open sky and spread-out prairie. He welcomed the solitude of a single campfire on a vast plain.

That was a big part of why Luke Jensen did what he did. The force of law and order was needed to protect good folk from bad. On the frontier, the reach of the government was sporadic and less influential the farther from population centers that you got. It made vigilance committees and bounty hunters necessary.

It satisfied Luke greatly to bring owlhoots down. Bringing Goldsmith to justice was going to be one of the most satisfying events in his career. *It's going to happen,* he silently told Goldsmith as he leaned on the shovel next to the graves where he'd laid the murdered family to rest. *Bet on it.*

Sarah had been, of course, dead. He woke up in Jenny's room on the second floor of the saloon because the town had been running out of places to house the wounded. The harried and overworked doctor had patched him up and then left it to the surviving saloon girls to tend to his dressings.

Trask's bullets hadn't broken any bones, the medico had told Luke, and the nerve damage didn't appear to be too bad. Might be a little lingering stiffness. The loss of blood had been the main thing, and Luke had made it through that.

He'd been luckier than most. A good number of folks had been killed or badly wounded in the raid by Goldsmith's gang. The street echoed with the sounds of saws and hammers as carpenters knocked together coffins. Soon enough, lack of lumber meant that bodies were buried wrapped in tarps or blankets.

Sheriff Red Conwell informed Luke on one visit that the town had just dug a pit to shove the outlaws' bodies in, after a photographer was paid to take pictures meant to be taken over to the Carlton *Chronicle*.

The sheriff also told him that Josh and Sarah had been buried next to one another. Luke was glad to hear that. He figured it was fitting.

Luke fretted for a couple of weeks, afraid the trail was going cold. He'd been wounded often enough to know that riding out too soon was a fool thing to do when facing hardcases, but the delay rankled him deeply. As soon as he could draw and point his pistol with his injured arm, he started making preparations over the doctor's protests.

The arm still tired easily and was sore after a day of hard riding, but the scar tissue was strong enough that moving didn't rip it open again. When he wasn't trailing Goldsmith's gang, he forced himself to work the shoulder, lifting his Remington up and down several dozen times or even his saddle on occasion to test its strength.

He wouldn't want to wrestle with it or spend the day driving railroad spikes, but it was on the mend. It was good enough for gun work. Today, however, the shoveling involved in digging five graves in the prairie soil had tested the arm to its limits. It ached and when Luke was finished, he couldn't lift his canteen without hot needles of pain jabbing into his flesh.

He made camp a short distance from the burned house. He spooked a small herd of antelope and watched them run. His fire was small and he ate a cold meal after rubbing some foul-smelling ointment on the shoulder that the doctor back in Hatchet Creek had given him.

Above him a nighthawk screeched a challenge. At one point, he saw yellow eyes watching him from the dark. Most likely a coyote. The poultice soon worked and he was able to sleep.

He dreamed about little girls screaming as their eyeballs popped from the heat of a fire.

The sodbuster must have managed to wound one of Goldsmith's men. The bullet entered low down in the gut, right above his groin. When Luke found the outlaw, he was under the shade of an oak tree, slowly dying.

The gang had taken his horse but left him whiskey. His eyes were fever bright as Luke rode up. The man had a heavy Schofield .44 revolver in his lap, but by the time Luke found him he was too weak to lift it. Flies buzzed around him in a little cloud. Sometimes he would raise his hand as if to shoo them away, but his gesture did little good.

"You're dying," Luke told him.

"Go to hell . . ." The words started out as a shout but they ended in a soft slur.

"You burned those folks."

"They turned their back on us after the war."

Luke didn't dignify that with a response. The man's lap was full of blood and the ground around him was muddy with it. When he studied the wound, he saw a pulsing squirt coming out of the hole in the man's belly. Every time his heart beat, it pumped more blood out onto the ground. The flies crawled around frantically, drinking it up.

Luke never failed to marvel at the sheer amount of red stuff the human body contained.

Luke pulled his canteen off his saddle horn and spat.

"Hot," he said. "Make a man thirsty."

Undoing the cap, he drank half the canteen down. This seemed to infuriate the delirious outlaw. Sputtering until spittle flew from his lips, he made inarticulate sounds of protest. He tried lifting the Schofield, but the big iron kept dropping out of his hand.

Luke lowered the canteen and wiped his mouth with the back of his arm.

"You said those people turned their backs," he said, voice flat. "Looks to me like Goldsmith did worse. It's like that fella said in *Don Quixote,* there is no honor among thieves. Your so-called brothers ran off and left you to die."

"I don't know nothing about what no damn Mexican said," the outlaw slurred.

Drool ran down the side of his chin. Flies crawled over his skin, but he was too weak now to even try to wave them clear. He attempted to lift the nearly empty whiskey bottle, but that proved too difficult as well. A long sigh escaped his lips.

"Cervantes was a Spaniard."

But the outlaw didn't reply. Luke studied him. His eyes were fixed and dilated. The opaque gray of death filmed them over. As Luke watched, the blowflies walked across the man's eyeballs.

Luke rode on.

At some point the gang split up. It happened around the Kansas-Colorado border. Luke couldn't be sure which group Goldsmith was with, the one pointed south to New Mexico, or the one headed north to Wyoming. He'd never had a chance to study Goldsmith's mount so he couldn't cut the track by the hoofprints.

He figured there was a town closer in Colorado to the south, and if he managed to catch any stragglers getting lazy then he'd know soon enough which direction Goldsmith had gone. Besides, everyone riding with the colonel needed to swing on the gallows.

He rode past several abandoned homesteads. Here, closer to Colorado, there were as many log cabins as sod houses. They stood like rotting skulls with dark coffin doorways, empty windows, and collapsed roofs. People had come, tried, failed, then moved on. Or died. Soon only the weeds and spiders and ticks would own the homes. After them came the snakes, hunting the multitude of mice. He never tried to shelter a night in one of the lonely places.

There were plenty of native tribes to contend with. In the past, the Comanche had raided this far west and north. These days, it was mostly Arapaho and Cheyenne with an occasional band of Sioux. Farther west, the White River Utes were making noises of discontent, although this was too far east to worry about them.

Still, trading posts run by former Comancheros had sprung up enough distance away from army forts to encourage tribal raiders to raid isolated homesteads and ranches and sell whatever loot they could find. Such operations were risky because the warriors might decide to raid the trading posts themselves, but these weren't the same Indians as when people had first pushed into Texas well before the war.

This generation of warriors liked easy access to ammunition and new firearms as much as any white. Mostly the truce held. Unscrupulous merchants made steep profits on items stripped from the dead of homesteads and wagon trains. That thought always put Luke in a dark mood.

So it was that when he came over a gentle swell on the eastern plains of Colorado, he was not particularly pleased to see one of the trading posts on Big Sandy Creek. He needed to ask for information about the men he was chasing, but he couldn't be sure of the reception he'd get. Merchants in the business of receiving stolen property on a regular basis often weren't eager to supply information about the thieves and robbers they worked with.

Someone will talk, he promised himself as he leaned over in the saddle and spat. *One way or the other.*

He rode slowly down the slope toward the large, rough log building. There was a split rail corral to one side and he stopped riding when he saw five saddled horses near the water trough. The group he'd been following numbered five. He wasn't going to bet his life by thinking it was a coincidence and rushing in.

The sun had been swallowed by low, dark clouds about noon. Now a chilly north wind swept across the grass, and the first drops of rain began falling. Luke swung his horse out wide. He wanted to approach the trading post from an unaccustomed side. The building was like an island in a sea of grass, so he wasn't sure there was an unaccustomed side. He'd avoid the front and back and that would have to do.

His problem was one of orientation, he felt. Not in the sense of cardinal directions, but in the sense of his mental state. He was a lot of things. A bounty hunter for one. When push came to shove, he was a cool gun hand and a steady killer. But one thing he wasn't, was a murderer.

He knew that if some of Colonel Goldsmith's boys were down there, they weren't coming peaceably. All they had to look forward to was a noose. If he gave them a chance by announcing himself and demanding their surrender, he'd lose the element of surprise to a force of greater numbers. That they would open fire on him immediately, he had no doubt.

He considered himself at war. A soldier ambushed the enemy whenever opportunity presented itself. He would need surprise if he was going to win out in this situation. While the question of tactics spun like a pinwheel in his mind, as he thought of first one plan and then another, one thought never occurred to him—to simply ride away. It never entered his head.

As he drew closer to the trading post, he heard someone playing a harmonica at a frantic pace. Men were shouting, their laughter loud and boisterous. They sounded drunk. Good. Dismounting, he eased around the corral. Discipline had fallen away since the split with Goldsmith, he reckoned. The men had set no sentries. That was a strong indication the colonel wasn't with this bunch.

He catfooted along the wall of the log structure toward a greased paper window. Men were whooping and shouting, excited and celebratory. He wondered if maybe they were gambling. He tried picking out voices and heard what he thought were five different ones. That didn't account for the proprietor. He needed to see inside.

Heading toward the back of the rectangle log building, he drew his Remingtons. The repeater was in its saddle boot. He needed to shoot fast and at close range. Even a carbine wasn't short enough to be ideal for this kind of work. He'd seen a few men using cut-down lever action Henrys or Winchesters, but he preferred the feel of wielding a pistol in such situations.

Coming around the corner of the trading post, he entered the dirt chicken yard and sent half a dozen hens scattering, clucking in panicked alarm. He froze, trying to tell if the men inside had been alarmed. There was no break in the wild rumpus, and he edged up to the back door.

The back door stood ajar, and he eased up to it, moving in a deliberate fashion. He bent and slowly peeked through the six-inch crack. Those were Goldsmith's men inside, all right, and they were having a party.

An old man with a white beard longer than the one Trask had sported played the harmonica with frenzied energy. This was due to the .44 hogleg one of the outlaws pressed into his ear. The other four men stood around a squat sturdy table. It was immediately apparent what they were so giddy about.

An Indian girl was lying on the table with her head pointed toward the door. Her buckskin dress had been torn mostly off of her. One of Goldsmith's men held her hands and hooted as another outlaw struggled to control her flailing legs. She twisted her head around enough for Luke to catch a glimpse of her tear-streaked face. She looked like she was just about to give up and stop fighting.

The other two men stood to either side holding jugs from which they gulped every now and then. As Luke watched, one of them reached out and cruelly pinched the girl's arm. He wrenched at her until she cried out in pain, and he laughed.

I can't kill them all, Luke told himself as rage welled up inside him. *At least one of them has to be alive . . . for a while.*

Luke let that icy river of rage sweep him away to a place of utter calm.

He came through the door without a sound. The first indication of his presence was when he shot the man holding the gun to the harmonica player in the face. Blood and brain splattered the rough-hewn logs of the wall as the area between his eyes and upper lip suddenly looked as if someone had taken an axe to it. He fell away from the old man, the .44 unfired. Luke had taken a chance on that, and he was glad the outlaw hadn't jerked the trigger as he died.

The old man dropped the harmonica and dived to the floor.

For a long moment, the drunk men stood stunned and motionless. Luke smoothly aimed the second pistol and shot the man holding the girl's arms in the back of the head. Scarlet splattered her body as the man jerked forward and collapsed.

These men were hardened outlaws and veterans, well

prepared to react to sudden, seemingly random violence. Surprise held them in its grip only for a heartbeat. Then the men holding the moonshine jugs dropped them. The jugs crashed to the floor. Each man reached for big pistols stuck in their belts. But even though they were fast, they couldn't beat a man who already had his weapons drawn.

Luke fired both Remingtons at almost the same time, the reports so close together they blended into one giant peal of gun-thunder. The range was under ten feet. Each of his bullets cracked through the sternum of one of the outlaws. They each stumbled backward and fell as the heavy .45 caliber slugs cored out their hearts.

That left the final outlaw.

He pushed himself back from the girl, moving so fast that he tripped and fell hard to the floor. He was clawing at his pistol but hadn't cleared leather when Luke darted around the table and took careful aim. The man looked up at him, face white with terror. Gunsmoke hung thick in the air, sharp enough to dull the stink of dirty bodies and raw grain alcohol.

"No! Plea—"

Luke fired.

His round took the man in his right arm, and he screamed. Luke stood over him, gunsmoke curling from the Remington's hot muzzle. His face was tight with anger, and his eyes were cold and hard as winter hail.

On the floor next to the wounded outlaw was a body Luke hadn't seen at first. It was an older Indian woman in buckskin dress and trading-post shawl. She lay face up as flies crawled across her vacant, staring eyes. She'd been brutally hacked to death with a huge Bowie knife. The bone handle of the blade now stuck from her belly in a rude insult. The woman's hands were wrapped around it.

Luke shot the outlaw in his other arm.

He screamed. As he was screaming, Luke stomped him in the groin, driving his heel where he thought it'd do the most damage. *Calm down,* he told himself. *This one has to live.* He forced his breathing under control and holstered one of the Remingtons.

"You," he said to the harmonica player, who had rolled over on the rough plank floor and was sitting up, wide-eyed and still scared. "You the owner here?"

The man swallowed, struggling to find his voice. After clearing his throat, he managed to answer.

"I am," he said. "Name's Eustace Milligan."

Luke looked at the girl. She was watching him with frightened eyes, curled up on herself on top of the table as she struggled to pull the tattered remnants of her garment around her. She wasn't having much luck with that.

"Are you all right?" Luke asked, hoping she spoke English.

She nodded once.

"Good, get dressed."

"She ain't nothing but a squaw!" the wounded outlaw protested. "Why are you worried about her? I'm hurt bad here!"

Luke pointed the barrel of his cocked Remington at the man's face. He wanted this no-good skunk alive for now, but the outlaw didn't have to know that.

"Talking is not a good choice for you at this moment."

The man blanched and nodded. He was bleeding heavily from the wounds in his arms. If they weren't seen to, he'd bleed to death soon. Luke couldn't let that happen. That the man wasn't in shock already, he put down to the alcohol coursing through his veins.

"How'd you like to live? You're worth five hundred

dollars to me, so if you expect to get out of here, you'd better do what I say."

"You're going to let me live?" the outlaw asked.

Luke squinted at his face, trying to recall the man's name from his brief sojourn with Colonel Goldsmith's gang. "Turner," he said. "You're Cleo Turner."

The man didn't answer.

"I take it back," Luke told him. "You're only worth three hundred at the moment. Of course, when I turn you over to the authorities at Fort Laramie, they'll add rape and murder and desecration of a corpse to your charges. That should get you up to five hundred dollars, which is respectable."

"Dese—what?"

"Mutilated. You burned bodies. I found that settler family."

"I never!" Turner protested. "That was the colonel. Colonel Goldsmith loves burning people like a normal man loves getting him some—"

The Indian girl—Luke thought maybe she was Shoshone—streaked past him, a cheap hatchet in her hand. The sudden attack caught Luke by surprise and he was a second late, only managing to jostle her arm slightly as she brought the hand axe down.

The blade struck Turner in the side of the head and stuck there. Luke flung an arm in front of the girl and threw her back against the table.

"Stop!" he yelled. "I need him alive, damn it."

The girl leaned on the table and glared at him, eyes blazing as she spat what he was sure were vile curses in her own language, which confirmed her identity as Shoshone if he'd got the sound of it right.

Luke looked back at Turner, expecting the man to be dead. He blinked. Turner stared up at him with glassy eyes.

Scalp wounds bled heavily and he looked as if he'd done a swan dive into a slaughter pen. But he was still alive.

The hatchet jutted from his head like the handle on a pot. The blade was stuck into his skull about a quarter of an inch from what Luke could tell from where he stood.

"Did she scalp me?" Turner's words were slurred. From the loss of blood or because of the whiskey he'd guzzled down earlier, Luke didn't know.

The pupil of one of Turner's eyes was drawn down tight and the other one was dilated so far you couldn't see the iris. Luke looked back at the hatchet, trying to comprehend what he was seeing.

"Lord have mercy," the old man said.

"Did she scalp me?" Turner repeated.

"No, she didn't scalp you," Luke said. "She stuck an axe in your head."

"There's an axe in my head?" This seemed puzzling to Turner.

"Damn right, there's an axe in your head," the old man said. "You murdering son of a—"

"Well, pull it out!"

"I'm disarming you first," Luke informed him.

"Pull it out!"

Turner was not in a mood to be reasonable.

Luke kept the Remington trained on Turner and used his other hand to pull the man's pistol free. He slid it across the floor toward the trader, who picked it up. Luke continued searching Turner. Long ropes of drool had started collecting at the corner of his mouth and dripping into his beard. He worked his jaw back and forth, his throat making hard little clicks every time he swallowed.

There was a sheath for a knife on the gunbelt, but the knife was missing. It was probably the one stuck in the

Indian woman, Luke figured. He found a straight razor in one boot and a two-shot derringer in the other. He kept both. Reaching around to the small of the outlaw's back, he found a Colt Navy .36. He slid that over to the old man.

"Who are the women?" Luke asked. "Will they have family to come look after them?"

"I am the family," Milligan said with a bitter voice. "That was my wife. The girl's my daughter, Rosie."

That simplified things, at least. He was going to be trailing Goldsmith north. He didn't need a band of justifiably outraged braves tracking the man as well.

Milligan broke down crying. Though he held little sympathy for a man who might have dealt in goods stolen in situations all too similar to this one, Luke heard the genuineness of his grief.

"I am truly sorry for your loss," Luke said.

"Pull the axe out of my head!" Turner wailed.

Snarling, Luke reached over and yanked the blade free. The wound looked like a ravine and immediately welled up with blood. If he wanted Turner to lead him to Goldsmith, he would have to dress the man's wounds.

"You got any laudanum?" he asked the trader.

"Not for him!" Milligan cried.

"Look, I appreciate your feelings, I truly do. But there's twenty bad men just like this lot that went north, led by the worst of the bunch. I guessed wrong and followed these varmints here. But I need him alive and fit enough to ride."

"Rosie done put a hole in his head."

"That is unfortunate," Luke agreed. "But I need him to be able to ride."

The interior of the trading post was close and crowded. Every kind of antler rack or horn known to the plains or mountains had been mounted on the wall. There were so many prongs and tines sticking out that a drunk man would need to be cautious that he didn't stumble and impale himself.

The place was crammed with tables and they were mounded with bolts of cloth, trading post knives of an inferior quality, steel traps, piles of furs, liquor, small mirrors, and boxes of ammunition. The Indian girl, Rosie, had stepped off to one side and wrapped a blanket from one of the tables around her while Luke talked to her father.

He caught the flash of motion out of the corner of his eyes and whirled. He was in no position to stop the girl except to shoot her, and he wasn't going to do that. He was rising to his feet and uncocking the Remington when she reached Turner.

She grabbed the outlaw by the long greasy hair dangling over his forehead, now streaked crimson with his blood. Rosie held one of the trading-post skinning knives in her hand. Luke shouted at her, but she was cat-quick.

Turner screamed in pain as she jerked his head back, then started shrieking as she used the blade to scalp him. The skin made a wet tearing sound as she peeled it back and then ripped it clean off. Throwing the knife to the other side of the room, she showed Luke the bloody scalp.

"Mine," she said.

Luke had to clear his throat to speak. "Sure," he said.

Turner was alive, though getting worse for wear by the second.

"She scalped me!" he managed to moan.

"Oh," Luke agreed, "she surely did."

CHAPTER 17

Luke dug a grave for the old man's wife, the exertion making his still-healing arm ache again. He hadn't had to bury anybody for quite a while before today, and now it seemed like he was digging a grave every time he turned around.

Eustace stood off to the side, a gloomy expression on his white-bearded face, and nipped from a jug as he watched Luke laboring. Between drinks, he talked aimlessly of his life. He had come west and followed Jim Bridger toward the end of his career in the late 1830s and early '40s. St. Louis had still felt like the edge of the world, back in those mountain man days, he said.

After binding up the outlaw's wounds to stop the bleeding, Luke had made Turner drink enough laudanum to be in a senseless stupor and then tied him, sitting up, to one of the hitching posts in front of the building. He'd learned his lesson by now and insisted that Rosie not be left alone with Turner. She had good reason to kill him, but when he made the request that she leave Turner alone, she'd just shrugged.

"Let him hang. I have his scalp."

Luke couldn't be sure how sincere she was, though, so he figured he'd best err on the side of caution.

When the grave was ready, Eustace roused himself from his drinking and grieving enough to help Luke lower the blanket-wrapped body into the ground. Luke decided digging the grave was enough. Somebody else could cover it up.

He left the father and daughter tending the grave and went over to Turner. Luke stood over the incapacitated Turner, knife in hand. He looked down at the man, feeling the weight of the blade in his grip. He knelt and took each boot in turn. Sleeping the morphine sleep, Turner didn't stir. Luke made a mark on each of Turner's heels, then came to his feet and headed for the corral.

Entering the enclosure, he stripped the saddles off the outlaw horses and brushed them down before doing the same with his mount. Any money, along with the saddles and guns, he left with them. He asked for the loan of a tack hammer and awl, which Eustace gladly gave him. When he was finished with the chore he'd set for himself, he gave them back.

Once the laudanum wore off a little and Turner began to come around, Luke slung each dead man over his mount and then cut Turner loose and tied him into the saddle. He slid the straight razor he'd appropriated into the man's back pocket. The outlaw looked at him dully, not quite comprehending what was going on. Smiling, Luke tucked the pain medicine into Turner's shirt where it wouldn't fall out.

"A little ways up the trail, you can cut yourself loose," he said. "Your arms ought to work well enough for that. You're wanted, so I wouldn't head for any of the nearby towns." He looked the owlhoot in the eye and lied. "From

Fort Bent all the way to the south Platte, they know to look for you. I rode through them tracking you."

The wounded man just glared at Luke with sullen eyes. He was starting to understand more now. The bounty hunter had caused him so much pain he was afraid to speak out of turn. He cast his eyes nervously around after a moment, though, as if he were looking for something . . . or some*one*.

Luke grinned. The man was terrified Rosie would take another crack at him.

"You can tell Goldsmith that hell is coming. That's the only reason you're still alive and the only reason I'm not taking you back to a hang rope."

The man looked on the verge of saying something, but Luke stepped back and slapped his horse on the rump. The startled animal jumped and began trotting away across the grassland. Luke stood for a while and watched the man riding north until he became a speck on the horizon.

The old man shook his hand and wished him well. Rosie was nowhere to be seen.

"I thank ye ag'in for your help," Eustace said. "I guess those old boys would have done for me and Rosie both if you hadn't showed up."

Luke touched the brim of his hat in acknowledgment. Turning his horse, he took his grisly mule train of bounties and headed north.

This wasn't a bad day's work, he thought. But things were just getting started.

He turned in the bodies and collected the bounties at the nearest town and then rode his back trail looking for Turner. Less than forty-eight hours had gone by since Turner rode away from the trading post, and soon enough

Luke found the trace. He'd tapped in two X's on either side of Turner's mount's shoes, and the track was readily identifiable.

Coupled with him being fairly sure the wounded outlaw was headed to southeastern Wyoming, it was easy enough to guess his path. Luke swung out wide around settlements and when he stopped to ask questions at the little ranches or homesteads in that path, they frequently reported missing chickens or piglets. Turner was exhausted and hungry, but not desperate enough to risk venturing into a town.

Luke began to worry that the man might collapse and die on the trail before he was able to rejoin Goldsmith's gang. Despite that, they made it out of Colorado in a reasonable time and crossed over into Wyoming. But then he began finding empty bottles of Mariani wine along the way.

More potent medicine than wine, it explained how the wounded outlaw was dealing with both the fatigue and the pain of his wounds. A bottle of Vin Mariani a day could keep a man in the saddle for a long time.

His hunch was that Goldsmith would have designated rendezvous points when the gang split up, and that Turner would make his way to one of these. A day into Wyoming, he cut Turner's track on the other side of a feeder stream to the North Platte and realized that the way Turner was heading coincided with the direction a large group of riders had been headed. Those tracks were older, fainter, but still readily identifiable. Goldsmith was close. Luke felt it in his bones.

In a shallow valley he came across a sheep massacre. Forty or fifty animals had been killed and left to rot. He saw bold coyotes eating carcasses at the edge of the meadow and the place was alive with crows. His slow canter made them take flight and they rose in the air in a black cloud, harsh caws echoing wildly.

Luke inspected the sheep casually as he rode through, and it was obvious they'd been shot and left to rot. Big cattlemen had always coexisted uneasily with homesteaders and smaller spreads. Neither group held much patience for sheepherders. The friction frequently erupted in violence. Down New Mexico way, Luke knew, the Colfax County range war that had started back in '73 was still going on.

Hell, Clay Allison had burnished his already considerable reputation as a gunhawk during those early battles in Colfax County.

Luke avoided such conflicts when he could, though with his skill with a gun, he could have earned top dollar. Inevitably, his upbringing and history caused him to side with settlers over cattlemen and landowners. That wasn't the profitable side of the battle and frequently cattle associations had the law on their side. Or in their pocket.

A man could only do what he could do. Luke chose to take his money eradicating one evil man at a time.

The stench of the sheep carcasses brought him back to the present. His horse tried shying, as disturbed by the stink as Luke was. Rather than fight with the mount, he gave the animal its head and they galloped clear.

They followed clear wagon tracks up into the foothills of the Medicine Bow Mountains. First part of the Cherokee Trail, the area had seen several mining booms. He assumed he was heading toward an old mining town, but he hadn't ridden this area much before, so he wasn't sure what he would find.

It was beautiful, stark country. And he enjoyed the ride for a while. But as the elevation increased and the hills and canyons began pressing in on all sides, the atmosphere changed. Stands of trees gave him uneasy feelings like he was being watched, or that someone would ambush him.

He followed Turner's track until he found the horse dead by the side of the trail. Wolves had been at the belly and he was mildly concerned a grizzly could be attracted by the horse flesh. He inspected the animal and saw a worn spot on one forelock and a bullet hole in the animal's skull.

There was a now familiar empty bottle of Mariani wine on the ground.

He supposed the animal had come up lame and Turner had put him down and continued on foot. The other possibility was that he'd checked the forelock and seen to the shoes only to notice the marks Luke had branded them with, then killed the horse to try and throw the bounty hunter off the scent.

Luke didn't favor the latter thought, though it was possible. Men didn't like to be afoot in wild country. Goldsmith's men were cavalry, not fur-trading mountain men. They'd sooner cut off their feet than travel cross country the way Kit Carson had. No, if Turner had discovered the marks, he would have risked riding into a town to sell the horse and purchase another.

The outlaw was on foot with only one hope of shelter— the settlement wherever those wagon tracks led. There was no place else to go. Luke gigged his horse and started off at a trot.

He found the preacher hanging a man just before dusk.

CHAPTER 18

The crowd outside of Golgotha Rock was hungry for blood.

Golgotha Rock was in the fading glory of its boom. What had started as a river of copper had, over several years, dwindled to streams. The town hadn't given up the ghost and died yet, but it seemed the vultures were circling.

Luke slowed his horse to a walk as he saw the mob standing on the flats outside of the town proper. A big tamarack pine stood at the center of a small clearing. A rope was tied to a stout branch and the rope came down in a noose around the neck of a sullen-looking man with a bushy mustache and haystack hair.

The crowd was arrayed in a half-circle around the hanging tree and a preacher man stood in the back of a buckboard. Black, flat-brimmed hat, black trousers, black coat. White, collarless shirt buttoned all the way up to the throat. In one hand he held a Bible and in the other a whip. As Luke drew nearer, he could hear the fire-and-brimstone sermon erupting from the man's throat. The crowd shouted choruses of *Amens!* and *Hallelujahs!* to punctuate his points.

He stopped to listen, pulling his horse up at the edge of the crowd. The preacher had a deep, clear voice. Luke had no trouble hearing the sermon. The man's voice carried.

"A dark door has opened in Golgotha Rock, I tell you, friends! A door has opened and Satan has walked through!"

The preacher was so bombastic, it was hard to ignore the man's voice, but Luke did his best. He studied the man about to hang. He assumed it wasn't a lynching when he got a glimpse of several men with tin stars on their shirts in the congregation.

And that's what it is, he thought. *A congregation. Not a crowd or a mob, but a congregation.*

He realized he recognized the criminal. It wasn't one of Goldsmith's outfit, but a hardcase from the New Mexico Territory, John Hamilton Little. Sometimes called Short Little because his brother stood six and a half feet tall. Horse rustler, bank robber, an owlhoot with eleven deaths on his gun. At least. Stringing him up was no injustice.

"And this man turned his eyes away from God," the preacher was shouting, "and took the hand of the devil!"

Luke, who'd seen his share of hangings, was just about to guide his horse around the congregation, when the preacher reached the pinnacle of his sermon.

"Meet your maker, sinner!"

The bullwhip in the preacher's hand cracked hard. The lash stung the outlaw's horse on the rump, and it bolted forward. The outlaw's eyes grew wide in startled shock at the sudden action. He went up as he was jostled from his saddle and then dropped hard.

The crowd had held its breath at the preacher's motion, but despite the moment of quiet, Luke didn't hear the telltale *crack* of John Little's neck snapping. They'd mis-tied the knot, he realized. The devout citizenry of Golgotha Rock was going to have to watch the condemned man strangle.

It was unsavory, but knowing the crimes John Little had committed, Luke couldn't summon up any sympathy for him as he kicked and swung.

Luke turned to ride the short distance into the town when the crowd next to him parted and a man stepped up to him. The man wore a black Stetson over a chambray shirt and starched jeans tucked into snakeskin boots. The man also wore a star on his chest.

"Marshal," Luke said with a slight nod as he reined in.

The man was tall and built like a trail hand, lean and rough. His face was lined and his goatee and mustache salt-and-pepper. His eyes seemed to stare right through Luke's. They were the eyes of a man who had killed and found joy in that killing.

"Welcome to Golgotha Rock, stranger," the marshal said. "Town ordinance requires you to hand over all firearms for the duration of your stay. That going to be a problem?"

Such ordinances were common. As long as he knew it was evenly enforced, Luke had little problem agreeing to the terms. The marshal waited. Luke couldn't tell from his expression if he hoped Luke would do as asked or hoped that he did not.

"No problem," Luke said. He nodded toward where John Little hung, face purple, tongue lolling. "I'd hate to cross you, since you sure can foul up a hanging."

The marshal turned his head to the side. He blinked, and his eyes, which had seemed to see past Luke before and into the middle distance, now focused on him. There was curiosity in their focus, and a little annoyance.

"Who says we fouled it up?"

Luke sighed, regretting that he'd let his tongue get away from him. Getting crossways with the town marshal wasn't the best move at a time like this.

"Do I turn them in at your office, I presume?"

The marshal nodded. "That's right."

Luke touched his hat. "I'll go do that now."

The marshal watched him go, but as he rode away, it was the eyes of the preacher upon him that Luke felt the most. Luke had recognized him almost as soon as he rode up.

The preacher was one of Goldsmith's men.

Luke could tell right away that something was odd about Golgotha Rock. Like all boom towns, it was alive and well as darkness descended. Light spilled out into the street from several busy establishments. Saloons, gambling dens, brothels, were all doing a brisk business despite the size of the crowd that had turned out to watch the hanging.

As he let his horse amble along toward the sheriff's office, Luke noticed other things as well, occurrences he didn't normally associate with boom towns. For one, some of the businesses were closed. Not closed for the night, like the apothecary or mercantile might be, but shut down for good. They were boarded up, and tacked on their doors were public announcements and something else: wooden crosses.

Religious people frequently shut down establishments of ill repute, but usually that only happened once the boom had faded and the community had shifted to less volatile forms of economics such as farming. At the beginning of booms, churches were not a force for change.

Luke had seen the pattern many times before. There was money to be made off miners or cowboys or railroad workers, and tent city Sodom and Gomorrahs sprang up to service the labor force. The only women around at all were whores and saloon girls.

Those women could rise to positions of wealth and power inside a boom town. They could hold sway with city councils, marshals, and sheriffs and even the less risk-averse banks that showed up usually in the second wave of a boom. But gradually, the tents gave way to more permanent structures. Men who were going to stay started looking around for wives, and more women came into the area. Families grew. Schools and churches were built.

As proper church-going women increased, so did the pressure to remove the wilder, less-savory, elements of the town. Madams and dance hall girls were no longer important pillars upon which a town's economics were built. Instead, they were sinful and in need of being driven out.

Once they were gone, the only women remaining were wives and mothers. Women the city council and banks didn't need to deal with because it was their husbands who controlled all the finances of note. Then a town was tame, civilized, and the wilder elements were pushed west, chasing a frontier that shrank more every day.

Even now, Luke knew the frontier was fading away and would likely be gone in his lifetime. The thought made him restless and morose if he allowed himself to dwell on it. He belonged in the wilderness, and he didn't know what would become of him once there was no longer one.

Second, there were a larger-than-normal amount of streetside preachers present. People loved a good revival meeting. Listening to sweating, furious preachers harangue against the wages of sin and the searing fire of hell was a big form of entertainment. Preachers were performers. To have one of them around, such as the man leading the hanging, was normal in even the rawest of boom towns. But not counting the hanging pastor, Luke passed three separate fire-and-brimstone street shouters as he rode along Golgotha Rock's main street.

He came up to the marshal's office and threw his reins over the hitch rail. The wooden structure was sandwiched between a dry goods store on one side and a diner on the other, both closed. There were no windows in the front of the building, but light showed around the door.

Luke opened the door and stepped in. A beefy, red-faced deputy looked up from a newspaper. There were cigarette makings on the desk in front of him. The room was sparsely furnished with a desk, a potbellied stove, a coat rack, and several chairs. A gun rack on the wall held several rifles and shotguns. The deputy was no more friendly than the marshal.

"What do you want?"

"I want a receipt for my guns."

"Town ordinance against carrying guns."

"Yes, the marshal told me. That's why I'm here."

"You talked to the marshal?"

"Yes," Luke repeated. "That's why I'm here, to turn in my guns."

"There's a town—"

"A town ordinance," Luke cut him off. "Yes, I know."

The deputy scowled. Luke waited patiently. Finally, apparently not seeing a reason to refuse, the deputy stood up and led him to the back. He snatched a ring with five large keys hanging from it off a nail on the wall. The jail held three cells, each with a barred window, an army cot, and a bucket. Each of the cells held a sleeping occupant.

Across from the jail cells was a large oak standing dresser. A massive padlock like the kind stagecoaches used on payroll boxes secured the doors. The deputy undid the lock and opened the dresser. Inside, a multitude of rifles and pistols, each with an attached tag, were stored.

Luke stood there as the deputy laboriously filled out a receipt for both Remingtons and the Winchester. After the frustrating conversation at the start, the deputy did little talking. It was a state of affairs that Luke preferred, although the man kept a sullen look on his face that began to try his patience.

"There you go."

The deputy handed him a receipt and locked up the cabinet. At the front of the office, the door opened and Luke heard the jingle of spurs as someone walked in. He and the deputy emerged from the back and Luke saw the marshal. The man stopped walking and looked at Luke.

"You sign them guns in?"

Luke spread his arms as if to say, *What else?*

The marshal sat on the edge of the desk. Ignoring Luke, he began using the deputy's makings to roll a cigarette. Luke inspected the room and noticed something missing. There were no wanted posters tacked up. The deputy walked over quickly and struck a match as the marshal finished rolling his smoke.

The marshal ignored that, struck a wooden match, and lit the cigarette himself. The deputy glared at Luke as if the slight was his fault. The marshal inhaled and then released a cloud of smoke.

"You don't have any wanted posters up," Luke said.

The marshal looked at him. "Nope."

"Why not?"

"I don't want any idiots getting it into their heads that they should play at being a lawman. I got no use for bounty hunters."

"Interesting."

"What do you do for a living?"

"Hunt bounties."

The marshal remained silent, studying Luke. The cigarette dangled from his lip, strings of smoke trailing up the side of his face. Luke touched the brim of his hat.

"Be seeing you, Marshal."

The man said nothing, and Luke stepped into the street, closing the door behind him.

CHAPTER 19

Outside, he stopped to inhale deeply and looked around trying to find a hotel. Absentmindedly, he looked down and saw the mark he'd carved into Turner's boots. The print was plain in the dust of the street, there was no mistaking it.

Providence.

"Good to see you again," he said, even though Turner wasn't there to hear it.

He walked out into the street, casually following the steps through the dust. He didn't know why Turner would have come into Golgotha Rock. He assumed it was some sort of version of what he and Trask and Josh had been sent to Hatchet Creek to do, only on a more involved scale. Maybe the man he'd seen pretending to be a preacher was on the same errand. Luke hadn't recognized any of the other street preachers he'd seen as he rode in, but that was no guarantee they weren't members of Goldsmith's gang.

Luke moved along the boardwalk past a few doorways and then stopped. He studied what he'd found. A plain wooden cross had been nailed to the front door of a dark store.

The sounds from the street faded into the background as he tried the door, found it unlocked, and stepped inside the store. It was dark inside the mercantile, like the burrow of some animal. The air smelled stale, and something had died somewhere. The greasy stink of rotting flesh hung in the air, bonded to the dust motes floating like balloons through the single, bone white bar of moonlight shining inside the store.

Luke waited for his eyes to adjust, listening carefully. The dimness lessoned and he began making out shapes in the dark. Tables, barrels, support posts. He stepped forward and the floorboards creaked beneath his feet. Dust was thick on every surface. The piles of tools in barrels were rusty and splintered.

His foot struck a bulging bag of grain. The old fabric ripped and mold-infested wheat covered in squirming worms spilled out. The organic rotten smell of a swamp rose around him, and he jerked his head to the side in disgust.

From somewhere farther back in the building, a floorboard creaked. Luke froze, ears straining. Except for his knife, he was unarmed at the moment. He had a couple of spare pistols in his saddlebags that he hadn't mentioned to the marshal or the deputy. He'd planned to get one of them and tuck it behind his belt at the small of his back, where his shirt would conceal it, but he'd taken this ill-advised stroll first. He could only hope that anyone he faced wasn't packing iron, either.

He waited, patient as a hunter. His eyes grew more accustomed to the gloom every moment. Faint light filtered through the dirt and smeared grime of the storefront windows. He heard a rustling closer at hand and turned.

A fat rat perched on a gunny sack. Its beady eyes gleamed pink in the moonlight as the rodent watched him. It looked sleek, greasy, and well fed. Where there was one, there were others. It was always that way with rats.

A floorboard creaked again. The sound had come from a different part of the store. Luke turned smoothly in that direction. His breathing slowed and he waited. While searching the store interior with his eyes, his gaze fell on an empty wine bottle sitting on a rough table made from the slats of some old buckboard.

The cork was missing and only about a quarter inch of liquid remained. He recognized the bottle immediately. Vin Mariani, more commonly called Mariani wine. Some Italian chemist and patent medicine inventor had created the drink in 1863. Coca leaves were mixed with red wine. The alcohol mixed with and extracted cocaine from the leaves, making for one powerful kick.

Luke knew of cocaine. It was as legal as morphine or heroin and could be purchased over the counter at apothecaries. Saloons in Denver sold pinches of the drug to be snorted like snuff for the same price as a shot of decent whiskey.

He picked up the almost empty bottle and brought it to his nose. He sniffed delicately. There was no vinegar smell of wine gone bad. This had been opened and drank recently. Carefully, he returned the bottle to the table.

Another floorboard creaked behind him.

From the other direction, where he'd heard the first sounds, something wooden *thunked* onto the floor. Someone began walking slowly, dragging something heavy along with them. In a moment, a second thump sounded from toward the front of the store. This was followed by a third from behind him.

He was surrounded.

Turner's voice called out, mocking.

"Just tell me one thing," the man said. "Did you really ride with Red Legs, or is you a dirty rotten, yellow-bellied Johnny Reb scum?" The hate in the man's voice was sincere.

"Stars and Bars forever," Luke said. "I guess being a noble child of the Union didn't keep you from becoming a child burner."

"I told you," Turner shouted, "that was the colonel!"

"You ride with him."

Luke turned in a slow circle, trying to find the three men he knew were closing in on him. The sound of whatever they were dragging was as loud as nails on a chalkboard now. He reached for his knife, then saw something else leaning against a wall filled with old sledgehammers and hay rakes. He took up the pitchfork in both hands.

In a sudden rush, footsteps came thumping out of the dark from behind him. Luke spun, bringing up the pitchfork as he dropped to one knee. He saw a dark shape charging at him, an axe or pick handle held up to cave in his skull. He thrust.

The force of the pitchfork tines slamming into the attacker's body reverberated down through the haft. Momentum rocked Luke back even though he was braced for the impact. The man stood revealed in a bar of moonlight. An axe handle tumbled from his fingers and clattered to the floor.

The tines, wicked long and rusted, had penetrated the man high up on the abdomen and sank most of the way in. Luke watched the outlaw's mouth work. A bubble of bright blood, nearly pink in the moonlight, blew out of his mouth. It popped, and blood gushed out to stain his beard and shirt.

Someone shouted, an angry, inarticulate cry, and both remaining sets of feet thundered toward him. Luke jerked the pitchfork free and it came loose from the meat of the man's body with a *snik*. He spun toward the closest attacker. The man was only in silhouette, but he held his heavy pick handle like a Chicago White Stockings batter swinging for the fences.

Still on one knee, Luke caught the powerful swing crosswise on the haft of the pitchfork. The wood-on-wood contact made the handle hum like a tuning fork, stinging his grip. Driving his legs into the floor, Luke rose out of his crouch, pressing hard against the other man who was grunting with the effort.

A figure he assumed was Turner rushed toward him. Still pushing against the second attacker, Luke lashed out with his boot. His heel drove into the side of an old butcher table piled with canned goods and he kicked out hard.

The table slid across the floor, spilling cans, and slammed into the charging man's thighs. The figure squawked in pain and surprise and Luke recognized Turner's voice. The pressure against his pitchfork suddenly went away and he stumbled. He ran up hard into a counter and the man took another overhand swing.

He caught the blow again on the haft of his pitchfork. The wood handles clacked together. The man swung again as Luke's back bent painfully over the counter where he couldn't find any purchase. He caught the blow again. They struggled hard as the man leaned in. They were close enough for Luke to smell the wine on his breath.

Desperate, knowing Turner was coming to the other

man's aid, Luke lashed out. Rolling his weight back on where his shoulders were pinned to the filthy countertop, he lifted both feet, jackknifed his knees, and drove his boots into the man.

The man staggered back, grunting hard as the wind gushed out of him. Luke didn't hesitate. Twisting the pitchfork, he rammed the tines into the man's throat just under the jaw. The man stiffened and came up on his toes. He opened his mouth, but nothing came out other than a wet gurgle.

Turner ran at Luke.

The bounty hunter tried pulling the pitchfork clear, but the tines were stuck in the man's skull. Luke shoved the dead body from him, and the corpse fell heavily, taking the pitchfork with it.

Turner brought his axe handle down like a man driving a railroad spike. Luke rolled clear.

The axe handle smashed hard into the counter where Luke's body had been just a split-second earlier. Turner jerked the axe handle up and swung again. Luke stumbled back and just sidestepped the blow.

His right hand came down on a table and brushed an old lantern. Snatching it up, he flung it at Turner to create some distance. The lantern struck Turner in the head, shattering glass into his face. Turner yelled in pain. Luke flipped the table out of the way and dodged Turner's next two wild swings.

The man panted heavily. He couldn't be fully healed from the wounds he'd taken back at the trading post. He obviously thought that three on one would have evened his chances in a hand-to-hand melee. That hadn't worked out. Now he was fading fast.

Luke dodged around a shelf and scooped up several dented cans. Turner came around the other side, trying to push Luke back into the store. When he started down the aisle between the two shelves, he was silhouetted against the murky light bleeding in through the windows of the storefront.

Luke threw the cans. Both bounced off Turner's head with meaty *thunks*. The outlaw stumbled under the unexpected blows, crying out. Luke charged.

Putting his shoulder down, Luke drove into Turner. His momentum carried them like a freight train, and they slammed into the display window. The glass shattered and they plunged through. They landed hard on the boardwalk, and Turner shoved Luke clear. The axe handle was gone. The collision had knocked it out of Turner's hands.

Luke rolled and came to his feet. Turner was just as quick. In the better light of the street, Luke saw the glassy sheen to the man's hugely dilated pupils and remembered the Mariani wine. Cocaine was giving the outlaw fuel and strength he shouldn't possess with his still-healing injuries. Luke wondered how many more empty bottles were in the abandoned store.

Grinning a lunatic smile, Turner pulled a Green River skinning knife from a sheath on his belt. His scalp was wrapped in dirty, blood-stained bandages that obviously hadn't been changed recently.

"Going to cut you, Reb."

Luke drew the Bowie blade he'd taken from Daniel Yellow Dog. Green River knives were thick, sturdy butcher blades used by trappers and buffalo hunters. It kept a keen edge and had some weight behind it, but the Bowie was practically a Roman short sword in comparison.

"Nice haircut you've got there, Cleo," Luke replied. "The barber sends her regards."

Turner screamed a crazed, high-pitched wail that reminded Luke of a panther screech. It didn't seem like a sound that would come out of a human throat. It startled him as Turner lunged. He jumped back, but the man's jittery, intense speed was lethally quick. Like a striking snake, the Green River knife struck the arm that was already bruised by the axe handle.

The blade opened an ugly gash on Luke's forearm, and blood welled from the wound, soaking the sleeve of his shirt red. Luke retreated. He heard someone shout from down the street but didn't pay attention. His focus was entirely on that Green River knife.

He feinted with the Bowie, pushing Turner back. Turner laughed, a cackling, unhinged sound. More voices shouted, and people ran toward them. Turner ignored everything and lunged again. Inebriated, the outlaw overextended himself in a stabbing thrust as Luke sidestepped him. The strike looked like an exaggerated fencer's lunge.

Luke didn't hesitate. He struck three times. First slash to the inside of the elbow of the arm holding the Green River skinning knife. The second a backhand cut that opened up a wound on Turner's chest. Bringing the Bowie around again, he cut the back of the arm not holding the knife.

"Where's Goldsmith!" Luke demanded.

He hadn't left Turner alive after the trading post raid just to hack him to death in a mining town. He needed to locate Goldsmith, and he knew the crazed colonel was close.

Turner didn't give him the chance.

Despite the cut to the inside of his arm, the outlaw

hadn't dropped his knife. He sprang toward Luke, stabbing wildly. Luke reacted without conscious thought. Ramming his free hand into the man's injured elbow, he blocked the thrust as Turner rammed into him.

Luke's knife entered Turner's body just below the ribs, and hot blood gushed across his hand. Turner gasped and slapped at Luke's chest ineffectually. Luke pulled his knife free, and the body hit the ground. Panting, he turned.

A small crowd had gathered and stood silent for a moment. Turner scratched weakly at the boardwalk. Blood was a spreading black lake around his body. The outlaw shuddered.

"Make way, damn it!"

Luke turned to face the marshal. He wiped the blade of his knife on his leg and put it away. The lawman approached, pistol drawn. His face was expressionless, and Luke couldn't read his mood.

"I've got some bounties to turn in," Luke said.

The marshal stopped short. He didn't bother looking at the dead body until Turner's final death rattle pulled his attention away for a moment. He looked back at Luke.

The lawman slammed the barrel of his Peacemaker into Luke's temple and dropped him to the ground.

CHAPTER 20

Luke wasn't unconscious. He was awake but couldn't function, couldn't make his limbs do what he wanted them to do. He was in a twilight awareness where he couldn't understand words and the pain where the marshal had laid the heavy Peacemaker upside his head was everything. He would blink, and when he opened his eyes, it was as if he were waking from a sleep that had lasted hours.

The crowd was shouting but he didn't know about what. The marshal barked something but the words were a jumble in Luke's mind. Rough hands grabbed him under the arms and started dragging him. He heard someone moan in pain, the sound surprisingly close, then realized it was him.

His eyes felt heavy and he let them droop for just a moment. When he opened them again, he was being hauled through the marshal's office door. His feet dragged along the floor, scraping the boards. Someone said something. He didn't know what.

He blinked again and when he opened his eyes next, he bounced on one of the cots in the cells. Metal slammed on metal and he turned his head to look. A lightning strike of pain went off in his head. His face was covered with something hot and sticky.

Vision blurry, he tried making sense of what he was seeing. He heard a faint *click* and the sound centered his addled brain. The marshal stood about six feet away, on the other side of the jail-cell bars. He'd just shut the door and turned the key.

In his mind Luke said, "What the hell are you doing?"

What came out sounded like a man with a mouthful of marbles trying to read scripture. The marshal cocked his head to one side, a bemused look on his face. The deputy from earlier stood behind him next to a fat man also wearing a deputy marshal badge.

"What was that, bounty hunter?"

He chuckled and in response the two deputies brayed like donkeys with laughter.

"He sounds like he's got buffalo patties in his mouth!" the fat deputy guffawed. "Ain't that so, Marshal?"

"Shut up, Chubbs," the marshal said. Chubbs shut up. The marshal looked at Luke. "What was that?" he repeated. "I rang your bell pretty hard, I guess."

Luke didn't repeat himself. He didn't trust that he could speak yet. His mind was beginning to clear, but slowly. The more aware he grew, the more the pain intensified. He bit down hard and forced himself to sit up.

"You better sleep it off," the marshal advised. "The territorial judge will be here by the end of the week. He'll get you settled then."

"Those men are wanted," Luke got out. He more or less said it right. "They're part of the Goldsmith outfit. Wanted down Nebraska and Kansas way."

"I told you," the marshal said. "I don't like saddle tramps playing at being lawmen. Not in my town."

"That doesn't change the facts," Luke said. "Those men are wanted, and I had a legal right to pursue them."

The marshal smiled. It didn't reach his eyes.

"Then why are you in jail?"

"You got a circuit judge coming through, right? Isn't that what you just said?"

The marshal didn't answer.

"I'm not exactly a stranger to appearing in court. And for this territory, that court means Judge Charles Pierce."

The marshal was deathly still. He stared at Luke so intently his eyes glittered. Luke continued talking, voice even and unhurried.

"I know Pierce," he said. "I've been before him for trials with bounties I've brought in alive, and he's been part of the certification for paying out on my dead bounties. Hell, a couple of years ago, he and I shared a stage in the Dakota Territory. He isn't going to go along with you pistol-whipping me for bringing in a legitimate bounty."

The marshal walked away but then stopped by the door and spoke without turning around.

"We'll see how this plays out."

"Luke!"

Luke came out of his sleep. He felt groggy, and his head hurt immediately, but it wasn't the same as last night. Sunlight came in through the window. He sat up and winced at the pain in his head, but it was already less than it had been before. Blood had crusted on his face and he didn't have any water to rinse it off.

"Luke!" The voice was feminine.

Blinking he turned his head in the direction of the voice. He was confused. He didn't know anyone in Golgotha

Rock. Certainly not any women. A small figure stood on the other side of the bars. He squinted, bringing his eyes into focus.

"Katey?"

He knew he sounded baffled, maybe even a little stupid, but it felt like his brain was an ore-hauling locomotive trying to pull out of the station. It was inching along, but picking up steam. The figure on the other side of the bars was Katey, the young whore from Craig's Fork.

"Yes, it's me," she said. "Luke, you need to listen to what I'm saying!"

"What is it?"

From the front he heard a grunting, like the breathing of a man chopping wood. He looked at Katey.

"What are you doing here?"

"Me and Misty May left Craig's Fork. Buffalo Hump refused to leave, said the outlaws would come back once they didn't fear bounty hunters getting them no more. We weren't making no money. You scared off all the potential clients."

Luke tried to smile. "You didn't belong in Craig's Fork," he said. He gestured vaguely. "I don't think you belong here, either. I wish you'd try Denver."

She smiled. "We'll see. These old miners are doing pretty well for themselves right now. Which means we're doing pretty well for ourselves."

Luke nodded. "Just came to say hello, then?"

Katey leaned in. "Luke, they mean to lynch you."

Luke absorbed the news in silence. "The preacher?" he asked after a moment.

She nodded. "Preacher Brown. All the street-corner Bible thumpers are shouting out about you, but he's the one who gets the townsfolk riled up enough to stretch someone's neck."

Outside in the office the deputy was making stuttering, dog-like howls. They didn't have much time.

"I take it the marshal isn't big on standing him down?"

"Never does. I volunteered to bring you food from the diner next door. I put a skeleton key in there. Misty May volunteered to distract the deputies so we could talk."

"Whooo doggie!" the deputy shouted. The situation in the front office had reached a conclusion.

"When will they come?" Luke asked. "Tonight?"

"Yes."

"Then I'll make it work. Thank you, Katey."

"Yellow Dog told me he was going to cut my face like the Cheyenne do to their women when they're unfaithful." She drew a line across her nose indicating the path of the knife. "If you hadn't come along when you did, I would have been ruined. You saved all three of us girls that day." She touched his arm through the bars. "Now hide this under your pillow."

She produced a Colt Navy .36 from the folds of her dress and slid it through the bars of the cell door. Luke quickly hid it under his pillow.

"Thank you," he said.

She rose, leaving the small pail with the cloth over it behind.

"I'll be back for dinner," she promised.

About an hour later, Deputy Chubbs left the office, leaving Luke alone in his cell. Immediately, Luke rose and went to the cell door to try the skeleton key Katey had brought him. Before he could do that, the front door opened again.

Cursing silently, he stuck the key in his back pocket and wandered casually over to the cell window to look out through the bars. Boot heels clicked on the floorboards behind him. He didn't turn around. The cell window looked out on the edge of town. Beyond a green meadow with a snowmelt creek running through it stood a cluster of pine trees. Beyond them, the walls of the shallow canyon sloped gently upward toward the foothills of the Oxbow Mountains.

"Take a good long look," the preacher said. "That's your last sight until I stretch your neck tonight."

Luke turned. The man he'd recognized as being a member of Goldsmith's gang stood before him, smirk firmly in place.

"Brown," Luke acknowledged. "You traded being an owlhoot for being a preacher man. Interesting choice."

"Who says you can't be both," Brown snickered. "The only thing I'm sorry about is that the colonel won't be here to see you die."

"You should invite him, if he's so close by."

Brown gestured toward the side of his face where Goldsmith's scars were. "The colonel is a hard man to forget," he explained. "Those wanted posters you got out for the rest of us weren't so bad but," he shrugged, "a man shaves, or gets a haircut, or lets his hair grow out and his beard get long. Wanted posters ain't always so helpful."

"I know what you look like."

"But you're going to be dead."

"How the hell did you get people to follow you?"

"Wasn't hard. Hell, before the war I *was* a pastor. I went to seminary and everything. I'm afraid I may have strayed from the righteous path since we looted and burned Georgia."

"Yeah," Luke said. "I'm sure you miss that life real bad. That doesn't explain how you buffaloed the marshal, though."

Brown's face was so gaunt that it looked like a skull when he grinned, the flesh pulled tight and thin over jutting bones. "No buffaloing needed. The marshal rode with the colonel and Sergeant Major Trask in the war, too."

"How's Trask doing? Oh, wait . . ."

That knocked the grin off Brown's face. He pointed a long, trembling finger at Luke. His voice was tight with rage as he spoke. "Tonight you die, bounty hunter, so best make your peace."

"I'm not so good at making peace," Luke told him. "I'm a lot better at making war."

"We'll see!" Brown snarled.

Luke casually turned his back on the man, dismissing him like a king with a peasant. Brown swore, then turned and stomped off. As the office door banged shut, Luke continued staring out at the trees.

CHAPTER 21

The skeleton key didn't work. Luke spent ten minutes repeatedly trying before giving up in frustration. Katey brought him dinner, and this time the deputy called Chubbs sauntered into the cell block after her. He leaned against the locker holding the confiscated weapons and sneered at Luke.

"Gonna hang you," he said. He said it like he thought it was the punchline to a joke.

"For what?" Luke asked mildly. "Doing your job?"

Chubbs straightened from his casual pose, his body going rigid with anger. "Them was the wrong boys to be killing. They was good upstanding citizens! Folks in these parts don't tolerate the killing of good, upstanding citizens."

"So you mean everything would have been just fine if I'd shot you?"

However Chubbs had expected the conversation to go, it wasn't. His face was red with fury. He tried speaking but choked on the words. Luke was somewhat amused at how easy it had been to rattle the deputy. Chubbs stalked out, leaving Katey there with the dinner pail.

She hesitated and didn't approach the cell until they

heard Chubbs guffawing in the front office, as well as Misty May's high-pitched fake giggles. Katey looked back over her shoulder and then pressed close to the bars.

"We have to hurry," she said. "Chubbs ain't one to last any longer than it takes him to eat a piece of pie. Meaning . . . fast."

"I got that," Luke nodded. "The skeleton key didn't work."

"Damn it!"

"You tried," Luke said. "That means something."

"I ain't done yet."

She cocked her head to the side, pondering the problem. Behind her, Misty May's voice was clearly audible.

"Well, then, lock that door, Chubbs," the prostitute said. "I ain't going to handle this myself, though I guess I could if I had to."

Katey looked at him, eyes searching. "If I could wave a magic wand, what would your escape look like?"

"I don't care how I get out," Luke said. "But I hate the idea of leaving my Remingtons."

Katey smiled. "Now *that* I think I can help with."

"That's it, big hoss," Misty May urged Chubbs. "Now you're getting the idea!"

"Wait here," Katey whispered through the bars to Luke.

"Katey, wait—"

She waved an impatient hand at him, and Luke fell silent. He crowded the front corner of his cell and pressed his face into the iron bars. From this position he could just see into the front of the marshal's office. Chubbs and Misty May weren't visible, but he could still see Katey.

She had pressed herself up against the wall. She was clearly visible if Chubbs turned his head, but she moved too slow to make any motion that might register in his peripheral vision. The key to the weapons locker hung from the peg of a coat rack. Carefully, Katey stretched out and reached for the key.

Misty May must have seen what Katey was trying to do. "Easy, big hoss," she warned in her raspy voice. "I don't get to enjoy it so much, not many men are like you."

"That's right," Chubbs gasped. "I'm special."

Katey took the key from the hook.

"You're special!" Misty May shouted back, covering up any sound the key might have made as it came off the hook.

Katey began slowly stepping back toward Luke.

Chubbs didn't seem to comprehend the idea of slowing down. Suddenly, Luke heard dull, meaty thuds and knew the deputy must be punching Misty May in the back of the head. The prostitute gasped.

Katey made it around the corner as Chubbs snarled at Misty May. The prostitute let out small cries of pain. Katey leaped forward and shoved her hand between the bars, catching hold of Luke's arm as he started to draw the Colt Navy from behind his back.

No! she mouthed silently, urgently.

Though it twisted his guts, he stopped. He nodded once and she turned and unlocked the cabinet. She knew his guns by sight and gave him the Remingtons. He stuffed them behind his belt next to the Navy Colt as she locked the cabinet.

"Whoooeee!" Chubbs yelled, voice cracking.

Katey went around the corner and replaced the keys on the peg without missing a step, and Luke released a pent-up breath.

"If that's the way you act when somebody offers you a freebie," Katey said, "then maybe you shouldn't get any more freebies." Her voice was cold with suppressed anger.

Deputy Chubbs chuckled. "Guess your kind can do as they're told or end up on the wrong side of Pastor Brown's vigilance committee."

Katey helped Misty May stand. Luke could see them now. Misty May's usual spitfire demeanor was gone. Once her clothes were straightened up, Katey walked her to the door. Chubbs was still chuckling as she stopped. Without turning around, she spoke.

"You know who the marshal's favorite is right now, don't you, *Deputy* Chubbs?"

The deputy stopped laughing.

"I guess if I were to get real sad and not be in a sporting mood anymore," Katey continued, "then I guess he'd likely not be too happy with whoever put me in such a dour mood."

Luke smiled as he could all but see Chubbs's jaw dropping open. Taking Misty May with her, Katey left the office before he could reply.

"I ain't scared of you!" Chubbs shouted at the closed door. He sounded like he was trying to convince himself of that as much as her. "Whore!"

Luke sat down and began eating his dinner. Depending on how this evening turned out, it could very well be his last meal.

Katey didn't show at suppertime. Deputy Chubbs, grumbling, would have to get his own supper.

"I doubt you'll need much food in a couple of hours," he sneered at Luke.

Luke ignored him and the deputy left. Imagining the lynch mob stringing up the prisoner seemed to restore the deputy's good mood after his encounter with Katey. Luke wondered how he was going to parlay his guns into an open jail cell. It wasn't going to be easy to get enough of a drop on the lawmen to get the keys.

If he couldn't get the keys before the mob came, he'd open fire and force them to shoot him. It was a better death than getting his neck stretched while people cheered.

"Hey, Luke," Katey whispered.

Surprised, Luke turned and found the young woman standing at the window to his cell and grasping the iron bars.

"Hurry!"

Luke stepped over to the window, and she began shoving a rope through the opening to him.

"Tie it around the bars," Katey urged him. "We need to get you out of here, fast!"

Luke looked past her, and in the fading light he saw a wagon with a team of mules hitched to it. Misty May sat on the seat, looking back over her shoulder at the jail.

"Where'd you get the wagon?" Luke asked Katey as he looped the rope around the bars and began knotting it securely.

"Stole it, of course," the young prostitute replied. "It was Misty May's idea."

Luke grunted as he finished tightening the knot. "And a good one. Go!"

Katey stepped back from the window and nodded to Misty May, who slapped the reins against the backs of the mule team and called out softly to the animals.

Inside the cell, Luke hoped fervently that the mules wouldn't balk and refuse to move—as mules were often known to do.

These brutes must have been well-trained. They leaned forward into their harness almost instantly. The rope, which was tied to the wagon's framework behind the seat at its other end, sprang taut. Inside the cell, Luke braced his feet, gripped the bars, and leaned hard against them, adding his weight to the force trying to pull them loose.

With a gritty grinding of masonry, the bars began to shift in their moorings.

Luke let go and stepped back. Misty May called to the mules again. After a moment that seemed longer than it really was, the bars suddenly broke loose and flew outward, taking chunks of the surrounding wall with them. Dust flew, making Luke cough a little as he waved it away from his face.

Where the window had been was now a ragged opening, large enough for him to wriggle through it.

He still wore his empty gunbelt. He pulled the Remingtons from behind his belt at the small of his back and pouched the irons in their accustomed holsters. No need to keep them concealed now. The crash of the window breaking out was going to draw some attention, so he had to hurry.

He caught hold of the edges of the opening, pulled himself up and through, and dropped head-first to the ground outside the jail.

Grunting at the impact as he landed, he rolled over and came to his feet, guns seeming to spring into his hands as if by magic. Misty May had stopped the wagon, and Katey stood by anxiously.

"You're all right?" she asked.

"Yeah," Luke told her, "and you two need to get out of here, now!"

He had heard startled shouts from the street in front

of the marshal's office. From the sound of it, the members of the lynch mob had showed up and were starting to realize that they might lose their intended victim.

Katey jumped in the back of the wagon, and Misty May whipped up the team again. The mules took off and the wagon rolled off into the dusk, the rope with the attached bars and pieces of wall bouncing along behind it.

Hearing rapid footsteps, Luke swung the other way, toward the alley next to the building.

Two townsmen in flour-sack hoods charged down the passage. One held a double-barreled 12-gauge shotgun while the other wielded an old Army Colt. One was tall and built like a lumberjack, the other shorter and rounder. They yelled curses when they spotted Luke and aimed their weapons at him.

The Remingtons boomed in his hands.

The attackers stopped like they had run into a wall. Twin red blossoms burst from the flannel shirts above their hearts. They folded up, dropping their guns as they did so.

Luke pouched the Remingtons and scooped up the fallen shotgun. After a moment's consideration, he also took the Army Colt. He might not have a lot of time to reload.

People were shouting all over town now, angry, confused sounds that came from everywhere at once. The lynch mob was in full swing. The town was laid out in a series of H-shaped streets so that it spread from one side of the narrow valley to the other. He could easily find himself surrounded. He had to keep moving.

He ran down the back of the buildings, shotgun ready. A man in a grungy peacoat and a hood over his head stepped out the back door of a boarding house and fired

at him. The bullet struck the side of a building next to
Luke, and he fired a barrel of the shotgun on the run.

The buckshot took the shooter in the chest, leaving
bloody, mangled flesh. The man fell backward and died,
heels drumming the earth. Men shouted from behind Luke.

Reaching the two-story boarding house, he leaped over
the dead body and ducked inside. He was at the rear stairs
and he went up without hesitation. The stairs turned back
on themselves halfway up, and as he turned the corner a
man appeared above him.

Luke almost triggered the 12-gauge but saw that the
man was unarmed just in time. He wasn't going to kill anybody who wasn't trying to kill him. The man blanched and
stumbled backward in protest, holding empty hands up de-
fensively as Luke pushed past him. Choosing the door to
a room facing back toward the marshal's office, he kicked
it open and went inside.

The room was narrow with only a bed, dresser, and
chair. Luckily, it was empty. The fella who lived here probably was out looking to kill Luke right now.

Luke hurried to the window and threw it open, seeing
that the roof of the adjoining building was only a few feet
below him. A shot came from the door behind him and
chewed splinters from the window frame next to his face.

Luke turned and triggered the shotgun's second barrel.
The man who'd fired the shot ducked back in time, and
most of the blast peppered the wall. Throwing the empty
12-gauge away, Luke slid through the window.

He half jumped, half fell, plunging downward and landing on hands and knees on the adjoining building's roof.
He scrambled to his feet and yanked the Army Colt from
his waistband where he had stuffed it.

The man who'd taken the shot at him a moment earlier

appeared in the boarding house window and fired quickly, but the shot was rushed and flew wide. Luke put a round into the wall just below the window and drove the man back behind cover.

He'd kill the corrupt marshal and deputies. He'd kill every man wearing a lynch mob hood, but he wouldn't kill any of the regular townsfolk unless they backed him into a corner and seemed intent on killing him.

"He's on the roof!" the boarding-house tenant shouted.

"I should have shot you," Luke panted as he raced.

He ran fast, boots clunking on the rooftops. He cleared the diner and landed on the marshal's office. A shot winged past him. Turning, he fired back at the man in the boarding house, pulling the round wide and driving him into retreat.

Someone shouted from across the street, and he turned to see the second story balcony of a bordello. On the balcony, a lynch party member in a flour-sack hood fired at him with a Henry .44 lever action. Luke stopped, carefully aimed, and killed him with a single shot. The man flipped over the railing and dropped to the ground.

Luke ran hard to give him some momentum and leaped from the edge of the marshal office's roof to the next building. More people were shouting in the street, and he heard increasing cries of "He's on the roof." His heart pounded in his chest and his breathing grew ragged as sweat soaked his shirt.

Down the line of roofs in front of him, two men in white flour-sack hoods, armed with pistols, appeared from somewhere. Shouting, they opened fire on Luke. He took a knee beside a parapet façade and snapped off two quick rounds. The men separated, diving in different directions.

One popped up, and Luke shot him in the head at thirty yards. The hood hiding the man's face jerked oddly to the side and then blood soaked the material as he slumped dead. The other man fired several times. The hard, flat *bangs* rolled across the roofs and lead hornets buzzed through the air to either side of Luke. The man was jerking his shots.

Luke lined him up, thumbing back the hammer on the Army Colt.

The man snapped off two more poor shots, screaming "He's here! He's here!" as he did so. Luke ignored them and squeezed his trigger. He fired twice, putting both rounds into the man's chest. The hooded man flopped to the roof and lay unmoving.

Luke was up and running. He sprinted across the distance and hurled himself onto the roof of the last building. Throwing aside his stolen Army Colt, he took each of the dead men's pistols in either hand. Running to the edge, he looked down and saw a narrow flight of stairs leading up to a second-floor door. He dropped onto the small wooden platform in front of the door.

Just then, a hooded lyncher came out of the door in a bull rush. The door slammed into Luke and drove him up against the railing, causing him to lose his grip on the pistol in his left hand. He grunted under the impact and staggered, off balance. The man tried driving the muzzle of his pistol into Luke.

Luke twisted to the side and snatched the man by his shirt sleeve, keeping the barrel wide of his body. They struggled for a moment, straining sinew against sinew and then Luke twisted sharply and brought his stolen .45 up. Jamming it under the man's chin, he pulled the trigger and blew the top of the man's head off.

Luke let the man crumble and turned to thunder down the stairs. Like a howling wind, Luke suddenly heard the preacher's voice shouting, ranting, urging the crowd to kill him. A handful of the lynch mob came around the corner of the building off the main street and headed toward him. They raised their weapons in unison as he ducked behind the back edge of the building.

A wall of lead flew past him in a swarm of lead hornets that made the all-too-distinctive *hiss-spat* of rounds flying too close. Dropping to a knee, he stuck the stolen pistol blindly around the corner and fired all the rounds left in a hail of cover fire.

Throwing the empty gun to the ground, he made for the back door of the building next to him. He took out a Remington as he kicked the door in and then slammed it shut behind him. He was in a short hallway that led into one of the mercantiles. Ahead of him, tables and shelves filled with dry goods made a maze. It reminded him too much of the closed-down store he'd found himself in last night. He was being driven like a fox before hounds.

Through the plate glass windows of the storefront, he saw twenty armed men in flour-sack hoods milling back and forth. He thought that brought the lynch mob to something like thirty men. He didn't see any regular townsfolk. They seemed to have gone to ground, leaving the hooded killers to their hunt. Then the crowd parted and he saw the marshal and both deputies.

He darted left as he came out of the short hall and into the store's main room. Suddenly, bullets hammered through the back door, traveled the length of the store, shattered the plate glass window, and dropped two of the lynch mob outside.

As the back door flew open and some of the hooded men charged in that way, the lynchers out front turned their guns on the store and began firing. Luke threw himself down behind the counter and kept low. A hail of bullets ripped both directions through the store for a furious handful of seconds as the two groups unwittingly fired at each other, not realizing that they were gunning down their own allies. Men screamed as bullets struck flesh.

Bodies fell in front of where Luke hugged the floor. Outside, the marshal's voice boomed out commands.

"Cease fire! Cease fire! Stop shooting, you damned fools!"

The gunshots tapered off and no more bodies rushed from the back hall. Luke came up in a crouch, gun in each hand. As the firing stopped, he stepped from behind the counter. Bodies lay on the floor in growing pools of red. In the rear hallway, the last of the vigilantes stood staring at his dead friends. When he spotted Luke, he stiffened and jerked his gun up.

Luke killed the man with his right-hand gun.

With his left, he began firing on the confused crowd that had just been told to stand down. He dropped three men in half as many seconds.

"It's him!" someone shouted. "He's still alive!"

Chubbs the deputy appeared in the swirling mass of masked vigilantes. Remembering the man's brutal assault on Misty May, Luke fired his Remington. The slug opened an untidy third eye in the deputy's forehead and he went down in the street like a puppet with its strings cut.

Luke spun and threw himself down, diving forward as more bullets poured into the store from the street. He snatched a Winchester off the floor that one of the dead lynchers had dropped. Bullets cut through the air above him.

He crawled outside and worked the lever on the rifle as he came to his feet. He saw the line of ponderosa pine he had studied from inside his jail cell but decided he'd never cross the open meadow before more vigilantes came. He'd be an easy target running in the open.

To survive, he was going to have to hurt the lynchers bad enough that fear of him was stronger than their bloodlust.

That meant killing more of them.

CHAPTER 22

Standing, he brought the rifle to his shoulder and shot the first man coming around the corner of the building. He worked the lever, fired again, then sprinted down the alley toward the staircase he'd used while coming off the roof.

He saw men scurrying for cover. One took a position behind a horse trough and fired a large cap and ball pistol at him. Luke returned fire and the man went facedown into the dirty water.

Bullets whizzed past him. In Luke's experience, few men were good shots under pressure. The reason some men rose to prominence as gunhawks was not because they were all that much faster or more accurate. They survived to let their legend grow because they were the calmest. It wasn't the shakes that ended a gunfighter's run, it was a loss of nerve.

Luke bounded up the steps to the outside landing, taking them two at a time. He knew that if he ever stopped for very long, he would realize how exhausted he was. But as long as he kept moving, that urgency would fuel him. Tossing the Winchester up onto the roof, Luke leaped, caught hold of the roof's edge, and pulled himself up and over.

Two rounds punched into the wood where his legs had been a second earlier. Rolling, he came up with the rifle.

He realized something as he'd taken his peek at the street. Not counting the marshal and his deputy, there were only a handful of men left from the mob and the general citizenry of the town had not rallied behind the lynchers.

For the first time since escaping from the jail, Luke began thinking he could pull this off. He fought to bring his breathing under control. He had to get the marshal. With him gone, the rest would scatter.

He came up in a crouch and began running back the way he'd come across the roofs. Beyond the boarding house was the stable where he'd put his horse. He risked a quick look over the edge and saw the marshal dart down the alley behind him. If they fanned out and got superior vantage points, what was left of the lynch mob could make life very hard for him.

Bullets struck the building like hail. The rounds slapped into the wood, spraying splinters and whizzing by his face. Changing directions, Luke raced for the back of the building. With the Winchester ready, he rolled over the side, hung from his free hand for a moment then dropped to the ground and landed in a crouch. As he popped upright, he worked the lever on the Winchester.

From the right, a member of the lynch mob came around the corner of the building, a Walker Colt in his hands. He fired hastily as Luke dropped to one knee and brought the Winchester to his shoulder. The rifle cracked as the vigilante's bullet whipped over Luke's head.

The Winchester slug drove into the man's chest. He crumpled to the ground as blood poured from his body to stain the ground. Working the lever, Luke spun back to his left.

The marshal came around the corner, hands filled with his guns. Obviously expecting Luke to still be on the roof, his eyes grew comically large in surprise. Luke felt a grim, hard smile tug at his lips as he fired.

The round struck the marshal low in the stomach, doubling him over. He fired his pistol into the ground. The rhythmic, metallic clack of the lever action working was music in Luke's ears. The marshal stumbled back, hand going to the wound in his stomach. He looked up, hate bright in his eyes, and tried aiming his pistol.

Luke fired again.

A neat hole the size of a coin appeared in the corrupt lawman's Adam's apple and blood sprayed out the back of his neck in a fine mist. Crimson bubbled up and rushed out of the marshal's mouth as he fell back. He hit the ground hard and lay still. Gunsmoke hung between the men.

Luke worked his Winchester, seating another round. He was ready to keep fighting as silence settled over the town. No one else was brave enough to try to assault his position, he realized. The diehards and drunks had been killed. Those left were taking up defensive positions and seemed willing to wait it out.

Entering the back door of the general store, he cautiously made his way forward. There were bodies piled in the back hallway, bodies littered on the street beyond the shot-out windows. The dead and wounded were strewn like playing cards and everywhere reeked of gunsmoke. Inside the building it stunk like a slaughterhouse. It reminded him of the war.

Keeping back from silhouetting himself, Luke looked

outside, taking quick peeks without exposing himself too much. He saw a few armed men hiding behind wagons, store windows, and horse troughs. Most had taken off their flour-sack hoods. He didn't see more than five. One of them was the remaining deputy.

He was crouched behind a large wooden barrel filled with ten-penny nails, according to the sign tacked on it. He took a quick peek every few moments and then ducked back.

Luke doubted the Winchester would penetrate the barrel of nails well enough to let him make the shot. Easing into a kneeling position, he lined up his sights. He rested his finger on the trigger and moved the blade of the front site just to the left of the barrel. He could just make out the deputy's knee.

"I'm not dead yet, deputy," Luke shouted.

"You're sure enough going to swing for this, Jensen!" the man replied. "You're going to hang for killing the marshal!"

"That marshal was corrupt, working with a lynch mob in extrajudicial execution."

"Extra jew . . . what?"

"I have a legal right to defend myself against unlawful actions. The territorial judge will clear me. I know the man. I was arrested for serving a legal bounty. You had no call to throw me in jail in the first place."

The deputy laughed. "You ain't gonna be seeing no judge—"

Filled with false bravado, the deputy risked taking a look around the edge of the barrel. Luke squeezed the trigger. The deputy's head jerked like a boxer taking an uppercut and a gaping cavity of a wound appeared where his right eye had been just a split-second before. The back of the man's head exploded outward and brains splattered on the unfinished lumber of the hardware store behind him.

"He's killed the deputy!" someone shouted.

Immediately a fresh hailstorm of bullets raged. Rounds came in from several directions at once. Tins and jars and boxes of dry goods exploded as Luke dropped to the floor. He hugged the ground waiting for his chance.

"Hold your fire!" a rough baritone yelled. "Hold your damn fire!"

Luke worked the lever on the Winchester and realized it was out of bullets. He tossed it aside and drew one of his Remingtons. Everything had grown quiet outside.

"Jensen!" the baritone called. "You in there?"

"I am until I decide to leave," Luke shouted back.

"This is Bob Jenkins, the mayor!"

"Nice to meet you. It seems the town council is going to have to appoint some new lawmen."

"That fact has not escaped my attention, I assure you."

"What do you want?"

"I want the killing to stop. There's been enough death already. There doesn't have to be any more."

"Bob, I'm not turning myself in to you. You want me, you best come in here and get me. I wasn't joking about holding out until the judge gets here." That was a bluff. He figured they didn't need to know that.

"The marshal's dead. You just killed the last deputy. The town's all shot up, and there's something like twenty men dead in the damn street!"

"What do you suggest, Bob?"

"Suggest?" The mayor laughed, but the sound was so

bitter it came out in a choking hack. "I *suggest* you get on your horse and ride the hell out of here."

"I have a few words for Pastor Brown. He's a wanted man."

"And *he* took off as soon as you killed the marshal. You want him? Hell, go get him!"

"I see anyone, I'm going to assume they're part of the lynch mob."

"Ain't nobody going to mess with you, Jensen. Just go."

"Where would Brown be?"

"He rode north, that's all I know."

Luke frowned. It would have to do. "All right!" he shouted. "Everyone stay back. I see a face, I'm blowing it off. No second chances."

"You have my word!"

Yeah, that's worth a whole lot, Luke thought.

Still, he had an opportunity here. He might as well play it out.

Luke left the store through the rear door and walked down the back of the buildings toward the stable. Curtains dropped over windows as he moved. No one wanted to risk drawing his ire. Looking along an alley, he checked the street. No one moved. The bodies still lay where they'd fallen. People were staying indoors.

It was a risk, but he couldn't stay out of sight forever. Sooner or later, he was going to have to test the supposed truce. He stepped out and walked across the street toward the bordello where Misty May and Katey worked.

He came in the door and saw a cadaverous man in a bowler hat and banker's shirt sitting by himself at a small bar. He was deathly thin, skin yellowed by what Luke guessed was consumption. He coughed into a red handkerchief and looked at Luke without fear.

"The grim reaper arrives on my door," he said. His voice was soggy gravel. He coughed into the cloth.

"Katey, Misty May?"

"You looking to blow off a little steam after you gun down an entire town?" The man chuckled. His eyes were fever bright.

"I have to ask twice?"

"You want Misty May, look behind the bar," the pimp shrugged. "Whores lead short, hard, and very sad lives."

Luke's stomach tightened. He stepped around the end of the bar. Misty May lay face up, buck teeth protruding. She'd been shot in the chest by what he thought was a .44.

"She caught a stray round?"

The pimp just looked at him. "Short. Hard. And very sad."

"Brown," Luke said. It wasn't a question.

"He came in ranting about you killing the marshal. He wanted Katey. Misty May stood up to him."

"But not you?"

He shrugged. "I'm unarmed."

"He took Katey?"

"And left."

"You still didn't try and stop him."

"I'm going to die very soon, bounty hunter. Soon enough."

"He say where he was taking her?"

"He did not."

Luke turned and headed for the door. Brown had ridden north, the mayor had said. The man hadn't mentioned that Katey was with him.

Most likely, Brown was heading to wherever Goldsmith was. Luke was willing to bet that under those hoods, some of the lynchers had also been former members of Gold-smith's prairie fire gang. By now, the colonel wouldn't have such a formidable army at his command. Luke had whittled down the odds considerably.

He helped himself to ammunition from the dead men. He took a canteen off the wall in the deserted stable, filled it at the pump, and saddled his horse. He slung the heavy sack he had filled with extra cartridges, from the saddle horn, then led the mount from the stable to one of the general stores. When he came back out, he had enough supplies to last for a week or more.

Luke Jensen left Golgotha Rock, Wyoming, and did not look back.

CHAPTER 23

There was enough moonlight for Luke to be able to cut Brown's trail north of town. It was easy to tell when one horse was being led by the reins by a rider on a different mount. Katey was on that second horse. Luke felt certain of that.

As he followed the outlaw into the lower Medicine Bow Mountains, he knew Brown might be leading him into a trap. The crazed preacher had taken Katey to ensure that Luke followed as quickly as possible, and he was running straight toward what the bounty hunter could only assume was Goldsmith and the rest of the gang. This forced Luke to ride slower. He had to read and anticipate the land, look for the places where Goldsmith could set up an ambush.

Overhead that harvest moon hung, fat and low and bathing the mountains in dull, red-orange light. It cast a stark, almost surrealistic illumination as he rode. The foothills grew thick with hawthorn and pine, twisting oak, and ancient alder. Night birds called from far back among the gnarled, twisting trunks. Shadows hung like black curtains, split at odd intervals by bars of hard moonlight swirling with dust motes. Small animals scurried through the tangled brush. Silence bled through like a stain as Luke made his way.

The tracks began following a road, an ancient path marked by deep ruts driven into mud by heavy cart wheels, flattened in the middle by the steps of men, horses, oxen. Luke knew there were numerous mines up here in the mountains above Golgotha Rock. It was common for bandits to haunt the roads and trails between isolated mining claims and the towns that serviced the miners.

A branch snapped in the woods.

Luke stopped his horse and peered into the trees, trying to get an idea of what was out there. After a moment, he urged his horse forward and soon came to a fork. One branch led west, the other north, farther into the mountains. He wished he'd had an opportunity to mark Brown's horseshoes the way he had Turner's. There was nothing he could do about it now, however. Dismounting, he knelt and studied the sign in the orange-tinted light of the moon. He walked back and forth a few paces, eyeing the strides of the horses.

North.

One horse with a heavy rider leading a second mount with a lighter load. No doubt. Brown was taking Katey north. Luke swung back into his saddle and rode on.

Luke drew up short.

The fetish hung from a rawhide thong looped around a low-hanging branch. A bundle of sticks and what he thought were bird bones. He wasn't enough of an expert to identify the tribe, but he knew a shaman's talisman when he saw one. Goldsmith must have led his men into an area held to be big medicine by whatever native tribes remained in these parts.

Normally, seeing something like that, Luke would have given the area a wide berth in order to avoid offending the Indians. He considered himself a Christian, even if a bit in need of redemption, but he still didn't see the point in disrespecting the religion of others when it could be helped.

This time, it couldn't be helped.

"Come on," he said to the horse, and heeled him forward.

He rode at a walk, Winchester out and across his saddle. The trail led between two low, rocky outcroppings and entered a valley. He heard a stream running a short distance ahead. The trees began crowding in on the path now. The tang of pine needles hung in the air like perfume.

The path grew narrower and rockier, more of a game trail than a road. He began seeing more of the dangling fetishes. They were hanging every few yards now. The bird bones had been replaced by those of small animals and the sticks with beaded strings and bits of mirror and metal. Soft chimes tinkled in the slight breeze. In the moon-shot darkness, a sense of eeriness grew stronger and stronger.

Luke reined in his horse and dismounted to take a better look around. The twisting trail cut through a heavy thicket like the path through a labyrinth. He could see no more than a few yards ahead because the trail turned on itself.

Deeper in the thicket, something rustled through the undergrowth. Luke paused, trying to track it. A twig snapped. The wind rustled through the branches and gently shook the dangling talismans. Chimes rang softly. To the other side of him, leaves suddenly rustled.

Rapid footsteps thudded dully behind him. Luke turned,

taking a knee and bringing his rifle to his shoulder. The horse blocked his view back up the trail and there was no space to turn him or pull him to one side. Frustrated, Luke flopped onto his stomach to try to spot his enemies through the horse's legs.

He caught a flash of fleeting shadow, followed by the rattling of sticks on bone as one of the fetishes was bumped, then silence. He cursed under his breath. In his worry over Katey, he'd pushed pursuit too hard and ended up caught in a deadly ambush spot.

Then, from farther up the trail, Katey screamed.

Riding or leading the horse wasn't an option without exposing himself to bushwhackers' lead. Katey didn't scream again, but once had been enough. He felt almost frantic to get to her and keep her safe. He couldn't give in to that urge, though. That would only get him killed.

Out of time, he made his best worst choice and led the horse into the trees then draped the reins over a tree branch. The breeze that had been blowing from his right as he made his way into the valley suddenly shifted. It blew directly into his face.

Instantly he smelled the faint but undeniably distinct odor of old death. His horse whined and shifted nervously. He didn't have time to calm the animal. Across the trail from him, deep in the brush, he heard more rustling.

Crouched, he slowly began backing out from the little thicket. He turned and froze mid-step. Directly in front of his face hung one of the stick-and-bone fetishes. Blundering through that would have been like setting off a foghorn.

He stepped carefully around the talisman, ears straining. Some distance away he heard a branch snap. He was sure he wasn't facing Indians. The men hunting him were too loud, too clumsy. This hollow might have been medicine ground for the Cheyenne or Blackfoot, but they weren't the ones closing in.

He moved quietly, paralleling the trail. He placed his feet down toe first so his boot would slide underneath the foliage and detritus of a forest floor. Once he was sure he wouldn't make any noise, he carefully lowered his heel. It was painfully slow going.

Just ahead of him the orange light of the harvest moon shone down in hard, bloody tinged shafts of illumination. The trees, lodgepole pine, grew more scattered. In the light of the moon, Luke saw the first scaffolding. Five feet off the ground on a pole framework, a rectangle of deer hide formed the platform on which a body rested.

The wind had worked the burial robe loose, and a boy's skull gleamed dully in the moonlight. Wispy strands of long black hair were lifted gently by the breeze. Luke edged forward. A shadow darted through the trees beyond the burial scaffolding.

The mounting tension pulled at Luke's nerves. It reminded him of the war. The waiting before the battle, the building anxiety until the strain grew so intense he wanted to scream. It haunted him.

Slowly, he eased his breath out through his nostrils. The sound of the stream was closer now. If he could make it that far, the bubbling music of the running water would mask his steps, allowing him to get closer in to where Katey was held. If she was still alive.

Easing forward, he saw more scaffolding placed among the trees. A few hardwoods had been utilized as burial trees. Bodies wrapped in buffalo robes were placed at varying heights in the branches, and the trunks were decorated with red and black stripes.

Something rustled to his right and he froze.

Silence.

He studied the next burial scaffold. The person resting there had been a warrior. As was the custom, he was buried with his arsenal, including knives and tomahawks. A horn bow and quiver of arrows hung from one notch in the framework. A long lance had been laid next to the body.

Luke frowned.

Once the firing began, he'd be night blind and deaf. So would his attackers, but they were many and he was one. Perhaps he needed to hold back on firing until he had no choice. Following his impulse, he picked up the lance. It had a ragged-edged flint tip some six inches long and was strong enough to pierce buffalo hide. He hefted it.

"That'll do," he whispered. "That'll do."

Luke moved in a crouch. He kept the Winchester ready. It was light enough to fire one-handed if he needed to. He held the lance in his left hand, point forward, ready to strike. He moved slowly, pushing toward the running stream just ahead.

The sound of the water grew louder, filling his ears. Keeping his eyes fixed, he slowly turned his head and scanned the terrain. He looked once, then repeated the motion. A shadow shifted among other shadows.

There.

Luke remained still with the patience of a lifelong hunter. After a moment, the shadow moved again and he made out a figure crouched at the foot of a tree. He edged forward. The tree was right on the edge of the stream. The clouds parted and the orange-red gleam of the moon played across the rushing water.

The stream looked shallow, maybe no more than knee deep, and about five yards wide. The water flowed over a gravel bed, the surface broken with white water where it traveled over stones. The man crouched by the tree wore a cotton duster and a battered old cavalry Stetson. He was holding a repeater. Luke couldn't tell which model.

Luke slid forward, hands tight on his weapons. The wood of the lance haft felt solid in his grip. Toe, heel, toe, heel. Closer in, Luke saw the long scraggly beard and thought he recognized the man from Goldsmith's gang. He didn't recall his name and it wasn't important, he wasn't adding up bounties quite yet.

Clearly impatient, the man rose off his knee into a half crouch and looked around the bole of the tree. Luke followed his gaze as he glided forward and saw the path was only a few feet beyond the man, screened by the low shrubbery of a juniper berry bush.

Luke's foot came down on a loose branch and it snapped loudly.

Startled, the man whirled, the whites of his eyes gleaming oddly in the moonlight. Luke reacted without thinking. Thrusting out with the lance, he slammed the spear point into the man's body. The blade slipped between two ribs and went deep.

The man grunted. His mouth came open and blood, black as ink in the moonlight, rushed out. He gurgled, gasping for air like he was underwater. Luke hauled back, ripping the lance free, then lashed out again. The spear point caught the man in the throat this time, and he went over backward.

The outlaw's heels drummed the earth briefly, but the sound was swept away by the flowing creek. He had died surprisingly quietly.

Luke took a knee, both hands on the Winchester now.

The lance stuck up out of the dead man's throat like a sign post.

Luke froze, watching the night and listening intently, trying to penetrate the darkness with his senses.

Goldsmith's crew were all veterans or experienced gun hands led by veterans. Their ambush would follow military guidelines, Luke figured. It would be L-shaped to provide for crossfire on the target but keep the men from inadvertently shooting each other. There'd be an anchor man on either side of the L, set just far enough out to catch anyone if they made it back out of the trap.

Most likely the man Luke had just killed was one of the anchor points. Not counting the one or two men who'd been positioned up the valley to drive him forward, most of the gang would be spread out directly along the trail just ahead of him. They'd be too close to one another for him to kill them one by one.

He needed to flank the group, penetrate to the rear, and try to pinpoint where and how Katey was being held. Carefully, now that he had the gang roughly placed, Luke began moving out to their left. Quickly he realized that wasn't going to work.

The brush grew too close here, too thick. An Indian might have ghosted through the trees and bushes, but Luke didn't think he had the woodcraft for it. Not to this degree. He paused, watching the trail.

Up the valley, much closer than before, he heard Katey scream. He half-jumped at the sound and whirled in that direction. The night was lit up about a hundred yards through the woods. A large bonfire had been lit and though Luke couldn't see it directly, orange light wavered through the tops of the trees, bright as a star, and making shadows.

The fire got going good enough for Luke to hear it now.

It grew in intensity and he began seeing flickers of orange flames through the densely packed branches and brush. Icy fists knotted his stomach. Goldsmith was capable of anything.

Luke moved forward, and as the breeze stoked the flames, the light from the bonfire penetrated the gloom even this far out. He was behind a line of five men. Luke stopped. He wasn't a backshooter. Except he had been during the war. Soldiers struck from ambush whenever possible. They brought more powerful weapons to the battle than their enemy whenever they could. War wasn't a duel, and nobody expected soldiers to behave as if they were in one.

Luke was at war here. These men were the enemy, and if Katey was going to live he had to kill them by fair means or foul. If he couldn't bring himself to bring war to these men, then he might as well leave and abandon Katey to her fate.

He wasn't going to do that.

Drawing the Bowie knife in his left hand and holding the Winchester in his right, Luke slipped forward. He moved slowly, carefully placing his feet. He saw the man closest to him clearly, and the one just beyond him. Beyond them, he thought two more lay in the lee of a fallen log, but they were cloaked in shadow. Even farther on, the dark silhouette of a man's head and shoulders was barely visible.

If he held off firing until he was among them, it would confuse things. The men positioned in the other arm of the ambush would think the shots were coming from their own people, firing at something they couldn't see. The men he'd be among would be expecting action from the trail. The situation tilted things in his favor.

But to keep the advantage he'd have to be in among them deep. No separation, close enough to touch. He wove his way through a little cluster of burial scaffolds. The breeze tickled the crude chimes. Eyeless skulls peered out from robes of buffalo and elk hide.

He came up behind the first man. Luke hovered behind him, crouched in the shadow of a live oak. The Bowie felt heavy in his hand. Carefully, he turned the blade over until it was pointed down from his fist.

Stepping forward, he drove the knife into the man's back at the base of the neck and a little to the left. He slammed it hard, and six or eight inches of the foot-long blade plunged into the man. That was more than enough steel to push through his lung and strike the heart.

The man grunted hard, then pitched forward and dropped into the bushes. The men closest to them were turning, but they were slow and stupid with surprise. Closing his left eye, Luke fired the carbine. The shot struck the man closest to him, who fell back limply. Luke yanked the Bowie knife free from the man he had stabbed, then threw himself to the ground as he worked the Winchester's lever.

The final man in the line turned in his direction, a massive double-barreled shotgun in his grip. The sound of it going off reminded Luke of the cannons firing at Vicksburg. The muzzle flash flared brilliant as the sun, and the boom muffled Luke's hearing as if someone had slammed cotton packing into his ears.

Buckshot punched through the air above his head. He'd been close enough that the shot was still spreading as it passed him and only the point-blank range saved his life.

The Winchester banged hard in his grip, and he realized he'd fired instinctively at the sound of the shotgun blast. The figure staggered. Luke rolled, working the lever. The man fired the second barrel and it blew apart a burial scaffold just above where Luke had been.

Debris erupted into the air and began falling, bones, body parts, broken bits of poles, travois, and bits of pelt. A rain of death. Momentarily deaf and half blind, Luke fired toward where the shotgun's muzzle flash had been. He got a dim impression of a figure flopping backward into the bushes.

Beyond the site of the brief battle, men were shouting, calling out, questioning what was going on. Staying low as a snake, Luke hurriedly wormed his way forward toward the running stream. He needed the stream to mask his movements.

Behind him, the other bushwhackers must have realized their compatriots were dead because a wall of gunfire opened up. Unable to hear the bullets burning close, he still felt their wind-rip as they sliced through the air above him. The men were shooting wild and nowhere near low enough.

Reaching the stream, he put a likely looking tree trunk between himself and what he took to be another four shooters. It didn't do to leave armed men at your back, but he had to keep moving, keep from getting pinned down. He had to fight like the Indians he'd faced, hit and run, hit and run. Attack, kill a few, retreat and draw the rest after him, killing a few more then retreat again and kill more until they ran, then follow and pick them off as they fled.

It was risky. It meant he had to be better than the men he faced, because if he faltered the superior numbers would easily overwhelm him.

But he was growing to hate Colonel Neville Goldsmith on a very deep personal level. Perhaps as much as the men who'd backshot him at the end of the war. His brother Smoke had done for them. Goldsmith and his men were Luke's to settle.

CHAPTER 24

He entered the stream in a crouch. The water was icy, and the swift current immediately tugged at his legs. Slick rocks shifted under his feet. He had to move without making too much noise, but the fast-moving stream made that hard.

He fought his way across to the other side and trudged out. He sank to one knee, letting the water drain from him. The shallow valley was higher in elevation compared to Golgotha Rock, and the air was cool. He'd get chilled very soon. He needed to get moving.

Suddenly, the night above him exploded into brilliant flashes. He winced away from the glare, caught by surprise. *Coston flares,* he thought. He automatically closed one eye. Invented in 1859, the Navy had made extensive use of them during the war. Fired from blunderbuss-looking pistols, the maritime flares burned intensely.

He held his arm up against the glare. Three flares drifted out of the sky, coming slowly back down toward earth. Their illumination was blindingly brilliant. He threw himself to the ground and lay absolutely still.

Men called out in the woods around him, organizing

into squads and beginning to spread out and hunt him. The dead ambushers had been found, and arguments were breaking out among the survivors.

As the flares drifted down to tree-top level and winked out, Luke opened his closed eye. He'd closed it in time to save his night vision and with it he could see almost as well as before. Men stumbled through the brush close to him. They were firing and maneuvering by squads now, not stalking him like deer hunters anymore.

He heard a distinct *crack* and immediately closed his good eye. Two more reports followed hard on the first, and the sky was lit up again. He went to ground, but the pursuers were much closer now.

"There he is!" someone shouted.

Bullets flew in his direction. Desperate to find cover, Luke haphazardly dog-crawled under a burial scaffold and threw himself behind a tree. Two wasp stings creased the back of his leg, inches from each other, and hot sticky blood began flowing.

Putting his back to the tree, he forced himself to his feet. His injured leg screamed with pain. Turning, he thrust the rifle around the edge of the tree and emptied it rapidly, working the lever action, firing without aiming, just laying down a wall of lead to provide cover and break the attackers' momentum.

The Winchester ran dry.

He dropped it and took off in a hobbling run. He had only a few moments before the men behind him began firing and advancing again. He darted around another large pine tree and put it between himself and Goldsmith's gang. Blood filled his boot.

He came out of a line of trees well past the Indian burial ground. He was at the foot of a low hummock topped by several house-sized boulders. Going to all fours, he scrambled up into them. Panting heavily, he cut down a narrow alley between two granite slabs and came out into the open again. To his right, back down a shale gravel embankment, the hollow narrowed. It ran into a promontory where the creek cascaded in a twenty-foot-high waterfall and fed the stream bisecting the shallow valley.

He stopped, sucking in lungfuls of air. He saw two things immediately.

The first was the mouth of a mine tunnel carved beside the waterfall, rough-hewn timbers forming the opening, an old coal oil lamp hanging from a rusty nail. There was a pile of weather worn, ten foot long four-by-four beams next to the tunnel. Obviously they had once been meant for shoring up tunnels.

From the tunnel ran a narrow-gauge railroad track that ended ten feet outside the mine tunnel where a cart used to haul debris from the mine lay overturned. The metal cart was rusted through in several places.

Next to the cart stood an unlit bonfire. Brush and chopped kindling were stacked in a sloppy pyramid around one of the four-by-fours, which had been driven into the ground so that it stood up vertically. Katey was bound to the post like a witch at trial. Her hair hung loose around her face and she'd been crying. Next to her stood Brown and Goldsmith. Goldsmith held a burning lantern while one sat on the ground at Brown's feet.

They're going to burn her alive, Luke realized.

As Luke watched in horror, Brown took a flare from a box opposite his lantern and fed it into a naval flare gun. He lifted the device and triggered another flare. It arched up into the night and exploded over the hollow. The glare cast undulating shadows across the running water and bare rock, causing the scene around the unlit bonfire to momentarily appear as if it were underwater.

Fresh anger bubbled up in Luke. In the time it took to breathe in, the anger became rage. Murderous rage. He'd been fighting for survival and the hope of reaching Katey. But to see the girl bound to a post and threatened with burning alive infuriated him beyond the ability to think straight.

The men he needed to kill were just below him. It was an uncertain pistol shot. He'd made shots that distance before, but not every time. When he fired, he wanted to be sure he killed.

Motion exploded out of the clutch of boulders to his left and slightly up the small hill. One of Goldsmith's men rushed out, a big Hopkins & Allen .44 revolver in his hand. He seemed startled to find Luke this close. Eyes wide, he lifted the pistol.

Luke twisted at the waist and drew his Remington. The outlaw had him beat, but the man wasn't a cool hand and his first shot went into the ground next to the bounty hunter. Luke fired twice. Two bloody holes opened up on the man's chest. He went over backward.

Luke spun back to the horrific scene in front of him.

Brown and Goldsmith were looking up at him in surprise. Brown had dropped the brass flare gun as he drew the Colt Single Action Army pistol he carried. Next to him, Goldsmith was hauling his own Peacemaker from leather, a lantern still held in his left hand.

Luke fanned his hammer four times.

The distance was too far for any real accuracy, but the sound of his .45 booming and spitting lead toward them distracted the two men. They turned to run, and Luke began bounding down the shale gravel incline. He grimaced as white-hot pokers of agony speared into his leg where the bullets had nicked his hamstring. He put one Remington away and drew the other.

Goldsmith dove behind the overturned cart as Brown instinctively went for the cover of the old pile of mining timbers. Luke came down on his injured leg in the scramble, and the screaming muscle failed on him. His leg buckled suddenly at the knee. He bounced off the incline and started tumbling.

He took the force of impact along his right shoulder and side and rolled crazily, out of control but stubbornly refusing to lose his grip on the Remington. The world spun with each jarring impact, and the gravel was jagged against his body as he struck and bounced. He finally reached the bottom and landed on his belly, gun ready.

He caught an impression of Brown rising up from behind the support timbers, aiming his Colt. Luke fired first. Brown jerked hard and blood exploded in a spray from his shoulder. Moving deliberately, Luke cocked the Remington and aimed as Brown fired.

Brown's bullet struck the ground next to Luke's head. Dirt sprayed his face. He flinched as he fired. But despite that, his bullet struck its target, the coal lamp thrown on the ground when Brown had dived for cover. It exploded with a crash, burning coal oil splattering the timbers and part of Brown's body. The outlaw's hair went up like a lucifer match.

Brown shrieked in agony. The sound was a keening wail that echoed down the hollow. Brown stood up, flames consuming his clothes. Like a human torch he stumbled, still screaming, toward the creek. Luke looked past him and saw Goldsmith staring in open fascination as Brown burned.

Luke fired.

His shot banged into the cart and ricocheted away. Goldsmith flinched back behind cover. The sickly sweet smell of roasting human flesh and burnt hair created a stomach-churning stench. Brown fell, sprawling out the length of his body, arm reaching for the creek. His face was melting like candle wax where the coal oil had splashed it. Some instinct for mercy guided Luke's hand, although it was a waste of a bullet during battle. He shot Brown in the head.

The outlaw went limp and the screaming stopped.

Goldsmith fired, kicking up a geyser of dirt next to Luke. From the tree line, the rest of the gang shouted, calling out to Goldsmith. Luke fired, driving Goldsmith back behind the cart again. The last of the gang were coming. He had to do something and do it fast or he'd be caught in a brutal, unforgiving crossfire.

Goldsmith's coal oil lantern suddenly arched out from behind the metal cart. In horror, Luke watched it trace its trajectory toward the stacked wood at Katey's feet. The young whore began screaming. The lantern crashed into the woodpile and shattered like fine China plates.

Instantly the wood caught fire.

"Save her or kill me," Goldsmith yelled. "It's your choice, Johnny Reb!"

Goldsmith sprang up and ran for the tunnel.

Luke was already in motion. Ignoring the fleeing outlaw, he sprinted toward the bonfire. Flames were spreading fast. He needed to save her before the last of the gang found them. Kicking wildly, he began scattering brush and kindling away from Katey. He knocked most of it away, but her skirt had caught fire and now she was sobbing as the fire spread.

Luke snatched at the dress, pulling it from her body. He swore as fire burned his hand but kept hold. He yanked his Bowie knife from its sheath and the blade swung down. The material of the dress ripped loudly and then he had thrown it away, his hand stinging and red.

Katey sobbed. She looked like a lost child in the tattered remnants of her now filthy dress. Purple bruises stood out in stark relief against the paleness of her flesh.

"When I cut you loose, get across the stream and hide!"

She was crying too hard to answer him as he sliced away the knotted rope around her slender wrists. The bonds parted and she fell forward, stumbling. Driven by fear for her safety, Luke didn't have time to be gentle.

"Go!" he shouted as he pushed her toward the creek.

She stumbled, then lurched into a run as he scrambled for the revolver Brown had dropped. Stooping, he picked it up as the first two men left the trees and entered the little clearing. Hand stinging, leg burning, Luke held the Army Colt steady and fired deliberately.

He centered the muzzle on the second man as the first fell backward. He rushed the shot and caught the outlaw high on the belly instead of in his chest. The man sagged, folding in on himself and wobbling unsteadily. Luke took better aim and blew the back of his head out in a fine misting spray of brain and blood and bone.

Muzzle flashes exploded out of the shadows along the tree line. Luke knew that if he didn't think of some way to even the odds, he'd be caught out in the open and cut down by superior numbers.

Like an answer to a prayer, his desperate gaze fell on the flare gun Brown had dropped.

Without thinking, he holstered the Remington and snatched up the flare gun. He spun as gunfire continued erupting from the tree line. Bullets whizzed by and several struck the dirt near him as he ran. A round passed so close that it tugged at the sleeve of his shirt.

Bending down, he snatched up the little wooden box of flares as he sprinted back. He almost ran for the metal cart but realized it was exposed to the mine tunnel where Goldsmith had fled. Instead, he dove for the pile of support timbers where Brown had tried making his own stand.

Luke hoped he'd have better luck.

He landed hard and rolled onto his back, head and shoulders flush up against the wood pile. He fed rounds into both Remingtons, keeping an eye toward the mine as bullets slammed into the wood, kicking up splinters.

He was worried about Katey, but if she'd made the concealment of the bushes and had sense enough to get down, she was already as safe as she could be in a situation like this.

"We got you dead to rights!" one of the men in the trees shouted.

Luke ignored the bait. Instead, he loaded the flare gun. He needed to give the outlaws something to think about other than himself.

Fire worked pretty damn well for that.

CHAPTER 25

Rolling left onto his stomach, into the open at the edge of the pile of timbers, Luke fired the flare gun and sent the brightly burning flare straight into a stand of blue-chip juniper, mountain sage, and cheatgrass. He rolled back as lead stormed at him in return. He loaded the flare gun again.

Luke rolled to his right instead of his left and popped out on the opposite side of the timbers. The maneuver bought him a second and he was able to put the flare directly into creeper vines around the foot of an Engelmann spruce. The oily bush caught almost instantly.

He rolled back. Two flares left. He had a good picture in his head of the edge of the clearing. He didn't need to expose himself needlessly. He stuck his hand over the wood pile and fired the flare gun on the level. He heard the crackling of growing flames and smelled smoke.

A fusillade of bullets tore into the wood pile. Splinters, sawdust, and wood chips rained down like hail in a storm. The din of the weapons echoed loudly off the rocky surrounding slopes.

Luke waited for a small break in the shooting and

then fired the last flare. He dropped the gun and drew a
Remington in his right hand. Rifle shots continued striking
around him but he thought the number of people firing had
dropped off as some of them maybe reloaded.

Luke eyed the mine tunnel, concerned Goldsmith would
emerge. He fired four rounds from the Remington, putting
them indiscriminately into the opening in hopes of driving
him back if the Union colonel was there. He heard his
shots ricochet but no one returned fire and he reloaded.

He looked out to his left. A grin split his face. The flares
had caught. One ponderosa pine was going up like a
Roman candle. Walls of flames the size of buckboard
wagons burned, spreading quickly. The fire roared.

Now men began shouting in panic and frustration. Shots
continued pouring in at the pile of timbers, but with each
moment the fire grew in intensity. Once fire caught hold
that strongly in the trees, nothing could stop it until it
burned out. Smoke hung like morning fog on the ocean,
filling the clearing.

Safe in his cover for the moment, Luke caught his
breath and let the fire grow even more. He scanned the
trees and shadows on the other side of the stream, hunting
for some clue as to where Katey had gone to ground. He
saw none.

Men were still yelling, but the shooting petered out as
the roaring flames drove the outlaws back. Unable to wait
any longer, Luke rose in a crouch and ran toward the creek
where he'd sent Katey.

The heat from the flames pulsed like a heartbeat across
the clearing. It was reflected back from the rocks and the
temperature climbed toward oven-hot. The smoke was
harsh and bitter in Luke's lungs, forcing hacking coughs
from him as fingers of it reached out to circle twice

around him. The lack of oxygen made him feel slightly light-headed. His irritated eyes ran with tears.

Those naval flares burned at something close to three thousand degrees, Luke knew. He'd never had a doubt they'd catch the trees on fire, but even he had been surprised at the degree to which his ploy had worked. As he waded into the creek, he began worrying that maybe it had worked a little too well.

The snowmelt was cool and the current less strong than it was lower down the hollow. It was a relief when he slipped into it. Crouching to get below the line of smoke filling the clearing, he crossed to the other bank and came out.

"Katey!"

There was no answer. Behind him there was a sound like a runaway train barreling out of a tunnel. The clearing glowed. Flinching away from the heat, Luke turned to see a two-hundred-foot-tall sugar pine go up like a pillar of fire in the Bible. Wood exploded as the heat cooked it.

"Katey!" he shouted.

"Here!"

She answered him from behind a tangle of raspberry vines. He hurried in that direction and saw a cleft in the rock face where she'd burrowed in. Her face and arms were marked with long, angry red scratches.

"Come on!" he shouted.

He had to shout to be heard over the fire. The skin of his face tightened where he was turned toward the conflagration. He'd wanted to go into the mine to follow Goldsmith. Now he realized they needed to reach the mine in order to survive. That meant going back toward the fire, but they had no choice. They weren't going to be able to outrun the flames.

Katey threw herself into his arms, and he allowed himself a moment to appreciate the feel of her, the feel of her being safe. She clung to him, trembling. There was no time. After a moment he gently pushed her away.

Beyond the wall of flame, a man began screaming. At the far side of where they stood, several bushes caught fire, cooked in the rising heat until they burst into flame. Smoke rolled into the box canyon clearing, making it harder and harder to breathe.

"Follow me!" he shouted over the roar of the fire.

The mine was their only hope. Even if the heat didn't bake them like biscuits in a Dutch oven, the smoke would asphyxiate them, and if they fell unconscious, they'd never wake.

But it was still their only hope.

He drew his Remington again as he pulled her along after him, back into the water.

As he stepped out onto the far bank, he fired into the mouth of the tunnel three times. If Goldsmith had stubbornly remained close to the opening, that should give him pause. They ran past the cart, lungs burning as they hacked out a seemingly endless series of coughs.

He threw himself against the side post at the opening, keeping Katey safely behind him. Out in the hollow another man screamed. Luke prayed his horse had made it out. Holding the pistol up, he risked a look around the edge.

Orange light illuminated the entrance and penetrated a short distance into the tunnel. The place was old and crumbling. It'd been a number of years since it had been in use. Loose dirt and rock from the tunnel sides and ceiling had fallen, making little mounds on the uneven floor. Water seeped down as if the stone were weeping and formed small puddles that eerily reflected the apricot light of the wildfire.

Beyond the first twenty feet lay only blackness. He saw no sign of Goldsmith.

"Let's go," Luke said. His voice was very grim.

They entered the mine, and the deafening cacophony of the wildfire was almost instantly muffled by tons of rock and earth. The light from behind them cast their shadows large on the visible rock. Letting go of Katey's hand, Luke took down an old lantern hanging from a spike just inside the entrance.

Smoke from outside had begun creeping into the tunnel. The cooler air was keeping it closer to the ground, but it was rising fast.

Pulling a lucifer match from his front search pocket, Luke struck it and miraculously the old lantern lit.

"Are you sure this is a good idea?" Katey asked.

Luke heard the fear in her voice.

"We have to go at least a little further back," he explained. "We have to go deeper than the smoke can reach until the fire dies down."

She nodded, face pinched with anxiety. Luke felt his heart go out to her. She was barely more than a girl. She'd suffered a lot in a short time and reacted bravely. He admired her heart.

"It's going to be okay," he told her. "I promise."

She nodded again and squeezed his hand for reassurance.

"Just don't leave me."

"I won't, I swear."

He set the lantern down and reloaded the Remington. When he was done, he handed the gun to the girl.

"Here," he said. "You know how to use it?"

She nodded.

"Good. Stay behind me and don't fire unless you have to."

Drawing the second revolver, he shifted it to his right hand and picked up the lantern. The mouth of the mine was definitely filling up with smoke. There was no time to waste. He advanced slowly, the lantern thrust out before him and at an angle.

He was painfully aware of how good a target he must make. He cocked the Remington.

The shaft ran in a straight line on an ever-increasing downward slope. Little effort seemed to have been put into keeping the mine in good repair. Luke only found a few places where newer beams had been fitted to shore up the walls. The entire operation had the feel of a death trap about it.

What sounded like a woman's shriek pierced the gloom and lifted the hairs on the back of Luke's neck. He stopped short, and Katey pressed in close behind him. The reverberation of the scream bounced down the tunnel past them.

"What the hell was that?" Katey got out.

"I think it was a cougar," Luke said. "Hopefully it's making short work of Goldsmith."

But they heard no shots or screams as they moved forward. It confirmed his suspicion that Goldsmith had fled and not stuck around.

"Did Goldsmith talk about another exit from this mine?" he asked.

Katey shook her head. "Not that I heard."

They pushed forward, the lantern lighting the way before them. After a few yards they came to a narrow branching shaft, obviously dug to follow a now-depleted vein of ore.

Luke stopped and studied the ground, looking for some sign as to which way Goldsmith had fled.

From the left-hand branch, a deep yowling growl emerged and adrenaline seeped into Luke like water soaking cloth. Cautiously, he lifted the lantern. Its glow crept up the branch tunnel.

Demonic yellow eyes appeared. Luke almost pulled the trigger on the Remington. He lifted the lantern a little higher. The tawny colored panther crouched on the tunnel floor, which was littered with pine needles. Six-inch fangs gleamed in the lantern light. The feline face was drawn back in a terrifying snarl. It was poised to spring.

Luke saw two dusky brown balls of fur tumbling over each other in their haste to retreat. The mountain lion was a mother with cubs. That strange, savage yowling built to a rising crescendo in its chest.

"It's a mother with cubs," he told Katey. "Start backing up slow. Don't run."

Katey said nothing but he felt her slowly retreating behind him. He took a careful step backward. The musty, wild stench of the beast and its fetid kills rankled in his nose.

"Easy," he told the big cat in a soothing voice.

It was the voice he used on frightened horses. He hoped it worked on cougars, too. He took a cautious step back. The big cat hissed at him, tail snapping back and forth. His finger rested on the smooth metal curve of the pistol's trigger. He didn't want to kill the cougar. Knew it was stupid not to, but couldn't bring himself to gun the thing down. If he did, he might as well go over and stomp the kittens to death.

Luke seriously doubted Goldsmith had harbored any similarly merciful compunctions. He had to admit it had been clever of the colonel to leave the big cat alive to slow him down. It raised his suspicions even more that there was a second way out of the mine.

He stepped back and the angry cat hissed a warning. Katey had stepped around the lip of the branch and into the main shaft. Luke smoothly followed her.

"Walk a few yards," he told her. "I'll catch up."

She did as instructed. Luke followed more slowly, still backing. If the cougar came around that corner it would be attacking and moving at speed. He'd likely have only a heartbeat of time to shoot before it was on him. He couldn't afford to turn his back.

The low chest-growl of the cougar echoed weirdly off the rock. Luke went farther into the mine. The cat let loose an ear-splitting scream that sounded for all the world like a woman in agony. Luke shuffled deeper. After several moments he felt confident enough to turn around.

"I can't believe we made it," Katey said. Her voice was breathless, as if she'd run a race.

"Murderous lunatic in front of us, angry mama cat with cubs behind us," Luke sighed. "We're right where we want to be."

CHAPTER 26

They moved down the tunnel. Luke could no longer smell the smoke. As they made their way deeper into the mine, he grew more and more convinced that Goldsmith was gone. After a couple of minutes, they came to a spot where the shaft bisected a natural cavern about the size of a house.

Tools now thick with dust had been stockpiled there. Coils of rope lay next to bundles of picks and shovels. There were several overturned wheelbarrows scattered about. The place had seen far less traffic than the front of the mine and Luke clearly saw the bootprints leading across the floor. Against one wall several wooden crates were stacked.

An eerie, otherworldly keening that seemed tinged with sadness floated out of the darkness. Luke stopped as the wail reverberated through the supply chamber. It sounded like mournful voices calling out in lamentation.

"I-i-is that another cat?" Katey whispered.

"No. Just the wind."

"This is Golgotha mine," Katey said. "The first mine they sank, the one that started the town."

"So?"

"So Golgotha is from the Bible. It means Place of Bones, or something. They named it after the Indian burial ground outside."

"Makes sense."

"A cave-in killed thirteen miners three years ago. They never recovered the bodies. I heard all about it in town. People still talk about it."

"It's not ghosts," Luke said.

Despite him being convinced of that, when the ululating moan drifted from the darkness, the hair along the back of his arms stood up. *Don't be stupid,* he told himself. *There's no such thing as ghosts.* It was an unnerving sound, though, and he'd be glad to hear the last of it.

"Come on," he told Katey.

They left the big chamber and once again entered the bleak darkness of the main tunnel as it continued on. They no longer smelled smoke, but now an oppressive musty odor formed around them. The wailing peaked and waned. He began to feel the sensation of being watched. The drip of water in the distance sounded unnaturally loud. Almost oppressive. Their breathing was loud in his ears. The walls of the mine were uncertain, threatening collapse. The thought of being buried alive made it difficult to breathe.

They came to a second fork in the shaft. In front of them, it ran downward into an abyss-like darkness. To the left, it continued straight, and he could hear the moaning sounds coming from that direction. He closed his eyes and felt air on his face.

"This way," he said.

They had barely started along that branch of the tunnel when the sound of a pistol being cocked echoed from the darkness beyond the lantern light's reach. Cold, distinctly metallic, and utterly unmistakable.

The sound saved Luke's life. If Goldsmith had been thinking clearly enough to have cocked the single action weapon before they penetrated this far into the mine, the outcome could have been much different.

Luke, already poised for action and tightly wound, dropped the lantern and threw himself backward into Katey. She screamed and staggered back.

The gun went off with a thunderous roar that slammed against Luke's ears like giant fists. The ricochet whined off rock and made a meaty *splat* as it struck the young whore. She screamed again as Luke grabbed her and bore her to the ground. The echoes from the gunshot created a terrible clamor in the tunnel. Luke came up on one knee, his body shielding hers just on the edge of the yellow glow from the lantern, which, surprisingly, hadn't gone out when Luke dropped it.

The Remington came up and exploded in the uncertain light, muzzle flashes splitting the gloom like lightning strikes. Bullets burned down the tunnel. The ground rumbled beneath him, and Luke felt his stomach drop away in fear as he realized just how unstable the mine was.

Dirt fell from the ceiling like rain. More dirt poured out to the floor as a section of one of the walls gave way. Katey was sobbing from the pain of her wound. There was no time to be gentle. Luke turned and shoved, pushing her into motion.

"Go! Go! Go!" he shouted.

Behind him Goldsmith kept firing. Bullets whizzed past above them. Luke shoved Katey forward, then threw himself on top of her as she fell. He felt the dampness of her blood soak his clothes, but he couldn't tell where she was shot.

"I'll bring the whole damn thing down, Jensen!" the outlaw shouted.

More dirt streamed down, followed by head-sized rocks. Goldsmith emptied his pistol and the sides of the shaft began to cave in. With a sudden crash that section of roof collapsed and plunged several thousand pounds of dirt and rock into the tunnel. Dust filled the tight space, and Luke choked on it.

Beneath him, Katey coughed violently, fighting for air as dust filled her mouth and nose. Tremors reverberated through the tunnel, shaking the floor beneath them. Timber joists groaned in protest. They sounded like wailing ghosts. Luke hugged Katey and waited for the world to come to an end—or not.

After a moment, the tremors stopped. Luke lay still, listening to the streams of loose dirt and pebbled rock spill out into the tunnel. Gradually the dust began to settle, and it was easier to breathe.

Luke put his lips next to Katey's ear. "Where were you hit?"

"My leg," she whispered back.

"Press your hand against it until I can help you."

Luke gently rolled off her. It was pitch black in the tunnel. They had lost the lantern, and he wasn't sure how much of the roof had come down. He could only hope the entire shaft wasn't blocked now. He crawled forward, hands searching.

He heard nothing more from Goldsmith. If Luke was lucky, the cave-in had killed the crazed outlaw. However, he doubted it would be so easy. He came up to the dirt pile. By a stroke of luck, his hand found the hot metal of the lantern.

He hissed in surprise as his skin was singed and drew his hand back. After a moment he probed for it again, finding the handle. With his other hand, he felt the mound of debris before him. He wasn't certain it reached the roof, but it did go up several feet. Enough to provide cover.

Taking another wooden lucifer match from his pocket, he snapped it to life with his thumbnail. Holding it up, he saw that the glass housing of the lantern had been shattered. However, the wick and some coal oil were still present.

Carefully threading the match between the jagged fingers of broken glass, Luke lit the wick. The lantern didn't work nearly as well, but it was better than the grave-like darkness without it. He lifted it. The debris from the cave-in filled the shaft to the ceiling. But off to the right side, the blockage looked shallow enough to dig through. They were safe from Goldsmith for now.

"Let's see that wound."

Luke crawled over and inspected Katey in the dim light. The girl looked pale and frightened. Her face was covered in dust. He moved the lantern down and saw that her dress was soggy with blood.

"How bad is it?" she asked.

He heard the fear in her voice. Setting down the lantern, he drew his Bowie knife and cut away the material surrounding the injury. It was ugly, but seeing it up close made him more optimistic than he had been.

"Through and through, and not too deep," he said. "Missed the big artery down there. You may have a limp, but we'll get you bandaged up and into town. You should be fine."

To insure that, though, she needed a doctor, and soon. He could do a good enough job of patching her up for now, but she still required actual medical attention. They couldn't go back out the front of the mine. The fire would still be burning out there. His horse had most likely fled to town, and the distance was too great to walk, especially with Katey being wounded.

"You won't leave me?" she asked.

She must have seen the apprehension on his face even in the gloomy lantern light. He smiled at her. Reaching out his arm, he used the back of his hand to gently stroke her face, the way he might a spooked horse. He shook his head.

"No. No, Katey, of course not."

She took his hand in her much smaller one and kissed it. The yellow flickering light glistened in her eyes where she held back tears.

"I'd promise you to pay you back for saving me," she said as she summoned up a faint smile, "but I think I might need some time to heal up first."

Luke laughed, glad to hear a little spirit in her voice despite their dilemma. He held her hand for a bit longer and then the moment passed. He sighed. No rest for the weary.

"I'm going to dig a hole through that cave-in," he said. "Then I'll crawl through and check for Goldsmith. Once it's safe, you'll have to follow."

"I can do it," she vowed.

Luke dug quickly. The labor was easy because the debris wasn't packed tight. Neither of them liked the way the remaining timbers groaned, but there was little choice but to continue. He made short work of the job.

He held up the lantern, trying to get a glimpse beyond. Two things happened. The flame flickered. Air was coming from somewhere up ahead. That seemed to prove his second entrance theory.

The second thing was that Goldsmith didn't fire at him. The colonel must have decided the tunnel collapse had done for them.

Luke got to work getting Katey through the opening he had made. As soon as she had climbed high enough on the mound of dirt and rock, he reached through and took hold of her arms to help her. In the faint light, he saw her biting her lip to hold back whimpers of pain and fear. She was determined, though, and after a minute she had squeezed through far enough for Luke to slide his arms under hers and pull her the rest of the way. She gasped as that made the wound in her leg hurt even more.

"As soon as we get out, I'll bind that up," he told her. "That ought to make it feel a little better."

He didn't know if that was true or not, but it wouldn't hurt anything for him to be encouraging.

They moved along the tunnel with Luke holding the weakly burning lantern in one hand and wrapping the other arm around Katey's torso. After a few minutes, they found the other entrance Luke had suspected all along.

A vertical shaft ran thirty feet straight up and at the top, through an opening the size of a church door, they saw stars in the sky. The air looked hazy from smoke, but they still saw stars. They could smell smoke, as well, but only faintly.

Against the wall, spiked into the earth, was a wooden ladder. Luke set the lantern down and tilted his head back to watch the opening while Katey leaned against the wall. Remington in one hand, he lifted the lantern and blew it out. Darkness closed in around them, but the hole above them actually seemed to lighten in contrast, midnight blue versus deep, deep black.

Climbing was going to hurt, but Katey had endured everything so far with the perseverance of a soldier.

"Almost there," Luke told her. "I don't want to get cocky and rush this. Slow and steady does it."

"Slow and steady," she echoed. "I don't think I could manage to rush, anyway."

Luke winced at the strain in her voice. She needed a doctor. The strain of climbing the ladder would likely start the wound bleeding again. There was no other way out, though.

Still watching the opening, he tested the ladder. The wood was rough and easily splintered, but it seemed secure. If Goldsmith caught them on the ladder, it would be bad. Luke knew he could still shoot fine with one hand holding on to a rung, but the advantage would be firmly on Goldsmith's side.

"Stay here," he told Katey. "Keep that gun ready. Press up against the wall, out of the way. When I get to the top, I'll check the area and call you up."

Her hand found his arm and clung to him.

"Don't leave me alone down here." Her voice was close to breaking.

"Katey," he said, voice low. "Katey, it'll be okay." He gently pulled his arm free. "You need to trust me. Have I ever let you down?"

In the dark, he sensed more than saw her shake her head in response.

"I haven't," he agreed. "And I won't now. It's too dangerous for us both to be on the ladder."

She nodded, and he squeezed her shoulder reassuringly.

He turned, but she grabbed him and kissed him hard. He kissed her back. Finally, after too long given the precariousness of the situation, they broke apart.

"Hurry," she urged.

Turning, he found the ladder and began climbing. It was slow but steady going. He climbed with only his left hand. With his right he kept the Remington cocked and ready. The smell of smoke intensified the higher he climbed. The old wood was rough and each grip he took threatened to leave his hand punctured by splinters.

At the top he paused, feeling like a damn prairie dog. He knew he had to stick his head out of the hole, but he also knew that was the most dangerous time. Slowly, he lifted his eyes above the rim.

He was on top of the hill that overlooked the hollow. Faint gray light in the eastern sky told him that dawn wasn't too far away and allowed him to see his surroundings. A stand of pine trees rose off to his right; the creek that ran into the waterfall was to his left. The opening had been made in a little clearing and he easily spotted the deep ruts of old wagon wheel marks on the ground.

No one fired on him.

He came up out of the hole in a rush, rolled across the top, and lay belly down with his back to the stream, pistol pointed toward the stand of trees. The smoke was a thin gauze here. The breeze was pushing it in the opposite direction.

Long moments crawled past.

In that time, his ears adjusted enough for him to hear the fire burning in the distance. He could imagine Goldsmith climbing out here, seeing the blaze and deciding to hightail it, either to a predetermined rendezvous point or just in headlong flight.

He decided on the former.

Goldsmith wasn't going to win any medals for unprovoked valor, but he was a steady hand. The colonel was capable of holding his own. He just approached violence with a criminal mentality. Luke was better than him, by quite a bit, and the man knew it.

Goldsmith would fight if cornered, and he'd strike from ambush or attack when the odds were in his favor. But face Luke down? Never.

Slowly Luke stood.

He walked to the copse of trees and inspected the area. He found fresh horse droppings and counted the hoof marks of two horses among the pine needles and sand soil of the dirt. Goldsmith had had saddle mounts hidden here, as Luke had suspected, and with his plans to ambush Luke and finally be rid of him gone awry, he had fled.

Again.

CHAPTER 27

Trying not to think about how many of the gang might have survived the fire and still be lurking around, Luke built a travois and dragged Katey back to Golgotha Rock. It took two days because the terrain was rough, but mostly it was downhill.

After all the havoc that had been wreaked in the town because of him, he figured the citizens might start shooting at their first sight of him. That turned out not to be the case. The marshal and his two deputies had ruled Golgotha Rock with iron fists, like the outlaws they truly were. Folks had been scared of them, but they hadn't had any real affection for the star packers.

Likewise, the hooded lynchers had been mostly outsiders, and those who weren't had been drunks and troublemakers. The decent settlers weren't sad to see them go, or the street preachers who had drifted in after Brown. Most of them were actually grifters who'd regarded the inhabitants of Golgotha Rock as easy marks.

So while the townspeople certainly regarded Luke with wariness and didn't welcome him with open arms, they didn't turn him and Katey away, either.

He even found his horse at the livery stable. It had made its way back to town, as he had hoped.

Despite Luke's best efforts, he hadn't been able to stop the spread of infection. He had cleaned Katey's wound with creek water before bandaging it, but he had nothing else with which to disinfect it. By the time they had reached Golgotha Rock, the smell coming from the wound had told Luke the bad news, but he had hoped against hope the doctor in town could do something to help.

The doctor saved her life but was unable to keep her from losing her leg. Luke had to help hold her down as the doctor sawed her leg off halfway above the knee. Even the laudanum the doctor had given her wasn't enough to completely blunt the agony.

Luke had been torn between following Goldsmith while there was still a trail to follow and staying with Katey. The young woman had no one else, so it wasn't much of a call. Katey needed him. He wasn't the only force for law and order on the frontier, but he was the only person in this girl's life.

While she writhed and moaned in delirium, he fed her soup and laudanum and bathed her feverish skin with cold rags. After the first week, he moved her from the hotel to a room in the house of the Chinaman who ran the town laundry, Ping.

Ping's daughter—Luke never got her name—shared her room with Katey and took care of her. Luke paid her enough to be a nursemaid that her father didn't resent her absence in the laundry. The doctor visited periodically to check that the amputation was healing.

"You should've gone off and let me die up there!" Katey told Luke bitterly by the end of the second week. "Ain't no one gonna want no one-legged whore!"

Luke figured that was true enough. At least not in the more upscale establishments where girls made good money and the customers weren't allowed to get too rough. He tried to comfort her as best as he could, but it wasn't very much.

When he'd been betrayed, shot, and left for dead, he had been cared for by Emily Sue Peabody and her father. Without them he would have died of the injuries he'd suffered when the snakes he rode with stole the Confederate gold they were supposed to be safeguarding, back there in the last desperate days of the war. So he stayed, though he was no doctor. There'd been a time in his life, more than one, where he'd been left vulnerable by violence. He took what opportunities he had to repay all those acts of kindness.

By the end of the third week, Katey had deduced a plan of her own.

"I know you can't stay much longer, Luke."

"I'll stay as long as you need me," he argued.

It made his guts tighten to think of the lead Goldsmith had acquired already. But, still . . . he'd grown even more fond of Katey as he witnessed the courage she displayed in healing and facing up to the reality.

She smiled. It was small and bittersweet. She touched his hand. "I know you're a rambler. And I know you want to kill Goldsmith more than you want to take care of me."

He opened his mouth to protest, but she stopped him with a lifted finger.

"It's okay," she said. "You don't need to apologize for who you are, not with me. I want you to kill him, too. But I need to ask you a favor."

"Anything."

"After you've settled things with Goldsmith, will you come back? Lippy, over to the Velvet Chamber Saloon, said I could play the piano at night. It's not much, but it'll keep me fed and a roof over my head until you can get back."

"Okay." Luke sensed she needed something else. He took both her hands in his. "What else can I do for you, Katey?"

"You can take me to New Orleans."

Luke blinked. The notion seemed to have come out of nowhere.

"You have family there?" he asked.

Katey shook her head. "No. But I know a place where I can work."

Luke blinked. "Work?"

Katey laughed out loud at his surprise. It was a genuine sound, the first he'd heard from her. "Oh, Luke!"

"What?"

"I'm going to have to work. There's a place in New Orleans that deals with, um, I'd guess you call 'specialties' girls."

"Specialties?" Luke repeated. He felt stupid, and he was no stranger to brothels, but he wasn't following.

"For customers with tastes that stray outside what most would call normal."

"Like circus freaks?" he asked.

The words had come out of his mouth before he could pull them back. He hadn't meant to imply Katey was a freak, but he didn't understand what she was trying to tell him. To his surprise, Katey barked out another one of her laughs.

"Why, I imagine the midgets and bearded ladies would do just fine there. And that's the thing, Luke. The girls who can do one-of-a-kind things *are* paid very well. They're not easily replaced so management tries to keep them happy. Maybe I can put enough away that I can open a parlor of my own someday."

"Well, I suppose that makes sense," he said with a frown. "Even if I don't quite understand it."

She smiled. "Just promise you'll at least get me as far as St. Louis. I can catch a riverboat to New Orleans."

"Katey, I promise to take you all the way to New Orleans once Colonel Neville Goldsmith is dead."

Katey poured them each a shot of rye. Smiling, she handed one to Luke and they lifted their glasses.

"Good," she said. "Now go kill him."

Ripped out by glacial violence, the ragged pyramids of the Cathedral Group were the tallest mountains among the Grand Tetons. The terrain there was stark, beautiful, and utterly unforgiving. Snow stayed year around above the timberline, but when winter came, the whole range could look like some desolate, arctic waste. Snow came hard and settled deep. It brought with it a bone-chilling cold that could stop a man's heart.

Mountain men and fur trappers had been using the area around Jackson Hole since the early 1830s. The territory's gold rush had ended almost five years earlier, but there was still enough gold to keep individual claims running. That reduced industry still needed services, so small towns, once flush with gold and armies of miners, were now quieter villages and hamlets.

Luke boarded the train in Cheyenne and followed a rumor west toward the Teton range. Night fell as the Union Pacific locomotive began its climb into the Cathedrals. Outside, the early twilight deepened into a velvet blue-black and cold, stone gray clouds gathered. Snow fell. He quietly watched it come down.

His train car was nearly empty. Most of the other passengers had already disembarked. The brakemen had uncoupled all but this passenger coach and the mail car at the last valley town. The train mostly pulled empty freight cars and flatbeds for returning timber coming back down the mountains.

There was a small family a couple of rows up from him: tired but kind-looking mother, father, little girl with quiet, solemn eyes, and a boy a couple of years older. The boy couldn't sit still. Beyond them was a drunk in a worn suit. Luke had him pegged as a gambler. The man was asleep now and snoring like a bear in hibernation. Up near the front of the passenger car, a grizzled old-timer wore gold-rimmed spectacles under eyebrows nearly as bushy as his beard and read a two-week-old copy of a St. Louis newspaper.

Outside the town of Cedar Falls, a homestead had been raided and burned to the ground. The family had been locked inside. Locals thought it was rogue Blackfeet or maybe Crow.

Luke didn't think Indians were responsible for that atrocity. As soon as he heard about it in Cheyenne, he knew it was Goldsmith, unable to control his unholy appetites, who was to blame.

The man had gone to ground for a while, but he couldn't fight his urge to burn. He wouldn't stop until someone put him down. This time Luke planned on following him straight into hell if that was what it took.

He looked out the window at endless white and deep drifts. It seemed hell was cold. Very cold. Thanks to two potbellied stoves, it was warmer by far inside than it was outside the coach. But that didn't mean it was actually warm. The family was bundled against the chill like arctic explorers. Luke himself didn't remove his brand-new buffalo skin coat.

The train slowed and the sounds of the engine's chugging grew strained. They were climbing. Outside Luke's window, the snow-covered valley began giving way to rugged, snow-covered foothills.

The conductor appeared, dressed all in black like an undertaker and with the same officious air of self-importance. He was a portly man with a ruddy complexion and the heavily veined nose of a chronic drinker. The man's lambchop sideburns were the largest Luke had ever seen. He thought they gave the man the appearance of an owl sticking its head from bushes. A drunk owl. The conductor cleared his throat.

"We are beginning the climb."

His voice was startling high and squeaky for a man of his girth. The little girl began giggling and the mother shushed her. The conductor eyed the child warily, as if fearing sudden attack.

"The grade will become quite steep," he continued. "I suggest you remain seated until we reach the top."

"How long will that be?" the old-timer with the newspaper asked.

The conductor made a great show of checking his gold pocket watch. He frowned down at the watch as if disapproving of what he found there. He harrumphed a bit.

"Two hours."

Why he needed to check his watch to come to that conclusion, Luke had no idea. The man nodded once, sharply, his double chin quivering. He smiled tightly beneath his drooping Walrus mustache as if pleased he'd been able to answer the query so accurately.

Suddenly the wheels screeched along the rails in a cacophony of screaming metal. The coach lurched and the conductor stumbled, driving his prodigious belly into the back of an empty seat. He grunted. The mother let out a short scream.

The train seemed to stall for a moment and the reverberations of the straining engine made the cars tremble. Then, slowly, the locomotive began inching its way upward again.

"What was that?" the woman demanded.

The conductor pushed himself back into a standing position. "That, madam," he said, "was an ice patch. You can rest assured that the Number Eighty-Seven has made this trip numerous times."

"I should hope so," the old-timer spoke up. "The price of a ticket was ridiculous."

The conductor did not seem impressed with the observation. Promptly breaking with his own advice, he began making his way down the train toward the mail car behind them. He passed by in a perfumed cloud of lavender water and whiskey.

The woman produced a picnic basket from the floor and passed sandwiches to the kids. Her husband, dour faced, refused his.

"You have to eat, John," she said.

Luke realized she was younger than he'd first thought. Barely out of her teens. She'd most likely had the boy when she was fifteen or sixteen. Her husband's salt-and-pepper hair marked him about a decade and a half older.

"I'm not hungry," he said.

The tone of his voice ended the discussion. Luke waited

for the man to soften his words, or make some small gesture of affection toward the woman or children. None was forthcoming. After a moment the man produced a well-worn Bible from his lap and began reading. The boy ate his sandwich quietly. The girl stared at Luke, eyes innocent of guile.

Luke liked kids. Maybe not enough to settle down and have his own, but their innocence and good nature always served to remind him of why he rode the trail he did. For children to prosper on the frontier, evil men had to be brought to heel.

Pulling his hat down over his eyes, he settled in for a nap.

CHAPTER 28

The explosion jerked Luke from his slumber.

He was awake and had identified the sound before he was fully conscious of making any decision. Several sticks of dynamite had just detonated somewhere nearby. Then he heard the roaring, rumbling sound and realized what was happening.

Luke sprang to his feet and lurched toward the windows on the opposite side of the train. He looked out, but it was pitch black. The rumbling noise grew large enough to swallow them. The men in the train shouted in confusion, the mother screamed as a wall of white suddenly appeared. The children cried out.

Operating on pure instinct, Luke threw himself back. The avalanche struck the train with hurricane force. Snow exploded through the windows as the arctic wall slammed into the coach. Freezing white pushed into Luke, shoving him to the floor.

Suddenly the train lurched to the side. In the next moment, the entire world seemed to turn over. Luke was tossed as if in the hand of a giant. He churned through the snow that enveloped him, trying to keep from being smothered.

Bone-chilling cold grasped him in a tight fist as his body lurched back and forth. He struck something hard and when he cried out snow filled his mouth, choking him. The sound of crashing metal fought the rumble for dominance, but the noise was too short-lived, and the thunder of the avalanche continued echoing.

His head came up hard against an immovable object and his vision exploded with stars. Then it went black and he lost consciousness. He had no idea for how long. When his awareness seeped back into his brain, he had no way of telling how much time had passed.

The sensation of driving forward had stopped, and the avalanche thunder dissipated. Finally, after long moments in total darkness, Luke spit out snow and gasped for breath.

He was entombed, surrounded by darkness and cold and silence. His legs were bent in different directions. One of his arms was trapped behind him. Luke couldn't tell if he was up or down. Cautiously, he tried widening a space in front of his face. He pushed some of the snow back, packing it into a hard pocket.

Everything in him screamed to flail and dig for the surface, to break free and find air, to suck in huge lungfuls of the stuff until the feeling of drowning and claustrophobia subsided. He couldn't give in to the fear.

He brought his hand up and awkwardly inched his fingers into the breast pocket of his flannel shirt. He always kept a few matches there. He found one but realized he was already starting to tremble with the cold.

He managed to light the match with a thumbnail. The lucifer head sprang to life, and he moved the burning match away from him. He studied the flame, watching which way it burned. It burned upward, warming his fingers as the fire ate the matchstick. He blew it out.

He'd come to rest facedown and had been too twisted around and stunned to tell. His body ached from the beating it had just taken. He was glad he hadn't started frantically digging; he would have only ended up burrowing deeper into the snowpack.

He contorted his body in little jerks, working to flip himself over. Finally, he was upright and he began clawing at the snow above him with gloved hands. He wore long-handled underwear, a flannel shirt, denim trousers, and a heavy winter coat, but the cold was oppressive. He trembled uncontrollably until his efforts began to warm his muscles.

It was getting harder to breathe. His exertion was forcing him to use larger amounts of oxygen. He could have survived the avalanche only to be smothered to death in the drift.

Somebody did this, he thought.

That explosion hadn't been some unlucky coincidence. Someone had meant to derail the train. Someone willing to kill women and children without a second thought. He'd heard of train robbers pulling up sections of track or blocking the rails, but only the lowest used derailing as a means to stop their target.

His hand pushed through the snow and suddenly broke free into the air. He scrambled to widen the opening. He saw the midnight blue of the sky appear before his eyes and lunge-jumped toward it. Snow was falling. Sweet, frigid air filled his gasping lungs.

He lay for a moment, exhausted, thinking of nothing but breathing.

After several minutes, Luke lifted his head and looked around. He knew he was still in deadly danger.

He was several hundred yards away from a rearing cliff face. The mass of snow made it hard to tell how far downward he'd been swept. If he looked to the left or right, he ought to be able to see the rail line somewhere. But for something like nearly half a mile in either direction, all he could see was the avalanche and the destruction it had caused.

To his left he saw a couple of empty flatbed cars sticking up like toothpicks in the snow. To his right the back end of the engine protruded like a black fist. Of his passenger car, he saw nothing. It had been absolutely buried.

Remembering the little girl, Luke became almost frantic. He had to help her. His heart pounded as he had no idea of where to start looking. They were miles outside of a town. By the time he trekked somewhere and brought back help, any survivors would have suffocated. If by some miracle they hadn't, buried under all that snow, then the cold would kill them.

He felt enraged by his sense of helplessness. His mind spun, frantic to find a solution to the seemingly insurmountable problem. Maybe the snow hadn't carried him out of the coach. Perhaps he'd dug his way up through a broken window and out of the train car without realizing it.

That would mean he was directly above the other passengers. Using his memory to measure the distance from his seat to that of the family, he began pushing his way through the massive drift. When he'd gone what he thought was far enough, he began calling out and digging with his hands.

His voice echoed off the lonely mountainside. It made him feel small and futile. He dug down until he was breathing like a man who'd just run a long foot race. He didn't find a survivor or even any evidence of the train coach. He stopped and breathed deeply, exhausted by his exertions.

Somebody did this, he thought again.

Somebody who would die for it.

The idea that outlaws might be responsible for this occurred to him for a second time, but when he considered it, the use of an avalanche to stop the train seemed particularly vicious and stupid. Look at how the cars were buried. How many men would it take to find where the train safe was located in all of this white mess?

He frowned.

There hadn't been a safe in their coach. That left either one of the empty cargo cars, the caboose, or the engine. If someone had done this to carry out a robbery, they'd be coming down the mountain to pick over the remains of the train.

He looked to where the locomotive stuck out of the deep drifts. That would be the first place the attackers would go. They wouldn't want to leave any survivors of the wreck alive. He didn't see anyone moving yet, obscured as his vision was by the falling snow, but he hadn't hallucinated that explosion.

He felt for his guns.

"Damn," Luke cursed softly.

One of his Remingtons had remained in its holster. The other was missing. He drew his remaining pistol and cocked the hammer back. He had fifteen bullets in the loops of his gunbelt. Not a lot of firepower to take on a gang of train robbers.

He saw the little girl clearly in his mind's eye; imagined

her stiff and blue and dead, eyes staring wide into nothing, buried until the spring thaw released her from an icy tomb.

If the men who'd done this wanted to search for the safe, then he'd be ready and waiting for them. With fresh determination, Luke began pushing his way toward the engine.

He kept sinking into the snow. It made the going brutally tough, but his anger was extremely good fuel. He was out in the open, far from cover. He used what concealment he had. He tried keeping the locomotive between him and what he thought was the most likely angle of approach, based on how the avalanche had come down.

The driving snow was a double-edged sword. It helped hide him, but he wasn't able to see anyone else who might be approaching. All he could hear was the wind. Falling snowflakes gathered on his eyelashes. He'd lost his Stetson in the wreck, and snow landed on his head where his body heat melted it. It ran like sweat down his neck and into his clothes. He knew as soon as he stopped moving, it would freeze solid.

If he didn't find shelter soon, he'd freeze to death.

A little closer to the locomotive, he came upon either the engineer or fireman. The man lay like a casually tossed rag doll. His back and neck had been broken so that the body was bent in all the wrong directions.

There was also a bullet hole between his eyes.

Someone had put the man down like a lame horse or sick dog. Luke frowned, then looked back toward the partially exposed locomotive. He hadn't heard a shot. It must have happened while he was unconscious. He'd obviously been out too long; the robbers had come and gone.

He jerked violently with his shivering and came out of his pondering. Ice had formed in his hair and the skin of his face was tight to the point of feeling brittle with the cold.

The cold could kill him.

He had to get moving. He was in trouble now and realized it. He forced himself to push forward. The muscles of his legs felt like clenched fists, and his hands were achingly numb. Frustrated, Luke holstered the one remaining Remington. Whoever had done this was gone anyway. He stuffed his hands up under his armpits. He was glad for the buffalo coat. It was a good coat. But it left too much exposed to save him on its own.

He shuffled forward through the drifts, the locomotive growing larger before him. As he drew closer, he saw the tracks of snowshoes now filling with fresh snow. Soon they'd be entirely obliterated. The knowledge felt far away, like a kite on a very long string. It was as if someone else were thinking these things. He wasn't sure anymore what they had to do with him. It was important, but he couldn't quite think of why.

He reached the locomotive and leaned against it for a moment. The interior was a dark cave through the broken glass of a window. Immediately below him he saw a hand-brake sticking from the metal floor and a panel covered with gauges. A light dusting of snow covered everything.

As he tried to climb inside the cab, his wooden limbs failed him and he fell roughly. He struck an iron wheel lever painted bright red, but it didn't hurt as much as it should have because his body was numb. He lay in a heap, chin on his chest. Something metal and unforgiving prevented him from raising his head.

His legs stuck up above him, almost straight out, and his arms were held in tight against his stomach. It was not a good position to be in. He forced his knees to bend and reached out with an arm to find purchase. His body wanted to breathe deeply at the exertion, but when he tried, he realized he couldn't open his mouth. The moisture of his breath had frozen his lips together.

Groaning as the skin tore, he forced his mouth open. Blood ran warm and coppery in his mouth and more of it froze on his chin. He kept his mouth open to prevent it from freezing again. He managed to push himself onto his side. It was dark here, but his eyes quickly adjusted to the gloom.

Something pressed hard into his arm and he scooted back from it. Coal shovel. He felt his eyes scrunch almost shut and realized he was grinning. He couldn't feel his cheeks. He had to hurry.

From outside in the blowing snow, a wolf wailed up into the sky. Luke felt a primal chill completely unrelated to the temperature gripping his spine. The wilderness did not care, he knew. The mountain and the weather and the wild animals would all kill him with utter indifference.

He struggled into an upright position.

There it was. The furnace.

Luke reached out with trembling hands and tried to work the lever. His fingers were slow and stupid and wouldn't do what he told them to. Frustrated, he shoved his shoulder into the lever and forced it open that way.

Metal screeched on metal, and the heavy door swung open a little. He managed to jerk his elbow into position just in time to stop it swinging closed again. The air in the furnace was much warmer than outside though no coal embers glowed.

Reaching in, he put his hand on a coal then placed his other hand over the first. Concentrating hard, he tried closing his hands. It worked. Somewhat. Coal in hand, he tried striking it against the edge of the furnace mouth. The lump cracked. He struck again and this time it crumbled into dust and chunks.

Careful as he could, he let the coal bits dribble out of his grip and on top of the other coal inside the furnace. Coal dust would light the small bits. The small bits would light the larger bits. Soon he'd have a coal fire burning.

If he could get a match out.

He couldn't feel his feet any longer. He wore thick socks, but his boots were made for riding, not kicking through snow banks. His body shook violently from the cold, as if he were convulsing. It was agony to get his hands burrowed inside his coat and shirt and then under his armpits. He hugged himself, rocking back and forth.

He looked at the little pile of coal dust, hungry for the fire it promised. If he could just get his fingers to work, damn it! He twisted back and forth at the waist, doing every motion he could think of to burn energy and warm himself, if only a little.

At last he felt like he could wiggle his fingers enough, and he withdrew his hands. The moment they touched frigid air they began cooling. He was in a race. He ripped the button off his shirt pocket. He didn't even try to work it through the opening. That would be a waste of precious time.

Holding one hand with the other, he crawled his fingers into the pocket. He felt something cylindrical and giving. Through the numb tips, he felt something rigid and straight. A match.

"Come on," he whispered to himself. "Don't give up."

When he spoke, he let his mouth rest for a moment. Immediately his lips froze together. He moaned in frustration. Carefully he got his thumb on one side of the match and tried pressing it into his fingers. He wasn't certain his purchase was adequate. His life depended on it. He slid his other hand around his fingers and squeezed as best he could.

The matches stayed in his grip as he slowly pulled his hands free. There were two of them trapped there. His eyeballs began to ache suddenly. He had a moment of panic as he realized the moisture in his eyes was freezing. He had no idea how far below freezing the temperature had to be to do that. Wyoming in winter was murderous.

His vision was gray and fading as he held the matches before him. His arms swayed. Carefully, he reached out and pressed the tips against the metal furnace. If these didn't light, he didn't think he'd have the strength left to dig more matches out of his pocket. This was it.

He laid the match heads against the metal. He couldn't press too hard because the sticks might break. But there had to be enough friction to strike the head. He pressed. His body convulsed with a sudden shudder. The matchsticks snapped.

He groaned but couldn't curse through his sealed mouth.

The matches were still in his grip, just broken partway down. He realized his feet and legs were no longer cold. He felt nothing at all below his belly.

He dragged the matches across the metal.

CHAPTER 29

They caught.

He touched the flame to the coal dust and it burst to life. The hungry fire spread readily to the crumbles and then to the lumps. Soon a proper fire was going in the furnace. He leaned close to the open door and let the life-saving heat wash out over him.

Once he was properly warm, Luke draped his buffalo coat over the window to stop snow falling inside. The metal interior of the locomotive cab held the furnace heat fairly well. He was almost comfortable. First the ice melted from him, then his clothes dried.

Now that he wasn't in danger of immediate death, he needed a plan.

He closed his eyes and leaned toward the firebox, letting more warmth seep into him. He dozed, waking every so often to shove more of the coal on the edges into the center where the fire burned.

The fire would not last forever. Only until dawn perhaps. While there were loose piles of coal collected in the corners of the locomotive cab, thrown there from the tender during the derailment, there wasn't enough to keep a decent fire going for more than several hours. He'd have to make the most out of the time he had.

When he'd thawed and dozed, he slid past the buffalo coat and crawled out of the window. The sun was coming up pale and yellow over the edges of the horizon on the east. It was slightly warmer than it had been during the night, but still bitter cold.

It had stopped snowing, so he took the robe, which now stank of smoke, and put it on. He set out to locate the dead man he'd found last night. The snowfall had obliterated everything. He paused for a moment, studying the mountains rising above him.

Luck was with him. The dawn was still new enough that darkness clung in the valleys and hollows. And there, up on the mountainside, he saw the winking yellow light of a fire.

He marked the place in his mind. He'd have no trail of snowshoes to track. He'd have to use dead reckoning. He trudged toward the spot where he thought he'd last seen the dead man and began looking in the snow.

The physical exercise kept him warm enough, and he soon found the body before the cold had gotten a real grip on him. The man was stiff as a board and his ears and back of his neck showed blue-black with lividity. Luke stooped and grabbed his ankles like the handles of a wheelbarrow and began dragging him.

It was brutally hard work, but it kept him warm. Once he got back to his hole, he climbed back down and spread his coat over the opening again. When he was sure the coal fire was still going in the furnace, he took several clumps of snow and ate them.

That way of getting water would have been ill-advised if he hadn't been close to an external source of warmth.

Eating snow for the moisture could cool a man's core by several degrees and hasten death.

After he'd replenished himself as best he could, he crawled out and began stripping the body. He had to wrench a kneecap out of place and break an arm at the elbow to get the man's clothes off. When he was done, he laid the garments next to the furnace to thaw.

He used the last of the coal to stoke the fire and waited for the clothes to dry. After a little while, he methodically began dressing for his journey. He wasted nothing. Every bit of covering could be the difference between life or death. It would be a race against the cold.

He layered the dead man's clothes over his own. When Luke had gone back for the body, he'd realized the man was indeed the fireman and not the engineer. On his first look, he'd failed to notice the long leather protective apron the man wore. That would be helpful on his journey.

He doubled his socks. Doubled his long johns. Doubled his shirts and then put on the heavy leather apron. Over that the buffalo coat. For weapons, he only had the Remington, fifteen extra shells, and his knife. He'd done more with less, he reckoned.

He'd have to keep his hands inside his coat as much as possible. He had brought gloves, but they'd been placed inside his warbag.

His life, or at the very least a few fingers and toes, absolutely depended on how quickly he made it to town. He'd find the track and follow it up the mountain. He figured another five miles. If a storm didn't come, he thought he'd make it.

He knew that once the train didn't arrive, search parties would be sent out. There was a possibility he'd meet them on the tracks. He couldn't afford to dawdle, but he felt good about his chances.

When he climbed out of the locomotive, he saw storm clouds piling up against the mountaintops above the valley.

Walking got easier once he made it past the avalanche and onto the track. The snow was knee deep here, and the ground relatively flat. It turned out the train had been much closer to Cedar Falls than Luke had first realized.

He came up over a slight rise in the saddle between two granite cliffs and saw the town below him. He breathed in sharply. The place looked in ruins. Smoke hung in a haze above charred, burned-out buildings. Timbers and joists leaned drunkenly, like blackened skeletons. Mounds of soot and ash stood out in sharp contrast to the snow.

The scent of fire and gunsmoke hung in the air. Here and there lonely, isolated buildings stood untouched by whatever conflagration had ripped through the mining town. Those structures were few and far between.

Goldsmith's come full circle in his mind, Luke realized. *He's bringing Sherman's March to the frontier.*

He was now convinced the explosion he'd heard during the train ambush had been set off by Goldsmith. Maybe a few owlhoots would dynamite tracks or a bridge to derail a train, but only a lunatic like Goldsmith would take the time to burn a whole damn town.

Luke studied the scene below him, soaking it in. Cedar Falls hadn't been large. Its boom had been relatively small. Built next to the rail line, it had boasted only one main street and no more than ten or twelve buildings. It wasn't as small as Craig's Fork, but it had never been close to the population of Golgotha Rock. He guessed it had held maybe a hundred full-time citizens with up to three or four times that number on mine paydays.

No one moved among the ruins and debris. No smoke curled from the two remaining homesteads to indicate survivors huddled around stoves for warmth. No lost children or stunned witnesses to the apocalypse wandered the street searching for loved ones. All was still. All was silent.

Cedar Falls was a graveyard. The bitter cold kept the lingering smoke close to the ground instead of letting it trail up into the gunmetal gray sky. The quiet was uncanny. Steeling himself for what he feared he'd find, Luke began walking.

Behind the clouds the weak, reddish-yellow smear of the sun was sliding toward the horizon and twilight. Luke had spent most of the day just thawing out and warming up and then getting here. With evening would come another killing cold. Luke could not afford to be caught without shelter and heat, or the winter would kill him long before he ever faced Goldsmith.

Closer to the town, he began coming across footprints. Fresh snowfall had filled the indentations in somewhat, but hadn't yet obliterated them. He found a line of snowshoe tracks coming out of the woods from the direction of a now frozen stream and going toward the town.

He followed them in closer and found himself not approaching by the main road, but coming up behind the line of buildings running perpendicular to the small train platform. It was impossible to tell how many men with snowshoes had begun this approach, but Luke was willing to bet one of them was Goldsmith.

The water tower beside the track had been shot to hell. A coal bin had been placed beneath it to keep the water unfrozen. The dozens of bullet holes had caused water to spill out and freeze in a pond around the tower. The ice gleamed a shade of blue much different from the snow.

There was the body of a railway worker frozen in the floored area. The face of the corpse was black, and the fingers, curled into claws and reaching upward, looked brittle as glass. Blood had pumped from the back of his head and pooled around him. It formed a scarlet and pink halo in the ice.

Luke noticed something sticking out from under the corpse. It looked like the finger of a glove. He reached down and tried to tug it free, but it was stuck. Grimacing, Luke tugged up on the dead man's coat until the body moved a little. He pulled out a pair of gloves the man probably had dropped when he died.

Those gloves might save Luke's fingers . . . and his fingers might save his life.

Luke skirted the frozen lake, eyes searching the burned-out buildings and charred ruins. He needed to keep the gloves on because of the cold, but he drew the Remington. The metallic click of the hammer going back was unnaturally loud.

He turned slowly, scanning the rubble. His breath sounded loud in the unnatural stillness. It formed silvery clouds in front of his face. The air tasted of ash. He stalked forward, coming down the narrow alley between two buildings. He looked through the rib cage of struts and charred timber.

Two corpses lay on the floor of the building to the left. By the size difference, he guessed a man and woman.

They'd died in each other's arms. Their flesh and hair had burned away, leaving grinning teeth exposed.

He came out on the main street. A few feet away a flash of color caught his eye. A woman in a red dress that would only have ever been worn by a saloon girl lay facedown in the snow. Raw meat and bone fragments showed in the little mounds the bullet wounds had made of her flesh. She was stiff as old stone.

He waited, but after a short time he felt himself starting to shiver and had to get moving again. He wandered like a ghost through the charred wreckage, taking note of the eternally quiet bodies. Everywhere was the stink of old smoke.

Suddenly, from across the town, he heard the sound of a door slamming shut. The sound was so abrupt and unexpected it caused Luke to jump as if he'd been attacked. His finger tightened on the trigger in automatic response, but he was too experienced to accidentally trigger the weapon.

Using the jagged remnants of walls and collapsed roofs for cover, Luke edged his way toward the far side of town from which he'd heard the sound. There, a short distance from where the livery stable's corral stood, was a log homestead. A dead man in a red flannel shirt was sprawled, frozen, across a wood pile.

Eyeing the way the cabin windows faced, Luke slipped forward at an angle. If there were survivors, they'd probably shoot first and ask questions later. He didn't blame them. If it was Goldsmith or any men low enough to ride with him, then Luke could expect nothing but death. Which he was ready to return.

He set his feet down carefully, not wanting the sound of his boots pushing through the snow crust to carry. Step, step, stop. Listen. Wait. Step, step, stop. He stalked the occupants of the homestead the way a cougar does its prey. As he drew closer, he thought he heard the sound of a man's voice. Then laughter.

At least two then.

He remembered the battle at the trading post. There were similarities here. He needed to make sure what kind of people he was dealing with. The last thing he wanted to do was bring more pain and violence to this town. Or what was left of it.

He continued stalking forward.

Coming up to the homestead, he put his back against a wall and waited. Over his head icicles the size of Bowie knives hung like stalactites from the eaves. Luke's nose burned from the cold. First chance he got, he needed to find something to cover his face. Carefully, he inched his way toward a glass window.

He paused, listening.

"The colonel will be back by nightfall," one of the voices said.

"So what?" a second voice answered. Luke could tell he was drunk. "Horses aren't going to help us in this weather. That crazy hombre burned down the town we have to hole up in for the winter. We ain't riding no damn horses past that avalanche, either. Leastwise not until spring."

"Colonel will think of something."

"To hell with that! I ain't no soldier boy like you. I don't believe just because he was some damn big deal officer that he's always right!"

Maybe they'll kill each other and save me the trouble, Luke thought.

"Well," the first voice said, "either way he's coming. When he does, you can just give him your opinion to his face."

"To hell with that," the second voice snapped. "It won't be just him coming. He'll be bringing those outlaw Crow with him."

"So?"

"So they're going to want the girl, and there's five of them."

"I reckon we better all have our fun before then," the other man said with a crude laugh.

"Hell yeah, we should!"

"Then we should kill her so they can't get none."

This declaration came out in a hacking guffaw. A feminine voice began sobbing, her terror obvious.

Luke eased a slow, even breath out through his nose. He had to act.

CHAPTER 30

Luke had found that there were several types of outlaws. Owlhoots like the James-Younger gang for example, were dangerous, no doubt about that. They stole at the point of a gun, and if you crossed them at the wrong moment, you could wind up in a pine box. But they held to their own sense of ethics, and would offer no insult to a woman.

They were criminals, but not degenerates. They didn't torture, they avoided bloodshed, and they did not rape. They needed to be brought to justice, but they were not despicable human beings. Quite a few outlaws were like that. Often the horse thieves and cattle rustlers operated under this rough code.

Then there were the marauders.

Marauders were remnants of a frontier before the war. They came out of a hundred years of lawless borderlands. Their raids were like guerrilla strikes that left all in their path slaughtered. They killed with callous impunity and sadistic pleasure. Rape was as much the goal as gold. They sold their victims, Mexican, Indian, or white, into the slave trade south of the border.

Marauders were men who'd come to the wilderness and lost their humanity. Since the end of the war and the push of the railroads, those sorts had diminished even as hostile natives had also been reduced. But they were far from gone.

Luke had seen more than enough of varmints like that in his quest to extinguish the evil wolves plaguing decent folks. But he was hardened to his work. He knew it was common among the men he hunted. It was, in part, integral to why he hunted them in the first place. The callous abuse of women made him see red.

He risked a glance through the window. Seething hate warmed his body. The woman wasn't old enough to be called a woman. She was a girl. Dressed in only a gingham dress, she shivered as she fed kindling into a potbellied stove. Her arms were purple and black, her young face swollen. There were bite marks on her neck. And she was cold, shaking with it.

Two men in buffalo robe coats watched her, passing a jug of what Luke assumed was corn whiskey back and forth. He didn't recognize them from Goldsmith's gang. He was pretty sure he'd killed or scattered most of those men. Goldsmith had recruited more scum.

He forced himself to stay calm and take stock of the situation. He decided quickly that the cabin served as some kind of supply cache for Goldsmith. Barrels and crates of dry goods were stacked along a back wall. Rows of rifles in various calibers had been put together in piles like Indian wickiups. Piles of furs sat on the floor. There were kegs of beer and numerous liquor bottles. As far as Luke could tell, it seemed the loot from the town had been stored here.

Pulling back from the window, he leaned against the wall. Given the amount of supplies, these two had to be rear guards. That meant Goldsmith could be returning, possibly very soon, with whatever constituted the rest of his outfit.

The girl cried out. Luke heard the men's rough laughter. He closed his eyes. He wasn't going to leave her. He drew the Remington and cocked it. Without bothering to disguise the sound of his footsteps through the snow, he tromped around to the front door. Placing the pistol behind his leg, he pounded on the door with his other hand.

"Open up, damn it!" he hollered. "I got word from Goldsmith."

There was a long, pregnant pause, followed by the sounds of heavy boots on the floorboards. Luke pounded the door again.

"Hurry the hell up!"

The footsteps stopped at the door. The wooden dowel handle that worked the sliding bolt slammed backward and the heavy door swung open. In the doorway stood a big man, well over six feet. Even in the bulky buffalo robe coat it was easy to tell he weighed more than two hundred and fifty pounds. His skin was a burnt copper that, along with his beardless face, suggested he bore a lot of Indian blood. His eyes, red-veined and muddy brown, opened wide in surprise when he saw Luke standing in front of the cabin.

Luke lifted the Remington from behind his leg and shot him in the face.

Time slowed down for Luke Jensen.

The outlaw jerked backward. The Remington boomed again. The girl screamed. The shriek rang out, high and clear as a musical note.

The body twisted as it fell, and as Luke came into the homestead he stepped over the bloody corpse. His head moved on a swivel, eyes hunting, the barrel of the .45

tracking. He caught a flash of motion and turned. The second man lunged for a .30 caliber Sharps rifle lying on a butcher block table.

This outlaw was also dressed in a buffalo robe coat but was as different as night and day from the first man, tall and cadaverously thin. His scraggly beard and long greasy hair were both the bright orange-red of the Irish.

His hand closed around the rifle's stock. Luke thumbed back the hammer and carefully aimed down the barrel of the Remington. The man had the Sharps in both hands now. He turned, swinging the rifle to bear.

Luke squeezed the trigger. The man grunted as the gun boomed. Again the girl screamed. Luke cocked the pistol. The man, bleeding heavily from the shoulder just above his heart, grabbed the crying girl and hauled her to her feet in front of him. He produced an ugly looking, bone-handled Bowie knife with a long, wide blade.

"Back off!" he shouted. His teeth were black with rot.

The edge of the knife pressed into the girl's throat. She stared at Luke with terrified eyes. Tears rolled down her cheeks and cooled on her skin in the cold. Luke aimed the Remington at the man.

"Put it down or I'll bleed the little slut like a pig," the man warned.

He pressed harder and the knife blade opened a thin line of blood on her throat. The girl gasped. Luke remained silent. The Remington held steady.

"I said drop it!" the man yelled.

Luke shook his head. He stepped forward.

"No," he said. "You kill that girl, I shoot you half a second later. Her death is your death."

"I'll kill her!"

"You'll kill us both if I put down my pistol. Since she dies either way, I don't aim to join her."

Luke stepped forward.

"Stay back!"

Luke stopped.

"What's it going to be?" he asked. "You can still live."

"I'll kill her!"

Luke stepped forward.

"You already said that," he pointed out. "You know you'll die. This cabin where you want to die?"

The outlaw said nothing. He looked like a man trying to cipher out a difficult arithmetic problem but finding himself unable to add all the numbers up.

"Is . . . this . . . where . . . you . . . want . . . to . . . die?" Luke shouted.

The man shoved the girl forward. Crying out, she stumbled forward. Smooth as a dance partner, Luke sidestepped and caught her body with his left arm. The man dug at the butt of a Hopkins & Allen revolver stuck in his belt.

His frantic hand clawed at the handle. He got his grip on it and began yanking it clear of his pants. His frightened eyes never left Luke as he drew down. The wound in his shoulder pulsed, his racing heart pumping blood out in a scarlet waterfall.

"To hell with you!" the man shouted.

The pistol was almost out. Luke squeezed his trigger twice. The man wrenched backward, the pistol tumbling from his hands. The two .45 caliber bullets struck, one atop the other, directly in the middle of the man's sunken chest.

He struck the table as he fell and sent it skidding backward. Finding no purchase, the outlaw fumbled on the floor. Blood rushed out in a lake as the man quivered his last, but the temperature was so cold it began congealing rapidly.

Luke looked down at the girl he held.

"You better get some warm clothes on," he told her.

She fainted.

Luke looked nervously out the window.

It got dark early in the high country this deep into winter. Already the sky was turning black as the twilight deepened. He watched the woods, searching the tree line for any sign of movement. He had no idea from which direction Goldsmith would make his approach.

He glanced back at the girl. He'd covered her in blankets and homespun quilts and had also stoked the stove thoroughly. After he'd gotten it open, he'd taken the time to bring in two days' worth of wood for the stove. He was vulnerable when he left the cabin and didn't want to be outside any more than he had to.

If Goldsmith returned to a chimney puffing smoke, he'd just assume it was his men inside and make his approach. If he saw Luke out there chopping wood then everything changed, and not in the bounty hunter's favor. He'd dragged the bodies out and covered them with snow. They'd keep fine under a fresh blanket of white.

He needed the girl to wake up so he could question her.

The situation was frustrating. She seemed to be doing nothing more than sleeping peacefully, but she also didn't stir. She potentially had information that could help him, but he understood the trauma she'd been through.

He discovered a fire-blackened cook pot and when he lifted the lid he'd found son-of-a-gun stew. The dish was a cowboy staple. It wasn't exactly fine dining, he reflected, but it was nourishing. He put it on the stove and began searching for plates and utensils.

He found a tin plate and a fork, took them to the stove and began stirring the stew before dishing some out.

Behind him, floorboards creaked.

He stiffened, the hair on the back of his neck lifting. He smelled woodsmoke and musty dust. Setting down the ladle and plate, he slowly turned.

The bedding he'd prepared for the girl was empty. It lay silent on the floor like a rumpled nest. The girl was gone.

He heard the gentle scuff of a bare foot on the wooden boards. He turned, stomach sinking at the strange potential of the situation.

She stood next to the butcher block table with her back to one of the windows. She was silhouetted by the uncertain gray light. Her hair hung in a tangled curtain before her face. Her eyes burned fever bright out from behind the dirty strands. Her skinny arms dangled loose as ropes down by her sides.

In her hands she held the dead outlaw's Bowie knife.

"Hey there," he said. He kept his voice gentle. "My name's Luke. I'm not with those men—"

The girl threw back her head, exposing heavily bruised elfin features. She howled an anguished cry that startled Luke so badly he took a step back.

"Easy," he said. Had the torment snapped the girl's mind?

The cry cut off, and the girl studied him. He saw nothing but pain in her blue eyes, no trace of humanity or comprehension. She lifted the knife.

The blade looked ridiculously large in her small hands, like a knight's sword or heavy cavalry saber. It gleamed dully in the gloomy light seeping in through the window.

"I'm not here to hurt you—" Luke began.

The girl screeched again, the noise as piercing as nails on a chalkboard. She launched herself at Luke, knife raised over her head.

"Easy!" he shouted.

He jumped backward, avoiding her maniac slash. She grunted in primal fury and swung the blade at him. He danced to one side, but this time the tip managed to catch and rip the front of the bulky coat he wore. The outlaw had been greasy and grime covered, but he'd kept his blade well maintained and razor sharp.

"Hey!"

Drawing back her thin arm, the girl thrust wildly with the knife as she leaped at Luke. He jumped backward, but his heel caught on a pile of animal hides.

His arms windmilled almost comically as he nearly toppled and fought to keep his balance. Cat-quick, she sprang at him and he was forced to jerk his head away or lose an eye.

Already off balance, he fell and landed hard on his back. The girl sprang, landing on his chest and knocking the wind from him. Her arm scythed down as she plunged the knife toward his throat.

His gloved hand caught her arm at the wrist and held it in a vise-like grip. The girl spat, eyes burning, and writhed atop him as if struck by lightning.

Luke couldn't believe her strength in the clutches of her delirium. His free hand came up, found her waist, and shoved hard as he jerked himself onto his side to unseat her. She shrieked in rage. He shoved and she tumbled away.

Scrambling to his feet, he looked around for a rope or anything he could use to restrain her. Yowling like a wild-cat, she sprang at him, relentless. He stumbled backward, narrowly avoiding having his upheld hand sliced by the knife.

"Easy! Take it easy! I don't want to hurt you!"

Dancing sideways, he put the butcher-block table between himself and her. He needed a plan to constrain her without hurting her. She flung herself around one side of the table, and he moved to the other.

His dodge took him past the window. Glass shattered. The shock wave of a bullet so large it felt like a slap across his face passed in front of him. The report of a heavy caliber rifle rolled down across the snow.

CHAPTER 31

Luke stumbled back in surprise. The sound of the rifle had been massive, he suspected a .50 caliber buffalo gun. That was powerful enough to punch holes even in the logs forming the homestead, depending on the range. He threw himself flat and saw the girl lunge toward him.

She darted, quick as a snake striking, around the table, stabbing viciously with the knife. More rifles erupted outside and bullets smacked into the homestead walls and punched out the window glass. The front door was transformed into a splintered sieve as a dozen bullets cracked through it. In a fit of adrenaline, Luke shoved the butcher block into the girl's path.

The heavy table struck the girl and the impact threw her to the floor. Luke scrambled around the corner and dived on her before she could recover. He landed hard on top of her and she cried out. He saw one hand still wrapped around the bone handle of the knife.

He caught her wrist and slammed her hand into the floor before she could slash at him again. The girl snarled, feral, but clung to the weapon. He did it again. More bullets ripped through the air above them. The girl released the knife and sobbed in emotional anguish, her killing rage abruptly broken.

The Bowie knife slid across the floor and clattered against the wall. Beneath Luke, the girl lay motionless, crying. He felt sickened by the need to use physical force with her. But as more bullets riddled the homestead, he realized he had bigger problems.

"I'm not with them!" he said in the girl's ear. "I don't want to hurt you. The men who hurt you are back, they're trying to kill us. I won't let them, but I can't do that if you keep trying to kill me, damn it!"

The girl stopped crying. She lay beneath him, still and silent.

"Do you understand?" Luke asked.

Slowly, the girl nodded.

Luke breathed a sigh of relief and realized the firing had stopped.

He frowned. The sudden silence could mean Goldsmith and his men were making their approach. He had to move quickly. He looked at the girl. He couldn't be sure if she was playing possum or not. He might get up only to find her trying to kill him again as soon as his back was turned.

He had to do something, though. Standing still wasn't an option. Act or die.

"Don't try and kill me," he warned.

Keeping low, he made his way toward the window. He approached it at an angle to avoid exposing himself and scanned the outside. He saw nothing. Still moving in a crouch, he crossed to the second window and repeated his look.

He saw one of Goldsmith's gang finish a sprint out of the tree line by throwing himself behind the charred timber of a burned-out building. Luke ducked back quickly.

"Get against the back wall and lay down," he told the girl.

He edged cautiously toward the front door. Gray-blue streams of light slanted through the bullet-riddled wood. He dropped to one knee beside the door and cracked it open.

Immediately, a barrage of bullets hammered the door. Wood planks cracked as if splintered by axes. Lead slugs flew through the homestead. Bullets cracked glass and crockery and rattled off the potbellied stove to hammer into the huge collection of loot stuffed into the one-room building.

Throwing himself belly down, Luke kicked the door shut. He looked around for the girl, worried that she'd take the interruption as a chance to knife him in the back. He found her where he'd told her to go, huddled in a fetal position against the back wall. There were bullet holes in the logs only a foot above her. She trembled violently and had begun sobbing again.

White hot rage rekindled in Luke's breast as he saw the terrified girl.

"This ends *now*," he vowed.

No matter what, he promised himself, *I will kill Neville Goldsmith today. No matter what it takes, I will finish this.*

"It's okay, honey," he told the girl. He crawled across the floor toward her. "I'll get you out of here."

Reaching the butcher-block table, he used his feet to turn it over. It landed on the floor with a loud, sharp clatter. Standing on its side, it made a four-inch thick bulwark. Still crawling, he put his shoulder against it and pushed it right up to the girl.

Bullets knifed through the chill air above him. Now he

heard men shouting outside, although he couldn't make out the words over the gunfire. They were going to rush the homestead. Soon, if not immediately.

Desperation drove him to his knees even though it exposed him to danger from stray rounds. Ignoring the pain and weariness that coursed through his entire body, he began throwing sacks of flour and meal in front of the overturned table. When he had a good stack of them, he rolled heavy casks and kegs in front to add to the barrier.

Running footfalls crunched through the snow outside. Popping up, he brought the Remington out and risked a look through one of the windows. He recognized one of Goldsmith's men by the long facial scar that split his beard along the jaw. The man ran toward the cabin, holding a Winchester across his body. Their eyes met and the man cursed. He tried to bring the rifle around into play.

Luke shot him and then threw himself down, having caught a glimpse of the outlaw going backward as the slug plowed into his chest. Bullets struck the homestead in a wave from that side. A random keg of beer was struck several times and began spurting its contents onto the floor.

Luke holstered his pistol and shouted, "I need your help, girl!"

Without waiting for a reply, he swept up several of the gang's stolen rifles and matching boxes of ammunition. He tossed them over his makeshift fortress.

"Load those as fast as you can," he ordered.

There was no question in his mind that a girl raised on the frontier would know exactly how to load and handle a firearm. The girl had stopped crying, and while she didn't answer him, he heard the unmistakable sounds of weapons being loaded.

Taking a .10 gauge, he snapped it open and loaded two rounds before putting fistfuls of shells into his pocket. He left two out on the floor next to where he crouched. Raising the shotgun, he cocked the hammers and pulled the twin triggers one after the other.

The shot punched holes through the door large as fists and sailed out into the deepening twilight. It was like knocking a window into a wall. Luke peered outside as he reloaded the .10 gauge. Just as he feared, he saw men darting toward the cabin. As he snapped the shotgun closed, the top of the door blew apart as a .50 caliber round punched through it. The report echoed like a thunderclap.

He'd made his hasty fighting position at an angle to the door so the round was not only high, but off to his right. That was good. He felt good about his defense in general but had no real illusion about it stopping a .50 caliber slug.

"Keep loading," he told the girl. "And tell me your name," he added.

She stopped feeding bullets into an Army Colt and raised her head to look over the top of the makeshift fortress. When she gazed at him, her brown eyes were clear of the madness he'd seen gripping them earlier. He hoped they stayed that way. When she spoke her voice was slow, solemn.

"Clara Wheeler," she said.

"Nice to meet you, Clara," he replied. "I'm Luke Jensen."

He didn't have time to say anything else. A tall, hatchet-faced and pockmarked outlaw Luke recognized but had never spoken to appeared in the window. Luke shifted, swinging the shotgun up. The man thrust his own Schofield pistol through the fangs of broken glass. Luke pulled one of the triggers before the outlaw could fire. The man's face disappeared in a smear of scarlet blood and shattered bone.

He fell away, and Luke shifted. A second outlaw appeared at the window just as the door was kicked in. There was no time to draw and fire. Luke triggered the second barrel and the buckshot caught the man coming through the door in the belly. He collapsed forward on himself even as Luke dropped the shotgun and threw himself behind the crude bulwark.

The table jerked under the impact of a .45 caliber slug and the crack of the pistol seemed insignificant after the brutal booms of the shotgun. Luke raised the Army Colt and thumbed back the hammer.

He fired once in the general direction of the other window to provide cover then popped up as he worked the single action again. The outlaw was swinging back into the window from his instinctive duck. The barrel of his pistol thrust toward Luke.

Luke fired a split second before the man, and a red hole appeared in the outlaw's neck. Blood sprayed as the bullet punched its way clear through and formed a crimson halo behind his ear. The acrid stench of burned powder filled Luke's nose. Gunsmoke hung in a haze.

The body of the outlaw who'd charged into the cabin had fallen in such a way that the front door was pinned open. Luke had an unimpeded view out the doorway.

He saw a muzzle flash as a heavy rifle slug buzzed into the room, followed hard by the deep-throated *crack* of the rifle.

"Give me the Sharps!" he said. His voice was tight with strain.

He reached back without looking and the .30 caliber

rifle was thrust into his hand. He swung it up to his shoulder and cocked it.

"Get flat!" he ordered.

Sighting in on where he'd spotted the muzzle flash, he fired. He ducked low as the shooter returned fire. A cask of meal exploded like a bomb, sending the foodstuff into the air like confetti. He scrambled around to another spot and cocked the Sharps again. He knew the inside of the cabin was dark to those looking inside and that his own muzzle flash would stand out like a lightning bolt. He couldn't fire from the same position twice.

A man armed with a Winchester sprinted out of the woods and flung himself down behind some burned timber beams just as Luke drew a bead. Luke froze, adjusting his aim. He could only guess how many men Goldsmith had left after the battle and fire in the hollow outside Golgotha Rock. Couldn't be a lot. Luke had sent a whole bunch of them across the divide.

Then Goldsmith yelled.

"You're done now, Jensen," he shouted.

Luke didn't bother answering. He was too busy drawing a bead on the man with the Winchester. An uneasy feeling told him not to take the shot, however. He thought maybe the sniper was using him to flush Luke's location out. He'd take the shot on the outlaw and then the marksmen would finish him. He'd seen Confederate sharpshooters using the same trick during the war.

"I don't know how the hell you survived that train wreck," Goldsmith continued, "but I'm going to finish you now!"

Luke ignored him. The colonel hoped he'd answer back and give the Sharps .50 caliber man an indication of where he was. Luke didn't plan on making it that easy for them.

He shifted. The girl was crying again. His breath frosted in a silver plume in front of his face, and it was only then that he noticed the potbellied stove had gone out.

"Put on more coats," he told the girl. "The fire has gone out."

Before she could answer, Luke heard another rush of footsteps crunching through the snow outside. He swung the .30 caliber Sharps around. He'd have to throw himself flat immediately after pulling the trigger or the sharpshooter would finish him.

Instead of a human silhouette however, what came through the window was a lit lantern. The thing sailed in and cracked open with a crash. Kerosene spilled, soaking everything within range of the splash. The flame from the wick flickered amid the busted glass, then caught.

Yellow flames sprang up, hungrily consuming everything they touched. Luke swore. The girl had gone silent.

Outside Goldsmith cackled like a madman.

CHAPTER 32

"Clara!" Luke yelled.

"What?"

He spun around to face her. He was a little surprised that she had actually answered him. Behind him, yellow flames began leaping toward piles of goods and climbing the wall. The fire spread rapidly. Even if it meant his death, he enjoyed the warm weight of it on his back. He took a fresh Sharps from the pile of weapons Clara had loaded.

The girl looked at him with wide eyes. She was scared but eerily calm. Like a person who knew better than to even struggle. Like a bird with a broken wing looking at a snake. This obvious fatalism only served to motivate him more to save her.

To save her, he was going to have to put her in danger.

Taking up a Colt Navy, he cocked the .36 and handed it to her. She took it from him and looked down at the pistol, then back up at him. He cupped her under the chin with one hand and stared into her eyes.

"Listen to me well," he said.

Clara nodded.

"I'm going to get into position," he told her. "When I

give you the nod, you fire the pistol over the top of the table. But as soon as you pull the trigger you have to drop straight down. Straight down, do you understand? Straight down."

Again she nodded.

"Just shoot toward the door," he said. "Don't worry about hitting anything. Just fire and drop. Can you do that?"

Again she nodded.

"Say it."

"Fire and drop," she recited. "Fire and drop."

"That's a good girl," he said.

Hurriedly he took up a position toward the middle of the overturned table. Directly to his front was the crack between two barrels. Through the space he could see out the door. The room was filling with smoke. It'd kill them soon enough. Smoke poured out the window on the side the fire burned and more smoke had begun migrating toward the open door.

They had to hurry or soon their vision would be so obscured by smoke he couldn't hope to shoot with accuracy. He cocked the Sharps and released his breath. The stock of the rifle settled into the pocket of his shoulder, and his cheek formed a tight bond with the smooth wood.

He kept both eyes open but the right one centered on the rifle sights. It would be instinct shooting, pure reflex and automatic coordination. He was lethal with that type of shooting with his Remington. He felt confident of his ability to do it with a Winchester or shotgun. But the Sharps was a different beast, a different sort of marksmanship. He clenched his teeth.

Nothing to it, he thought, *but to do it.*

"Okay, Clara," he whispered. "Fire."

Clara popped up out of her crouch at the opposite end of the table and fired the cap-and-ball pistol she held in both hands. The .36 caliber handgun banged. The recoil threw her arms upward and she was already spinning back like a dancer on the stage.

The cannon-sized muzzle flash of the sharpshooter's .50 caliber Sharps flared brilliant from just above a snow-covered log about seventy-five yards out in front of the homestead. Mind blank, lungs empty, Luke shifted, sighted, squeezed the smooth metal curve of his rifle.

The recoil pushed smoothly back. Gunsmoke plumed from the barrel. The fire had reached the roof and began eating its way across. Out in the snow, the dark outline of a figure fell over the log and shuddered in a spastic tumble. Luke saw a long rifle, what the Indians who'd interacted with the Hudson Bay Company trappers had called a *long carbine* thirty or forty years earlier.

The .50 caliber Sharps bounced off the front of the log and plunged into the snow drift on the other side. A dead man in a wide-brimmed black hat and buffalo robe coat sprawled over the log. Even from almost one hundred yards away, Luke saw the dark sheen of his blood as it pumped out on the snow.

"Hell, yes!" he shouted.

Remembering the girl, he turned quickly, eyes frantically searching for her. She sat huddled in the corner against the back wall. She still had the Colt Navy in her hands. The barrel was more or less pointed at him. He couldn't see her eyes because her unbound hair had fallen across her eyes.

She'd cocked the pistol, he saw.

"Clara?"

He spoke softly despite the spreading fire. He kept his voice calm and tried to find her eyes.

"They hurt me," she told him. Her voice came out dull. Her expression was slack. He couldn't read what emotions she might be feeling.

"Honey, there are still men out there. I will stop them from hurting you again." He lowered the Sharps to the floor. "I'm not with them."

In a bit of random weirdness, he noticed that the sleeve of the coat she'd climbed into was puckered just above the shoulder. Even a quarter-inch closer and the .50 caliber round would have ripped her arm from her body and she'd have bled out before he could save her.

"Clara?"

The girl lifted the Colt.

Bundled up as he was, a fast draw was impossible. All Luke could do was grasp for the rifle he'd laid down. He was slower than the girl by a long, slow country mile. She lifted the pistol in both hands, using both of her thumbs to cock the hammer on the cap-and-ball Colt, the barrel lifting until the dark hole of the muzzle filled his vision.

He felt the stock of the Sharps rifle beneath his fingers and he closed his hand around it. He saw Clara's knuckles whiten as she pulled the trigger. Her hair fell back and he saw her eyes blazing with rage and hate.

This is how I die? he had time to think before the gun went off.

He winced backward as the weapon exploded inches away from him. He felt the heat of the muzzle flash. A sudden ringing erupted in his ears, and all other sound faded away instantly. He blinked. Realized he was alive.

Somehow the girl had missed him from an arm's length away.

She lowered the pistol and screamed at him. He couldn't make out her words over the ringing in his ears. But the madness was gone from her eyes and she was shouting at him. Time seemed to slow, to lengthen out like salt water taffy as his brain spun through scenarios to explain what was happening.

Then, like a roulette wheel spinning to a stop on the number a gambler had picked, he understood. His brain snapped into focus and time returned. Dropping the Sharps, he reached out and took the pistol from Clara's hand. The ringing receded into the background. Spinning, he thrust the pistol over the table side, scanning for targets.

A new outlaw leaned heavily against the doorframe. His pistol hung at his side from a limp arm. His free hand had found the wound in his chest just to the right of his heart, the wound that Clara had given him, and he was looking at the fresh blood staining his fingers.

Luke shot him again.

The bullet caught the man just to the left of the first wound and he flopped backward out the door. The fire had reached the other side of the one-room homestead now. Luke saw a line of fire eat its way toward a huge pile of stored ammunition. The rounds would start cooking off in the heat any minute. When that happened, this place would become so lethal with buzzing rounds that their death was assured.

Luke vaulted over the table, bounced off a crate, and rolled away from the door. He took it as a good sign when no one fired at him. Perhaps there was hope. On hands and knees, he threw his shoulder against a barrel containing something he didn't have time to identify.

He strained against its weight, grunting wildly with the effort. The barrel slid across the floor, and he rammed it up against the wall beneath the window on the side of the room not totally engulfed in fire.

"Clara!" he shouted.

Smoke billowed around him. It seared his lungs, and he began coughing violently. Heat blasted into him as the fire consumed everything in its path, sounding like a rushing locomotive in his ears. He couldn't see the girl any longer.

Using dead reckoning, he crawled back toward the girl.

"Clara!"

His head came up hard against something unforgiving and stopped cold. He felt like he'd been bludgeoned with an axe handle. He touched the object and realized it was the heavy butcher block table. When he ran his fingers across it, he felt dozens of pockmarks where bullets had slammed into its surface.

He couldn't see or hear the girl.

Grasping the edge of the table with both hands, Luke heaved. It grated across the floorboards as he shoved it clear. Once he could slip past it, he crawled behind his makeshift defenses. Heat from the fire eating up the ceiling pushed down on him like the hand of Satan.

"Clara!"

"Luke!"

Coughing, he reached through the smoke and grabbed the girl. She came easily into his arms. Pressing her tightly against his chest, he crawled awkwardly back the way he'd come. He couldn't breathe, his lungs spasmed from the smoke, and he felt light-headed and dizzy. He couldn't allow himself to stop.

Superheated air spilling through the window from inside mixed with the cold air outside and created erratic drafts. The smoke billowed like curtains parting and he saw the barrel he'd shoved against the wall. He pushed Clara toward it.

"Climb!"

She looked at him, eyes blurry. She was slow and sluggish as if she'd swallowed laudanum. He shook her roughly. Her head snapped back and forth like a rag doll, making him feel sick in the pit of his stomach. She needed clean air.

Abandoning his original plan, Luke scooped her up. Using his teeth, he pulled his glove from his right hand and drew the Remington. The skin on his face and scalp tightened so painfully from the heat he thought they might split like the fabric of an overstuffed gunnysack.

Now I know how the witch Hansel and Gretel shoved in the oven felt, he thought.

Some distant, disassociated part of his brain scolded him that this wasn't the time for such silliness, and he realized how much he needed clean air himself. His vision grew black.

Snarling, he swung the Remington, clearing away the last jagged fangs of glass. One-handed, he shoved the limp girl through the window and dropped her into the snow.

"Run!"

He staggered, then coughed wildly. He turned, intending to race out the front door in an attempt to try and draw any remaining fire, but he met only a volcanic wall of heat. He staggered back.

Suddenly the air was alive with bullets cooking off. The fire had reached the ammunition.

Turning, he plunged through the window.

Sailing into the frigid air and landing in the snow was like diving into a pool of cool water. The sensation was bracing, and his sluggish thoughts sped up as wholesome air filled his protesting lungs. Snorting in more air, he looked around for the girl.

To his relief he saw her pushing herself up from the snow a few feet away. He looked around and lifted the Remington. They'd had little choice but to flee the burning building, but it had, as Goldsmith no doubt intended, left them vulnerable once they were outside.

No gunfire erupted from the tree line. No men shouted. He tried remembering how many he'd killed since the attack had begun, but his head was still too cloudy to count. It was possible the gang was finally wiped out.

But he hadn't seen Goldsmith fall.

He helped Clara to her feet. She already looked better. He bent down and spoke in her ear.

"Run," he told her. "Run that way, to the tree line. I'll find the rest of them, if there are any left."

She didn't argue. Nodding once to show she understood, she spun and ran across the snow in the direction Luke had indicated. Satisfied there was little else he could do to help her, Luke made his way toward the front of the homestead.

The building was a blazing inferno now. Smoke gushed from the openings, and the timbers of the roof groaned loudly, threatening to collapse. Flames licked toward the sky and heat pulsed from the conflagration. Unconsciously, Luke held up his free hand toward the searing heat away from his face as he rounded the corner.

Goldsmith stood in front of the building. His eyes shone with near religious fervor as he hungrily watched the fire. The glare of the flames undulated across his scars and reflected off melting snow to create a dome of light in the thick darkness that had settled down during the battle.

The colonel held an Army Colt in one hand, but his arms were spread before the fire like Christ on the Cross. He grinned like a lunatic. Luke lifted the Remington.

"Drop it, Goldsmith!"

Goldsmith's smile grew wider, more frenzied as he rolled his eyes toward Luke.

"I want it all to *burn*," he said, voice coarse as old sandpaper. "The whole world. I want fire to eat it all up until only ash remains."

"I said drop it, damn you!" Luke shouted.

"When I find that little slut you saved," Goldsmith went on as if Luke hadn't spoken, "I'm going to burn her, too." He laughed, a raw, ugly sound. "I like hearing the eyeballs on the little ones pop."

He said the last as if confiding a great secret to a good friend. He faced Luke. His grin threatened to split his head open.

"Drop it or I'll kill you."

Goldsmith cackled. "Pop-pop-pop-pop!"

Furious, Luke stepped forward. He was between Goldsmith and the front of the burning homestead now.

It was all he could do to keep from murdering the man where he stood. He wanted the outlaw to swing. He wanted to be drinking good whiskey with Katey when the executioner yanked back the lever and the trapdoor opened beneath the lunatic's feet.

Goldsmith smirked at him. "Their screams come to me in my dreams. Happy, happy dreams."

The outlaw turned the Colt with a casual flick of his wrist. Both men fired at the same time. The gunshot reports tripped hard, one over the other, in almost perfect concert. Luke grunted as the bullet punched into him. He felt his ribs down low crack, and searing pain exploded through him as the bullet tumbled out from the side and struck the back of his arm.

His gun fell and he staggered.

Goldsmith's right shoulder jerked and blood flew where Luke had pulled his shot high. The impact whipsawed the outlaw's arm back and the man's own pistol flew into the snow as he stumbled. Holding the wounded shoulder in his left hand, Goldsmith glared at Luke wildly.

Luke dropped his uninjured arm toward his belt where he kept his Bowie knife. Roaring, Goldsmith charged. Giving up on the knife, Luke swung hard at the rushing man. His punch glanced off Goldsmith's shoulder, and the man slammed into him.

Fighting wildly, they fell backward into the burning building. Heat enveloped them.

Luke landed on his back. Goldsmith clawed at his face. Luke couldn't get his injured arm to work, and his side screamed with agony where the outlaw's bullet had struck him. White-hot flame shone brightly through the dark, billowing shrouds of black smoke. They were battling in hell.

Goldsmith's fingers found Luke's eyes and gouged. Concentrating on the arm that worked, the bounty hunter reached up and took hold of Goldsmith's ear. With a brutal motion, he squeezed hard then yanked downward.

Goldsmith screamed as his ear tore free from the side of his head. Hot blood gushed out, soaking through the material of Luke's glove and turning it gummy. Overcome with pain, Goldsmith stopped trying to blind Luke and attempted to knock his arm clear instead.

The blow to the inside of Luke's elbow knocked his arm wide. In the intense light of the fire, Luke saw blood spurting wildly from Goldsmith's head where the ear had been. Some of the scarlet flood splattered his upturned face. Directly above the colonel, fire raged. Luke heard the ceiling groan again and knew it was only moments away from collapsing.

Goldsmith snatched his own knife free and tried plunging it down into Luke's throat. Luke bucked hard and swung his good arm up to block the stroke. The material on the sleeve of his coat suddenly burst into flame. Goldsmith's coat was ablaze in the back. The point of the knife came down and sliced into the muscles of Luke's forearm.

He screamed as the knife stabbed through the other side of his arm. Goldsmith yanked it back and forth, trying to free the blade. Luke shoved upward with both knees and twisted. The violent bucking unseated the outlaw. Calling on the last vestiges of desperate strength, Luke snatched his arm clear of Goldsmith.

The knife remained buried in his arm as the hilt broke free of Goldsmith's grasp. The colonel's hair went up like a match head, forming a halo of fire. Forcing his screaming muscles to work, Luke rolled away. Goldsmith shrieked as his pants and the front of his coat caught fire. Shrieked again as he tried to rise. Luke made it to his feet. The sleeve of his coat was fully on fire now. He staggered out the door, body awash with pain.

He stumbled toward a melting drift, the snow near the blaze like slush now, and plunged his burning arm into the mess. The frigid sensation was as welcome as the warm rush of morphine.

Screaming, Goldsmith stumbled out of the homestead. He was on fire from head to toe. He tried to run but tripped after only a few steps. Luke saw the flesh on the unscarred side of his face melt like wax. Though still thrashing, Goldsmith suddenly went silent, and Luke knew the fire had seared his lungs and vocal cords.

The man fell face first into the snow and lay unmoving. Luke watched the flames consume the last of his clothing. Before his eyes, Goldsmith turned from a vile human being into a burned-out cinder.

"I hope there's enough left to collect the bounty . . ."

He sat down heavily. He was exhausted. Exhausted enough to sleep right where he'd settled. He was going to need the girl to pull the knife free of his arm and patch him up. If he was lucky, she would snap again and use it to cut his throat while he slept.

Near delirious, he chuckled.

"It's always something," he muttered. "Nothing can ever be simple."

Nothing but death.

Three weeks later

Katey's fingers strayed idly over the piano keys. She turned back and forth, the stool on which she sat turning with her. It was early yet, and the Velvet Chamber Saloon in Golgotha Rock wasn't doing much business at this hour.

The place would be more crowded later. According to Lippy, the owner and bartender, having Katey here had been good for business. She was surprisingly skilled at the piano, and she was still pretty, even missing a leg. The loss wasn't even that apparent under the long dresses she wore. The customers liked having her around.

Lippy brought over a glass of brandy and set it on the piano. She picked it up, took a sip, and then realized he was still standing there, looking toward the door with a strange expression on his face.

Katey turned on the stool, saw the man standing in the entrance with the late morning light behind him. The floorboards creaked a little as he came in and started across the saloon toward her. He moved stiffly, as if he had bandages wrapped tightly around him, and his right arm was in a black silk sling.

"Luke," she breathed.

Lippy took the glass out of her hand and put it back on the piano before she could drop it.

Katey reached for the crutch leaning against the wall beside her. Luke Jensen lifted his left hand and told her, "Just stay there. I'll come to you."

"The hell with that," Katey said. She grabbed the crutch, stood up, and hurried to meet him.

TURN THE PAGE FOR AN EXCITING PREVIEW!

Johnstone Country. Forecast: Deadly.
Will Tanner is no ordinary lawman.
He's a force of nature. But when he's outnumbered by
rustlers, outgunned by outlaws—and stalked by a killer
fresh out of prison—he's in for the fight of his life . . .

There's a storm brewing . . .

. . . in Oklahoma Territory, and this time,
it's deadly serious. Local cattle ranches are being targeted
by Texas rustlers—and the only man who can keep it
from turning into a bloodbath is U.S. Deputy Marshal
Will Tanner. The newly married lawman hates to leave his
beautiful bride Sophie, but duty calls—for better or
worse. In Tanner's experience, it's usually worse.

An unexpected confrontation with outlaws is just the
bloody beginning. Then an escaped convict catches
wind of the fact that Tanner killed his brother.
Now Tanner is really in the crosshairs.

Tanner knows he's riding straight into a perfect storm
of vengeance and slaughter, with only one way
to end it—a hailstorm of hot lead.

National Bestselling Authors
**William W. Johnstone
and J.A. Johnstone**

THE VIOLENT STORM
A Will Tanner U.S. Deputy Marshal Western

Live Free. Read Hard.
www.williamjohnstone.net
Visit us at www.kensingtonbooks.com

CHAPTER 1

Making a journey he had made many times before, Will Tanner guided the buckskin gelding through a gap in a long line of hills that led into the Sans Bois Mountains. The gap was actually one end of a narrow passage that led through the hills and ended at a grassy clearing at the foot of a mountain. On the other side of the meadow, built against the base of the mountain, stood the log cabin of a man named Merle Teague. A little, gray-bearded man, Merle had become a friend of Will's, just as the original owner of the cabin had. It was built by a quaint elf-like man named Perley Gates, who had also become a friend of Will's. But one day, Perley abandoned his cabin and left for parts unknown. Will had gotten into the habit of stopping to camp there whenever he was traveling into certain parts of the Nations. It was on the way and a convenient distance from Fort Smith. And he was always welcome because he usually brought coffee and tobacco. More times than not, he was able to enjoy a supper of fresh venison. So, one of the first things he looked toward was the large oak next to the porch where Perley, and now Merle, hung their fresh killed venison to skin and butcher. He smiled to himself when he saw the carcass hanging from that tree on this occasion.

Merle spotted him as soon as he left the cover of the trees at the end of the passage. He dropped his skinning knife, picked up his rifle, and brought it to his shoulder before he realized who it was. "Will Tanner!" he exclaimed, delighted. "You musta smelled some of that fresh meat on the fire over yonder." He nodded toward the firepit at the opposite corner of the porch.

"Howdy, Merle," Will said. "That's something new. That firepit wasn't here the last time I came by. You're makin' a regular palace outta this place." He was glad to see the little old man was getting by. He pulled the buckskin and his sorrel packhorse to a stop in front of the cabin. "That's a dandy firepit you built there, with that low wall of rocks around it. You can sit right there on the rocks while you tend your cookin', can't you?"

"You sure you wasn't here since I built it?" Merle asked. "Has it been that long since you was here?"

"Six or eight months, I expect," Will answered. "Anybody up in that cave?"

Merle knew Will was referring to a cave up on one of the mountains that was a popular hideout for fugitives on the run. It had earned the name of Robbers Cave. "I ain't been up that way in a week or so. But if there is somebody holed up there, they ain't stumbled on me yet. And they usually do, so I reckon ain't nobody up there right now."

"Well, the least I can do is help you get rid of some of that deer meat," Will said. "I'll take care of my horses first." He pulled his saddle off Buster and the packsaddle off the sorrel, then turned them loose to go to the stream that cut through the meadow. He put his saddle and the packs up on the porch, then he commented, "I like a good cup of coffee with my venison, and I don't see your coffeepot settin' out anywhere."

"I'm sorry about that," Merle said. "I've been outta coffee beans for three months."

"Did you throw your coffeepot away?"

Merle grinned sheepishly. "No, I didn't throw it away. I knew you'd show up here again, so I kept it ready to go."

"Well, get it out and put some water in it," Will chuckled. "Here's a twenty-pound sack of coffee, ground, it ain't beans. That oughta last you a little while." Merle could not speak, for grinning so wide. "I brought you a sack of sugar, too. What about smokin' tobacco? Did you give that up, too?"

"About two days after I gave up coffee," Merle managed, still beaming like a kid at Christmas.

"Well, I reckon you can start again," Will teased. "You didn't throw your pipe in the fire, did you?"

"I swear, Will, if I had the money, I'd be happy to pay you double for this stuff."

"Hell, it's a fair trade for some fresh deer meat," Will replied. "I don't get to go deer huntin' like I used to. I brought you some flour. I bet you're outta that, too."

Merle just shook his head as if he couldn't believe his good fortune. Without further delay, he ran into the cabin, came back with his coffeepot, and went straight to the spring to fill it. "I knew this was gonna be a good day when I woke up this mornin'." They enjoyed a big supper of venison and fresh coffee and a long visit while Merle finished butchering his deer and prepared a good portion of the meat to be smoked on a rack that Perley Gates had made for that purpose. It was later than either man's usual bedtime when they finally turned in, Merle in the cabin, and Will in his bedroll on the porch.

"I swear," Lester Camp whispered to his partner, "I didn't think they was ever gonna go to sleep, but I reckon it was worth the wait."

"I'll say it was," Carl Babcock replied. They had trailed the old man after he had killed a deer they had been following for more than a mile. Lester had wanted to shoot the old man and take the deer right then and there, but Carl talked him out of it. He persuaded him to wait and follow the old man to see if he had anything else they could use. He figured the deer was theirs for the taking, even if he didn't have much else they could use. "I don't know if we woulda ever found this place, if he hadn't led us here. Then this other feller comes along, ridin' a dang good lookin' buckskin horse and leadin' a packhorse loaded with supplies. It can't get much better'n this." He grinned wide with pleasure over the happenstance, knowing it was just plain luck.

"Ain't no trouble takin' care of the feller on the porch," Lester figured. "That old man might be a chore to get outta that cabin. Might have to burn him out."

"I hope not. We could use that cabin," Carl reminded him. "We mighta made a mistake waitin' for dark to take care of that old man."

"I thought it was you that wanted to wait and let him skin that deer and butcher it for us," Lester declared. "Besides, you saw how quick he had that rifle up when the other feller showed up. I don't care how old he is, it don't take much strength to pull the trigger on that Henry rifle he was holdin'."

"I say we oughta wait a little bit longer to make sure

they go to sleep," Carl suggested. "And while we do, I'm gonna slip up to that little corral they put the horses in and lead that buckskin over closer to our horses back there. I mean to have that horse, so if anything goes wrong, and we have to run, I'm takin' that horse with me."

"Hell, ain't nothin' gonna go wrong," Lester insisted, while he watched Carl sneak back to the horses they had tied on the other side of the meadow to get a rope. He almost chuckled as he watched Carl going to the trouble of sneaking up to the corral where he removed the two rails that served as a gate. The horses started walking out of the corral, so Carl waited and stopped the buckskin. He quickly fashioned an Indian bridle with his rope, then led Buster halfway across the meadow before tying him to a small bush. Then he returned to take his place beside Lester.

"You ready?" Lester asked, and Carl said that he was. Lester drew his long skinning knife from his belt and tested the edge of the blade with his thumb. "When I cut this jasper's throat, if he don't make enough noise, I will. And when that old coot comes running out to see what's wrong, we'll give him a belly full of lead. All right?"

"Why don't you just shoot him?" Carl asked.

"If I shoot him, that old coot inside will grab his gun and bolt the door, and we'll have to shoot up a lot of cartridges tryin' to get him outta there," Lester explained. "Might have to set fire to the cabin to get him outta there before it's over. But if I cut the other feller's throat, I'll holler like hell, and the feller inside will come a-runnin' to see what happened. He might have his gun with him, but he'll be out of the cabin. And that's when you'll cut him down."

"All right," Carl answered. "You be careful."

"Always am," Lester replied. "Don't worry, I'll leave him with a great big smile, right under his chin." He got to his feet again, and hunkering over in a crouch, he approached the sleeping figure on the porch. Carl aimed his pistol at the cabin door and waited.

Lester paused at the edge of the porch to listen for sounds from the sleeping man. There were none, thanks to a contented belly, Lester figured. *Good,* he thought, *best way to die, with your belly full of deer meat.* He climbed onto the tiny porch and crawled over to his victim, whose back was turned to him. Even though he was on his side, his victim was turned more toward his stomach, so Lester didn't have a clear view of his throat. He laid a hand gently on his shoulder and slowly rolled his body toward him. The sleeping man offered no resistance, but as the body turned, the barrel of a Colt .44 six-gun came into view, and it was aimed straight at his face. "Was there something you wanted?" Will asked, his voice soft and calm. Lester Camp made the last and worst mistake in a long line of mistakes in his life. His reaction was to try to stab Will. With no time to think, Will pulled the trigger at the same time he tried to block the hand holding the knife. The result was a .44 slug sent into the forehead of Lester and a cut on Will's left arm.

Shocked almost to a state of paralysis, Carl nevertheless managed to fire a couple of rounds at the porch, but Will held Lester's body in front of him to catch both bullets. He returned fire then when he saw the spot the shots came from and rolled off the porch to take cover behind Merle's firepit. In a panic then, Carl didn't like the position he now found himself in, so he decided to run when he realized that Will didn't know exactly where he was in the darkness. It was so dark in the narrow valley between the mountains that Will didn't know Carl was running until he caught an image of a dark figure moving across the meadow. Will had no way of knowing how many his attackers were before, but now, he felt sure they had only been two. So he scrambled out from behind the low rock wall of the firepit and gave chase, ignoring the fact that he was without his boots.

Running as fast as he could manage, Carl was already out of breath when he came to the buckskin he had left tied to a bush. He untied the horse and jumped on his back. When he kicked the buckskin with his heels, Buster kicked his rear legs straight up in the air, with only his front feet on the ground, causing Carl to go flying over his head to land hard on his backside. Stunned for a few moments, he looked back to see the dark form of Will Tanner running toward him, and behind him, Merle Teague jumped off the porch to give chase as well. Again in a panic, Carl reached for his six-gun, only to find it missing from his holster, having lost it when Buster bucked him off. Almost crazy with fear now, Carl looked all around him for his missing handgun, crawling one way, then another until finally he found it. With Will almost upon him, he frantically fired one round and missed before he was struck in the chest by a round from Will's .44. He went down at once and never moved again. Hearing Merle puffing behind him as he ran to catch up, Will said, "He's done for. It's over." He then knelt beside the body and took the pistol out of Carl's hand, then slowly released the hammer. He realized then, that had the man been able to pull the trigger again, he probably would not have missed, for he was so close by that time.

"What in tarnation?" That was all Merle could think to say at the moment. "Was there any more of 'em?"

"Don't think so," Will replied.

"Are you all right?"

"Yeah, I'm all right. That one back there at the porch managed to give me a little cut on my arm, but that ain't my worst problem. I ain't got my boots on and I feel some sore spots on the bottom of my feet from runnin' after this jasper."

"That horse of yours is kinda particular about who rides him, ain't he?" Merle asked.

"Not so much," Will answered. "He'll let pretty much anybody ride him as long as it's me." That prompted him to remember. "The direction he was runnin' in was that way." He pointed to some trees on the other side of the meadow. "So I reckon we'll find their horses over that way somewhere. I'll go see if I can find 'em."

"While you're doin' that, I'll go back to the cabin and get a lantern so we can take a look at these two buzzards," Merle said.

"That's a good idea," Will japed. "They mighta been some of your relatives come to visit you."

"If they are, we treated 'em the right way," Merle replied, then turned to go back to the cabin to fetch the lantern. Will walked toward the edge of the clearing until his eye caught the movement of forms big enough to be horses in the darkness of the trees. At that point, he drew his weapon again, confident that he wouldn't need it, but cautious enough to make sure he didn't blunder into a third person left to hold the horses. There turned out to be just the two horses, as he expected, so he untied their reins from the tree branches and led them back toward Merle's corral. He put all the horses in the corral and pulled the saddles off the two would-be assassins' horses. Then he went over and joined Merle, who was taking a close look at Lester on the porch. He picked up his boots, but decided against putting them on, since he had already torn the bottom of his socks and caked them with dirt.

"I brought their saddlebags over," Will said. "Thought I'd throw 'em on the porch, so you can look in 'em to see if there's anything worth something in 'em. I'll bring the saddles up, too, and you can see if you can trade them for something, but I wouldn't get my hopes up on 'em. You recognize him?"

"Never seen him before," Merle said. "He's just another one of those drifters who robbed somebody, or killed somebody, and came up to the mountains to hide. Don't know him, and I don't know his partner, but they were sure fixin' to settle your grits, weren't they?"

"Yep. Neither one of 'em gave me any choice. I had to shoot both of 'em."

"I sure thank the Lord you came along. This was my lucky day when you showed up."

"Well, I'm glad I happened to be in a position to help," Will responded. "Those two weren't plannin' to leave anybody in this cabin alive."

"Oh, hell," Merle snorted. "I weren't talkin' about them two tryin' to kill me. They'da played hell tryin' to smoke me outta this cabin. I was talkin' about the coffee and the tobacco you brung me."

"Right," Will replied. "What was I thinkin'? Bring your lantern and let me take a look at the other fellow." They walked back out in the meadow to Carl's body and Will took a quick look. "I don't know him either," he told Merle. "Did he have anything on him?"

"A Colt .45 Army revolver and a knife, eighty-five cents

in his pocket, and that's all," Merle answered. "Oh, and a pocket comb. You want it? You've got hair."

"I don't want it," Will told him. "You feel like diggin' a hole tonight to put these two jokers in, or you wanna wait till mornin'?" Merle chose morning, saying he'd rather go back to bed now. That suited Will fine, so he dragged Lester's body off the porch to lie in the yard till morning. He moved his bedroll away from the puddle of blood Lester had left on the porch and retired to try to make up for some of the sleep the visit had cost him.

They were up early the next morning, in spite of the little interruption in their sleep the night before and enjoyed another meal of fresh-killed venison for breakfast. They gave their two guests a rather undignified burial on the backside of the mountain before Will set out again on the trail to Atoka. "How long you figure you'll be down that way?" Merle asked. He was wondering if Will might stop by on his way back to Fort Smith.

"I don't know for sure," Will told him. "After I see Jim Little Eagle in Atoka, I'm gonna ride on over to the other side of Tishomingo. Tom Spotted Horse wired Fort Smith about some cattle rustlin' goin' on over near the Red River. So I don't know how long I'll be gone."

"What about all this stuff we ended up with after we stuck these two fellers in the ground?" Merle asked, already pretty sure what Will's answer would be.

"I figured it might be a little more trouble for you, but the next time you ride over to McAlester for supplies you'll have a lot more to trade for 'em. And you won't have to wait for me to show up to have coffee."

"I 'preciate it, Will. That's mighty generous of ya. I

might keep one of them horses, that roan. He looks in pretty good shape and that sorrel I've been usin' for a packhorse is gettin' so dang old he ain't gonna be good for much of anythin' pretty soon."

"Yeah, that roan looks like he's got a lot left in him, and you oughta get something for the bay, too," Will allowed. "Well, I'd best get in the saddle. I've got a good day and a half's ride to get to Atoka. Maybe by the time I get there, Jim will have taken care of the problem, himself."

CHAPTER 2

Will and Buster put in a long day after leaving Merle that morning. He wanted to arrive in Atoka around noon the following day because he planned to eat dinner at Lottie Mabre's dining room, which she had recently started calling Lottie's Kitchen. It was next door to a rooming house owned by her husband, Doug, and started out as the dining room for her husband's boarders. In short time, the quality of Lottie's cooking became quite well-known, and consequently, the favorite place to eat in the little town. As much as he had enjoyed the fresh venison, he was hankering more toward a good homestyle dinner with some biscuits or cornbread and butter. So after a day's ride that he figured to be close to forty-five miles, he rode into Atoka a little after noon. He decided to eat first, then ride out to Jim Little Eagle's cabin on Muddy Boggy Creek. He knew Jim's wife, Mary Light Walker, would insist on fixing him something to eat, if he had not already eaten. The food would be good but not what he was hankering for on this day.

He pulled Buster up before the hitching rail in front of Lottie's and dismounted, wrapped the reins of both horses around the rail and paused only a moment to admire the new sign that proclaimed the dining room to be Lottie's Kitchen. "Will Tanner!" Louise Bellone called out when she saw him come in the door. "I thought you musta died."

"Howdy, Lou-Bell," he greeted her by the name she was called by all her friends. "I couldn't die till I had one more dinner at Lottie's."

"So you're sayin' one more dinner here will kill you?" Lou-Bell replied. "I don't know if you oughta tell Lottie that or not."

"You know what I meant," he said. Knowing she was japing him, he gave up immediately. He knew better than to get into a battle of wits with Lou-Bell. "What's for dinner today?"

"Lottie made meatloaf," Lou-Bell said, not willing to give up that easily, "and it's pretty deadly. But if you wanna be sure, we can fix you up with something that's guaranteed to do the job."

"Just bring me the meatloaf and whatever else goes with it and maybe that'll do the job," he said. She shrugged and headed for the kitchen to fill a plate for him, passing Lottie on her way out of the kitchen with the coffeepot. He went into the back part of the room and sat down at one of the small tables, instead of taking a seat at the long table in the center.

"Howdy, Will," Lottie greeted him. "Is Lou-Bell giving you a hard time?" She turned the coffee cup right-side-up on his saucer and filled it with hot coffee.

"She always does," Will admitted. "I think she knows she's got a sharper wit than I have, and I know when I'm over-matched."

Lottie chuckled and said, "Sometimes I think I oughta

put a gag in her mouth, but I'm sure half my customers come in here just to swap lies with Lou-Bell."

"Well, I'm in the other half," Will said. "I come in here because the food is the best in this part of the country."

"Why, thank you, sir," she responded, "I certainly appreciate that." She stepped to the side then to give Lou-Bell room to place his dinner on the table.

"Here you go, Deputy Tanner," Lou-Bell announced as she set his plate down. "Hope it does the job," she japed and gave him a wink. She turned to Lottie then and said very softly, "Look who's coming in the door. I kinda hoped they wouldn't be back today."

Forgetting Will for the moment, Lottie said, "Well, let's not sit them at the big table today. Go tell Fred to clear the dishes off that table over there by the window. I'll seat them there." Lou-Bell went at once to the kitchen and Lottie turned toward Will again. "I'll check with you in a little bit." She started to leave, pausing only a few seconds when Will asked a question.

"Who's Fred?" During the many times he had eaten there, he had never seen anyone named Fred.

Lottie quickly explained, "You probably remember Lila, the elderly lady who used to work here as our dishwasher. She came down with arthritis so bad she couldn't work anymore. We couldn't find anybody to take her place, so her husband came in to do her job till we found someone else, and he's still here." She hurried away then to intercept the two men coming in the door.

"Good afternoon, gentlemen," Lottie greeted them. "You've come back to see us again."

"You said that like you're surprised," Clyde Vickery

responded. He turned to look at his partner. "Didn't she, Sonny?"

"Maybe she's sayin' we ain't welcome," Sonny Doyle answered.

"We try to welcome everyone here," Lottie said. "We hope that everyone who eats with us is considerate of everyone else who's eating here. I'll call your attention to the table we've provided in the corner for firearms and ask if you'll be considerate of the other customers in the room and leave your weapons on the table until you're ready to leave. Yesterday, you refused. I'm hoping that today you'll leave them on the table. How 'bout it, you wanna make the rest of my customers feel more at ease?" Her earnest request failed to wipe the smirks off either face.

"How 'bout it, Sonny? You wanna make her customers feel more at ease?"

"I don't give a fat rat's ass whether her customers feel at ease or not," Sonny answered him. "I just care about how I feel, and I feel uncomfortable when I'm settin' in the back of the room full of sodbusters and my .44 is layin' on a table up front."

"Well, there you go, sugar plum," Clyde told her. "I reckon you've got your answer. Now the smartest thing for you to do is to bring us plenty of food and don't let none of them other customers bother us, and everythin' will be just fine."

Lottie hesitated. She glanced over at the opposite back corner at Will, already eating, apparently paying no attention to the two men she was talking with. She couldn't decide whether to ask him to order the troublesome two out of the building or not. Maybe these men had no intention of causing anyone any trouble and just wanted to eat and get on their way. Finally, she made a decision. "All right, gentlemen, I'm gonna seat you right over here at a table by the window, best table in the room. It'll be cleaned off and set up with clean knives and forks." She led them over to the table. "Have a seat, and I'll go to the kitchen and get your dinner ready."

Clyde and Sonny looked at each other with surprised grins on their faces. "Now, that's more like it," Clyde declared.

Watching from the kitchen door, Lou-Bell grabbed Lottie's arm when she walked into the kitchen. "What did you tell them?"

"I decided the best way to handle them is to treat 'em like a couple of kings, feed 'em good and fast, and get 'em out of here as quick as we can. Don't give 'em anything to complain about."

Surprised by her plan of action, Lou-Bell was quick to remind her. "We've got a genuine U.S. Deputy Marshal settin' right across the room from them. Why don't we just tell Will to order them out of here?"

"That was my first thought, too," Lottie answered while she set two plates next to the stove and put two healthy slices of meatloaf on each one. "But those two refuse to take their guns off, and if we get Will to throw them out of here, I'm afraid there might be a gunfight. Then we would be endangering the lives of all our good customers in here. I'd rather try this approach first and save Will for the last resort."

Lou-Bell thought about it for a moment, then shrugged. "I don't know. Maybe you're right. It wouldn't be too good if it turned into a gunfight in here. But I ain't sure your idea will work on those two ignorant saddle tramps. I don't think they're house-broke."

"I'll wait on 'em if you don't wanna," Lottie suggested, even though she was of the opinion that Lou-Bell was far more bulletproof to insults and crass remarks than she was.

"Oh, hell, no," Lou-Bell came back at once. "I'll serve 'em with a sweet smile, no matter how bad they misbehave." Fred came from the back sink with an empty dishpan and walked around them on his way to clear off the table by the window. "Clear off those dirty dishes, Fred, and we'll set those gents up with enough food to keep their mouths shut."

Out in the dining room, Will cleaned the last little bit of grease from his plate, using a piece of biscuit for a mop. Contrary to what Lottie and Lou-Bell thought, he was very much aware of the guns still riding in the holsters of the two rather raunchy-looking men seated at the table by the window. He knew that Lottie had a policy of no firearms in the dining room, unless you were a lawman. He was curious as to why Lottie was making an exception for them. So he decided to have another cup of coffee and stick around for a while. He made an attempt not to be obvious about his interest in the two drifters. They hadn't broken any laws that he was aware of, just refused to remove their weapons in the dining room. That was Lottie's law, but not one a deputy marshal was called upon to enforce. Hopefully, they'll just eat and be on their way, he thought. It didn't take long for him to find out.

"Let me clean up this table a little bit for you fellows," Fred Polk said, and started picking up the cups and dishes left on the table.

"Who the hell are you?" Clyde demanded, thinking the old man had been sent to wait on them since they wouldn't surrender their guns. "Where's that sassy gal that waited on us yesterday?"

"Lou-Bell," Fred replied. "I reckon she'll be servin' you. I'm just cleanin' up the table for her."

"He's just the dishwasher and the cleanin' woman, Clyde," Sonny remarked. "Ain't that right, old man?"

"I reckon you could say that," Fred answered. "I'm just tryin' to help Lottie out a little bit till she finds another dishwasher."

"We wouldn't want him handlin' our food, anyway," Sonny continued taunting the old man. "If somebody drops a dish on the floor, he has to clean it up. Ain't that right, old man?"

"I reckon I'd most likely be the one to clean it up," Fred allowed.

"Oops." Sonny grinned and slid a coffee cup to the edge of the table to let it drop off and smash into pieces. He and Clyde both chuckled as Fred tried to clear the rest of the table before any more dishes fell. "You better check this table," Sonny continued. "I don't believe it's level."

"I didn't know you was a carpenter, Sonny," Clyde blurted gleefully. "Maybe you oughta take a look at this table to see if you can see what's wrong with it." He took hold of the edge of the table and came up with it till all the remaining dishes slid off on the floor. "Sorry about that, old man. Looks like you've got a bigger mess to clean up. Come on, Sonny, we're gonna have to move to another table."

"You're gonna be movin' farther than that."

So absorbed in their harassment of an old man, Clyde nor Sonny were aware of the man who got up from the table in the opposite corner until they heard him speak behind them. Both turned to discover the dead-serious eyes of Will Tanner. Sonny was the first to challenge the stranger. "Mister, you'd best turn your behind around while you still can and mind your own business."

"This is my business," Will replied. "Now, you and your partner have shown everybody that you're not fit to eat with civilized folks. So both of you start walking toward that door."

Amazed, the two drifters exchanged puzzled glances before Clyde sneered, "And what if we don't? You gonna throw us out?"

"I'm gonna give you the chance to walk out of here peacefully," Will answered him, and pulled his vest aside to show his badge.

"A lawman!" Clyde exclaimed, then broke out with a grin. "This is Injun Territory. You ain't got no jurisdiction in Injun Territory. So you can just go to hell."

"I'm gonna explain this to you just one time," Will said. "This badge says I'm a U.S. Deputy Marshal. I *am* the law in Indian Territory for every white lawbreaker like you two sorry scabs who think you can do anything you want in The Nations. That ends all the discussion we're gonna have on that subject, so start walking toward that door. You better hope you've got enough money to pay for all those dishes you broke. You're lucky that table ain't broken." He glanced at Lottie who was standing frozen like everyone else in the dining room now. "How much are those dishes worth, Lottie?"

Still too flustered to think straight, Lottie could only stammer for a few seconds before she blurted out, "It's not that much. Just take them out of here. They don't have to pay for them."

Seeing she was too upset to think, Will asked, "Would a dollar cover it?" She said yes immediately, so Will looked back at Clyde and said, "Put a dollar on the floor beside those dishes." He could almost see the thoughts racing through the crude man's head as he snarled and raised a hand that hesitated over his holstered pistol. "Don't even think about it," Will warned, and drew his .44 to enforce the warning. He had hoped to avoid the appearance of a gun in the dining room, but Clyde had hesitated long enough to warrant his concern. "A dollar," he reminded him.

His eyes blazing with anger, Clyde reluctantly reached in his shirt pocket and pulled out a small roll of bills. He peeled a dollar off the roll and dropped it to fall in the middle of the broken dishes, then looked defiantly at Will. "I wonder how tough you'd be if we took it outside and you faced me with that pistol back in your holster."

"That would make me as stupid as you," Will answered. "Now, I'm tired of messin' with you two, so walk right on out that door." With little choice, since his gun was already out and aimed at their backs, they did as he ordered. Once outside, he said, "I'm arrestin' you for disturbin' the peace and destruction of private property. That's three days in jail."

"Three days in jail?" Clyde exploded. "Hell, man, I paid for those broke dishes!"

"That's right," Will replied. "The jail time is just for disturbin' the peace. It woulda been five days for both counts." He let them stew over that for a few seconds, then continued. "I'll tell you what, I'm in a pretty good mood today, so I might cut you fellows a little slack. We ain't got no real jail here in Atoka, so I use the Choctaw jail, which ain't nothin' but an old smokehouse they turned into a jail. It's gonna be a little cramped-up for ya, dependin' on how many drunken bucks the Choctaw policeman has in there right now. So, I'm gonna give you a choice, the Choctaw jail, or get on your horses and ride outta town right now. What's it gonna be?"

"I reckon we'll ride," Clyde said, and untied his horse's reins and backed it away from the rail. Sonny, the silent witness to the confrontation between Clyde and the deputy marshal, was astonished by his partner's apparent surrender, especially when they had him outnumbered two to one. And when Clyde's horse backed away from the rail and blocked Will's vision of him for a couple of seconds, Sonny didn't hesitate. He reached for his six-gun and raised it halfway before Will put a round into his right shoulder, causing him to drop his weapon and stagger backward several steps.

"You ain't had time to grow any common sense, have you?" Will asked. "I oughta put a round in your head, so you'd have something inside that empty space." Stunned for a few moments, Sonny clutched his wounded shoulder with his left hand. When he thought to pick up his six-gun and made a motion to do so, Will said, "Leave it right where it is. Can you ride?" Sonny didn't answer, so Will looked at Clyde and said, "Get him outta here, before I decide to throw him in that smokehouse jail and throw the damn key away." Clyde immediately went to help Sonny, and Will watched while he got the wounded man in the saddle. While Clyde was busy with that chore, Will picked up Sonny's .44 and emptied the cylinder and checked to be sure there was not one in the chamber. Then he dropped it into Sonny's saddlebag. "You gonna be able to take care of that wound?" Will asked.

"Nope, but I know somebody who can," Clyde answered. "Maybe we'll see you again some time."

"Is that a threat?" Will asked, his six-gun still in his hand.

"No, it ain't no threat. I was just sayin', that's all," Clyde quickly replied.

"Get on your way, then," Will said, and stepped back out of the way. He stood there to watch them ride out of town. Near the end of the street, they passed a rider coming into town, who gave them a concentrated looking over. Will smiled when he recognized the rider as Jim Little Eagle.

"Will Tanner," Jim called out as he pulled up next to him and slid off his horse. "One fellow back there look like he been shot. Was that you?"

"Yeah, that was me. Couple of drifters makin' trouble in Lottie's. It got outta hand, so I had to ask 'em to leave."

"You not put 'em in jailhouse?" Jim wondered.

"I'll be honest with you, Jim, I didn't wanna burden you with 'em, and I sure as hell didn't wanna take 'em with me. I didn't bring a jail wagon with me, and I've got to go on out to the Chickasaw Nation after I leave here. That's why I decided to run 'em outta town and hope they don't come back for a while."

"Better you shoot 'em. Then they don't come back," Jim said. "I hear one shot just before I get to town."

"I put a bullet in one of 'em's shoulder. He tried to go for his gun when I'm standin' there with mine in my hand. His partner said they didn't have to see the doctor, said he knew somebody who could take care of it. I don't know where he was talkin' about."

"I know where they go," Jim declared. "That's the reason I send wire to Marshal Stone and ask him to send somebody for little problem we got." Will knew Jim always asked Stone to send him, and it was usually for the sale of whiskey to the Indians.

"Has to do with those two fellows?" Will asked.

"Them and others just like them," Jim said, nodding slowly to emphasize the gravity of the problem.

"Don't tell me those women we left to operate Mama's Kitchen down the road have started sellin' whiskey, after all their promisin' to run a law abidin' eatin' place." Will remarked. It had not been that long ago that he and Jim Little Eagle had worked together to close down an illegal saloon and whorehouse no more than three miles from Atoka. Run by a crude man named Tiny McGee, in partnership with a Texas cattle rustler named Ward Hawkins, Tiny was selling whiskey in Indian Territory to white man and Indian alike.

"No," Jim quickly assured him. "Those women do like they promise, sell food and rent rooms." He nodded toward the door of Lottie's Kitchen. "They give them some competition. What I wire Marshal Stone about is new place. Man named Reese Trainer build cabin on Clear Boggy Creek, twelve miles east of Atoka. I think he build big house, must have big family, but he not build house. He build saloon, sell whiskey. I tell him no sell whiskey in Choctaw Nation. He tell me mind my own business. I tell him deputy marshal come to see him. He tell me mind my own business."

"I'll take a ride out that way after my horses are rested up. You ready to go with me?" Will asked. Jim said that he was and suggested that Will could leave his packhorse at his cabin, assuming that Will would camp at his place on Muddy Boggy Creek, as he often did. Will was agreeable with that, so he went back inside the dining room to pay Lottie for his dinner. She and Lou-Bell both thanked him for getting rid of their troublesome customers even though there was no guarantee they would never come back.